Praise for and h

"Marta Perry is synonymous with sweet,
loving romance!"
—*Romantic Times BOOKclub* on
A Father's Place

"...a splendid romance beautifully
demonstrating the
multiplicity of love."
—*Romantic Times BOOKclub* on
A Father's Promise

"Marta Perry's *Hero in Her Heart* is a highly
emotional story, loaded with excellent
conflict and heart-tugging romance."
—*Romantic Times BOOKclub*

"*Hero Dad* shows the power of God and family
to overcome trials. Detailed characterization
brings the story to life."
—*Romantic Times BOOKclub*

MARTA PERRY

Father Most Blessed

A Father's Place

Steeple
Hill®

Published by Steeple Hill Books™

STEEPLE HILL BOOKS

Steeple
Hill®

ISBN-13: 978-0-373-65267-9
ISBN-10:   0-373-65267-4

FATHER MOST BLESSED AND A FATHER'S PLACE

FATHER MOST BLESSED
Copyright © 2001 by Martha P. Johnson

A FATHER'S PLACE
Copyright © 2001 by Martha P. Johnson

www.SteepleHill.com

Printed in U.S.A.

CONTENTS

Books by Marta Perry

Love Inspired

MARTA PERRY

has written everything from Sunday school curriculum to travel articles to magazine stories in twenty years of writing, but she feels she's found her home in the stories she writes for Love Inspired. She was a 2005 RITA® Award finalist.

Marta lives in rural Pennsylvania, but she and her husband spend part of each year at their second home in South Carolina. When she's not writing, she's probably visiting her children and her beautiful grandchildren, traveling or relaxing with a good book.

Marta loves hearing from readers and she'll write back with a signed bookplate or bookmark. Write to her c/o Steeple Hill Books, 233 Broadway, Suite 1001, New York, NY 10279, e-mail her at marta@martaperry.com or visit her on the Web at www.martaperry.com.

FATHER MOST BLESSED

For it is by grace you have been saved, through faith, and this not from yourselves: it is the gift of God—not by works, so that no one can boast.

—*Ephesians* 2:8-9

This story is dedicated with love and gratitude to the siblings and spouses who add so much richness to our lives: Pat and Ed, Bill and Molly, Herb and Barb, Gary and Arddy, and Chris.
And, as always, to Brian.

Chapter One

A man who lived in a twenty-room house ought to be able to have silence when he wanted it. Alex Caine tossed his pen on the library desk and stalked to the center hallway of the Italianate mansion that had been home to the Caine family for three generations. The noise that had disrupted his work on a crucial business deal came from beyond the swinging door to the servants' area.

Frowning, he headed toward the sound, his footsteps sharp on the marble floor, and pushed through the door to the rear of the house. He'd told his ailing housekeeper to rest this afternoon, so there should have been no sound at all to disturb his concentration. But Maida Hansen, having taken care of him since the day his mother died when he was six, tended to ignore any orders she didn't want to follow.

Well, in this case she was going to listen. If he didn't find the right words for this delicate negotiation, Caine Industries might not survive for another generation. There might be no company at all to leave to his son.

He winced. What would his grandfather or his father have said to that? They'd assumed they were founding a dynasty to last a hundred years. They wouldn't look kindly on the man who presided over its demise.

The noise came from the pantry, down the hall from the kitchen. He seized the doorknob and yanked.

The figure balanced precariously on the step stool wasn't Maida. Maida had never in her life worn blue jeans or a sweatshirt proclaiming her World's Greatest Teacher. His heart stopped, and he looked at the woman he had thought he'd never see again.

"What's going on?"

She spun at the sound of his voice, wobbled and overbalanced. Her arms waved wildly to regain control, but it was too late. The step stool toppled, sending her flying toward him. Pans clattered to the floor. In an instant his arms had closed around Paula Hansen.

The breath went out of him. Carefully he set her on her feet and stepped back, clamping down on the treacherous rush of feelings. Paula—here in his house again, looking up at him with what might have been embarrassment in her sea-green eyes.

With an effort he schooled his face to polite concern and found his voice. "Paula. I didn't expect to find you here. Maida didn't tell me you were coming."

Maida's time outside her duties was her own, and she was perfectly free to have her niece stay at the housekeeper's cottage whenever she wanted to. But in the almost two years since the plane crash, since what had happened between them, Paula hadn't returned to Bedford Creek.

"She didn't tell you?" Surprise filled Paula's expressive face. She tried to mask it, turning away to right the step stool.

"No, she didn't." If he'd known Paula was on the estate, he wouldn't have betrayed shock at the sight of her. In fact, he'd probably have found a way to avoid seeing her at all.

"But I thought she…" Paula stopped, seeming to edit whatever she'd been about to say. "My school just got out for the summer yesterday, so I'm on vacation now." Again she stopped, and again he had the sense of things left unsaid.

She'd been on vacation two years ago, when she'd come to Pennsylvania to spend the summer taking care of his son. It had seemed the perfect solution. He had needed someone reliable to care for Jason until kindergarten started in the fall. His house-keeper's niece needed a summer job. Neither of them had anticipated anything else.

The June sunlight, slanting through the small panes of the pantry window, burnished the honey blond of her hair. Her hair was shorter now than the last time he'd seen her, and it fell in unruly curls around her face. Her green eyes still reflected glints of gold, and that vulnerable mouth and stubborn chin hadn't changed.

Tension jagged along his nerves as images of the last time he'd seen her invaded his mind—lightning splitting the sky outside the small plane; the brief hope the pilot would manage to land, shattered when the plane cartwheeled and flames rushed toward him; Paula, several rows ahead, trapped in a mass of twisted metal. If an unexpected business trip hadn't put him on the daily commuter flight the same day that Paula was leaving to go home, what might have happened? Would someone have pulled her from the jammed seat to safety?

"Is something wrong?" She pulled her sweatshirt sleeves down, frowning. "You don't mind that I'm here, do you?"

"Of course not. I'm just surprised." He tried for a coolness he didn't feel. "It didn't bother you, flying back into Bedford Creek again?"

"No." She shook her head, then smiled ruefully.

"I suppose it might have, if I'd tried to do it. I drove up from Baltimore."

Her admission of vulnerability startled him. The Paula he remembered had been proud of her self-reliance and determined not to accept help from anyone. Even after the accident, when he'd awakened in the hospital and learned her family had taken her home to Baltimore for medical care, his offer of financial help had been quickly refused.

"Driving instead of flying sounds reasonable to me," he said. "I don't enjoy getting on a plane now, either."

His own admission shocked him even more. Alexander Caine didn't admit weakness, not to anyone. His father had trained that out of him when he was about his own son's age.

"I haven't been on a plane since..." Paula's gaze flickered away from the scar that accented Alex's cheekbone.

His mouth stiffened, and he read the reaction he should have gotten used to by now. "The plane crash," he finished for her, his tone dry. "You can say the words, you know." He didn't need or want her pity.

"The drive up wasn't bad—just long." She seemed determined to ignore his reference to the crash. She stared at the rows of shelves with their seldom-used dishes as if she really didn't see them.

Then her gaze shifted to him. "As I said, I'm on vacation, so I was free to come when Aunt Maida needed me." Her expression turned challenging. "You have noticed she's in pain lately, haven't you?"

He stiffened at the implication of neglect in her pointed question. Of course he felt responsible for the woman who'd cared for his family all these years. But it wasn't Paula Hansen's place to question him.

"I've asked her repeatedly about her health," he said. "She keeps insisting she's fine."

She lifted her eyebrows, her gaze turning skeptical. Paula's face had always shown her emotions so clearly. A picture flashed into his mind of her lips close to his, her eyes soft.

No. He pushed the errant thought away. *Don't go there.*

"Aunt Maida always insists she's fine. But you must have noticed something."

"She's been tired and limping more lately." He reached behind him for the door, hoping he didn't sound defensive. He was wasting time in this futile discussion—time he didn't have to spare. "I told her to take it easy this afternoon. She does too much." He glanced at the pans scattered on the worn linoleum. "Instead, she seems to have enlisted you as assistant housekeeper."

Her chin came up at that, as if it were an insult. "I'm glad to help my aunt."

The last time she'd been here, it had been for her brief job as Jason's nanny. Alex tried again to ignore the flood of memories of that time: the laughter and warmth she'd brought to this house, her face turned toward his in the moonlight, the moment he'd forgotten himself and kissed her—

Enough. He'd gotten through the remainder of her stay in Bedford Creek by pretending that kiss had never happened. Paula was probably as eager as he was to avoid the subject.

"I've already told Maida to rest more," he said. "She won't listen."

"It isn't just rest she needs." She stared at him, a question in her green eyes. "You really don't know, do you?"

"Know what?" He couldn't erase the irritation from his tone. "What are you driving at, Paula? I don't have time for guessing games."

Her eyes flashed. "She can't put it off any longer. Aunt Maida has to have hip replacement surgery."

Surgery. The implications staggered him. Maida, the rock on which his home life depended, needed surgery. He fought past a wave of guilt that he hadn't guessed what was going on.

"No, I didn't know." He returned Paula's frown.

"I wish Maida *had* told me, but if she didn't want to, that was her right."

"She didn't tell you because she didn't want you to worry."

Paula clearly didn't consider protecting him from worry a priority. Antagonism battled the attraction he felt just looking at her. Maybe it was a good thing she annoyed him so much. It reminded him not to let that attraction get out of control, as it had once before.

"That's ridiculous," he said shortly. "If she needs the operation now, she has to have it. There's no question of that."

Even as he frowned at Paula, his mind raced from one responsibility to another—his son, the factory, the business deal that might save them. His stomach clenched at the thought of the Swiss firm's representative, due to visit any day now. He'd expect to be entertained in Alex's home. How could Alex swing that without Maida's calm, efficient management?

"My aunt knows this is a bad time for you. That's probably why she hasn't told you."

He sensed Paula's disapproval, although whether it was directed at him or her aunt, he didn't know. "I'll manage," he said curtly. "I'll have to find someone to fill in for her, that's all."

He knew when he said it how futile a hope that was. An isolated mountain village didn't boast an army of trained domestics ready for hiring. He'd be lucky to find anyone at all in the middle of the tourist season.

"It won't be easy to hire someone, will it?" She seemed to read his thoughts.

"No, I'm afraid Maida has spoiled us." He should have known things couldn't run so smoothly forever.

"Aunt Maida thinks she has a solution, if you'll go along with it."

He realized Paula was carefully not looking at him, and that fact sent up a red flag of warning. "What is it?"

Paula took a deep breath and fixed him with a look that was half embarrassed, half defiant. "She wants you to hire me as her replacement."

For a long moment he could only stare at her. Paula—back in his house, cooking his meals, looking after his son. Given what had happened between them the last time she worked for him, he couldn't believe she'd be willing to try it again.

One thing he could believe, though. Having Paula Hansen in his house again wouldn't just be embarrassing. Having her there, seeing her every day, no matter how desperately he needed help—that would be downright insane.

The expression on Alex's lean, aristocratic face showed Paula only too well exactly what he thought of her aunt's idea. Why on earth hadn't Aunt Maida told him before Paula arrived? Maida knew this situation would be difficult. She'd said she'd prepare the way. Instead, she'd brought Paula here without saying a word to Alex about it.

Of course, Aunt Maida couldn't have known her niece would go weak-kneed at the sight of Alex Caine.

"I see." Alex's tone was coolly noncommittal, and the polite, well-bred mask he habitually wore slid into place.

It was too late. Naturally he wouldn't come right out and tell her he didn't want her in his house again. But she'd seen his swift, unguarded reaction. Her heart sank. She should have known he wouldn't agree to this.

"Where is Maida? We need to talk about this."

"She's not here." She took a deep breath and prepared for an explosion. *Oh, Aunt Maida. Why didn't you tell him?* "She's already checked into the hospital in Henderson."

He started to speak, then clamped his mouth closed. Maybe he was counting to ten. She could only hope it worked.

"She's scheduled for surgery tomorrow." She might as well get it all out. If he intended to explode, he'd just have to do it once. "I guess she thought I could help out here, at least until you make a decision about replacing her.''

''You said she didn't want to worry me. Did she think this wasn't worrying—going to the hospital and leaving you to break the news?''

The fine lines around Alex's dark eyes seemed to deepen. She longed to smooth them away with her fingertips. The urge, so strong her skin tingled, shocked her. She couldn't think that, couldn't feel it.

She didn't have a good answer to his question. ''I thought she planned to tell you. When we talked on the phone last week, she said she would.''

Maida had sounded so desperate. *''I need you, Paula. Jason needs you. That child is hurting, and you might be the only one who can help him.''* Maida must not have wanted to risk telling Alex, and his finding some other solution to her absence. She could only pray Maida was right.

''Why didn't you tell me, then?''

Alex's intense, dark stare seemed to pierce right through her, finding the vulnerabilities she longed to hide. She took a deep breath, trying to quell jittery nerves. She'd known it would be difficult to come back here. She just hadn't anticipated *how* difficult. If Aunt Maida knew how hard this was for her—

No, she couldn't let Maida know that. She'd agreed to do this thing, and she had to do it.

''I am telling you. I mean, now you know, don't

you?'' She clenched her hands together, hoping he
didn't realize how much of her attitude was bravado.
"Look, all I know is that she said she'd tell you. I
thought it was all arranged. That's why I'm here—''
she gestured toward the scattered pots "—trying to
fix dinner for you and Jason.''

Alex looked if it was the worst idea he'd ever
heard. If he sent her packing, she'd never have a
chance to make up for the mistakes she'd made the
last time she was here.

"I can cook, you know," she assured him. "I
learned from the best.'' Maida had insisted on giving
her cooking lessons every time Paula came to visit.

*"Of course you're going to get an education and
have a profession,"* Maida would say. *"But it never
does any harm to know how to cook."*

He looked at her skeptically, and her doubts rose.
Why was this so difficult?

*Lord, if this really is the right thing to do, please
let me know it.*

"Dinner tonight isn't important.'' His voice was
clipped. "I'll take Jason out for a hamburger—he
always welcomes that. As for the rest of it, I'll make
a decision later. You can go to the hospital to see
Maida. Tell her I'll be there tomorrow.''

She nodded, trying not to react to his tone. As heir
to the Caine family fortune, he'd probably been born
with the commanding manner that assumed compli-

ance with his orders. The quality never failed to irritate Paula, but Alex had a right to make his own decisions about his staff. And if she did work for him, he'd also have a perfect right to give her orders and expect obedience.

Seeming to consider the matter settled, Alex turned toward the front of the house.

She wanted to let him go, because his disturbing presence upset her equilibrium and made her silly heart flutter. But she couldn't. There was too much yet to be settled. She had to convince him that she was the right person for this job.

She caught up with him at the swinging door marking the boundary between the family's part of the mansion and the servants' section.

"Alex—" She put her hand on his arm to stop him, and was instantly sorry. Through the silky broadcloth of his shirt, his skin warmed to her touch. He wore the dress shirt and tie that was part of his usual attire, but the sleeves were turned back at the wrists, exposing a gold watchband that gleamed against his skin.

She pulled her gaze from his hands, fighting for balance, and focused on his face, instead. It didn't help. He bore lines he hadn't two years ago, and the narrow scar that crossed his cheekbone added an attractively dangerous look to his even, classic features.

She snatched her hand away. "I mean, Mr.

Caine.'' She felt her cheeks flushing. Observing the proprieties might help keep things businesslike between them. It might prevent a recurrence of what happened two years ago.

He stopped, looking down at her, his dark eyes unreadable beneath winged brows. Then he shook his head.

''You've been calling me Alex since the first time you came here. You were only about Jason's age.''

She nodded, deflected by memories of the past. At least Alex seemed able to put his antagonism aside for the moment and remember a more peaceful time. That had to be a good sign.

''I was eight. And homesick as could be. You showed me where the children's books were in the library and told me to help myself.''

She'd been awestruck when Alex Caine, only child of the town's richest man and the prince in the Caine castle, had made the effort to be kind to her. She'd felt like Cinderella when he'd led her into the elegant room lined with books and shown her the window seat next to the fireplace where she could curl up and read. Not that she'd ever done it when there was a chance his formidable father might find her.

''So we're old friends.'' The smile that came too rarely lit his lean face, causing an uncomfortable flutter somewhere in the vicinity of her heart. ''Alex will do.''

"Alex," she repeated, trying not to linger on his name. "You know how stubborn Aunt Maida can be. I'm sure she was just doing what she thought would cause the least trouble. If she could have delayed the surgery, she would have, but the doctor insisted."

She wanted to say the words that would convince him to let her stay, but she couldn't find them. Instead, she swung back to her worries about Maida.

"She told me Dr. Overton retired. Someone else took over his practice."

"You can have confidence in Brett Elliot," he said promptly, apparently reading her concern. "He's an excellent doctor, and I'm sure he's recommended the best surgeon." A hint of a smile touched his lips again. "And I'm not saying that because Brett's an old friend."

She suddenly saw herself as a child, peering from the housekeeper's cottage toward the swimming pool. A teenage Alex entertained two other boys: Mitch Donovan and Brett Elliot, his closest friends.

"Aunt Maida seems to trust him. That's the important thing."

He nodded, hand on the door. She could sense the impatience in him, as if he wanted to be elsewhere, as if only his deeply ingrained politeness kept him standing there.

She probably should let this go, but she couldn't. She took a breath. "I know Aunt Maida's suggestion has put you on the spot. But it really would ease her mind if she knew I was staying.''

She knew instantly she'd pressed too hard. He seemed to withdraw, putting distance between them even though he hadn't moved. His face set in bleak lines.

Alex had never looked that way when she was growing up. He'd always been surrounded by a golden aura nothing could diminish. But that had been before his wife left, before he'd spent too many weeks in that hospital himself.

"Let's get the immediate situation taken care of first,'' he said. "You settle Maida at the hospital. If she needs anything, she just has to ask.''

"I know that. I'm sure Maida does, too.'' She tried to deny a wave of resentment that he could so easily grant any wish of her aunt's, while she couldn't.

He clasped her hand, sending a surge of warmth along her skin and stealing her breath. Then he dropped it as abruptly as if he'd felt that heat.

"Maida will be glad to have you with her for the operation. I know how much she enjoyed it when you worked here.''

He almost seemed to stumble over the words, as if he found this situation as awkward as she did. It surprised her. Smooth, sophisticated Alex had never been at a loss for the right phrase. That ability was something else the upper crust seemed to be born with.

All the things she didn't want to say about the time she worked in the Caine mansion skittered through her mind. Still, it wouldn't hurt to remind him that his son already knew her. "I appreciated the chance to take care of Jason. How is he?"

"Fine." His face seemed to stiffen again. "Looking forward to summer vacation after the rigors of second grade."

She had the sense of something suppressed, something he didn't want to say about his son, and thought again of Aunt Maida's worries about the boy.

"He used to be such a happy child. But his mother went away, and then Alex was in the accident and in the hospital all those weeks. Jason's changed. He's all curled up inside himself, and I don't know how to help him."

"I'm looking forward to seeing him." She tried to keep the words casual. "Does he really want a fast-food burger, or did you just make that up?"

"Believe it or not, he does. Maida and I try to educate his palate, but he's very much a seven-year-old in his tastes." The skin at the corners of his eyes crinkled. "I think you gave him his first trip to get fast food when you took care of him, didn't you?"

"I'm afraid so." She remembered it as if it were yesterday. Jason's excitement at ordering from the counter, the awed look on his face as he sat across from her in the booth. The feelings that welled up at how much he resembled his father. That emotion struck her again, as strong as if someone had hit her.

Lord, what's happening to me? I thought I was over this.

Alex's dark, intent gaze penetrated the barrier she'd so carefully erected to shield her errant emotions. "What is it? What's wrong?"

"Nothing." She looked up and summoned a smile that felt tight on her lips. "Everything's okay."

She'd like to convince him. She'd like to convince herself. Alex couldn't know that, thanks to the accident, for nearly two years she hadn't been able to remember the crash or the months that had preceded it.

He didn't know that the memories of the time she'd spent in this house had fallen out of the hidden recesses of her mind a week ago, as fresh and as emotional as if they'd happened yesterday.

And prominent among them was the fact that the last time she was here, she'd fallen in love with Alex Caine.

Chapter Two

"Dad, is Maida going to come back?"

The forlorn note in his son's voice touched Alex's heart. What did Jason fear? That Maida had gone away and would never come back, like his mother?

Careful, careful. "What makes you think she won't come back?"

Alex glanced across the front seat of the car. Jason, who'd seemed happy enough at the restaurant, now sat clutching the plastic action figure that had come with his meal.

He frowned down at the figure, then looked up, his small face tightening into the mask that frustrated Alex as much as it did Jason's teachers.

Where has he gone, Lord? Where is the sunny little boy Jason used to be?

He felt almost embarrassed at the involuntary prayer, and his hands tightened on the wheel with determination. He was all Jason had, and he wouldn't let him down.

His son shouldn't have to worry, about Maida or anything else. Naturally he'd had to tell Jason something to explain Maida's absence, but he'd said as little as possible.

"She's just tired," he said now, trying to sound cheerful. "She needs to rest more. It's nothing you have to be concerned about. She'll be back before you know it, and everything will be fine."

They passed twin stone pillars and swung into the driveway. Paula, still wearing the jeans and sweatshirt that seemed to be her uniform, was bending over the trunk of a disreputable old car in his garage. She looked up at their approach, and he pulled into the bay next to her. When he got out, she was already explaining.

"I hope this is okay. Aunt Maida said you wouldn't mind if I parked my car here." She glanced down the row of empty bays, a question in her eyes.

"No problem. I got rid of the other cars after my father died."

Nobody needed five cars. His father had insisted on trying to relive the old days, when a full-time chauffeur had taken loving care of a fleet of vehicles, a full-time gardener tended the roses, and Maida supervised a staff of three indoors. Now they made do with a cleaning company and a lawn service, with Maida watching Jason when he wasn't in school.

He waited for Paula to make some comment, but her attention was fixed on the small figure coming around the car.

"Jason, hi. It's good to see you again."

Jason nodded warily, always seeming on guard with strangers. Not that Paula was exactly a stranger, but at his age, two years was a long time.

"Hey, you got the green Raider." She touched the action figure Jason held. "Good going. He's the best, isn't he?"

His son's protective stance relaxed a little. "One of the guys in my class says the orange one's better, but I like the green one. He can do cool stuff."

"He sure can. Did you see the story where he rescued the princess?"

"Yeah. And when he set all the horses free. That was neat." Jason's face grew animated as he talked about the latest adventure of his action hero.

How had Paula gotten past his son's defenses so quickly? Alex felt something that might have been envy, then dismissed it. She was a teacher—she should be good with children.

Paula pulled a duffel bag from the trunk, and Alex reached out to take it from her. It was heavier than it looked, and for a moment their hands entangled.

"Rocks?" he enquired, lifting an eyebrow.

"Books." She made an abortive movement, as if to take the bag back, then seemed to think better of it. "I never go anywhere without them."

He glanced into the car's trunk. One cardboard carton overflowed with construction paper, and a plastic Halloween pumpkin poked improbably from another. "It looks as if you've brought everything you own."

He meant the comment lightly, but a shadow crossed her face. It told him more clearly than words that how long she stayed depended on him. She shrugged, turning to pull out another bag.

"Most of this stuff is from my classroom. I loaded it up the last day and didn't take the time to unload before I left to come here."

"I'll carry that one." Jason reached for the small bag.

"Thanks, Jason." She smiled, surrendering it to him, then hefted a box out and slammed the trunk. "I think that's it." She glanced at Alex. "If you're sure it's okay for me to leave the car here?"

"It's fine," he said firmly. He'd rather see that poor excuse for a car hidden behind garage doors than parked in his drive. Lifting the duffel bag, he led the way around down the walk toward the rear of the house.

The setting sun turned the swimming pool's surface to gold as they neared the flagstone patio. He hadn't done the water exercises for his injured leg today, and it took an effort to walk evenly carrying the heavy bag. He'd already seen Paula's expression at the scar on his face. He didn't want to see more pity if she caught him limping.

What did she really think about this idea of Maida's? Had it made her remember what happened between them the last time she was here?

One kiss, that was all. It was ridiculous to worry about the effect of one kiss. Of course he shouldn't have done it. She'd been working in his house, and that alone made her out of bounds to him.

Even if that hadn't been the case, he'd learned something when his wife's death, so soon after she'd left him, had made patching up their failing marriage impossible. Even if Karin had survived, even if she'd come back to the small-town life she detested, he'd known then that finding the love of a lifetime was an illusion. Reality was raising his son properly and maintaining the business this whole town relied on. He didn't intend to chase any more romantic rainbows.

So what was he doing watching Paula's smooth, easy stride, eyeing the swing of blond hair against her shoulder when she looked down to smile at Jason? He should have better sense.

She paused at the pool, bending to dip her fingers

in the water. "Nice. I'll bet you're in the pool all the time, now that school's out."

Jason shrugged. "Mostly my dad uses it. To make his leg better."

Alex braced himself for the look of pity, but she just nodded.

"Good idea."

"If you'd like to use the pool while you're here, please do." He disliked the stilted tone of his voice. Paula's presence had thrown him off balance. She was part of an embarrassing incident in his past, and she was also a reminder of the plane crash.

But she'd probably long since forgotten about that kiss. As for the accident, that was something every survivor had to deal with in his own way.

"Thanks." She stood. "I don't know if I'll be here that long."

Her words challenged him, but he wouldn't be drawn in. He'd ignore that particular problem for the moment. Jason had gotten several strides ahead, leaving them side by side. As they headed for the housekeeper's cottage, Alex lowered his voice. "How did Maida seem when you visited her? I hope she's not too worried about the surgery. Or about not having told me. She needs to concentrate on getting well, rather than worrying about us."

She hesitated, frown lines creasing her forehead.

"She seems to trust the doctor to put things right. We didn't talk long."

"That sounds a bit evasive."

She shot him an annoyed look. "Don't you think it would be more polite not to say so?"

He'd forgotten that directness of hers. It made him smile—when it wasn't irritating him. "I'm worried about Maida, too. Remember?"

"Are you?"

"Yes." All right, now he was annoyed. Maybe that was a safer way to feel with Paula, anyway. "Believe it or not, you're not the only one who cares about her."

Her clear green eyes seemed to weigh his sincerity. Then she nodded with a kind of cautious acceptance. "The surgeon says she should come through the operation with flying colors, and then Brett will supervise her rehabilitation. That'll take time, and he wouldn't guess how long until she can come home."

He glanced at his son. "I haven't mentioned the surgery to Jason. I just said Maida needed a rest. The less he knows, the better."

She frowned as if disagreeing, but didn't argue. She moved toward his son. "Just put that on the porch, Jason. I'll take it in later."

She dropped her bags and sat down on the step, then patted the spot next to her. "Have a seat and tell me what's been going on. I haven't seen you for a long time."

Jason sat cautiously, seeming ready to dart away at a moment's notice.

Had Alex been that shy when he was Jason's age? He thought not, but then his father had always insisted on the social graces, no matter what he actually felt. Maybe, if his mother had lived, things would have been different. He stood stiffly, not comfortable with sitting down next to them, not willing to walk away, either.

"Bet you're glad school's out for the summer," Paula said. "I know my kids were."

Jason glanced up at her. "You have kids?"

"My students," she corrected herself. "I teach kindergarten. My school finished up yesterday, and everyone celebrated. Did you have a party the last day?"

Jason nodded. "We played games. And Maida made cupcakes for me to take."

Alex hadn't known that, but, of course, it was the sort of thing Maida would do. He shifted uncomfortably, trying to ease the pain in his leg. With the crucial business deal pending, he'd had trouble keeping up with anything else lately, including second-grade parties. He should go in and get back to work, but still he lingered, watching Paula with his son.

"I'll bet the kids liked those," she said. "Maida makes the best cupcakes."

Jason nodded, glancing down at the step he was scuffing with the toe of his shoe. Then he looked up at Paula. "Did you come here to teach me?"

"Teach you?" she echoed. "Why would I do that? School's out for the summer."

Jason shrugged, not looking at either of them. "My dad thinks I should do better in school."

Shock took Alex's breath away for a moment. Then he found his voice. "Jason, I don't think that at all. And it's not something we should talk about to Paula, anyway."

Paula ignored him, all her attention focused on Jason. Her hand rested lightly on his son's shoulder. "Hey, second grade is tough for lots of people. I remember how hard it was when I had to start writing instead of printing. My teacher said my cursive looked like chicken scratches."

"Honest?" Jason darted a glance at her.

"Honest." She smiled at him. "You can ask Aunt Maida if you don't believe me. She probably remembers when I used to try to write letters to her. Sometimes she'd call me to find out what I'd said."

She'd managed to wipe the tension from Jason's face with a few words. Alex didn't know whether to be pleased or jealous that she'd formed such instant rapport with his son. Paula seemed to have a talent for inspiring mixed feelings in him.

Her blond hair swung across her cheek as she leaned toward Jason, saying something. The impulse to reach out and brush it back was so strong that his hand actually started to move before common sense took over.

Mixed feelings, indeed. The predominant feeling he had toward Paula Hansen wasn't mixed at all. It was one he'd better ignore, for both their sakes.

Paula stood on the tiny porch of the housekeeper's cottage the next morning, looking across the expansive grounds that glistened from last night's shower. The sun, having made it over the steep mountains surrounding Bedford Creek, slanted toward the birch tree at the end of the pool, turning its wet leaves to silver. The only sound that pierced the stillness was the persistent call of a bobwhite.

The stillness had made this secluded village seem like a haven to her when she was a child. She'd arrived in the Pennsylvania mountains from Baltimore, leaving behind the crowded row house echoing with the noise her brothers made. Four brothers—all of them older, all of them thinking they had the right to boss her around. Her childhood had sometimes seemed like one long battle—for privacy, for space, for the freedom to be who she was.

Here she'd stepped into a different world—one with nature on the doorstep, one filled with order and quiet. She couldn't possibly imagine the Caine mansion putting up with a loud game of keep-away in its center hall. It would have ejected the intruders forcibly.

Paula glanced toward the back of the mansion, wondering how much Alex had changed it since his father's death. The room on the end was the solarium. She remembered it filled with plants, but Alex had apparently converted it to a workout room. She could see the equipment through the floor-to-ceiling windows.

Next came the kitchen, with its smaller windows overlooking the pool. She should be there right now, fixing breakfast for Alex and Jason, but Alex had made it very clear he didn't want that.

Aunt Maida wasn't going to be happy. The last thing she'd said the night before had been to fix breakfast. Paula's protests—that Alex had told her not to, that Alex hadn't agreed to let her stay yet—had fallen on deaf ears.

Maida's stubborn streak was legendary in the Hansen family. Paula's father was the same, and any battle between Maida and him was a clash of wills. She vividly remembered the war over Maida's determination that Paula go to college. If not for Maida, Paula might have given up, accepting her father's dictum that girls got marriage certificates, not degrees. Her dream of a profession might have remained a dream.

But Maida wouldn't allow that. She'd pushed, encouraged, demanded. Paula had worked two jobs for most of the four years of college, but she'd made it through, thanks to Aunt Maida.

She leaned against the porch rail, watching a pair of wrens twittering in the thick yew hedge that stretched from the housekeeper's cottage toward the garage. If only she could find a way to help her aunt, to help Jason, without being a servant in Alex Caine's house.

She and Jason had played on the flagstone patio when she was his nanny. They'd sat in the gazebo with a storybook, and he'd leaned against her confidently, his small head burrowed against her arm. She remembered, so well, the vulnerable curve of his neck, the little-boy smell of him. He'd look up at her, his dark eyes so like his father's, sure he could trust her, sure she'd be there for him. And then she'd gone away.

What am I supposed to do, Lord? If Alex said no, would she be upset or would she be relieved? Only the guilt she felt over Jason kept her from running in the opposite direction rather than face Alex Caine every day and remember how he'd kissed her and then turned away, embarrassed.

Infatuation, she told herself sternly. It was infatuation, nothing more. She would stop imagining it was love.

She remembered, only too clearly, standing in the moonlight looking up at him, her feelings surely written on her face. Then recognition swept over her. Alex regretted that kiss. He probably thought she'd invited it. Humiliation flooded her, as harsh and scalding as acid.

She'd mumbled some excuse and run back to Aunt Maida's cottage. And a few days later, when she'd realized the feelings weren't going to fade, she'd made another excuse and left her job several weeks earlier than she'd intended, prepared to scurry back to Baltimore.

The flow of memories slowed, sputtering to a painful halt. Her last clear recollection was of Alex lifting her suitcase into the limo next to his own, saying he had to take the commuter flight out that day, too. Then—nothing. She'd eventually regained the rest of her memories, but the actual take-off and crash remained hidden, perhaps gone forever.

When she'd recovered enough to ask questions, her parents had simply said she'd been on her way home from her summer job. If she'd remembered then, would she have done anything differently? She wasn't sure. The failure had lain hidden in her mind.

Now, according to Aunt Maida, anyway, God was

giving her a chance to make up for whatever mistakes she'd made then. Unlike most of the people Paula knew, Aunt Maida never hesitated to bring God into every decision.

Whether Maida was right about God's will, Paula didn't know. But her aunt was right about one thing—Jason had changed. Paula pictured his wary expression, the way he hunched his shoulders. The happy child he'd been once had vanished.

Of course, he was old enough now to understand a little more about his mother's leaving. That traumatic event, followed so soon by the plane crash that injured his father, was enough to cause problems for any child. And he must know that his mother wouldn't be coming back. Maida had told her the details that hadn't appeared in Karin's brief obituary—the wild party, the drunken driver. Paula frowned, thinking of students who'd struggled with similar losses.

A flicker of movement beyond the yew hedge caught her eye. Between the glossy dark leaves, she glimpsed a bright yellow shirt. She'd thought Jason was at breakfast with his father. What was he doing?

She rounded the corner of the cottage and spotted the child. The greeting she'd been about to call out died on her lips. All her teacher instincts went on alert. She might not know Jason well any longer, but she knew what a kid up to something looked like.

Jason bent over something on the ground, his body shielding it from her view.

She moved quietly across the grass. "Jason? What's up?"

He jerked around at her voice, dropping the object he held. The crumpled paper lit with a sudden spark, a flame shooting up.

She winced back, heart pounding, stomach contracting. *Run!* a voice screamed in her head. *Run!*

She took a breath, then another. She didn't need to run. Nothing would hurt her. *It's all right.* She repeated the comforting words over in her mind. It was all right.

Except that it wasn't. Quite aside from the terror of fire that had plagued her since the accident, what was Jason doing playing with matches? Another thought jolted her. Was this connected with his father's narrow escape from a fiery death?

Carefully she stepped on the spark that remained, grinding it into the still-wet grass. The scent of burning lingered in the air, sickening her.

She looked at Jason, and he took a quick step back. "Where'd you get the matches, Jason?"

His lower lip came out. "I don't know what you're talking about. I don't have any matches."

"Sure you do." She held out her hand. "Give them to me."

Maybe it was the calm, authoritative "teacher"

voice. Jason dug into his jeans' pocket, pulled out the matchbook and dropped it into her hand.

She closed her fingers firmly around it. She wouldn't let them tremble. "Where did you get this?"

For a moment she thought he wouldn't answer. He glared at her, dark eyes defiant. Then he shrugged. "My dad's desk. Are you gonna tell him?"

"I think someone should, don't you?" It would hardly be surprising if Jason's unresolved feelings about his father's accident had led to a fascination with fire. Not surprising, but dangerous.

"No!" His anger flared so suddenly that it caught her by surprise. His small fists clenched. "Leave me alone."

"Jason..." She reached toward him, impelled by the need to comfort him, but he dodged away from her.

"Go away!" He nearly shouted the words. "Just go away!" He turned and ran toward the house.

She discovered she was shaking and wrapped her arms around herself. Jason had made his feelings clear. His was definitely a vote for her to leave.

Alex put the weights back on their rack and stretched, gently flexing his injured knee. Brett Elliot, one of his oldest friends as well as his doctor, would personally supervise his workouts if he thought Alex was skipping them. And Brett was right; Alex had to admit it. The exercise therapy had brought him miles from where he'd been after the accident.

He toweled off, then picked up his juice bottle and stepped through the French doors to the flagstones surrounding the pool. The water looked tempting with the hot June sunshine bouncing from its surface, but he had another goal in mind at the moment. Jason was off on some game of his own. It was time Alex talked to Paula. He had to find some graceful way to get them both out of this difficult situation, in spite of the fact that he hadn't yet found someone else to replace Maida.

His timing seemed perfect. Paula was coming around the pool toward the house, dressed a bit formally for her. Instead of her usual jeans, she wore neat tan slacks and a bright coral top—probably a concession for a trip to the hospital. She briefly checked her swift stride when she saw him, and then she came toward him.

"Good morning." He tossed the towel over his shoulder and set his juice bottle on the patio table. *Business,* he reminded himself. "I hoped I'd have a chance to see you this morning."

Paula rubbed her arms, as if she were cold in spite of the June sunshine. "Aren't you going to the factory today?"

"Not until later," he said. "I'll work at home for

a while, then stop by the hospital to see how Maida's doing.'' He hesitated, looking for words, but since Paula was so direct herself, she should appreciate the same from him. "We should get a few things settled."

For just an instant Paula's eyes were puzzled, as if she'd been thinking about something else entirely. Then she gave him a wary look and took a step back.

"I have to leave for the hospital." She glanced at her watch. "I want to be there when Aunt Maida wakes up from the operation."

"This will take just a few minutes. We've got to discuss this idea of Maida's." He knew he sounded inflexible, but he didn't want to put this off. The longer he waited, the more difficult it would be.

He pulled out a deck chair for her. Looking reluctant, she sat down. He settled in the seat next to her and instantly regretted his choice. They were facing the gazebo at the end of the pool. They shouldn't be having this conversation in view of the spot where he'd kissed her.

But it was too late now, and maybe it was just as well. That embarrassing episode should make her as reluctant as he was to pursue Maida's scheme. He'd give her an easy way out of this dilemma, that was all. And she'd be ready to leave.

Paula tugged at the sleeves of her knit top. Apparently she did that whenever she was nervous, as if she were protecting herself. He tried not to notice how the coral sweater brought out the warm, peachy color in her cheeks, or how the fine gold chain she wore glinted against her skin.

Stick to business, he ordered himself. That was a good way to think of it. This was just like any business negotiation, and they both needed to go away from it feeling they'd gained something.

"Be honest with me, Paula. You don't really want to work here this summer, do you?"

She glanced up at him, a startled expression in her eyes. "What makes you say that?"

To his surprise, he couldn't quite get the real reason out. *Because the last time you were here, I kissed you and created an awkward situation for both of us. Because in spite of that, I still find you too attractive for my own peace of mind.*

No, he didn't want to say any of that. He tried a different tack.

"You probably had a teaching job of some sort lined up for the summer, didn't you?"

She shook her head, a rueful smile touching her lips. "There's not much teaching available in the summer. I was signed up with a temp agency for office work."

"Office work?" He couldn't stop the surprise in his voice, and realized instantly how condescending it sounded. "Why? I mean, couldn't you find anything else?"

Her expression suggested he didn't have a clue as to how the real world worked. "Kindergarten teachers aren't exactly on corporate headhunters' wish lists, you know."

"But aren't there courses you want to take in the summer?" He didn't know why the thought of Paula taking temporary work to make ends meet bothered him so much. His reaction was totally irrational.

"I can't afford to take classes." She said it slowly and distinctly, as if they spoke different languages. "I have college loans to pay off."

Belatedly he reminded himself he was supposed to be dissuading her from working for him. "Even so, I can't imagine that you'd want to come here to cook and take care of Jason, instead."

He saw immediately that he'd said the wrong thing. In fact, he'd probably said a lot of wrong things. Paula had that effect on him.

She stiffened, and anger flared in her face. "Cooking is honest work. There's nothing to be ashamed of in what my aunt does," she snapped, and she gripped the arms of the deck chair as if about to launch herself out of it.

"No, of course not." He seemed to be going even farther in the wrong direction. "I didn't mean to imply that."

She stood, anger coming off her in waves. "I really have to leave for the hospital now, Alex. I've told my aunt I'm willing to fill in for her here as long as necessary, but, of course, you may have other plans. Either way, it's up to you."

She spun on her heel before he could find words to stop her. He watched her stalk toward the garage, head high.

Great. That was certainly the clumsiest negotiation he'd ever attempted. If he did that poorly in the business deal, the plant would be closed within a month.

Paula had thrown the decision right back into his lap, and she'd certainly made her position clear. If he didn't want her here, he'd have to be the one to say it. Unfortunately, where Paula was concerned, he really wasn't sure what he wanted.

Chapter Three

Alex hadn't hired her, and maybe he wouldn't. But she couldn't just let things go. Paula pulled into the garage late that afternoon, aware of how pitiful her junker looked in the cavernous building. Aunt Maida was still groggy from the successful surgery, but she'd soon be well enough to demand a report. Paula had to be able to reassure her.

She walked quickly to the back door of the mansion. A small bicycle leaned against the laundry room door, reminding her of Jason and the matches. She should have told Alex, but their conversation had veered off in another direction entirely, and she hadn't found the words. Maybe she still hadn't.

Even the geranium on the kitchen window sill seemed to droop in Maida's absence. Breakfast dishes, stacked in the sink, made it clear that when Alex said he'd fix breakfast for himself and Jason, he hadn't considered cleaning up. She turned the water on. It wasn't her job. Alex hadn't hired her. But Maida's kitchen had always been spotless, and she couldn't leave it this way.

This was for Maida, she told herself, plunging her hands into hot, sudsy water. Not for Alex.

She'd been angry at Alex's implications about the housekeeper position, but she'd been just as guilty of thinking Maida's job less important than her own. Now it was the job she needed and wanted to fill— if only she could erase the memory of Alex's kiss.

Enough. She concentrated on rubbing each piece of the sterling flatware. She'd come here to make up for the past by helping Jason through this difficult time. That was all.

She heard the door swing behind her and turned. Jason stood staring at her. For a moment he didn't move. Then he came toward her slowly. He stopped a few feet away.

"I came to say I'm sorry."

"Are you, Jason?" Was it regret or good manners that brought him here? Maybe it didn't really matter. At least he was talking. That was better than silence.

"I shouldn't have yelled at you." A quiver of apprehension crossed his face. "Did you tell my dad?"

"No." She pulled out a chair at the pine kitchen

table. "I think Maida has some lemonade in the refrigerator. Want a glass?"

He nodded a little stiffly. "That would be nice."

He was like his father, in manner as well as in looks, she thought as she poured two glasses of lemonade. Same dark hair and eyes, same well-defined bone structure, same strict courtesy.

He didn't have the stiff upper lip to his father's degree of perfection, though. He watched her apprehensively as she sat down across from him.

"I don't want to tell him." The words surprised her. Surely she should—but if she did, she'd never get beyond the barrier Jason seemed to have erected against the world. "I think *you* should, though. It's pretty serious stuff. You could have gotten hurt."

"I won't do it again." Dark eyes pleaded with her. "Promise you won't say anything. I won't do it again, honest."

She studied his expression. Even at seven or eight, a lot of kids had figured out how to tell adults what they wanted to hear, instead of the truth. But Jason seemed genuinely dismayed at the result of his actions.

She took a deep breath. *Let me make the right decision. Please.*

"Okay, Jason. If you promise you won't do it again, I promise I won't tell."

His relieved smile was the first one she'd seen

from him. *Like his father,* she thought again. A smile that rare made you want to forgive anything, just to see it.

Jason didn't seem to have inherited any qualities from his mother. Did he miss her and wonder why she'd disappeared? Maybe by now he'd made peace with his loss.

She watched as he gulped the lemonade. Guilt seemed to have made him thirsty. Finally he set the glass down, looking at it, not at her.

"Is Maida really going to come back?"

The question startled her. "Sure she is. Why do you think she wouldn't?"

"I heard Daddy talking." He fixed her with an intent gaze. "He told me she just needed to rest a while, but I heard him tell somebody on the phone that she was in the hospital. Is she going to stay there?"

Never lie to a child; that was one of her bedrock beliefs as a teacher. If something was going to hurt, going to be unpleasant, a child had the same right as an adult to prepare for it.

"Only for a little while," she said carefully, remembering Alex's determination to shield his son. "She had to go into the hospital to have her hip fixed."

His face clouded. "I don't want her to stay there. Can't Dr. Brett just give her some medicine?"

The bereft tone touched her. "I know you don't want her to be away, but medicine won't fix what's wrong. She had to have an operation, and they gave her a brand-new joint. Now she has to stay at the hospital and do exercises until she's better."

"Like my dad does for his leg?"

"Sort of like that." She seemed to see Alex again in the workout clothes he'd worn that morning, and her mouth went dry. "Then when she's well, she'll be able to come back."

His gaze met hers, and she read a challenge in it. "You didn't come back. Not for a long time."

It was like a blow to the heart. Jason was talking about when she'd been his nanny. Maybe, underneath the words, he was thinking about his mother, too.

She longed to put her hand over his where it lay on the table, but he was such a prickly child that she was afraid of making him withdraw. She prayed for the right words.

"I want you to listen, Jason, because I'm telling you the truth. Maida loves you. If she could have skipped the operation to stay with you, she would have. She's going to come back, and in the meantime, you'll be okay."

"Are you going to stay?" His lips trembled. "Are you? I know I said I wanted you to go away, but I didn't mean it. I want you to stay."

Guilt gripped her throat in a vise so tight she

couldn't speak. She'd asked God to show her what to do. Was this His answer, in the voice of a troubled little boy?

She cleared her throat. ''I'm not sure, Jason. But I'm going to talk to your daddy about it.''

''When?'' Urgency filled his voice. ''When?''

Somehow, whatever it took, she had to convince Alex to let her stay. She stood. ''Right now.''

Alex had been trying to concentrate on work for the past half-hour, but all he could think about was how he'd manage the coming weeks. His business, his family, his home were too intertwined to separate.

He didn't have any illusions that it would be easy to replace Maida. First of all, no one *could* really replace her. She was the closest thing to a mother Jason had.

Tension radiated down his spine. Jason had had enough losses in his young life. It was up to his father to protect him from any more.

It was also up to his father to provide for his future. If this deal with Dieter Industries didn't go through, and soon, the Caine company would be on the verge of collapse. Their hand-crafted furniture would go the way of the lumber mills founded by his great-grandfather. Probably not even his private fortune could save it. Several hundred people would be out of work, thanks to Caine Industries's failure.

He didn't have the luxury of time. Dieter was sending someone over within weeks. Alex had to be ready, or they all lost.

He glanced up at the portrait of his father that hung over the library's tile fireplace. Jonathan Caine stared sternly from the heavy gold frame, as if he mentally weighed and measured everyone he saw and found them wanting. He would no more understand the firm's current crisis than he'd be able to admit that his mistakes had led to it.

His father's stroke and death, coming when he heard the news of the crash, had seemed the knockout blow. But Alex had found out, once he took over, just how badly off the company was. And he'd realized there were still blows to come. He'd spent the past two years trying to solve the company's problems, and he still didn't know if he could succeed.

This was getting him nowhere. Alex walked to the floor-length window and looked down at the town—his town. He knew every inch of its steep narrow streets, folded into the cleft of the mountains. Sometimes he thought he knew every soul in town.

Caines had taken care of Bedford Creek since the first Caine, a railroad baron, had built his mansion on the hill in the decade after the Civil War. Bedford Creek had two economic bases: its scenic beauty and Caine Industries. If the corporation went under, how would the town survive? How would he?

The rap on the door was tentative. Then it came again, stronger this time. He crossed the room with impatient steps and opened the door.

"Paula." That jolt to his solar plexus each time he saw her ought to be getting familiar by now. "I'm sorry, but this isn't a good time."

"This is important."

What was one more disruption to his day? He wasn't getting anything accomplished, anyway. He stepped back, gesturing her in.

"Is something wrong?"

She swung to face him. "Have you made a decision about hiring someone to replace my aunt?"

He motioned to a chair, but she shook her head, planting herself in the center of the oriental carpet and looking at him.

"Not yet," he admitted. "Summer is tourist season in Bedford Creek. Everyone who wants a job is probably already working."

He couldn't deny the fact that Maida had been right about one thing. Paula could be the answer to his problems. But the uncomfortable ending to her previous stay, his own mixed feelings for her, made that impossible. He couldn't seem to get past that.

"You have to have someone Jason can get along with." She hesitated. "I couldn't help thinking that he's changed."

He stiffened. "My son is fine." *Fine,* he repeated silently.

"He seems to believe you're disappointed in his school work."

Her clear, candid gaze bored into him. "He misunderstood," he said shortly. "Jason is very bright." He glared at her, daring her to disagree.

"Yes, of course he is. But that doesn't mean school is easy for him."

"Paula, I don't want to discuss my son with you. Jason is fine. Now, is there anything else?"

She looked at him for what felt like a long moment, and he couldn't tell what was going on behind her usually expressive face. Then her eyes flickered.

"Just one thing. You should hire me to fill in until Maida is well again."

Paula's heart pounded in her ears. She hadn't intended to blurt it out like that. She'd thought she'd lead up to it, present her arguments rationally. Unfortunately, she didn't seem able to think in any sensible manner when she was around Alex.

That in itself was a good reason to run the other direction. *"You didn't come back, not for a long time."* Jason's plaintive voice echoed in her mind. No, she couldn't let him down. He needed someone, and she was the one he wanted right now.

Alex wasn't answering, and that fact jacked up her

tension level. He was probably trying to find a polite way to tell her he'd rather hire anyone else but her.

He walked to the other side of the long library table he used as a desk. It was littered with papers, and supported an elaborate computer system. Maybe he wanted to put some space between them, or maybe he was emphasizing the fact that this was his office, his house, his decision.

But there, beyond him, was the window seat where she'd curled up as a child. There, on the lowest shelf, were the storybooks she'd read. She had a place here, too.

He looked at her, a frown sending three vertical lines between his dark brows. "Are you sure this is something you want to do?"

She took a breath. At least he hadn't started with "no." Maybe he was willing to consider it. "Jason knows me, and Aunt Maida would feel better. I'm sure she'd call me five times a day from the hospital if the doctor would let her, just to be sure everything is all right."

"That's not what I asked." His gaze probed beneath the surface. "How do you feel about it, Paula?"

How did she feel about it? Mixed emotions—that was probably the best way to describe it. But Alex didn't need to know that. "I want the job. I think I can do it, although I don't have much experience."

She remembered Aunt Maida's concerns, and plunged on. "I know you have some important entertaining coming up in the next month. If you're worried about that..."

What could she say? She couldn't claim expertise she didn't have. She'd never put on a fancy party in her life, and she didn't think her usual brand of entertaining was what Alex was used to. He'd probably never ordered in pizza for guests.

"I'm not." He glanced toward the portrait above the mantel, then away. "It's important, of course, but I'll hire a caterer for that, in any event. Maida's job would be to oversee the staff."

It sounded like a breeze compared to the elaborate cooking she'd been imagining. If someone else was doing the work, she ought to be able to manage a simple dinner party. "I think I could do that."

His gaze assessed her, and she stiffened. Maybe she hadn't lived all her life in a mansion, but she was smart enough to work her way through college. How hard could this be in comparison?

"Actually, that's not my concern at the moment." He looked impossibly remote, as if he viewed her through the wrong end of a telescope. "I want to know how you feel about working for me again, after what happened the last time you were here."

It was like a blow to the stomach, rocking her back on her heels. She hadn't dreamed he'd refer to it, had assumed he'd ignore what he probably saw as an unpleasant episode. Or that he'd forgotten it.

"That's all in the past," she said with as much firmness as she could manage. "You apologized. You said we'd pretend it never happened." He'd done a very good job of that, as she knew only too well. The humiliation she'd felt when he'd said those words brought a stinging wave of color to her cheeks. "Why are you bringing it up now?"

"Because I don't want it hanging between us," he said. "I don't want you to spend your time here worrying that I'll make the same mistake again."

A mistake, that's what it was to him. A moment of weakness when the moonlight had tricked him into a brief, romantic gesture he later regretted. Well, he was never going to know it meant any more than that to her.

"Please, forget about it." She forced herself to keep her voice steady and unconcerned. "I already have."

She had, of course. For nearly two years she'd forgotten it entirely. Maybe she'd have been better off if she'd never remembered. But just a week ago, the memory had popped out from behind the locked door in her mind. The doctors couldn't explain why. They'd said she could remember any time, or never.

She swallowed hard. What else might be hiding there? She still didn't remember anything about those moments when the plane went down. Would she suddenly find herself reliving every painful second of the crash?

"Good." He was briskly businesslike. "In that case, we can start with a clean slate between us. If you're really willing to take on this position, it seems to be the best solution for everyone."

She tried to smile. *Position* was a fancy word for it. She was about to become an employee in his house. And she'd have to do it without ever letting him know how she felt about him.

"The best solution for everyone," she echoed. "We couldn't ask for better than that."

She had to find a way to keep her relationship with Alex businesslike—pleasant, but businesslike. She was just another employee to him, and as far as she was concerned, this was just another job. It was no different than if she'd been filing paperwork in someone's office.

Well, maybe a little different. If she were filing papers, she wouldn't be working for someone who tied her heart in knots.

Chapter Four

Paula put the carafe of coffee on a tray and glanced at the schedule Maida had taped to the kitchen cabinet, tension dancing along her nerves. Okay, so far she was on target, although it had probably taken her twice as long as it would have taken Maida. It was a good thing she'd decided to get up early this morning, Paula thought as she headed through the swinging door to the front of the house and up the stairs. Next on the agenda was to take the coffee to Alex's room.

The second-floor hallway was as big as the entire living room in the apartment she shared with another teacher back home. She pushed the thought away. If she let herself make comparisons like that, she'd be too intimidated to do her job.

She tapped first, then opened the heavy door—more English oak. She remembered Maida showing her around the mansion on an earlier visit, explaining how one of Alex's ancestors had imported the paneling and brought artisans over from Germany to create the stained glass. Maida had been as proud as if it belonged to her.

"Paula, good." Alex strode into the bedroom from the bath, still buttoning his shirt. He stopped, looking at her. "Is something wrong?"

"No. Nothing." *Nothing except that I didn't anticipate how this much intimacy would affect me.* She forced down the flutter in her stomach and lifted the tray slightly. "Where would you like this?"

Instead of telling her, he took the tray, his hands brushing hers briefly. Her skin seemed sensitized to his touch, reacting with awareness in every cell. For an instant his gaze held hers. Was there more than business-as-usual in his eyes? Before she could be sure, he turned away and set the tray on the mahogany bureau. He busied himself pouring out a cup of coffee, his back to her.

She'd like to beat a retreat back to the kitchen, but Maida had said Alex would give his daily orders now. *Orders.* Paula swallowed a lump of resentment. She didn't take orders well; she never had. But she couldn't argue with Alex the way she would have with her father or brothers. In this situation, he was the boss, just as he had been when she was Jason's nanny. Their kiss hadn't changed that.

She pulled a pad and pencil from her jeans pocket. She'd taken the precaution of coming prepared, and the sooner this was done, the sooner she could escape. But Alex didn't seem to be in any hurry.

"Do you have some instructions for the day?" she prompted. Somehow "instructions" sounded fractionally better than "orders."

He glanced toward her, the lines around his dark eyes crinkling a little as he gestured with his coffee cup. "Let me get some of this down first. Then I'll be able to think."

She nodded, glad he couldn't know how dry her mouth felt at the moment. This was just too awkward—standing in Alex's private sanctum, watching him drink his morning coffee, noticing the way his dark hair tumbled over his forehead before he'd smoothed it back for the day. But she didn't have a choice.

She forced herself to stand still, glancing around the room to keep from staring at him. The heavy forest-green drapes and equally heavy mahogany furniture darkened the room, and the deep burgundy tones of the oriental carpet didn't help to brighten it. The room looked like a period set, in a museum. In fact, it probably was a period piece, but in a private home. She doubted that the furniture had been changed in several generations.

Had Alex had a colorful little boy's bedroom once, like Jason's? She smiled at the thought. She'd have to ask Maida. Somehow the idea of Alex with a cowboy or astronaut bedspread made him seem more like a regular person, instead of the blue blood who always stood slightly apart from the crowd.

Alex's cup clattered onto the tray, and he swung toward her. "Now, about the day's schedule—" His tone was businesslike, and her image of a little-boy Alex vanished.

"You'll need to see to Jason and the meals, of course. I won't be home for lunch, but I expect him to have a balanced meal. I'm sure Maida's talked to you about all that, hasn't she?"

"Yes." She tried to match his briskness. This was what she'd wanted, wasn't it? Brisk and businesslike, so she wouldn't imagine things she couldn't have. "And I have her schedule of the daily work, and when the cleaners and gardeners come." She poised the pencil over the pad. "I just need any special instructions."

"Hand me that tie, please."

For a split second she stared at the pad, confused, then realized what he meant. She took the striped tie from the dresser and handed it to him. He knotted it expertly, barely glancing in the mirror.

"Today I think it best if you concentrate on Jason. He's bound to feel a little apprehensive about Maida's absence. Try to keep him occupied."

He held out his hand. This time she'd caught on, and she had the suit coat ready to put into it. Again their hands touched, and a faint tingle warmed her fingers. She snatched her hand away quickly.

"I may bring a business contact back to the house this afternoon," he went on, "so please be sure there's coffee brewed and some sort of savories ready."

Her mind went blank. "Savories?"

"Cheese puffs, that sort of thing. Maida always serves something with coffee when people are here." He picked up his briefcase.

Pretzels or cookies probably weren't what he had in mind, she decided. "I'll see what I can do."

"I'll need you to pick up some dry-cleaning—" He was already out the door, and she hurried to follow.

"You can do that when you go to visit Maida. And don't forget to check on shirts to go to the laundry."

She scribbled on the pad, trailing him down the stairs. *Jason, dry-cleaning, laundry, coffee.* What else? Oh, yes, the savories, whatever they were going to be. Maybe she'd been just a bit optimistic in thinking this would be a breeze.

Alex stopped at the bottom of the steps, turning

suddenly. Their faces were on a level, only inches apart. Her breath caught.

"And tomorrow morning the coffee could be a little stronger."

"Stronger, right."

He turned away, heading for the dining room. She started to breathe again. So much for her idea that working for Alex could ever be cool and businesslike.

She'd really ended up with the worst of both worlds, she realized. As Alex's housekeeper, she would be in as close contact with him as a member of the family. But Alex would treat her like a servant, because in his eyes that was all she was.

Alex pulled into the driveway, sending a swift glance toward his passenger. He couldn't go so far as to say Conrad Klemmer's visit had gone well. The representative of the Swiss firm had been stiff, even seeming a little uncomfortable. Perhaps finishing their discussions in Alex's home would loosen him up a little.

It had better. Alex's stomach tightened. With any luck, a pleasant meeting in the library, sipping coffee and eating Maida's cheese straws—

But Maida wasn't here. Paula, quite aside from the totally inappropriate feelings she'd roused in him, was an unknown quantity when it came to running the house. This morning, in his bedroom, she'd seemed off balance. Or maybe he was projecting his own feelings onto her. It had certainly unsettled him to have Paula bringing him his coffee, handing him his tie. He hadn't anticipated the effect on him when she'd come in with his morning tray instead of Maida. He'd tried to act as if it were business as usual, but he probably hadn't succeeded.

Klemmer leaned forward, scanning the mansion from its pillared portico to the octagonal cupola on top.

"You have a lovely home," he commented in British-accented English. He glanced beyond the house, where the thickly wooded hillside swept sharply up to a saddleback ridge. "And a wonderful view."

"Thank you." Alex pulled to a stop and opened the door, surveying the landscape for any disorder and finding none. "We can finish our conversation in greater comfort here. My housekeeper should have some coffee ready for us."

He hoped. He led the way along the walk skirting the bank of rhododendrons, still heavily laden with flowers, that screened the front of the house from view. This meeting would be successful when he had a commitment from Klemmer to bring a full team in to negotiate the deal. Until then, the whole thing could fizzle away into nothing, and his last, best hope of saving the company would be gone.

"I'll get it!"

The shout from the front lawn startled him. They rounded the corner. Paula backpedaled toward them, a fielder's mitt extended. A baseball soared over her head.

He reached for the ball, seeing disaster in the making. He was a second too late. Klemmer caught it.

Paula, wearing her usual jeans and a T-shirt, skidded to a stop inches from them. Beyond her, Jason stood holding a bat, looking horrified.

They ought to be embarrassed. This was hardly the impression he'd expected to make on Klemmer. And it certainly wasn't the welcome he'd told Paula to prepare.

"I'm so sorry." She burst out, her cheeks scarlet. "I didn't mean... We were just practicing a little hitting."

"So I see." He bit off a retort. He couldn't say the words that crowded his tongue. Maybe that was just as well.

Klemmer was already reaching out to shake hands. "What a pleasure to meet your lovely family. This must be Mrs. Caine. I am Conrad Klemmer, your husband's business associate."

He wouldn't have thought it possible for Paula's flush to deepen, but it did.

"No, I—"

"Paula is my housekeeper." He kept his voice calm with an effort. "And this is my son, Jason."

Fortunately Jason remembered his manners. He dropped the bat, came quickly to them and extended his hand.

"How do you do, sir."

Klemmer darted a quick, speculative glance at Paula. Then he smiled. "It's a pleasure to meet both of you."

That speculative look only added more fuel to Alex's anger.

"Jason, will you show Mr. Klemmer to the library? I want to speak with Paula for a moment."

Jason nodded. "This way." He scampered up the steps and opened the door. "I'll show you."

The instant the door closed behind them, Alex turned to Paula, anger making his voice cold.

"Is this your idea of entertaining my business associate?"

"No, this is my idea of entertaining your son." Her green eyes sparked with answering anger. "That was my priority for today, remember?"

There might be some justice in her comment, but he was too annoyed to admit it at the moment. "I distinctly remember telling you I might be bringing an important business associate back with me this afternoon. I didn't expect you to greet him with a fly ball."

He saw her stubborn jaw tighten. "The coffee is

ready, and I found some of Maida's cheese straws in the freezer. Why shouldn't I play ball with Jason?''

"I don't care what you play with Jason," he ground out. "But the back lawn is the appropriate place for baseball, not the front. Jason should know that, even if you don't."

He knew how condescending it sounded the instant the words were out. But before he could say anything else, Paula had turned toward the door.

"I'll bring your coffee to the library." The words were coated with ice. "It will just be a moment."

The library. Klemmer. Alex followed her quickly. The Swiss businessman had to be his major concern right now. He had to salvage what was left of this meeting, if he could.

Then he'd worry about straightening things out with Paula. He wasn't sure which of those would be the more difficult.

Paula resisted the urge to clatter the baking sheet as she pulled cheese straws from the oven. That would be immature and childish. But it would feel so satisfying.

Using a spatula, she slid the straws onto a wire rack to cool for a moment before she took them in to the library. The cheese straws weren't the only things that needed to cool off. If she didn't get her temper under control, she wouldn't dare face Alex and Mr. Klemmer.

Well, she had every right to be angry. Alex had spoken to her as if she were beneath his consideration. As if only a barbarian would play catch with a child on the front lawn.

A reluctant smile tugged at her lips. Alex should see her neighborhood. Kids played ball anywhere and everywhere, including in the street.

The smile faded. Things were different here. She'd known that from the start. She'd known, too, that it was her responsibility to fit into Alex's world, and not the other way around.

Maybe, if she'd stopped to think about it, she'd have realized that the manicured front lawn wasn't intended for a game of catch. But it had been the first thing she'd suggested all day that brought a spark of enthusiasm to Jason's eyes, and she couldn't ignore that.

She wouldn't apologize for it, either. She arranged the coffee and cheese straws on a heavy silver tray, then picked the tray up, suppressing a nervous flutter in her stomach. She'd show Alex that she could be the perfect housekeeper, if that was what he wanted. But she wouldn't apologize for playing with his son. Jason could use a bit more play in his life.

The militant mood carried her down the hallway and right up to the library door. Then she paused, again needing to push down the apprehension that danced along her nerves. If Alex was still angry... well, he'd just have to get over it. She was doing her job. She tapped lightly, then opened the door.

The two men sat in the leather armchairs on either side of the fireplace. Was it just her imagination, or did Alex look worried?

She dismissed the thought. Alex, with his air of always being in perfect control, didn't worry about anything.

"Just put the tray here, please." Alex nodded to the inlaid coffee table between them.

She set the tray down, sensing Alex's quick assessment of it. Apparently satisfied, he nodded.

She poured the coffee into fragile china cups, careful not to let even a drop fall on the gleaming surface of the table. It wasn't until both men were served and she took a step back that she realized she'd been holding her breath.

Ridiculous, she scolded herself. She was being ridiculous to put so much pressure on herself to do this perfectly. And equally silly to imagine Alex would notice, or care.

"Will there be anything else?" she asked.

"That's fine, Paula." Alex's tone was cool and dismissive.

Well, all right. She could take a hint. Maybe he

expected her to bow her way out of his presence, like a servant of a medieval king.

She nodded briskly and spun away. The sooner she got out of here, the better. If they wanted more coffee, they could pour it themselves.

A couple of hours later, she hadn't exactly forgotten her irritation as she started supper, but it had been reduced to a slow simmer. Cooking, she'd discovered, was good for her disposition. Intent on Maida's chicken casserole recipe, she heard the kitchen door swing open. She turned, expecting Jason. But it was Alex, apparently back from delivering Klemmer to his hotel.

Her temper bubbled up again, as if their disagreement had been moments ago instead of an hour ago. "If you're here to deliver a lecture, don't bother." She dried her hands on a linen tea towel.

"Lecture?" His dark brows arched. "What lecture did you have in mind?"

"I got the message. No ball playing on the front lawn."

He held up his hands as if surrendering. "No lectures, I promise. I just came in to see if you had any more hot coffee."

The mild response took the wind out of her sails. It was tough to stay angry with someone who seemed to have forgotten the quarrel. She managed a smile.

"This is a Norwegian kitchen, remember? There's always coffee."

Alex took a heavy white mug from the shelf and filled it. He took a long swallow, then stood staring down at the mug. "I owe you an apology."

That was the last thing she'd expected to hear him say, and it left her momentarily speechless.

He turned toward her, the faintest of smiles curving his firm lips. "I take it you agree."

"I..." She didn't seem to have anything to say. Her anger had slid away, and she didn't know what to replace it with. Maybe it was easier to hold on to the anger, because it provided a protection from feelings she didn't want to recognize. "You don't need to apologize to me. I work for you. If you have a problem with what I'm doing, you have to tell me."

He leaned back against the counter, and the lines of worry in his face were unmistakable. She'd told herself the richest man in town didn't have anything to worry about, but clearly she'd been wrong.

"The point is, I hadn't told you not to play ball on the front lawn. And I certainly shouldn't have spoken to you so sharply." He shook his head. "It wasn't your fault."

She wanted to tell him that it wasn't anybody's fault, that it was perfectly normal for a little boy to play ball on his own front lawn, but she couldn't.

Obviously what was normal in her world wasn't in his.

"I hope your guest wasn't upset." She tried a smile. "At least I didn't give him a concussion."

Alex's face relaxed a fraction. "Thanks to his quick reflexes. I hadn't warned him he'd need a batting helmet when he came."

"Seriously, if you think I should apologize to him, I will." And what had happened to her fine conviction that she didn't owe anyone an apology?

"Not necessary. He has other things on his mind, anyway."

She wondered if expressing concern was beyond the limits of her job. "You look as if you do, too."

For a moment she thought he'd tell her it wasn't her business, but then he shrugged.

"Is it that obvious?"

"Pretty much." She could hardly say that she'd made a profession of studying him the last time she was here, or that she still remembered his every mood as if it had been yesterday.

"I suppose..." He frowned, then shook his head. "Maybe it's best if you know what's going on. What did Maida tell you?"

That Jason was lonely. That you were lonely. No, she couldn't say that, either. "About the business? She said you had some big deal going on, something that would happen this summer. She was worried about entertaining the visitors.''

"I wish that were all I had to worry about." The lines between his brows deepened, and again she had that ridiculous longing to smooth them away.

"What is it, then?" It had to be something serious, to make him look like that.

"If this deal doesn't go through—" He paused as if he didn't want to say anything else. "If it doesn't, I'm going to lose the company."

"But..." She grappled with the idea, trying to get her mind around it. It seemed impossible. "But you've always been the biggest employer in the county. How could this happen?"

"Changing markets, bad decisions." His face was grim. "It doesn't take much, not in today's economy. If this deal with Dieter Industries goes through, it will open up a whole new marketing opportunity for us. If not, the company will go under."

"But so many people count on Caine Industries." That probably wasn't the most comforting thing she could have said.

"Half the town." His hand tightened on the coffee mug until the knuckles turned white. "Half the town directly, and more than that indirectly. If I can't pull off this deal, I'll let all of them down."

The pain he was trying to hide caught at her heart.

"It's not just your responsibility. There are other people involved. No one will blame you."

He shot her a skeptical glance. "You can't believe that, Paula. If Caine Industries goes under, everyone will blame me—most of all I will blame me. And there won't be a company to leave to my son."

She didn't have any words to deal with something like this. Apparently the prince in his castle wasn't safe from the world's problems, after all.

"I'm sorry," she said at last.

He shrugged, pushing away from the counter. "I thought you should know what's at stake, because you're a part of it. These people from Dieter have to be entertained, and they expect it to be in my home. That means you have to keep things running properly."

No more ball games on the front lawn, in other words. Why hadn't Maida explained all this to her? Because she'd been afraid Paula would run at the thought of it?

Or because she knew one little boy was in danger of getting lost in the midst of all this high-powered business.

Paula realized Alex was waiting for some response from her. She looked up, meeting his gaze. "I'll do my best," she said. *My best for Jason, and for you.*

Chapter Five

The prince in the castle, the man who had everything, stood on the verge of losing it all. *No, not all*,
Paula corrected herself, drying the silverware from
breakfast the next morning. The Caine family fortune
would probably survive the loss of the company that
bore its name. But for a proud, private man like Alex,
the blow would still be severe. When he'd said there
might be no company to leave to his son, she'd
glimpsed a secret agony in his eyes that he probably
didn't guess he'd revealed.

He wouldn't like it that he'd exposed so much of
his inner life to her. She knew that instinctively. He
wasn't a man who confided his troubles willingly or
easily. Probably no one in Bedford Creek understood
just how important this business deal of Alex's was
to all of them.

Paula stared absently out at the June sunlight slanting over the mountain, gilding the pool. Aunt Maida didn't know how crucial it was. She'd never have kept that from Paula. *"Take care of Jason."* Maida's voice rang in Paula's mind. *"Find out what's bothering that child."*

Paula found herself counting the number of times Jason had smiled. Twice the day before, when they'd been playing ball. Once today, when she'd made a happy face with syrup on his pancake.

She clasped wet hands on the edge of the sink. *Dear Father, if Maida's right, if you do have something for me to do here, please show me my task.*

"Washing-up prayers," Maida called them. She always said she could feel as close to God standing at the sink as she could in church.

Movement on the patio caught Paula's eye. Alex skirted the pool, then headed for the empty cottage the gardener had occupied, back in the days when estates like this one had live-in gardeners. As she watched from the window, he opened the door and went inside.

She'd probably never have a better chance to catch him where Jason couldn't overhear. Maybe God was answering her prayer already, giving her an opportunity to talk to Alex about Jason's needs. She dried her hands and hurried out the back.

Curiosity overtook her as she approached the cottage. What had brought Alex here? She knocked.

The door swung open promptly, but before she could see inside, Alex's tall frame blocked the space.

"Paula." He didn't sound particularly welcoming. "I'm rather busy. Can this wait?"

"I'd like to talk with you before you leave for the plant. May I come in?"

She took a step toward the door. Alex didn't back away. Instead, he stood like a solid barrier, his frown a warning signal.

"We can discuss whatever it is this evening. I really don't have time now." His tone suggested that anything she might wish to discuss was far less important than his agenda.

She fought to control her temper. She wanted to involve him in making plans for Jason, not alienate him. "I want to talk with you about Jason, and I'd like to do it where there's no chance he'll overhear." Again she made a slight movement toward the door, and again his immobility stopped her. For a moment he just looked at her, frowning.

Then he stepped out of the cottage and pulled the door closed behind him. She heard a lock snap.

She lifted her eyebrows. "I wasn't planning to break in. You didn't need to lock it."

His frown deepened. "I keep some plans I'm

working on in there,'' he said. ''The office stays locked so they won't be disturbed.''

In other words, he didn't get away from work even when he was at home. She wondered if he had any idea just how compulsive that sounded.

He took her arm, leading her a few steps away from the cottage, and her skin warmed as if she'd walked into the sunlight.

''All right, what's so important?'' He shot back his shirtsleeve to consult his watch. ''I have to be down at the plant in less than half an hour.''

''I want to talk with you about Jason.''

''You already said that. What about Jason?'' That faintly defensive tone she'd noticed before threaded his voice.

Carefully, she thought. Say this carefully. ''I'm a little concerned about him. I know this is a difficult time for him with Maida in the hospital, but he seems so withdrawn.''

''Withdrawn?'' She had the sense that his muscles tightened. Hers seemed to clench, too, as if preparing to fight or run. ''My son is not withdrawn.''

She tried to force herself to relax, tried to smile. ''You make it sound like a communicable disease.''

He didn't smile back.

''Alex, I'm just afraid he's worrying too much about things, instead of talking them over with people he trusts.''

"You can't expect him to trust you immediately. He probably barely remembers you from the last time you were here."

"I realize that." *Even though I remember him, and you, as if it were yesterday.* "I didn't necessarily mean me. Is he talking to you about Maida, or about anything else that worries him?"

His face hardened. "I've already told you, I don't think it's wise to discuss illness with him. I don't want him to worry—that's why I protect him from such things."

"But—"

"He is my son, Paula. These decisions are mine to make, and I'm raising Jason the best way I know. Now if that's all, I really have to get to the plant."

She was losing him, losing the chance to make him see that Jason needed something he wasn't getting from the people in his life. There had to be something, some positive step she could take right now for that child. Maybe it was time, as her brother Keith, the football player, would say, to drop back and punt.

"What about his friends?" She blurted the words out before Alex could walk away. "I haven't seen any of Jason's friends since I've been here."

"You've only been here a couple of days." He looked harassed, as if she were a small dog nipping at his heels. "Jason has friends."

"Where are they? Wouldn't it be good for him to

be playing with them every day to distract him from Maida's absence?'' She had to press whatever advantage she had.

"He has friends at school."

"It's summer vacation. What does he do for friends during the summer?''

Alex gave an exasperated sigh. "We don't exactly have neighbors to run in and out, Paula.''

True enough. The Caine mansion, sitting on land that seemed carved out of the hillside above the town, was alone and isolated. A steep, winding lane led from the mansion to the nearest street, far below.

"Then we ought to be making an effort to get him together with his friends, even if I have to drive him. Don't you agree?'' A plan, somewhat hazy and amorphous, began to take shape in her mind.

"Yes, I suppose so." He took a step away. "Look, I have to go. You're right, Jason needs to see his friends. I'll trust you to arrange it. Do whatever you think is best.''

She nodded, the plan becoming clearer by the moment. "You can count on it," she said, watching as he strode away, obviously eager to get to work. Well, she was just as eager to get to her work, now that he'd given her a green light.

Alex might be a little surprised when he found out what she thought was best for his son—and maybe for him, too.

*   *   *

He had just enough time to swim his laps before dinner, Alex decided as he arrived home that afternoon. He tried to ignore the pain that radiated down his leg, but it demanded attention. He might succeed in denying weakness to everyone else, but he couldn't deny it to himself.

Too much stress, too little exercise. He knew exactly what Brett would say, whether he spoke as a doctor or a friend. And Brett would be right. Alex had too many people depending on him to let physical weakness get in the way of doing what he had to do.

"Jason?" He called as he entered the center hallway, but no one answered. Perhaps Jason and Paula had gone somewhere.

He started upstairs to change, trying to push away memories of that conversation with her that morning. She'd been persistent, he'd give her that. Her face, intent and serious, formed in his mind before he could block it out. In fact, her presence seemed to linger in the house even when she wasn't here, refusing to leave him alone.

All right, he was too aware of Paula Hansen. He accepted that, he admitted it. But that didn't mean he was going to act on it. There wasn't room in his life right now for anything other than his son and the business deal that might save them. His relationship with Paula would stay strictly business. That was what he'd promised her, and that was the way it would be.

Ten minutes later, towel over his arm, he walked out to the pool area. Paula and Jason hadn't gone anywhere; they were in the pool.

Paula glanced up, saw him and waved. Sunlight glinted on her blond hair and turned her warm skin golden. She wore a green swimsuit that matched her eyes. He swallowed with difficulty.

Hiding any suggestion of a limp, he crossed to the pool.

"This is a surprise. Jason doesn't usually like the water."

"Sure I do, Dad," Jason said quickly. But the tight grip he had on Paula's hand gave him away.

"If you want us to get out…" Paula began.

"No, of course not." He dropped the towel and stepped into the water. "There's plenty of room for all of us. I'd better get my laps in before Brett Elliot sends the exercise police after me."

Her face relaxed in a smile. "He is a good doctor, isn't he. He's been in to see Maida so much, and every time it perks her up."

"He cares." He could say more, could tell her how only Brett's determined intervention had brought him as far as he'd come in recovering from the effects of the crash.

He could, but why would he? Where had it come

from, this longing to confide in Paula? She was his housekeeper. Listening to his personal troubles wasn't part of her job description.

"Well, I'd better get at it." He turned away quickly, before he could give in to the impulse to share anything else with Paula. Before he could let his gaze linger on her smooth, honey-colored skin or the freckles that splashed across her cheeks.

Stroke, kick, stroke, kick. The familiar pattern soothed him, and he felt tight muscles gradually relax, responding to the repetitive motion and the massage of the water. When he swam, he could block out everything but the movement and the water.

At least, usually he could. Somewhere about the fifteenth lap, he realized that he wasn't letting his mind float clear. He was listening to Paula and his son.

She seemed to be coaxing Jason to trust the water to hold him up. If she succeeded, she'd be doing a better job than Alex ever had. He'd tried to get his son interested in swim lessons, but Jason had always held back. He'd finally realized the boy was afraid, and he hadn't known quite what to do about it. His own father would have bullied him into conquering the fear, but that wasn't the way he wanted to raise Jason.

"There, see?" Paula had kicked off and pushed

herself through the water to Jason, then grabbed his hands. "I trust you to catch me. You want to try it?"

Alex stood at the shallow end of the pool, half turned away from them, not wanting Jason to think he had an audience, and listened.

"I guess so."

Jason sounded reluctant. Alex wanted to intervene, wanted to tell Paula not to push the boy. But just this morning he'd told her to do what she thought was best for Jason. He shouldn't second-guess her already.

He glanced toward them. Paula didn't even seem to notice that he was there. All her attention was focused on his son. Her smile encouraged Jason, and she held out her hands to him.

"I won't let you sink, honest. I promise."

Jason nodded, shivering a little as a breeze swept across the pool. Alex saw his skinny chest rise as he took a breath. Then, his gaze fixed on Paula's face as if it were a lifeline, Jason launched himself through the water.

"All right!" Paula grabbed his hands and helped him upright. "You did it, Jason. And you didn't sink one little bit."

"I did it, didn't I." Jason grinned. "I really did it."

"Good job, Jason." There was, unaccountably, a lump in Alex's throat, along with maybe the smallest bit of jealousy that Jason had tried for Paula something he'd never tried for his father.

Jason glanced at him, startled, as if he'd forgotten his father was in the pool. Paula held out her hand, inviting Alex to join them.

"Maybe Jason will float to you, if you promise not to let him sink." The faintest stress suggested that *promise* was the operative word.

Alex didn't need Paula to tell him how to react to his own son. He hoped his look made that clear. "Jason knows he can trust me." He held out his hands. "Come on, Jason."

His son seemed to mentally figure the distance between them. "Come a little bit closer, Dad."

He almost coaxed Jason to try it, but Paula's eyes held a warning that might as well have been shouted. He swallowed his resentment and took a giant step forward. "How's that?"

"Okay." Jason bounced a little, as if working up his nerve. Then he pushed off, face screwed up, hands reaching toward Alex.

Alex grabbed him. "Way to go, son." He grasped a small, wet shoulder. "Good job."

Jason looked up at him, all the reserve gone from his dark eyes, at least for the moment. "I did it!" He turned, reaching out for Paula, and she swam a stroke or two closer to take his hand.

"You sure did." She stood, water streaming from sun-warmed skin, and smiled at them.

The smile went straight to Alex's heart and lodged there, making one thing abundantly clear. Ignoring Paula would not be an easy thing to do.

Paula's breath caught in her throat. Did Alex have any idea how devastatingly attractive he looked at that moment? He and Jason wore identical, laughing expressions, and the tenderness in his gaze when he looked at his son made her want to cry. As for the expression in his eyes when he looked at her—no, she must be imagining that.

She had to keep her mind on her job. Right now, that meant unlocking the puzzle that was Jason, and part of the answer had just played itself out right in front of her. One of the things Jason needed, maybe the most important thing, was a closer relationship with his father.

She didn't doubt that Alex loved his son—loved him more than life itself, probably. He just didn't seem to know how important it was for a seven-year-old to feel love, not just hear the word. If only Alex were willing to listen to her, she could help him understand.

"Alex, I—"

The telephone rang, so close it startled her. Then,

as Alex turned and swung out of the pool, she realized he'd brought his cellular phone out with him.

"Just one minute," he said, drying his hand and then picking up the phone.

In an instant she knew that playtime in the pool was over as far as Alex was concerned. His gaze turned inward as he concentrated on the call, and she could almost see him donning his corporate armor. Without looking back at them, still talking, he went into the house.

She tried to swallow her disappointment. Alex had business to take care of; she could understand that. It didn't have to spoil Jason's afternoon. She held out her hand to the boy.

"How about another try, Jason?"

But all the interest and happiness had gone out of Jason's small face. Shivering, he climbed out of the pool. "Don't want to."

"We don't have to go in yet," she said. "We could play a game of water polo."

"I don't like water polo." He grabbed a towel and started for the house. "I don't like swimming at all." He ran inside, slamming the door behind him.

Paula climbed slowly out of the pool. Jason might say he didn't like swimming, but she had a pretty clear idea what was bothering him. And it had much more to do with his father than with the pool.

She toweled her hair, feeling it curl over her fingers as it began to dry. She'd look like a poodle if she didn't blow-dry it, but she probably should have started dinner already. She pulled on her terry robe and headed for the kitchen.

Paula had no sooner gotten in the back door than Alex came hurrying toward her. Somehow he'd found time to pull on jeans and a knit shirt, and his dark hair was slicked back, still damp from the shower.

"Paula, thank you. That's the most interest Jason has ever shown in swimming. I'd about given up."

She clutched the robe around her, embarrassingly aware of how disheveled she must look. "I'm glad." She edged past him. "I really have to get changed and start dinner."

He shook his head, smiling. "Why are you embarrassed? I saw you in your swimsuit in the pool."

She didn't know why there was a difference between playing in the swimming pool with Jason and standing so close to Alex in the narrow hallway, but there was. And she didn't intend to say that to him.

"It's not that," she said. "I just don't want dinner to be late." She managed a smile. "My boss might not like that."

He touched a wet curl, turning it around his finger. His hand came within a millimeter of her cheek, and her skin tingled as if he'd caressed it. "Right now, your boss is very happy with you." His tone teased her. "You could probably burn the biscuits, and he wouldn't say a thing."

She wanted so badly to lean toward him. Just the slightest movement would bring them together. Her treacherous memory told her exactly how his hand would feel against her face.

She stepped back, instead. "I'll remind you of that when I put dinner in front of you. Now, I really need to get started."

His hand closed around her wrist. "Just one second. I wanted to tell you that your success in the pool with Jason gave me an idea for something that might make this time a bit better for him."

"That's great." Was she really going to get her wish so easily? Had Alex seen how much it meant to Jason when the boy felt his father's encouragement?

"One of the high school coaches gives swimming lessons to kids in the summer. I hadn't even considered hiring him, since Jason wasn't interested, but now I think that's just the thing."

"Swimming lessons?" Her heart fell. Jason didn't need lessons from a stranger. He needed his father.

"It's perfect. Lessons will give him something to think about and keep his mind off Maida."

"Alex, I'm not sure that's what Jason needs right now. Maybe it would be better if you taught him."

"Me?" He looked at her as if she were crazy. "I

don't have time to do that now. Besides, kids usually learn better from someone other than a parent.''

''Jason was excited because you were there. I'm not sure he'd be equally happy about swimming with someone else.'' In fact, given the way the child had left the pool, she was sure he wouldn't.

But Alex wasn't listening. He turned, headed toward the front of the house. ''I'll try and reach him now. Thanks, Paula.''

''Alex, I don't think...''

It was too late. He'd already charged through the swinging door.

Typical, so very typical. If Alex approached his business with that energy and directness, he'd undoubtedly saved the company several times over. He hadn't even heard anything she'd said.

She ran her hand through wet curls, seeming to feel again Alex's gentle touch. She forced her mind away from that moment in which they'd stood so close. She couldn't afford to let herself think about that.

She'd asked God to show her what she was supposed to be doing. And now God had given her the answer, in language so clear she couldn't possibly ignore it.

God had given her a chance to make up for the mistakes she'd made the last time she was here. Maybe that was why her memories had come back when they had. God had known she'd need them to accomplish her task.

No matter how difficult it was, she'd have to put her own needs and feelings aside for the time being. She had to help bring the prickly, private father and son closer together. And she suspected she really had her work cut out for her.

Chapter Six

❦

"Are you sure this is going to be all right with my dad?" Jason's dark eyes filled with concern the next afternoon.

Paula tried to push down her matching concern and speak with a confidence she didn't feel. "Your dad won't care one way or the other if I have a pet in the cottage. And I need something to keep me company while Aunt Maida is in the hospital." She opened the door to the animal shelter. "Come on. You've got to help me pick out just the right puppy."

The long room was filled with kennels on either side, and their entry signaled a chorus of yips and howls. Every dog there seemed to be proclaiming, *Pick me, pick me!*

"So many dogs." Jason's tone was awed. "How can you decide?"

She ruffled his hair. "That's why you're along. When we find the right one, we'll know."

And when Alex found out about this, what would he think? She tried to assure herself that what she'd said to Jason was true. Technically, this puppy was going to be hers, at least until Alex saw that it made a difference in his son's life.

Besides, he'd said she should use her own judgment about getting Jason together with friends. Somehow she felt a puppy might be just the right friend for Jason now—a creature that would depend on him and love him unconditionally.

And if she ended up having to take the dog back to Baltimore, she'd deal with that when the time came. But with that in mind, maybe a small breed would be best. She could just imagine what her roommate would say if she came home with a huge dog.

"Oh, Paula, look." Jason leaned against a large pen filled with puppies of every description, all barking and tumbling over each other.

The attendant smiled. "Shall I let the two of you into the puppy pen to make your choice?"

Paula tried to dismiss the image of Alex's frowning face. "Let's do it."

They were engulfed in a melee of puppies the instant they entered the pen. Laughing, Paula removed a beagle from her shoe. The little cocker spaniel might work. It shouldn't get too big. She looked at Jason. "What do you think?"

Jason was on his knees. A fluffy yellow pup had planted suspiciously large paws on his shoulder and was licking his face. The boy looked up, his eyes filled with longing that clutched her heart and wouldn't let go. "This one, Paula. Please, this has to be the one."

"What is it?" she asked the attendant, a sense of foreboding filling her.

The girl grinned. "A yellow Labrador. Great dogs."

"Large dogs." She banished Alex's face firmly from her mind. "Okay. He's the one." Jason's joy was worth any number of confrontations with his father.

A few hours later, she wasn't so sure. She hurried to finish dinner preparations, her stomach tied in knots over Alex's impending return. Jason and the puppy, playing on the kitchen floor, slowed her down, but she didn't feel comfortable letting them out of her sight yet.

She scooped the puppy out of her way as she bent to open the oven door. "Here, Jason. Keep him away from the hot stove. We don't want him to get hurt." She lifted out the casserole dish. "Have you thought of a good name yet?"

Jason frowned, forehead wrinkling in an imitation

of his father. "Goldy would be nice, 'cause of his color. But that sounds like a girl's name, and he might not like that."

She suppressed a smile. "What about Nugget? You know, like a gold nugget."

"Nugget." He tried the name, then tickled the puppy. "You like that, boy? You want to be Nugget?"

The puppy wiggled, licking his face.

"He likes it!" Jason declared. "His name is Nugget."

Paula's heart turned over at the sheer happiness in his face. She hadn't seen Jason look like that since she'd come here. His closed-off, somber expression had vanished. Now he looked like any normal seven-year-old should. Surely Alex would see that and would understand what she was trying to do.

"I'm going to carry this into the dining room." She picked up the casserole dish. "You hold Nugget so he doesn't get out."

Two things happened at once. Paula pushed through the door between the kitchen and the dining room, and Jason lost his hold on the puppy's collar. Paula felt a brush of fur against her legs, then lifted the casserole out of the way as Jason charged after the puppy.

"Grab him, Jason!" She deposited the casserole

dish on the waiting trivet and dived after the golden blur. "Don't let him get out."

She skidded across the marble floor of the hallway in Jason's wake. Her feet tangled with the throw rug; she lost her balance and sat down heavily. Nugget danced just out of her reach—his paws scratching a pair of highly polished brown wingtips.

Alex, who'd just come in the front door, bent over and picked up the wriggling puppy. He held it at arm's length, and his expression looked just as ominous as she'd imagined it might.

"What, exactly, is this?"

The glib explanation she'd prepared died in her throat. "A puppy."

His frown deepened. "I can see that it's a puppy. Whose puppy is it, and what is it doing in my front hall?"

She scrambled to her feet, trying to find some reasonable words.

"He's Paula's, Dad." Jason gathered the fur ball carefully into his arms. "I helped her pick him out. His name is Nugget."

"Nugget." Alex's expression didn't lighten, but she thought she saw him ruffle the puppy's ears before he pinned her with that frowning gaze. "Tell me exactly why you need a dog *now,* of all times."

"Well, I..." All her assurance shriveled at that frown.

"Paula gets lonesome in the cottage by herself at night," Jason piped up. "She needs Nugget to keep her company."

"She does, does she?" Alex's gaze softened slightly as he looked at his son. "Well, why don't you take Nugget out on the lawn for a while. Paula and I have to talk."

"Okay." Laden down with puppy, Jason trudged to the swinging door. "I'll get his leash, Paula. And I'll be really careful."

"I know you will." Suppressing the urge to run out the door after them, she turned to Alex. "If there's a problem with my having a pet in the cottage…"

His dark brows lifted. "But he's not in the cottage, is he?"

She couldn't deny that. "He's so little, I didn't want to leave him alone. He and Jason were playing in the kitchen while I cooked supper. I never intended for him to get into this part of the house."

Alex leaned a little closer, and she had the sudden feeling that he was using up all the air in the hallway. How else could she explain her sudden breathlessness?

"You're lonely in the cottage at night?" His tone made it a question. "Ms. Independence, the woman who's not afraid of anything?"

She shrugged. "Everyone's afraid of something."

What are you afraid of, Alex, besides losing the company? What keeps those barriers between you and the rest of the world?

He studied her, his gaze so probing that it was as if he could see right through her. "Who picked out the puppy?" he asked abruptly.

"Jason did."

He lifted an eyebrow. "I see. And who named the puppy?"

She had to stiffen her muscles to keep from fidgeting. "Jason and I both did."

"I see," he said again. His expression didn't change, but she realized that was amusement lurking in his dark eyes. She was right—he did look straight through her. At least he wasn't demanding she take the dog back.

"Really, Alex, he won't be any trouble at all," she said quickly. "I'll keep him out of your way. I promise." She held her breath.

"I did tell you to do whatever you thought best for my son, didn't I? But this wasn't quite what I had in mind."

She chose her words carefully, not wanting to imply that she knew better than he what Jason needed. "I just thought it might help to take his mind off things right now. There's nothing like a puppy for occupying a small boy."

A smile tugged the corners of his lips. "And then

there's the little matter of keeping you company at night." His voice dropped. "We don't want you to get lonely."

"N-no I won't," she stammered. He was too close, way too close. With the spicy scent of his aftershave teasing her senses, she could hardly think coherently. She took a step back, putting some space between them. "And I will keep him out of your hair."

Alex gave a quick nod. "I don't like disorder in my life, Paula. See that the puppy doesn't bring any, and we'll both be happy."

She wanted to point out that disorder was a chronic and even desirable state when it came to puppies and small boys, but she was afraid to press her luck. At least Nugget could stay. "I'll see to it."

Alex stopped her as she started toward the kitchen. "One other thing, Paula. I have a church committee meeting here tonight at eight. I'd like you to serve coffee and dessert." He raised his eyebrows. "Unless you'll be busy puppy-sitting then."

"Coffee and dessert, right." Her mind scrambled among the possibilities, coming up empty. "I'll take care of it. And dinner will be ready in five minutes."

When Jason and the puppy came into the kitchen in answer to her call, she was frantically leafing through Maida's wooden recipe box. How could Alex calmly expect dessert to be served to guests, just like that? What would her aunt have done?

"I'm ready for supper," Jason announced. "What are you doing?"

"Looking for a dessert I can fix in no time flat. Your dad wants me to serve something to a committee he has coming here tonight." She hoped she didn't sound as panicky as she felt. If she'd known ahead of time, if she hadn't spent the afternoon at the animal shelter...

Jason rinsed his hands at the sink. He grabbed for the tea towel and knocked the recipe box over.

Paula caught it. "Careful. I don't want that to get broken."

"It's just an old box. We could get Maida a new one."

"I couldn't do that." She ran her hand along the box's polished surface. "I gave this to Maida when I was about your age. I did chores for a month to earn enough money to buy it."

"Really?" The concept was obviously out of his experience.

"Really. And I hoped just now I'd find a fast, easy dessert recipe in it, but I didn't."

"Why don't you call Ingrid's?"

She looked at him blankly. "Who's Ingrid and how can she help?"

Jason giggled. "Ingrid's a bakery. It's the one Maida uses for stuff like that. You just call and tell them what you want, and they bring it to the house. Then you put it on a nice plate and serve it.''

You put it on a nice plate and serve it. ''That sounds like a terrific plan.'' Always assuming the bakery would still be open, of course. But during tourist season, every shop stayed open late. She wasn't sure whether she was happier over the answer to her problem or the fact that it had come from Jason. ''Thanks, Jason. You've really helped me.''

''It's okay.'' A faint flush colored his cheeks. He bent to say something to Nugget, then scurried into the dining room.

The puppy sat back on his haunches and stared at her, his tongue lolling in a silly doggy grin.

''I think we're making progress, Nugget,'' she told him.

With Jason, anyway. As for Alex…well, that was another story. The memory of those moments in the hallway flooded over her. If she could keep her feelings under control, she'd be better off. But that seemed impossible where Alex was concerned.

Alex pushed chairs into a semicircle in the library for the church fund-raising committee. He ought to be concentrating on the agenda for the meeting or on the appropriate amount for the donation he'd undoubtedly be expected to make. Instead, he was thinking about Paula.

Those moments in the hallway had gotten totally out of control. He seemed to stand back and look at himself in surprise. He'd been *flirting* with her—there was no other word that fit. It was the last thing in the world he should have been doing.

He saw again the wave of warm, peachy color filling her cheeks, saw the way her eyes sparked with indignation or clouded when she tried to think up a reasonable explanation for an unreasonable action.

He was spending entirely too much time thinking about Paula Hansen, he decided. All right, granted she had an appeal for him that he couldn't begin to explain. He still couldn't risk giving in to that attraction.

His mouth tightened. When his wife had walked away from their marriage and from their son, she'd made it clear that his small-town life wasn't what she'd expected from a rich man. He hadn't measured up for her, just as he'd never measured up for his father. He could accept that, and he could build a life without a romantic relationship.

And even if he wanted to expose himself to that kind of hurt again, he wouldn't risk Jason's happiness. His son had had too many people disappear from his young life. Jason wasn't going to be put in a position of learning to love someone and then having that someone leave.

Maybe Paula wouldn't leave, a treacherous voice whispered in his mind.

She did before, he reminded himself.

His rational side assured him this was the right decision. Anything between Paula and him had to be strictly business, for all their sakes. He'd put a guard on his emotions, and that little incident in the hallway wouldn't happen again.

The doorbell rang, and he went to let his guests in.

An hour later, the fund-raising committee had made progress on plans for the new campaign, and he had begun to wonder what had happened to Paula and the coffee. Almost as soon as the thought formed in his mind, the door opened. Paula, burdened with a large tray, entered.

"Why don't we take a break," he suggested. "I see Paula has brought some refreshments."

He had to smile. Paula, apparently determined to be the perfect hostess, had changed from her usual jeans to a skirt and blouse. He couldn't help noticing that the sunny yellow of the blouse brought out the gold flecks in her eyes.

You weren't going to notice things like that, he lectured himself. Before he could move, Mitch Donovan had leaped to his feet to take the tray from Paula.

"Let me give you a hand with that." Mitch balanced the tray while she cleared a spot for it on the cherry table against the wall. "It's good to see you again, Paula."

Paula looked a little startled at suddenly being the center of attention. Maybe it didn't fit in with her idea of a housekeeper's role. If so, she'd forgotten something about Bedford Creek, Alex thought.

"I think you know most of these people," Alex said. "You remember Gwen Forrester."

The older woman smiled. "How is Maida doing?" Her voice was warm with sympathy. "I just heard about her surgery. It's just like her to keep it a secret. She never wants to accept help. I plan to go and see her tomorrow, if you think she's ready for company."

Paula barely had time to nod before Pastor Richie interrupted. "I'm sure she'd love it, Gwen. I went in today but she'd like to see someone besides me. And Paula, of course."

"You know Pastor Simon Richie," Alex went on. He'd gotten used to interruptions with this group. "And you remember Mitch Donovan, our police chief."

Mitch smiled as he helped himself to a cup of coffee. "I remember Paula from when she was Jason's nanny."

"And this is Ellie Wayne, our church organist." As people got up and moved toward the coffee service, Alex introduced the last member of the committee. Ellie nodded, her wary manner with strangers disguising her generous heart.

"You'll be coming to worship with us on Sunday, I hope." Simon Richie sugared his coffee generously. "Maida never misses, and she'll want to know everything that happens."

Before Paula could respond, Gwen Forrester began giving her suggestions for Maida's therapy. Alex exchanged a smiling look with Mitch. Since Gwen's daughter had married Bedford Creek's only doctor, she had begun to consider herself an authority on all things medical.

Mitch crossed the room to join him. "Nice to have Paula back again, isn't it?" he said softly.

Alex tried for a neutral tone. "I'm sure it's eased Maida's mind, having her here."

"Maida's, huh." Mitch lifted a quizzical brow. "Actually, it wasn't Maida I had in mind."

Most people in Bedford Creek wouldn't probe into a Caine's personal affairs, but Mitch wasn't most people. He'd saved Alex's life, once upon a time. Maybe he felt that gave him the right to ask what others wouldn't.

"She's good with Jason," Alex said, gaze fixed on Paula. She was laughing at some comment of Simon's, and he felt a stab of what seemed like jealousy. "Irrational." He stiffened with annoyance when he realized he'd said it aloud.

Mitch eyed him with some amusement. "What's irrational? The fact that she's good with Jason? Or are you talking about her effect on you?"

"Neither." He turned his back on the small group by the fireplace. "Paula's an employee, nothing more."

"Try that on someone who doesn't know you as well as I do," Mitch said. "You're attracted to her."

He knew Mitch would see through anything less than the truth. "I shouldn't be," he said.

"Why? She's free, you're free. There's no reason—"

"Alex!" Gwen's call was peremptory, and he swung toward her. "You have to convince Paula to come to the church picnic Saturday. After all, you and Jason are coming. She can come with you."

Paula's cheeks were flushed. "I'm not sure that's a good idea."

"Nonsense," Gwen said briskly, her gray curls bouncing with emphasis. "You'll have to fix something, anyway, so you might as well come and enjoy it."

Paula glanced at Alex, and he wasn't sure what was in her eyes. Embarrassment at being singled out? He spoke before the silence could become awkward. "We'd like to have you join us, if you want."

"There, that's settled." Gwen beamed. "I'm going

to make my apple-crumb pies. Ellie, what are you bringing?''

Alex glanced toward Mitch, to find his old friend regarding him with amusement.

''Is that a date?'' Mitch asked softly.

''Certainly not,'' he said. He saw Paula slipping out of the library and knew he had to speak with her before the situation became awkward. ''Excuse me.''

He caught up with Paula at the kitchen door. She looked at him somewhat distantly.

''Is there something else I can bring you?'' she asked.

''What? No, that's fine.'' He frowned, not sure how to say what he felt he must. ''Look, I know Gwen's friendliness can be a little overpowering at times. If you don't want to go to that picnic, you certainly don't have to. I can make some excuse.''

She looked at him steadily for several moments, and for once her usually readable face didn't give anything away. ''Does that mean you don't want me to go?''

''Of course not!'' He always seemed to say the wrong thing to her. Or maybe she always took what he said the wrong way. He grasped her arm, and immediately knew he shouldn't have. He could feel her smooth skin warm at his touch. ''Look, I didn't mean it that way at all. I just meant that you shouldn't feel obligated. It's not part of your job. But Jason and I would enjoy having you come with us. Please."

A dimple appeared at the corner of her mouth. "I guess we should leave Nugget at home."

"Definitely." He smiled. "We'll give him a dog biscuit to make up for it."

"It's a deal." Still smiling, she turned and disappeared through the swinging door.

He stood for a moment, not yet ready to go back in the library and face Mitch's inquisitive gaze. What exactly had just happened here? He'd intended to keep his distance from Paula. He'd assured himself that what happened before wouldn't happen again. And instead, he'd committed himself to a social event with her.

It's not a date, he repeated to himself. He was just being hospitable to someone who was, after all, a stranger here.

He had to believe that was all there was to it.

Chapter Seven

By the next afternoon, Paula had been over the events of the previous day a hundred times in her mind, and she was no closer to deciding what they meant. One moment Alex had barked orders at her, the next he'd seemed to want...what? Friendship? Something more? She just didn't know.

"Come on, kids." She waved to Jason and Kristie, Gwen Forrester's granddaughter; they were playing with Nugget on the lawn near the pool. "You can go back in the water now. Jason, better put Nugget in his pen."

Having Kristie join Jason's swim lessons had been a stroke of genius, if Paula did think so herself. If Alex wouldn't teach his son, at least Jason would have the company of a playmate. Kristie, a year younger than Jason, was quick and adventurous. She'd stayed after the lesson to play, with the promise that they'd go back in the pool again later in the afternoon.

Paula sat on the pool edge, dangling her feet in the water, and watched the children play with a float in the shallow end. Timing was everything, she decided. Alex had arrived home moments before, and, true to his routine, he was changing to swim his laps. When he got to the pool, he'd discover he had company.

She stretched, enjoying the sun's heat on her back. Maybe she couldn't, and probably shouldn't, do anything about Alex's attitude toward her. But she ought to be able to influence how he behaved with his son.

This will work, Lord. Won't it? If I can just involve Alex with Jason, help him to loosen up and relax with the boy, it would be so good for both of them.

Her prayers lately always revolved around the Caine family, in one way or another. She watched Jason pull the float through the water, making motorboat noises and sending ripples across the surface. Jason seemed to be keeping his word to her. There had been no incidents with matches. And he certainly smiled much more since Nugget had come into his life. Now if she could build a few bridges between him and his father, she'd feel she was accomplishing something.

Alex came out the back door, saw them in the pool,

and hesitated for a moment before striding toward them. She suppressed a smile. Did Alex realize just how predictable he was? He treated swimming the way he did every other task in his life, approaching it with a determined work ethic. Of course, his swimming was therapy, but there was no reason why it couldn't also be fun.

He crossed the patio toward her, and a familiar tingle swept along her skin. *Keep your mind on the task,* she ordered herself.

"Hi." She looked up. He loomed above her on the pool deck, blocking the sun. "You have some company in the pool today. You don't mind, do you?"

"It's fine." To her surprise, he dropped his towel and sat down next to her. "I didn't know Kristie was coming."

Was there an undertone suggesting he should have known? He had told her to make arrangements about Jason's friends, she reminded herself.

"Gwen and I talked about it when she was leaving last night," she said. "She'd been looking for something to occupy her granddaughter now that school's out, and she thought swimming lessons would be perfect."

Alex's face relaxed as he watched the little carrot-top try to balance a beach ball on her head. "She's a cute kid."

Her breath caught. That was how he'd looked with

his friend Mitch the night before—off guard, as if he'd put away for a while the burden of being who he was. Why couldn't he seem to do that with his own son?

Maybe because it mattered too much. She thought again of those moments when he'd confided his concerns about the company. Alex was so intent on providing the proper lifestyle for his little boy that he didn't have time to play with him.

She remembered only too well the formal, intimidating presence of Alex's father. She'd been terrified of earning the elder Caine's disapproval on her visits. He certainly hadn't provided a role model for relaxed parenting. And like Jason, Alex had grown up without the softening presence of the mother who'd died when he was young. Maybe he just didn't know how to be closer to his son.

"Come on," she said, sliding into the water, cool after the heat radiating from the flagstones. She held out her hand in invitation. "Let's help the kids practice what they've learned."

For a moment she thought he'd follow her, but then he shook his head. "I have to get my laps in."

Of course he did. She tried not to feel disappointment. Changes wouldn't come in a day.

He walked toward the deep end, then paused, looking at her. "By the way, did the puppy serve his purpose?"

The sudden change of topic startled her, particularly since she'd been busy noticing the breadth of his shoulders. "What do you mean?"

"Your loneliness," he said. "Remember? You needed the puppy so you wouldn't be lonely in the cottage by yourself."

"Right." She couldn't stop a grin. "I'd have to say, he is a mixed blessing. He yipped until I gave up and let him spend the night on my bed."

He glanced toward the pen, where Nugget slept curled up on a rug. "It sounds as if that puppy knew how to get exactly what he wanted." He dove into the pool.

Maybe she could stand to cool off a bit herself. She submerged, then came up beside Jason's float, tilting her head back to let the water run off her hair.

"Why don't we practice your swimming," she suggested. Maybe when Alex saw what was going on, he'd be drawn in, just as he had their first time in the pool.

For the next few minutes she worked with the kids, careful to keep it fun. Kristie was more adventurous in the water than Jason, and her presence pushed him. He wouldn't want a girl, especially not a younger girl, to do something better than he did.

"Okay, let's practice blowing bubbles." She dipped her mouth under the water's surface, watching them closely.

Kristie put her whole face in, then came up sputtering. Jason, a little more cautious, screwed his eyes closed before trying.

"Good job!" Paula said when he'd come up again.

"Very good." Alex's voice, close behind her, made her jump. She'd been so intent on the children, she hadn't noticed his approach.

"I think putting your face in the water is the toughest part of learning to swim," she said, determined not to let him rattle her. "You two are doing great after just one lesson."

"I want to swim like you and my dad," Jason declared, bouncing on his toes. "I want to do regular strokes and go in the deep water and dive."

"You will." She pushed wet dark hair back from his eyes. "Give yourself a little time. Everything takes practice."

"Is Paula a good swimmer?" Alex gave her an innocent look. "I haven't seen her do anything but blow bubbles."

"I could probably give you a run for your money," she said.

"Is that a dare?"

"A race!" Kristie hopped up and down, clapping. "Have a race!"

"A race," Jason echoed. "Down to the end and back."

"Willing to put it to the test?" Alex's dark eyes held a challenge.

"You bet." She mentally measured the distance to the end of the pool. She might have overreached herself. "Jason, you be the starter."

Jason pulled himself to the pool deck and stood above them, raising his hand. "Ready, set, go!" he shouted.

Paula plunged into a shallow dive, surfacing with a strong, smooth stroke. It would take more than her best race to beat Alex. She churned through the water, glimpsing him from the corner of her eye. He didn't seem to be exerting himself at all.

They reached the end in nearly a dead heat, flipped and started back. *Outclassed,* she thought, watching him forge ahead of her effortlessly. She was definitely outclassed.

By the time she reached the end, he was standing there, smiling at her. She came up beside him.

"No fair," she gasped. "You're not even out of breath."

He seized her wet hands and pulled her upright. "Why is that unfair?" He grinned. "Because you lost? Maybe you'd like a handicap—say, three strokes?"

"More like five or six." She clung to his arm for a moment, getting her balance and her breath. Beyond Alex, she saw the children watching them. Kristie was grinning and clapping her hands. But Jason—Jason wore an expression she couldn't interpret.

She glanced up at Alex, to find he watched her equally closely. His expression was just as difficult to read, but whatever it meant, it made her heart contract.

"I don't want to!" Jason ran out of the kitchen the next afternoon, slamming the door behind him.

Paula sighed and bent to ruffle the puppy's ears. "Looks as if we've lost our charm, Nugget."

He woofed softly, and she almost thought his eyes reflected her own disappointment.

She'd been so sure she was on the right track with Jason. Now she regretted that her daily reports to Maida had been so optimistic. She'd hit a roadblock with the boy, and she didn't know what to do about it.

Since she and Alex had raced, since she'd caught Jason watching them with that odd expression, the boy had been difficult—sullen, locked away from her as if their growing friendship had never been. He didn't even seem to take pleasure in the puppy. Everything she'd suggested, including time in the swimming pool, had been met the same way. *"I don't want to."*

She heard the front door open and close—*Alex*—

and bent to put Nugget back in his pen. The puppy whimpered a bit, then began to chew on a toy.

I know how you feel, she told him silently. *I have to do something I don't want to do, too.*

But Alex had a right to know things weren't going well with his son, and she had a responsibility to tell him. She walked slowly to the swinging door and pushed through to the front of the house.

Alex stood in the wide center hallway, leafing through the mail she'd put on the heavy mahogany table. He glanced up at her step and smiled.

That smile had a regrettable tendency to take her breath away. "You're home from the plant early," she said, determined not to let him know his presence had an effect on her. "Is something wrong?"

"On the contrary." He dropped the envelopes back onto the table and came toward her. "Everything is remarkably good."

He looked lighter, as if a burden had been lifted from his shoulders.

"Really? What's happening?" She could use some good news to distract her from her worries about Jason and from her dread of telling Alex.

"I finished up my talks with Klemmer today."

Klemmer. It took her a moment to remember the representative of the Swiss firm—the man she'd nearly hit with a fly ball.

"And that's good?" she asked.

"More than good. He liked the plans I presented to him and recommended the firm to his company. His boss will arrive next week to negotiate the deal."

"Alex, that is good news." Without intending to, she reached out to him. He held both her hands in a firm, warm grip. For a moment they stood, hands clasped, very close together. Then she took a step back.

He released her immediately. "Yes, it is good. Not settled yet, of course, but they wouldn't come all this way if they didn't like what we have to offer."

"If it goes through—"

"It has to go through." His eyes darkened. "It's our last chance. So everything has to go perfectly."

She felt her nerves tense at his tone. Somehow she thought she was about to meet a hurdle. "Which 'everything' did you have in mind?"

"Among other things, I have to entertain them. I thought a small dinner party a week from Friday. Nothing too large, no more than twenty people."

She managed to keep herself from gasping. "Twenty?"

"We'll use a caterer, of course."

She could breathe again. No one expected her to cook for twenty.

"And we'll have the cleaners here an extra time," he went on. "Come to the library, and I'll give you all the information you'll need."

She followed him, trying to swallow her apprehension. She'd said she could do this. Now she had to live up to her word.

Alex riffled through a file before holding it out to her. Naturally he would have a file on entertaining. She thought again of her method of having guests, which usually consisted of ordered-in pizza. No, she was definitely out of her league now.

"That should have all the information you'll need, but if there's anything you don't understand, please ask me. I don't want any mistakes."

She held the folder, trying to think of a question to begin with, out of the many that crowded her mind. "Where are we going to seat that many people?"

He beckoned her to follow him again, and she trailed after him across the hall to the dining room.

"With the leaves in, the table seats sixteen. If there are more, the caterers will set up small tables. We'll talk about place cards and table arrangement when it gets a bit closer." He frowned at the heavy mahogany chairs, large enough to dwarf a normal human. "This room is tricky to arrange. I've always hated this furniture. The pieces we're making at the plant now are much more attractive."

She stared at him for a moment. "I don't understand. If you feel that way about it, why on earth don't you replace this...stuff?" She'd almost said *ugly stuff,* but caught herself in time.

"I couldn't do that." His response seemed almost automatic.

"Why not? It's your house."

His gaze lingered on the heavy oil portrait of his grandfather that hung over the dining room fireplace. "Sometimes I find that hard to believe."

His words were so quiet, he almost seemed to be speaking to himself. She wanted to argue, but instinctively she knew it wouldn't do any good. She'd been wrong. It wasn't his house, not in the way she understood those words. It was the Caine mansion, and right now Alex looked as if that were a heavy burden.

She frowned down at the folder. She had come into the hall intending to confide her worries about his son. But Alex already had his hands full. Maybe she should hold her tongue and try to handle this herself. Perhaps in another day Jason would regain his smile. *Coward,* a small voice said in her mind.

"I'll get started on this." She waved the folder.

Alex turned toward her, seeming to shake off the clouds that surrounded him. "Thank you." He reached out to clasp her hand again. The warmth of his grip shimmered along her skin.

"For what? It's my job." It was hard to sound casual when her heart clenched at his closeness.

"For being here. For helping me." His fingers moved caressingly along the back of her hand. "I'm glad you're back."

She wasn't sure she actually walked back to the kitchen. It felt much more like floating. She didn't want to look too closely at what she was feeling, because that might make it vanish, like mist on the mountain burned off by the sun.

Clutching the folder, she pushed through the door into the kitchen—and came to a halt. Nugget slept in his pen. The sauce she'd started for dinner simmered on the stove. But Aunt Maida's recipe box lay in the middle of the floor, broken into pieces.

Alex put another weight into place on the machine and slid onto the seat, hooking his legs behind the padded bar. Maybe if he pushed his body hard enough, he could keep his emotions at bay.

Ten repetitions later, he knew it wasn't working. His injured leg complained at the added weight, but that wasn't what bothered him.

Paula had caught him off guard. He'd told himself he had neither the time nor the inclination to get involved with her. He'd promised her that what happened the last time she was here wouldn't happen again. But each time he was near her, it became more difficult to keep that promise.

He forced himself into another set of reps, gritting his teeth against the pain. Brett would say Alex was pushing too hard. But Brett, newly married to the physician's assistant in his office, wasn't fighting a wave of longing for something he'd never have. He tried to remember feeling this way for his wife, but he couldn't. This was something new.

Is it so impossible? The treacherous question slid into his mind and refused to be dislodged. He'd convinced himself that happily-ever-after didn't exist, but his closest friends seemed to have found it.

He concentrated on his exercises, trying to bury the thought. It refused to be buried.

"Alex?"

The weights clanged down as he swung toward the sound. He hadn't heard Paula come in, but there she was, looking around the exercise room his friends had created in the old conservatory.

"I'm sorry. I shouldn't interrupt you when you're working out." She looked as if she wanted to back right out the door.

"Don't worry about it." He slid off the machine, willing his knee not to waver at the punishment he'd been dealing it. He grabbed a towel, feeling a wave of embarrassment at being caught this way. "I was about done anyway."

"I… There's something I need to talk with you about."

Whatever it was, she clearly didn't want to bring it up. He could almost see the reluctance surrounding her.

"All right." He tossed the towel over the machine.

"If it's something about the party, we can go over the notes together." He was astounded at the amount of pleasure generated by that thought. Paula hadn't just caught him off guard—she'd gotten under his skin.

"No, it's not the party. It's this—"

She held something out to him. Frowning, he crossed the room to her.

"That's Maida's recipe box, isn't it? What happened to it?" The wooden box that always sat on the counter next to the stove had been broken into several pieces.

"I'm afraid Jason broke it."

Her gravity seemed all out of proportion to the event. He took the pieces from her, turning them over in his hands. "I'd say, get a new box, but I know Maida prized this one." He smiled at her. "Because you gave it to her, as I recall. I think it can be fixed."

"That's not the point." She looked at the box, then up at him. "When I said Jason broke it, I didn't mean it was an accident. He broke it on purpose."

For a long moment he could only stare at her. Then anger kicked in. "What are you talking about? Why on earth would you think that?"

"I don't think it, I know it."

There was no matching anger in her face, only sorrow.

"Alex, I'm sorry. I feel like a talebearer, but I

didn't think I should handle this on my own. Jason was angry—he's been angry all day. And he broke the box deliberately. He told me.''

He wanted to say he didn't believe it, but he couldn't. ''Why? Why was he angry?''

She took an audible breath. ''He wouldn't tell me, but I think I know.'' Peachy color flooded her cheeks. ''He was watching us yesterday, in the pool. When we were…when we were close to each other. I think it bothered him. He's been angry ever since.''

''I can't accept that.'' The words were out before he thought about it. ''You must be wrong, about all of this. My son doesn't behave that way.''

A spark of anger lit her eyes at that. ''Why? Because he's a Caine? Because Caines don't have normal human feelings?''

Whatever softness he'd felt toward her was wiped from the slate now. He leaned toward her. ''I know my son better than you do. He's been taught what appropriate behavior is.''

''Appropriate—Alex, he's a little boy, and he's hurting.'' Her voice rose, impassioned. ''For some reason, he was bothered by seeing us together. I don't know why, but I know we can't ignore it.''

''I don't intend to ignore it.'' His grip tightened on the pieces of the box, but he kept his voice cool and controlled. ''Jason is my responsibility, not yours. I'll take care of the situation, if it exists. I don't care to discuss it with you any further.''

She jerked back as if he'd struck her. ''Fine.'' She was as pale now as she'd been flushed earlier. ''I'd nearly forgotten. I'm just the housekeeper. You handle it.''

She whirled and nearly ran out of the room.

Chapter Eight

This picnic was going to be no fun at all, Paula decided as she sat next to Alex in the car. At least, not if her enjoyment depended on the status of her relationship with Alex.

She glanced across at him, but if he felt her gaze, Alex didn't respond. Meanwhile, Jason moped in the back seat.

No fun at all.

"I'll bet lots of your friends will be at the picnic," she told Jason, trying to sound cheerful. After all, somebody had to.

"I wanted to bring Nugget." His lower lip came out in a pout. "He'd like a picnic."

Alex had flatly refused to bring the puppy, with good reason.

"Don't you think a picnic would be too exciting for a puppy?" she asked. "I know you'll enjoy it, but Nugget is still just a baby. He might be frightened of all the noise and people."

Jason clearly hadn't considered that. His gaze met hers in the rearview mirror. "But he'd be with me. He wouldn't be scared if he was with me. Besides, there'd be lots of good stuff to eat."

"For people, not for dogs," Alex pointed out. "Remember what the vet told Paula. Only puppy food is good for puppies."

"That's right." She welcomed the opportunity to agree with Alex on something, after the battle royal they'd had several days earlier. "You wouldn't want him to get sick."

"I guess." Jason acted reluctant to give up his grievance. "Can I give him a treat when we get home?"

"Sure." She smiled at him in the mirror, and after a moment got a hint of a smile in return.

At least her relationship with Jason had settled down. He wasn't quite as open as he'd been, but now he played with the puppy and went back in the pool. Whatever had been bothering him, whatever had led to his breaking the recipe box, he seemed to have gotten control of his feelings. Like his father, Jason always had to be in control.

Control was certainly the defining word when it

came to the Caine men. Alex had been rigidly polite to her since their quarrel. Maybe if she apologized for her outburst, things would get back to normal.

No, she couldn't do that. She probably hadn't been very tactful, but she'd said what needed to be said, and there was no one else to do that.

Alex stopped the car at the bottom of the steep lane, waiting while a cluster of tourists crossed the street, heading for the parking lot along the river. One woman carried a handmade quilt encased in a plastic bag over her arm, while another juggled three bags from Ellie Wayne's gift shop.

"Now you see why we have the picnic in the evening." Alex nodded toward the tourists. "The shops will close soon. No one would want to risk losing business during the tourist season."

It was the first conversational thing he'd said to her since their argument. Maybe that meant he was ready to put the disagreement behind them.

"I guess if you run a shop like Ellie's, you probably have to make money while you can."

He nodded. "There's not much market for handmade baskets and dried flowers in the middle of winter." He shot a sideways glance at her that was almost a smile, and the tension inside her began to ease. "Bedford Creek tends to hibernate in the off-season."

He turned up the steep street that led to Grace

Church. From the Caine mansion, the church steeple was clearly visible across the narrow valley. Maida had told her that an earlier Caine had donated the land for the church and even paid for the steeple, so he could have a good view of it from his windows. It took a bit longer to drive there, down and up the narrow, hilly streets, than it would take a sparrow to fly.

Bedford Creek seemed crammed into its tight valley, spreading upward from the river because there was no other place for it to go. Above the town the mountain ridge, dark with hemlocks, cut off the sky.

Paula looked out at narrow clapboard houses whose colorful window boxes were filled with pansies and ageratum. Bedford Creek dressed in its finest for the tourists who came to enjoy the mountain scenery and buy at the quilt store, the basket shop, the bakery, the candlemaker's. In addition to Alex's factory, tourism was the town's only source of income. Could it get by on that if the factory failed? She doubted it. No wonder Alex felt such a burden.

He pulled into the church parking lot. "Looks as if we'll have a good turnout." His unexpected smile erased the last vestige of tension from their quarrel. "Enjoy yourself, Paula. You're not here as part of your job, remember."

She smiled back, her spirits lifting. She just might enjoy herself at that.

Tables had been set up under the trees on the park-like grounds surrounding the church. To her relief, she saw some faces that were familiar from other years, other visits.

Alex took the picnic basket she was holding, then leaned close. "Don't let them overwhelm you," he murmured. "They're good at that."

She nodded, not trusting her voice. She was in danger of being overwhelmed, all right, but not by friendly church members.

But by the time she started through the buffet line, she wasn't so sure. She'd already given updates on Maida's condition to at least a dozen people and had promised to deliver get-well wishes. She tried to remember names, knowing her aunt would want to know who'd asked about her, but they began to blur in her mind.

As she reached for a scoop of fruit salad, Gwen bustled up to her, bringing the line to a halt. "Now, Paula, I have several quarts of homemade soup in the car to give you. Don't get away without it."

Paula looked at her blankly. Why was Gwen giving her soup? Was it something Maida had ordered and forgotten to tell her about?

"It'll do for lunches, and as soon as Maida comes home, we'll start bringing in suppers, too," the woman went on. "You'll have your hands full, running that big house and looking after Maida."

"You don't have to do that," Paula began, but Gwen went on as if she hadn't spoken.

"Probably I should line up people to stay with Maida right at first. Yes, that would be best. I'll let you know when I have a schedule set up."

"I don't need any help," Paula protested, but it was too late. Gwen had bustled away again, looking like a busy little brown wren on her self-appointed errand.

"You may as well let them help." The amused voice came from behind her, and she turned to find that Pastor Richie was the next person in line. The rotund, white-haired man smiled with sympathy. "I know Gwen can be overbearing, but everyone wants to help."

"But..." *I want to do it myself.* That would certainly sound ungracious, but it was what she felt. "The doctor wants Aunt Maida to go into rehab, so she won't be home for a couple of weeks at least. And I'm sure I can handle things, even when Maida comes home."

"Of course you can, but that's not the point, is it?"

She looked at him blankly. If that wasn't the point, what was?

Pastor Richie helped himself to a heaping spoonful of scalloped potatoes, then sighed. "I might be able to lose weight, if I could bear to turn down one dish. But then someone's feelings might be hurt.''

It took a moment to realize what he was saying. ''You mean people's feelings will be hurt if I don't let them help.''

He nodded, and his bright blue eyes were intent. ''That's true, of course. People here love Maida, so they're quite ready to love you, sort of by extension. But it's more than that. If you don't let them help, you might do them harm.''

''Do them harm?'' she echoed. Why on earth would her being independent harm anyone else?

''People need to be of service to others,'' he said. He added a dollop of cranberry salad to an already overflowing plate. ''It's a spiritual blessing, you see. You wouldn't want to deprive anyone of a spiritual blessing, would you?''

''No…no, of course not.'' Like Aunt Maida, the pastor clearly saw the world in spiritual terms.

He beamed. ''Then you'll let them help. You can always tell yourself it's for Maida, not for you, if that makes you feel better.''

She looked at him with surprise and respect. How had he known that was what she'd do? And what else did his wise eyes see when they looked at her?

''Paula, over here.'' She glanced toward the voice, to discover Mitch Donovan, seated with a group at one of the folding tables, waving at her to join them.

It wasn't until she reached them that she realized Alex was there. She hesitated, not sure whether he'd consider this appropriate. He'd told her she wasn't on duty at the picnic. Did that mean he'd prefer not to socialize with her?

He answered that by pulling out the chair next to him. "Join us, please."

She sat, very aware of his movements as he adjusted her chair and handed her a napkin. Would she ever get over this hyper-awareness when it came to Alex Caine?

"I think you know some of these people. Mitch, of course, and Brett."

Paula nodded to Brett. If she'd thought about it, she'd have realized Alex would be sitting with these two men. They'd long been his closest friends.

"This is Mitch's wife, Anne."

A beautiful, dark-haired woman looked up from the toddler on her lap and held out her hand. "Welcome to Bedford Creek, Paula."

"And you know Brett's wife, Rebecca. She's the physician's assistant at the clinic now."

"I'll see you often once your aunt is discharged from the hospital." Rebecca had a warm, sunny smile to match her auburn hair and peaches-and-cream complexion. "You'll be bringing her to the clinic for her checkups, I'm sure."

Paula nodded, a little overwhelmed with all this

friendliness. They acted as if she were Alex's guest, instead of his housekeeper.

Anne seemed to sense her discomfort. She turned the conversation to the current tourist season, urging Mitch to tell a story about the enterprising young man who'd tried to set up a souvenir shop in the town's park.

With the focus off her and the talk bouncing comfortably around the table, Paula tried to sort them all out. Anne was an attorney, she remembered hearing, and the toddler on her lap was adopted. Rebecca was Gwen's daughter, little Kristie's aunt, and she'd inherited her mother's warmth.

Paula noticed something else after she'd listened to them for a few minutes. With these people, Alex was at ease. With everyone else, as far as she'd been able to observe, the Caine shield stayed in place, marking the boundary between him and the rest of the world. But with Brett and Mitch, and perhaps with their wives, he was himself.

She saw his firm mouth relax, his eyes crinkle with laughter, and her heart seemed to cramp. If he ever reached that point with her…but there was no sense imagining something that would never happen.

Anne leaned across to her under cover of the general conversation. "That's our foster son, Davey, kicking the soccer ball with Jason and Kristie."

The lanky preteen towered over the smaller children, but he kicked the ball gently enough so that Jason had a shot at it. "He seems like a very nice boy."

Anne smiled with maternal pride. "He's come a long way, believe me. Mitch is terrific with him."

"I imagine you have something to do with it, too."

"I try." She stroked the soft curls of the sleepy toddler on her lap. "How are you doing with Jason? I know from Maida he can be a little difficult."

The urge to confide her concerns to a sympathetic ear was strong, but she resisted it. She didn't have the right to say anything about Jason, even to someone who was Alex's friend.

"I think we're getting along pretty well. I'm sure he misses Maida, though." Surely it was all right to say that much.

"Maida's been like a grandmother to that child." Anne seemed to read between the lines. She touched Paula's hand lightly. "Jason's had too many losses in his young life. And it can't be easy living up to the Caine name."

It was so near what she herself thought that she had to clench her teeth to keep from blurting something out.

Anne smiled. "If you ever need someone to talk to, just give me a call."

"Thanks." She had the sense that, improbable as it might seem, she'd made a friend. "I'll do that."

* * *

Nobody seemed able to make him as angry as Paula could with just a word. Alex smiled wryly as he walked slowly across the patio. Perhaps he needed to remind himself that the rest of the world wouldn't treat him with the deference most people in Bedford Creek did. Certainly Paula didn't. He suspected only her desire to keep her job had prevented her from saying even more than she had.

She seemed, without being aware of it, to have joined the select group that actually looked at him as just another human being. Certainly Brett and Mitch knew his weaknesses as well as he did himself, and didn't hesitate to call him to order if they felt he needed it. Now Paula had come on board, and he didn't know how to handle that.

He'd watched her at the picnic. He'd seen her fitting into his town, fitting into his life, as if she belonged here.

Nonsense. He tried to reject that idea out of hand. Paula worked for him. She neither wanted nor would welcome anything else.

She was the only woman willing to defy him. Maybe she was also the only woman who could really accept him.

That was a dangerous thought. He wasn't ready to take that kind of risk again. He—

A cry echoed through the gathering dusk, startling him. Was it a bird of some sort? Then it came again,

and he knew instinctively what he'd heard. *Paula!*
He began to run toward the garage, toward that panicked cry.

His heart thudded in his ears as he rounded the
building. She was in trouble, she was hurt, she—

An errant flame, stirred by the breeze, licked upward from the brush the lawn service had been burning earlier. He'd have something to say to them about
that. Then he saw Paula's face, and her expression
banished every other thought from his mind.

She was terrified. She stood backed against the garage wall, clutching the puppy in her arms. She
looked unable to move, and she stared, eyes wide and
frightened, into the flames.

"Paula!" He grasped her arm, pulling her away
from the fire. Another dry branch caught, flaring up.
He couldn't stop the images that flooded his mind—
the flames rushing toward them, working frantically
to free Paula from the seat, knowing that at any moment it could be too late…

That must be what Paula saw, too.

"It's all right." He turned her toward him, frightened at her reaction, and held her face between his
hands. His heart still pounded, but he willed his voice
to stay calm. "Paula, look at me, not the fire. It's all
right, do you hear me? You're safe."

For several seconds she didn't respond, as if she

couldn't hear him. Then, finally, she blinked. The terror was still in her eyes, but she focused on his face.

"You're safe," he said, longing to pull her into his arms and not daring to. "Can you stay right here while I get the hose and put that out?"

She swallowed, the muscles in her throat working. Then she nodded. The puppy wiggled and yelped, but she gripped it tighter.

"Good." His voice nearly betrayed him, but he wouldn't let it. He couldn't let her know how shaken he was by her reaction. "I'll just be a minute."

He let go of her tentatively. She took a gasping breath, then nodded again.

Alex hurried around the garage, grabbed the coiled hose and twisted the tap on. He ran back to Paula, ignoring the throbbing in his injured leg, and aimed the nozzle at the flames. Moments later, only a blackened circle marred the grass.

He brushed his hands on his pant legs as he went back to her. "The lawn service should never have left that brush pile behind the garages." Maybe talking would erase the shock from her face. "It's out now, and no harm done."

That had to be the stupidest remark he'd ever made. He desperately wanted the tension to be over. He wanted them both to smile and walk away.

But that couldn't happen, not now. This was one time when keeping a stiff upper lip and smiling through the pain wouldn't cut it. He put his arm around her gently and felt her tremble.

"Come on." He led her a step. "Let's go in the house. We need to talk."

She tried to pull away, embarrassment flooding her face. "No, I...I don't need to do that. I'm fine." Her voice seemed to gain strength as she spoke.

A few days ago he'd have accepted that. He'd have used it for an excuse to back away from a conversation that had to be painful for both of them. Now he couldn't. Paula's return had changed things. Her agony forced its way beneath his protective barrier, wrenching his heart. Pretending everything was all right was no longer an option.

He caught her hand, holding it firmly. "You're not fine, and we need to talk." He brushed his thumb over her knuckles, as gently as if she were a child.

She looked away from him. "There's nothing to talk about. I just have this stupid fear of fire."

"I can see that. And we both know why."

"I was chasing Nugget," she said, ignoring the reference to the accident. "When the flames flared up in front of me, I just panicked for a moment."

"Paula—"

"That's all it was." She tried to pull away.

He tightened his grasp on her hand. She was doing what he always did—tamping down the pain, ignoring it, ignoring anyone who brought it up. He was just beginning to realize how futile that was.

"I'm not satisfied with that explanation. You might get away with it with anyone else, but not me."

She looked at him then, and he read the pain in her eyes so clearly.

"I don't..."

He shook his head. "Don't even try, because I'm the one person in the world you can't fool on this subject. I was there, remember?" He never talked about the crash. He was going to. "Like it or not, we shared something terrifying and lived to tell about it."

Somehow those didn't seem to be the right words.

"No, not 'tell about it,'" he amended. "You haven't been talking about it, I'm sure of that. And maybe you need to."

"Talking won't make it go away."

"Nothing will make it go away, but we have to deal with it." Her pain was forcing him inch by painful inch from behind his own protective barricade. "I've got scars on the outside from the crash. But you—you're carrying your scars inside. And like it or not, we're going to talk about this."

Chapter Nine

Paula wanted to argue, to insist that she was all right, but she couldn't. Her stomach still churned, and the metallic taste of fear lingered in her mouth. She wasn't all right, and both of them knew it.

She let Alex pilot her into the house. He seemed to hesitate for a moment, as if trying to decide where to go, then led her into the sunroom that adjoined the kitchen.

The gathering dusk seeped into the room through the wall of windows, chilling her. Alex switched on a table lamp, and its golden glow banished the darkness.

"Sit down here." He pushed her gently onto the chintz sofa, then ran his hands down her arms. "You're cold. I'm going to make a cup of Maida's herbal tea for you." He shoved a hassock under her feet. "I'll just be a minute. Do you want me to take the dog?"

"No." The word was out before she had a chance to think about it. She stroked Nugget's soft fur, taking comfort from his warmth. "I'll keep him with me. You don't need to "

But he was gone. She leaned back against the over-stuffed cushions. The couch gave under her, cradling her body, offering further comfort. Maybe that was what she needed. Her legs still trembled, as if she'd run a marathon. She'd just relax a minute; then she could assure Alex she was fine and leave.

The small room, so out of place amid the formality of the rest of the mansion, welcomed her. Its soft colors were feminine and restful, and the dried flower arrangements and faded chintzes would have been appropriate in her parents' house. It hardly seemed possible that the same person who'd chosen mahogany bedroom suites suitable for Buckingham Palace had decorated this cozy haven.

She heard Alex's steps in the kitchen, their faint unevenness the only hint of his injured leg. Then he was back. He put a white pottery mug in her hands, sat down next to her and moved the sleeping puppy from her lap to a spot between them.

"Drink that. Maida's chamomile tea is guaranteed to make any trouble better."

She remembered all the times she'd sat across from Maida at the kitchen table, drinking her aunt's special brew, talking about anything and everything. Steam curled from the pale liquid, and she sipped cautiously.

Warmth suffused her, calming the quaking inside. Her muscles relaxed as the tension seeped away, leaving her limp and exhausted. As the last shadow of the nightmare vanished, she looked across at Alex, seeing him with a clarity she'd never before experienced.

He leaned back, his long fingers absently stroking the sleeping puppy. He seemed perfectly at ease, as if willing to wait all night, if need be, for her. Even the lines around his firm mouth had relaxed, erasing the formal reserve he normally projected. He was watching the puppy, and his dark lashes hid his eyes from her. His skin, tanned from his hours in the pool, contrasted with the white knit shirt he'd worn to the picnic.

He looked up suddenly, and their eyes met. Awareness of him shimmered along her skin and took her breath away.

"Better now?" His dark gaze probed.

"Yes." Her heartbeat accelerated, the tension returning. He was going to push her for answers, and she wouldn't be able to withstand him. He'd drag her weakness out into the light for both of them to see.

"This is a nice room, isn't it?" He ran his hand along the rose chintz arm of the sofa.

She blinked, surprised. That certainly wasn't the question she'd expected. He was giving her time, she realized. The hard questions still lurked, held in abeyance until he thought she could handle them.

She took another swallow of the tea. "It's a cozy room." She tried to smile, suspecting the result didn't look very convincing. "I've always thought this spot doesn't match the rest of the mansion."

"That's because my mother decorated it. My father insisted the rest of the house be left in its turn-of-the-century grandeur, but this room was hers." He touched the faded blossoms of a dried flower arrangement, his long fingers gentle. "She loved flowers. That's one of the few things I remember about her— the scent of flowers."

His words reached out and clutched her heart. Alex was exposing feelings he usually kept hidden. Maybe he did it because that was what he expected from her. He'd consider that fair. She might deplore Alex's arrogance, but she'd never doubted his fairness.

"I'm sorry." Her throat tightened. "It must have been hard, not having a mother when you were growing up." Her thoughts flickered to her mother, then Aunt Maida—two very different female influences in her life.

"Now my son is going through the same thing."

The lines around his eyes deepened. "The Caine family doesn't seem destined for 'happily every after.'"

"Jason will be fine." She answered the doubt under his words. "He just needs…" She stopped, not sure she should go on.

"What do you think Jason needs?" The usual defensive note was missing from his voice. He asked as if he really wanted an answer.

He needs the same thing you do. "He needs to open up to someone." She took a breath and waited—for an explosion, for him to freeze her out or give her that superior look that said her opinion wasn't worth hearing. For him to retort immediately that his son was fine, as he always did.

Instead, he put his hand over hers. "Isn't that what you need, Paula?"

There it was—the question he'd been waiting to ask, the question she knew she had to answer. "I don't know." The words didn't want to come out, but she forced them out, anyway. "Maybe I need courage. Maybe I'm really a coward, letting myself panic over a simple thing like fire." Her mind flickered to Jason and the matches. But he had been asleep for hours. He couldn't have had any thing to do with this.

"The accident—"

She swept on, the words suddenly rushing out now that she'd started. "You don't know, do you? I don't even remember the accident! It's wiped right out of my mind. So why should I have this stupid panic when I see flames? It doesn't make any sense."

"You don't remember anything about the accident?"

"Nothing." Her mouth twisted. "My family insists that's lucky. Maybe they're right."

He stroked her hand, in much the same way he'd stroked the sleeping puppy. "I'm not so sure. Maybe your conscious mind doesn't remember, but something inside you does."

She hadn't thought of it that way, but, of course, he was right. Something in her remembered and was terrified. "I feel like it's hiding there, in my mind." She took a shaky breath. "Just waiting to jump out and grab me."

"I'm sorry I didn't know." His fingers wrapped around hers. "I asked Maida how you were so many times, but she didn't tell me this."

"It makes me feel like a failure." The words tasted bitter. "I try to be strong, but in this…" *But I'm not.* She choked, and couldn't go on. She'd run out of steam, with her pitiful weakness laid out for both of them to see.

Alex took her hand and held it between his palms. His warmth and strength seemed to flow along her skin. "Paula, that's nonsense. You must know it. Nobody can go through what we went through and not have scars. Believe me. Do you think I don't have nightmares about the crash?''

She blinked rapidly to hold back hot tears. ''You're functioning. You don't let your fears paralyze you.''

''Maybe not, but everyone is different. You take any group of people and put them in a life-threatening situation, and each one of them will respond in a unique way.'' His hands tightened on hers. ''Believe me, I know. I've been through it twice.''

''Twice?'' For a moment she didn't know what he was talking about, but then half-forgotten words came back to her. ''I remember.'' She shook her head. ''A little, anyway. I overheard Aunt Maida talking to someone about you. But then when she saw I was there, she changed the subject.''

''She probably didn't want you to think about imitating our stupidity.''

'' 'Our'?''

''Brett's, Mitch's and mine. We came close to wiping ourselves off the planet on a class camping trip our senior year in high school.''

His words were light, but the rigidity of his jaw muscles belied that. He was trying to help by telling her this, but it was costing him.

''What happened?''

''A flash flood. You know how fast the streams can go up when we've had heavy rain.''

She nodded, unable to suppress a shiver. The valley was so narrow, there was no place for the water to go. "You were trapped, weren't you?"

"We were stupid. Or maybe just too immature to be let out alone. Each group in our class was supposed to find its way through the woods with a compass and a map. Instead, we got lost and ended up in an abandoned quarry with the water rising around us."

His voice sounded perfectly calm, but his hand clenched hers so tightly it hurt.

"You could have died." Just as they both could have died that rainy night at the airfield.

He gave a tight nod. "I slipped into the water. If Mitch hadn't grabbed me, within minutes I'd have been just a memory."

"But you did get out, all three of you." If he was trying to make her feel better about her pitiful weakness, he hadn't succeeded. "You survived that. You survived the plane crash. You didn't let either of those things keep you from moving on." If he did have nightmares, as he claimed, he'd beaten them into submission.

He seemed to realize how tightly he gripped her hand, and loosened his hold with a small, apologetic smile. But he didn't let go.

"I'm not making my point very well. All of us were affected by what happened. In the long run it made us stronger, but at the time it wasn't easy. For you, it's flames. For me, it's rain. I can't hear rain on the roof without breaking out in a cold sweat.'' He shrugged. "Other people didn't help after the accident. They either acted as if we were heroes for getting out or stupid for getting into the situation in the first place.''

That brought her startled gaze up to his face. "No one would blame you for an accident.''

"No?'' Something faintly mocking appeared in his eyes. "You don't remember my father very well if you think that.''

Yes, she remembered that rigid autocrat. "What did he say to you?''

"Just the usual sort of thing.'' His tone was light, but pain threaded through it, sharp and hard. "That I'd failed. I hadn't lived up to my responsibilities. I should have gotten excused from the trip, should have had better sense than to go in the quarry. My position as his heir was too important to risk on childish adventures.''

His words pierced her heart. Alex wasn't invulnerable, after all. He might try to convince himself that it didn't matter, but his father's harshness had damaged him. She actually found herself feeling pity for the man who had everything.

And she felt something else, too. Something she'd

been trying to deny but couldn't any longer, even if she could never say it aloud.

She was still in love with him.

Alex heard the pain in his admission, and it shocked him. What was he doing? He was saying things to Paula that he'd never said to anyone, not his closest friends, not even his wife. The lessons he'd learned early had been too deeply ingrained. A Caine didn't feel weakness. And if he did, he certainly never admitted it.

Paula was different. Karin had bought into the whole Caine mystique, but Paula never did. She saw him as a person, not just the Caine heir. He wanted to tell Paula the things he'd kept hidden in his very soul. He wanted to give in to that fierce attraction he felt every time he was near her. He wanted to stop thinking about what he should do or shouldn't do, and follow his instincts. For once in his life, he wanted to put his intellectual side on hold and just feel. Maybe, for the first time, he'd found someone with whom he could let down all the barriers.

She was looking at him with a mixture of emotions in her clear-as-glass green eyes—sympathy, tenderness, caring. Those feelings drew him in. They pulled him closer and closer to her. Close enough that he could feel the warmth that emanated from her skin. Close enough that he could smell the fresh, flowery scent she wore. Close enough that their lips could meet...

For once he wouldn't stop and analyze this. His hand moved, almost without volition, and he stroked her smooth cheek. He brushed back a strand of golden hair, and it clung to his fingers as if to pull him even closer.

Her breath went out in a soft sigh, moving across his cheek. He turned her face toward him, overwhelmed with a rush of longing and tenderness. His lips found hers.

She was soft, so soft. She moved closer, nestling into his arms as if this was the most natural thing in the world. The kiss deepened, saying all the things he couldn't find words for.

Finally she drew away. "Alex." She sighed his name, her cheek warm against his.

His breath came out unevenly. "That's been a long time coming."

She pulled back, looking into his eyes, and her hand rested over his heart. "Not for me."

He looked questioningly at her.

"That's another thing Aunt Maida didn't tell you. What happened then, when I was here before," she paused, as if preparing herself for something. "I didn't remember any of it. Working here, being Jason's nanny—it was all wiped out. I know my parents wanted me treated at the bigger hospital in Baltimore, but I didn't remember going back. My memories started again in the hospital there. I didn't remember that summer until Aunt Maida asked me to come back. And it was as if a door fell open in my mind, and there it was.''

He frowned, trying to assimilate her words. ''You mean, all this time, you hadn't remembered anything from that summer?''

She shook her head. ''I didn't remember. I still don't remember the actual crash—'' She broke off sharply.

Her eyes widened, and the hand that had rested over his heart gripped his shirt.

''Paula, what is it?'' She'd turned sheet-white. ''What's wrong?''

''The...the a-accident,'' she stammered. ''I didn't remember it. But now—'' She stopped again, her pupils dilating.

''Paula.'' He gripped her arms. ''You've remembered. Is that it?'' Something—maybe that kiss, echoing the one two years ago, or maybe talking openly about the accident at last must have brought it back.

She couldn't seem to answer. Then she nodded. Her eyes focused on the past, dark with pain.

He knew what she was seeing. He'd seen it often enough himself. The ground rushing toward them, the grinding crash, the crumpled seats and panicked passengers. The flames.

"Paula, it's all right." She didn't respond. He pulled her against him, wrapping his arms around her as if that would protect her from the images in her mind. "It's all right. It's over. You don't have to think about it any more."

"I don't want to." Her voice choked with tears. "I don't want to! All this time I couldn't, and now I can't get the pictures out of my head."

"I know, I know." He stroked her hair, and her pain surrounded his heart. "But it's a long time ago."

"Not for me!" She sounded almost angry, but her hands clung tightly and her voice was muffled against his chest. "It's right now."

He understood then. Time had blurred his memories of the crash. Bad as they were, the jagged edges had been smoothed away, eased by layers of other events, happier memories.

But not for Paula. Paula was experiencing it now as he'd experienced it those first few days in the hospital, when he couldn't close his eyes without seeing it all again.

He cradled her against him, rocking her as gently. Her hot tears soaked into his shirt. "Hush, it's all right." They were the words he'd wanted to hear someone say to him. "It was terrifying, but you're all right. There's nothing to fear."

Her pain pierced his control. *Lord, help her.* He so seldom asked God's help for himself, thinking that surely God expected him to handle his own responsibilities. But help for Paula was different. *Give her peace, Lord. Please. She's in such pain.*

All he could do was hold her, tightly, as if he could absorb the pain. He let her cry, and her sobs ripped through him, shaking him in ways he didn't begin to understand.

One thing was clear, though. His feelings for Paula couldn't be tidied away as convenient or unsuitable. Like it or not, she roused emotion in him that he wasn't prepared to handle.

Why not? Why couldn't he and Paula, like any other two people, find a way to build something together? He'd told himself he didn't believe in happy endings. Nothing in his experience had led him to think one could exist for him. But maybe, with Paula, things could be different.

They didn't have to be just employer and employee. They didn't have to fall into the roles life had assigned them. Paula was an intelligent, giving, lovely woman, not the child who'd looked at him with hero worship in her eyes. They could start again, put the mistakes of the past behind them, and begin as equals.

Gradually her sobs trailed off. The death grip she'd had on his shirt relaxed. Next, he thought, she'd become embarrassed. Independent Paula never wanted to admit that she'd shown what she'd call weakness.

She eased back, still in the circle of his arms, and rubbed her eyes. "I'm sorry."

He had to smile at the predictability of the words. "Don't be sorry. You've relived a terrible experience. Of course you cried—anyone would."

"I didn't just cry." She touched his wet shirt. "I bawled like a baby. You must be ready to run for cover."

"Not yet." His heart lifted. She was past the worst of it. *Thank you, God.*

"Right." She mopped her eyes with her sleeve. "Men hate it when women cry."

"Depends on the man." He touched her cheek lightly, brushing away the tear that sparkled there. "And the woman."

He felt the warmth rise in her cheeks at his words, and it made him want to kiss her again.

"I don't like behaving like a baby," she said stubbornly. "Especially—" The words broke off, and her gaze evaded his.

"Especially in front of me? Am I that much of an ogre?" He needed to make her smile again.

"No." A smile trembled on her lips. "Not an ogre. But you are my boss, remember?"

"That doesn't mean I can't also be…" He shouldn't push it, not when she was so fragile. He had to smile at the thought of her probable reaction if he called her "fragile" aloud. "A friend," he finished. "Haven't we always been friends?"

The word seemed to reassure her, and he sensed some of the tension leave her.

"A friend," she agreed. "You've gone above and beyond the call of friendship tonight."

"I've been there," he reminded her. "I know what it feels like."

She nodded. Her eyes narrowed, as if she approached the memory again, very cautiously. "I always wondered about it, even when I tried not to. What it was like, how I got out."

"Now you know." He moved a little away from her. "It will be easier now. You remember, so you can let the memories start to fade."

She frowned. "Is that what yours have done?"

"Most of the time." He had to be honest with her. "Sometimes the thoughts bother me, but most of the time, even if something reminds me, I can put it aside and go on."

How long? he wondered. How long until he could stop being the supportive friend and move to being the interested male?

Her forehead was wrinkled, her gaze focused on the past. "Put it aside," she echoed. "Not hear it, not see it." She shivered. "Not smell it. That's the worst. Maybe that's why I get so panicked around fire. I smell it, and I want to run. But I can't. I'm trapped…''

Her eyes widened as she stared at him. "That's true, isn't it? I was trapped."

Reluctantly he nodded. He didn't want her to think about that, but it wasn't in him to lie to her. "You were trapped."

"The flames. I couldn't get the belt loose. I couldn't move."

She was reliving it again; he could see that. He reached for her, longing to wipe the memories away, and knowing he couldn't.

"But you did. We both got out."

She shook her head as if trying to shake the image away. "I was trapped." She focused on him suddenly. "You got me out. I remember now. You came—you got me out of the belt."

"Paula…" What could he say? That he didn't want her to go there?

"You dragged me to the hole in the cabin." A shudder passed through her. "People were crying. You took my hands and lowered me out of the plane. You told me to get away."

"Everyone got out," he reminded her. "It could have been so much worse. Everyone got out alive."

"But you saved me." She reached toward him. "You saved me."

He realized what was happening, and the hope he'd

felt moments before turned to ashes. Paula wasn't looking at him like the woman who'd returned his kisses. She was looking at him like a starry-eyed, hero-worshipping child.

He drew back, fighting the fierce disappointment that swept through him. He couldn't do it. He couldn't pursue a relationship with Paula when she thought of him as some kind of a hero. Not when he was only too aware of how often he failed to measure up. They couldn't build anything on that.

Chapter Ten

"Come on, Jason. You can do it." Paula waved her mitt. "Throw it right in here."

Jason looked doubtful, but he pitched the baseball. His expression turned to astonishment when the throw made it across the makeshift plate and thunked into Paula's mitt.

Smiling, she stepped back and motioned one of the other peewee baseball players to take her place. When she'd learned the group of youngest kids from the church had no one to coach them, it had seemed a golden opportunity to involve Jason. And when a chance remark from Mitch at the picnic had informed her that Alex had been a pitcher on their high school team—well, that was too good to pass up.

She glanced at her watch. Alex should be home

from the plant soon, and this time they were playing where he could have no objection. The grassy lawn behind the garage was perfect for games, and even the most wildly hit ball couldn't damage anything. Or anyone. She thought of the Swiss businessman and winced.

But she wanted more than Alex's approval. She wanted his presence.

For Jason, she hurriedly reminded herself. This was for Jason, not for her. She stood back, watching the children, and tried not to think about what had happened between her and Alex on Saturday night. But it was useless. The memory wouldn't be denied.

Her cheeks heated at the thought of his kisses, and she could almost feel his strong arms around her, holding her protectively close. *Protected*—that was a good word for it. At a moment when reality had shattered around her, Alex had been a secure anchor.

That was all he had been, as far as he was concerned. She had to accept that. He'd been kind, and they'd both been a little carried away by the emotion of the moment. Maybe, for a few minutes, she'd dreamed their connection was something more.

But Alex's behavior in the days since had shown her the truth. He'd withdrawn from her, going back to his usual cool, urbane manner. The very tone of his voice had told her clearly that he regretted what had happened between them and had no intention of repeating that mistake.

At least he hadn't apologized. Her face burned at the thought. That would have been the final humiliation. He'd simply ignored the whole incident. Now she had to do the same.

She had to concentrate on the two people she'd come here to help. Aunt Maida would be home from the hospital soon, and Paula would have her hands full even with the aid of the church volunteers. And just as important, she had to make more headway with Jason.

She watched him toss the ball to Kristie, who promptly ducked. Jason had begun to smile again. Certainly that was progress. But she couldn't kid herself; the boy was worried about something. She could see it so clearly in the sadness that filled his eyes in unguarded moments. Whatever it was, he wasn't ready yet to confide in her. Maybe he never would be.

She wouldn't give up, she told herself as she went to help Kristie catch the ball. She'd come here to help Jason, and that's what she'd do, no matter who stood in the way.

"What's going on?" Alex's voice, coming so appropriately on the heels of her thought, startled her. Her heart cramped, and she took a firm grip on her emotions. *Be natural,* she ordered herself. *Pretend it never happened.* She swung around, looking for signs of annoyance in his face. But he was smiling.

"Baseball practice."

"So I see." He came closer. He wore his usual white shirt, but his jacket was thrown over one arm and his striped tie was loosened. She reminded her heart not to feel anything.

"Aren't they too small for this?"

"Not according to my brothers. They put a baseball in my hand when I was three." She grinned. "I'm not advocating that, you understand. This is the peewee team from the church. They want to start playing, but they don't have a coach."

He raised an eyebrow. "How are they?"

She lowered her voice so the kids couldn't hear. "Well, they can't throw. They also can't catch or hit. But they have lots of enthusiasm."

"In that case, I wish you luck. Sounds as if their coach will need it."

"I didn't volunteer myself as coach." She braced herself for an explosion. "I volunteered you."

"Me!" For the moment he looked too dumbstruck to be angry.

"Mitch told me what a good player you were in high school. He thought this was a great idea."

"He would." Alex looked as if he was thinking up a suitable punishment for his friend. "I'm afraid it's out of the question." He turned away.

She wasn't going to let him off that easily, not where his son was concerned. "Why?"

He looked at her blankly. Apparently that was something people didn't often ask Alex Caine.

"Why?" she repeated. "Why is it out of the question? The kids need someone to work with them. You have the requisite skills."

"I've already made a donation to the program."

"The kids need someone to give time, not money. You have a son who wants to play. Why shouldn't that someone be you?"

"That should be obvious." He wore the expression she thought of as the *royal look*—the calm assumption that anything he chose to do wouldn't be questioned.

"Not to me, it isn't." Somewhat to her surprise, she realized that Saturday night's events had made her bolder where Alex was concerned. She wasn't sure why, but it seemed a step forward. "Explain it to me."

He sent a harassed look toward the children, who'd begun to gather around Paula. "You should know why. The business I'm working on right now is important. It requires all my concentration."

"All the more reason why you should be getting some physical activity and relaxation," she said promptly, ignoring a twinge of caution. She was pushing hard, and she'd probably have her head bitten off for her trouble.

He raised his eyebrows skeptically. "And you recommend coaching small children for relaxation?"

"Are you going to coach us, Dad?" Jason's eyes widened. "Will you?"

Kristie, carrot-colored ponytail bobbing, threw herself at his legs. "Please, please, please," she chanted, clearly not awed by his status.

Over the mob of small children, Alex shot her a look that was both laughing and annoyed. "I'll get you for this, Paula. You and Mitch both."

The tension inside her eased, and she smiled. "I'm not intimidated by threats. Let's see what your fastball looks like after all these years."

"Too fast for a bunch of seven-year-olds," he said. "Even at my advanced age. Suppose you start with batting practice, while I go change."

She nodded, starting onto the field as the children hurried to grab bats. But as she passed him, he caught her arm, drawing her close to him. His dark eyes sparkled with laughter, and her heart seemed to turn over. He didn't often look like that, and when he did, the effect was devastating.

"I meant it, Paula. You and Mitch are in trouble."

She willed her body not to betray the effect he had on her. "At least that means I've got the police chief on my side," she retorted.

Laughing, Alex headed toward the house, his suit jacket slung over one shoulder. Paula kept her smile in place as she turned to the kids. Nobody was going to guess what she felt.

She'd created an opportunity for Alex and his son to grow closer, she reminded herself. That was what she'd intended. She hadn't intended to prove so clearly to herself that her feelings for Alex were completely out of control.

Paula had turned his world upside down, Alex thought as he raised the window shades in the old gardener's cottage the next afternoon. His studio flooded with light. Sunshine splashed across the wide, uneven oak flooring and touched the half-finished wood carving on the workbench.

He moved toward the carving of Jason he'd begun working on, his eyes assessing it, even while his mind continued on the by-now-familiar track. Paula, and the changes she'd brought to his life.

It was just like the last time she'd been in his house, he realized. She had a knack for turning the mansion into something other than the museum it so often felt like. She filled it with laughter, noise, small children. With Paula around, his son smiled.

The thought clutched his heart. Why hadn't he realized how little his son smiled? Jason's sober expression had become so habitual that Alex had begun to take it for granted—until Paula changed things.

He couldn't stop the smile that tugged at his own lips when he thought of that baseball team practice yesterday afternoon. She'd done it to involve him with Jason, of course, and she was remarkably good at not taking "no" for an answer.

But he'd had a surprise for her. If she wanted him to work with the children, she'd have to be involved, too. He wouldn't do it alone.

It was almost frightening, how much pleasure the idea of working with her gave him. He'd told himself there couldn't be anything between them for so many reasons, but she seemed to be breaking those walls down, one by one.

Unfortunately, the biggest wall still stood irrevocably between them. As long as she looked at him with hero-worship in her eyes, any other relationship was impossible.

He ran his hand over the grain of the carving, itching to get back to work on the piece. Carving soothed him, letting his mind wander while his fingers brought the wood to life.

A foolish waste of time. You have better things to do. It was remarkable how often the voice of his conscience sounded just like the voice of his father.

The knock at the door startled him. Quickly he tossed a cloth over the half-finished piece and went to answer.

"Paula." Somehow he wasn't surprised. He hadn't satisfied her curiosity the last time she came to the cottage, and she wasn't one to give up.

She held Maida's wooden recipe box in her hands.

"I found this on the kitchen counter. You've had it fixed." Her dimple flashed. "I'm so grateful. I hated the idea of explaining to her what happened."

"No problem."

He wanted to be happy for her, but the box was a reminder of her insistence that Jason had broken it deliberately. He'd thought of that each time he'd worked on it, and the accusation had leached the pleasure from the delicate repair job.

"If that's all…"

He should have closed the door more quickly. She moved past him as easily as if he hadn't spoken.

"Where did you have it fixed? I didn't realize there was a shop in town that did this sort of work."

He shrugged, groping for an answer. It was ridiculous to be so reticent about his hobby, but he couldn't seem to admit the truth to her.

In another second, the admission wasn't necessary. She saw the workbench. Her gaze shot from it to him.

"You repaired the box yourself, didn't you." She frowned. "I don't understand. Why didn't you tell me you were doing it?"

"I didn't think you'd be interested. What difference does it make who fixed it?" He took a half step toward the door, trying to ease her out. Having her here brought her too far for comfort into his inner life.

Paula ignored the hint, moving toward the drafting table. Her eyes widened as she took in the papers scattered on it. "Are these designs for the factory? I didn't realize you actually designed the furniture you make."

He swept the sheets together, unaccountably embarrassed. "It's nothing. I don't do all the designing, just a few of the lines."

She touched the top sheet. "That's the one Dieter is interested in, isn't it?" She looked up at him, perplexed. "Alex, I don't understand. Why are you so reticent about it? If I had a gift like this, I'd be proud."

"The designs are part of my job. Nothing to be excited about." He frowned down at the drawings. "It's true they're an aspect of the attraction our business has for Dieter, but certainly not all of it. Don't get the idea that I'm the Michelangelo of the furniture world."

He couldn't suppress his embarrassment that she'd found out. People at the plant knew, of course, but they'd learned not to comment. He'd started tinkering with designs when he was just a kid. He'd quickly found that his father didn't consider that the proper role for a Caine. He was supposed to run the plant, not play at being a draftsman.

"If you don't mind, Paula, I really have to get back to work. I'm a little short on time, especially since someone seems to have involved me in baseball practice."

He rather enjoyed the way she flushed and looked away.

"That's all I wanted. Just to say thank you."

She picked up the box, which she'd put on the table, and her elbow brushed the carving of Jason. Before he could grab it, the covering slid off.

Paula could only stare. She'd thought she understood Alex. She'd assumed she knew who he was—a rich man with no interest in anything other than his company and his family name.

But in the last few days she'd discovered facets of him she'd never expected. She'd seen the hero who had rescued her at the risk of his own life. She'd seen the gentle comforter who'd held her while she wept. And now she saw yet another side to the man she only thought she knew.

"It's beautiful." She reached out tentatively to touch the carving. Jason's face looked out of the warm, smooth wood. The piece was clearly not finished, but Alex had somehow suggested that lingering sadness that seemed a part of his son. She wondered if he even realized he'd portrayed that.

"It's not finished." Alex snatched up the cloth as if to hide this example of his artistry.

"No, I see that. But you've already caught his expression. That must be the most difficult thing." Her fingertips smoothed the figure's cheek. It was almost like touching the real thing, and her heart caught at the beauty of it. "Has Jason seen this yet?"

"No."

He flipped the cloth over the head, ignoring the fact that she still touched it. She took her hand away reluctantly.

"You want to wait until it's done, I suppose. But I'm sure he'd be fascinated at seeing his face appear in the wood."

Alex frowned, straightening a row of tools on the tabletop that didn't seem to need straightening. "I don't know that I'll show it to him. It's just something I've been playing around with."

"Not show him!" She reached out impulsively to touch his arm. "But it's wonderful. Any child would be thrilled." Didn't he realize that his love for his son came through in every line?

"It's more important that I provide properly for him, rather than wasting time on something like this." He looked as if the words tasted bitter in his mouth.

"Who said that?" she asked with sudden insight. "It sounds like a quote."

He shot her a look that was almost angry. "My father." He turned away from the workbench. "He had very little patience for wasting time. And he was right."

She wasn't sure how to respond to that. Probably

she didn't have the right to say anything, but she couldn't seem to stop herself.

Lord, show me what to say to him. I didn't understand.

"It's not a waste of time to do something just for the love of it," she said.

His mouth tightened until he resembled the portrait of his father that hung in the library. "It is when there are more important things to be done. Like saving the company, for instance—"

For a brief instant she saw the pain reflected in his dark eyes.

"If this deal doesn't go through soon, I'll be letting down a great many people, in addition to my son."

She tried to find the words that would comfort him, but she didn't have any. She couldn't spout platitudes in the face of his pain. Had she been wrong to push his involvement with Jason?

No, I can't believe that, Lord. Important business deal or not, a son needs his father's attention far more than he needs status or money.

"You can't hold yourself responsible for the welfare of the whole town," she ventured.

His swift gesture of rejection told her that had been the wrong thing to say.

"I am responsible." His hands tightened on the edge of the table until the knuckles whitened and the tendons stood out like cords. "Bedford Creek has always depended on the Caine family for its livelihood. Nothing's changed. If the factory goes under, half the town will be unemployed. That is my responsibility.''

"I'm sorry." It was all she could say. "I know you're doing your best for them. Everyone must know that.''

But did they? Did anyone, outside of Mitch and Brett, perhaps, really look beneath the surface to see the real Alex Caine? Or did they look at that polished, cool exterior and envy the man who had everything?

The way she had, she had to confess. All these years she'd seen him as some sort of privileged being, immune to the struggles that beset ordinary people like her.

Now, for some reason she didn't understand, he'd given her a look at the man beneath the shining surface—the person whose life was a constant struggle to do what was expected of him.

The saddest thing was that he didn't see that being perfect was impossible. And he didn't see the barriers that it put between him and everyone else in his life, especially his son.

Chapter Eleven

Why wasn't her plan working? Paula had been so sure God had brought her here to help Jason. She'd been convinced it was her opportunity to atone for leaving so abruptly two years ago. But if this was what God intended, why was she failing? With a sudden flare of temper at her own inadequacy, she kicked one of the two-by-four boards she was using to build a temporary ramp to the housekeeper's cottage.

"Is that a new construction method?"

Her heart thudded into overdrive at the sound of Alex's voice, and she turned to annoyance in self-defense. "Must you sneak up on me that way?"

He crossed the grass from the pool. "You were too busy beating up that defenseless piece of wood to hear me. What's going on?"

"That's the question I wanted to ask you. What's going on? Why didn't you keep your promise to Jason?"

She could see in an instant that he'd forgotten it completely—a blank stare, followed quickly by comprehension, then embarrassment.

"You forgot." She knew she sounded accusing, and she didn't care. "You made a promise to your son, and you forgot." He had told Jason at breakfast he'd be home before supper to practice with the team. But four o'clock came and went, and no Alex.

Dismayed by the children's pensive little faces, Paula had tried to engage them in batting and fielding practice. The other children had responded, but Jason had thrown his glove down and walked off the field. She hadn't had the heart to reprimand him, knowing the depth of his disappointment.

"Where is he?" He looked around, as if he expected to find Jason still waiting. "Was he very upset?"

"Of course, he was upset! What would you expect? Don't you remember what it feels like when the most important person in your life lets you down?"

She knew she'd gone too far, and she regretted the words almost before they were out of her mouth. Given what Alex's father had been like, that had to be a sore spot. But it was too late to call her hasty words back.

Alex's mouth tightened. "I'll tell my son I'm sorry, Paula." His implication was clear—he didn't owe an apology to her. "Where is he?"

"Brett and Rebecca took him out for pizza with Kristie. They should be back in about an hour." She sounded like a sulky child, even to herself. She tried to be honest. Was her sharp retort on Jason's behalf? Or was she thinking of her own disappointment? Her newfound empathy for Alex had become frayed around the edges the last few days. His preoccupation with the business to the exclusion of everything and everyone in his life had become so intense that all her efforts to bring him and Jason together were evaporating. Jason withdrew; Alex withdrew—she seemed to be the only person in the house who was actually *there*.

She glanced at her watch. "Or sooner. I've been working on this thing longer than I thought."

"What exactly are you doing?" He picked up the two-by-four, sounding as relieved as she was to get away from the difficult subject on which they'd probably never agree. "Are you and Jason taking up carpentry?"

Now that she had the opportunity, she was reluctant to ask Alex for help. She folded the instructions. "The physical therapist said I should rig up a temporary ramp to the porch, for when Maida gets home. So she won't have to tackle the steps every time she wants to get out.''

He held out his hand. She fought down a flare of resentment at the imperious gesture and gave him the paper.

He scanned it quickly. ''This doesn't look too difficult.''

''That's easy for you to say.'' Actually, it probably would be easy for him, given the unexpected skills she'd discovered he had. For that matter, she had yet to find the thing he didn't do well. ''I'm afraid I must be mechanically challenged.''

''I'll take care of the ramp.'' Alex slipped the paper into his pocket before she could snatch it back.

''No, you won't.'' She planted her fists on her hips. ''Aunt Maida asked me to handle this.''

He looked annoyed. She ought to be familiar with the expression by now, since he so often wore it when he looked at her.

Not when he kissed you, a small voice in her head reminded her. *Not when he held you.*

''I'm sure Maida expected you to take care of this by turning it over to me,'' Alex said. ''She'd know I'd have the ramp installed properly.''

''You mean, I can't do it the way you want it done.'' The fact that she probably couldn't only added to her frustration.

"That's not what I meant. This isn't a good use of your time, with the dinner party coming up. I'll have one of the carpenters from the plant stop by and do this."

"Maida is my aunt. I'd rather provide for her myself." She was using anger as a shield, and she knew it. But anger was the safest emotion she could feel where Alex was concerned. At least when she was angry with him, she didn't have to remember what his arms felt like around her.

Alex studied her for a moment. His dark eyes were as intent as if he studied a business plan. "The cottage belongs to me," he said finally. "I will modify it for Maida's needs. Why is this so important to you?"

His question pierced the shield of her anger, and she struggled to get it back. "Because I'm used to doing things myself, not ordering someone else to do them. Some of us didn't grow up having all this—" Her gesture took in the grounds, the pool, the mansion, maybe the whole town.

He didn't say anything, and she braced herself for an eruption. No, not an eruption. Alex was too cultivated to erupt. He'd give her the look that suggested she'd just crawled out from under a rock.

But he shook his head, suddenly looking tired.

"That's not quite what you imagine it to be, Paula. I won't try to convince you of that, because I probably couldn't succeed."

His calm, even tone brought a wave of embarrassment to her cheeks. Whether she was right or wrong, she shouldn't have spoken that way to him.

"I'm sorry. I—"

"You don't have to apologize for saying what you think of me. But I don't think you should be so proud of not accepting help, not when other people will have to pay the penalty for your pride."

"What are you talking about? What other people?"

"Maida, for one." He didn't sound angry, just matter-of-fact. "You'd rather build something you know won't work as well, so you can say you did it yourself."

His words stung, and she could tell he wasn't finished yet.

"And you won't let me help, even though I love Maida, too. I suppose that means my love is tainted by whatever privilege it is you imagine I possess. That's an odd kind of caring, Paula. I'm not sure Maida would approve."

She stared at him, her defenses crumbling and her eyes filling with tears. How could he cut her to the heart with a few words?

* * *

Alex's heart contracted when he saw the expression on Paula's face. He hadn't intended to hurt her, but he'd gone too far.

Maybe he was the one who needed to understand. He hadn't made any effort to find out why Paula felt as she did. He'd simply considered her stubborn independence an obstacle to what he knew was best. Did that mean he was as arrogant as she thought? He decided he didn't want to know the answer to that question.

"Paula." He reached out, wanting to touch her, knowing it was unwise. "I'm sorry. I don't want to hurt you. I want to understand."

She shook her head stubbornly, but her mouth trembled. "There's nothing to understand. I'm like everyone else."

Suddenly he didn't want to impose his will on hers or get his own way, even though he was convinced he was right. He just wanted to know what drove her.

"Tell me what's going on with you. Make me understand." He tried a smile. "In spite of the handicap of my imagined status, maybe I can."

He went to the steps, sat down and patted the spot next to him. That first night she'd done the same thing. Jason had sat next to her and connected with her in a way Alex still didn't quite understand.

The image of Jason's small face sent a twinge to his heart. Paula had been right about one thing: Alex had let Jason down tonight, and that was something he'd promised himself he wouldn't do. But Jason wasn't here now, and Paula was—a suddenly vulnerable Paula.

"Tell me what makes Paula Hansen tick," he said, trying to keep his voice light.

"Nothing out of the ordinary. Nothing important." She shrugged, obviously making an effort to sound casual, but she sat down next to him.

"It's important to you." For both their sakes, he had to stay detached. He had to be a friend, and nothing more. "Come on, Paula. Who are you really rebelling against?"

He knew at that moment that his shot in the dark had gone home. She crossed her arms over the Towson University T-shirt she wore, as if in self-defense. "I'm not. Not anymore, anyway."

"Why do I find that so hard to believe?" He tried to keep his voice gently teasing.

She shook her head. "Maybe I am a little overly independent. I don't think you'd understand why."

"Why wouldn't I?"

"Because you didn't grow up with four older brothers determined to protect you." There was a flicker of a smile at that.

"Doesn't sound so bad," he said, sure she hadn't yet reached the heart of the matter.

"Oh, really?" She did smile now. "Did you have an older brother who insisted on taking you to your first dance? Or one who threatened to beat up anyone who teased you? It got so bad, boys were afraid to smile at me."

"They loved you."

"They drove me crazy." She shook her head. "I had to fight them every step of the way. But it taught me to stand up for myself."

"And your father? Did you fight him, too?"

She rubbed her arms, the smile fading. "My father has some very old-fashioned ideas of what boys do and what girls do. Boys go places, they play sports, they get football scholarships if they want to go to college. Girls stay home. Girls are protected." Something in the timbre of her voice changed, betraying the emotion she seemed determined not to show. "I remember…"

He leaned a little closer, afraid to touch her because that might break the slender thread of connection between them. "What do you remember?" he said softly.

"I must have been about Jason's age." She looked down, her face soft and defenseless. "I had a teacher who really encouraged me. She recommended me for a special program for gifted kids. I remember coming home from school carrying the paper, so proud." Her hands clasped together.

He could almost see the little girl she'd been, blond

braids to her shoulders, face alight with eagerness. "What happened?"

"My father refused to enroll me." Her face tightened. "The teacher even came to talk to him, but he wouldn't budge. I sat at the top of the stairs and listened. 'A waste of money,' he called it. He wasn't going to throw good money away on foolishness. It wasn't worth it."

The vision of that little girl, huddled at the top of the stairs, hurt his heart. He knew what she'd felt when she'd heard those words. She'd felt *she* wasn't worth it.

Now, she'd reject sympathy. She'd interpret it as pity. "He sounds like quite a reactionary. He and my father probably would have had a lot in common."

She looked up, startled. Then, quite suddenly, she smiled. "I don't know which of them would have been more shocked at that comparison."

The tightness around his heart eased at her smile. "I'd say you turned out remarkably well, considering the obstacles. You got your degree in spite of him, didn't you?"

"With Aunt Maida's help. You should have heard the battle between them over that. On second thought, if you'd been listening, you might have been able to hear it from Bedford Creek."

"Maida is a special lady, isn't she. She's done as much, or more, for me over the years."

Paula raised her eyebrows. "Meaning you ought to be allowed to build the ramp for her?"

"I did have that in mind," he said. He sensed that she was eager to move away from the subject of her past.

Tears brightened her eyes for an instant, and she blinked rapidly. "I guess even a rich man ought to be allowed to give a gift of love."

He ought to say something light in response, but he couldn't. He'd been wrong. He couldn't go this far into her life and stay detached. Like it or not, he'd begun to care for her too much. All he could think was how close they were, and how much he wanted to close that gap and kiss her.

She looked at him, and she had to be able to read the longing in his face. Her eyes darkened, and he seemed to hear her breath catch.

Car doors slammed, and children's voices echoed from the driveway.

Paula pulled away from him, her cheeks flushing. "They're back."

His first thought was that Brett had rotten timing. His second was that Brett actually had pretty good timing, because in another second Alex would have moved his relationship with Paula in a direction he'd promised not to go.

"Paula, how nice to run into you."

Paula, arms full of packages, stopped, surprised to

be greeted by name on Main Street. Anne Donovan was just coming out of the candle shop. "I went to see Maida yesterday," Anne continued. "She's really doing well, isn't she?"

"The therapist says she'll be able to come home soon."

It felt like a deadline to Paula. The days were passing, and with them went whatever opportunity she had to do some good for Jason and his father. She'd thought that if she understood Alex better, she'd be able to help his son. Instead, she seemed only to have put her own heart in jeopardy. The memory of those moments on the steps the day before shimmered in her mind like a bubble about to burst.

"I'm so glad she's doing well," Anne said warmly. "Do you have time for a cup of coffee? We haven't had a chance to talk since you've been here." She nodded toward the café across the street.

Paula juggled packages to glance at her watch. "I do have half an hour before I pick up Jason. But I should get Alex's shirts—"

"Nonsense." Anne grabbed one of the bags. "You look as if you could use a break. Let Alex pick up his own shirts."

Paula couldn't help smiling as she followed the other woman across the street. Anne looked intimidating, with her glossy black hair and elegant clothes. But her easy friendliness was hard to resist.

Besides, she thought as Anne pushed open the door to the Bluebird Café, Anne's husband was one of Alex's closest friends. If anyone understood him, it was Mitch.

Anne dropped the packages on a blue-padded bench and slipped into the booth. Almost before Paula sat down, an older woman slid coffee mugs in front of them and poured with a deft hand.

"What'll you have with the coffee? I've got some currant scones fresh from the oven." The woman poised a pencil over a pad.

"No, I—"

"Two currant scones," Anne said quickly. "Cassie, have you met Paula Hansen?"

The woman nodded briskly. "Work up at the big house, don't you? I'll be right out with those scones."

She whisked away toward the kitchen, and Anne gave Paula an apologetic smile.

"Sorry about that. But Cassie takes offense if you don't eat something. And given the way she talks, you don't want her annoyed with you."

"I guess there are some interesting pitfalls to living in a place as small as Bedford Creek."

Anne nodded. "I've been here nearly two years, and I still don't understand all the ins and outs of it.

People imagine living in a small town is simple, but actually it's very complicated.''

"Because everyone knows everyone else?"

"Even back a generation or two." Anne stirred sugar into her coffee. "Take Alex, for example. Everyone in town knows his family history."

"They've always been the people living in the big house on the hill," Paula agreed. *Where they can look down at everyone else.* She couldn't help the thought.

Cassie reappeared and put plates in front of them. Paula broke a corner off a feathery light scone. Still warm, as Cassie had promised.

"It can't be easy," Anne continued, slathering butter on her scone. "Having everyone in town interested in what you're doing. It might make you put a shield up for protection."

She looked at Anne with increased respect. "Yes, I guess it might."

"A few people probably get past that, if they try hard enough."

"Maybe." She could hear the doubt in her voice. She'd tried, hadn't she? But each time she got too close, Alex pulled away.

She seemed to see him leaning toward her on the porch steps. He'd have kissed her, if Brett and Rebecca hadn't arrived when they did. But that hadn't been regret she'd seen in his eyes when he pulled away. It had been relief. He'd been glad they were interrupted.

"Trust me." Anne smiled, dropping the pretense that this was a theoretical discussion. "Alex is worth the effort to get close to him. He and Mitch go back a long way. They—"

"Coffee and gossip?"

Paula looked up, barely able to restrain a gasp. She'd been so intent on what Anne was saying that she hadn't heard Alex come in. She probably looked guilty, but Anne just smiled and slid over on the seat.

"You can join us, if you want. We aren't bashing men, I promise."

Alex sat, then looked enquiringly across the table at Paula. "Where's Jason?"

"At the library story hour." She gestured toward her packages. "I was picking up a few things we need for the dinner party."

"She's allowed a coffee break, Alex." Anne's voice was silky. "You don't want to get a reputation as a slave driver, do you?"

"I'm finished," Paula said hurriedly, deciding she really didn't want to sit across from Alex with Anne looking on. The woman saw too much. "I'll take the scone with me to eat later." She wrapped a napkin around it.

"I'll walk out with you." Alex stood, putting a bill on the table before Paula could open her bag.

Once they were on the sidewalk outside, she expected Alex to head down toward the plant. Instead, he walked beside her as she made her way uphill to the tiny library. In Bedford Creek, it seemed you were always going either uphill or down.

When he didn't say anything for half a block, she began to feel nervous. "Is something wrong?"

He looked at her blankly. "Why should anything be wrong?"

"Well, I thought you were on your way back to the office."

His rare, charming smile was like the sun coming out on a cloudy day. "I should be. But I'm playing hooky, just for the moment."

She smiled back, the tension inside her relaxing. Alex was treating her like a friend, instead of a housekeeper. That was the most she could expect, and she shouldn't let herself have silly dreams of something more. But there was something unresolved between them, and maybe this was a good time to bring it up.

"There's something I've been wanting to say to you all week, and I've never had the chance."

"What?" His dark eyes grew wary, as if expecting the worst.

"You don't need to look like that." She smiled. "It's not anything bad. It's just…I wanted to tell you how much I appreciate what you did in the accident.

'Thank you' doesn't seem enough to say to someone who saved your life.''

"That's not necessary." His tone was curt, and he turned away almost before the words were out. "I have to get back to the plant." He strode off, leaving her staring after him.

One instant he'd been smiling down at her, warm and approachable. The next he'd turned into a cold, distant stranger.

Chapter Twelve

By the next day, Paula had had twenty-four hours to think about that exchange with Alex on the street, and she still didn't understand his reaction. She stood at the linen closet, counting out napkins for the dinner, trying to concentrate on anything but the memory of the look on Alex's face when he'd turned away from her.

She clenched the napkins, as if she could use them to wipe away the image. It didn't work. Nothing would push it out of her mind, not even the rush and tension of the dinner preparations.

The linens stacked carefully in her arms, she started down the stairs. She hadn't taken two steps into the downstairs hallway before the caterer grabbed her arm, nearly sending the clean linens to the floor.

"Ms. Hansen... Oh, sorry." The woman caught the stack as it toppled. "I have to talk with you."

"Is something wrong?" Judging by the expression on Janine Laker's face, something was amiss, and Paula braced herself. Janine and her brother were supposed to be the best caterers in town, in addition to running the finest restaurant. They'd do a wonderful job, everyone said, but they had high expectations of the resident staff. Meaning her.

"The cleaning people are supposed to be finished in here." Janine glared at the man running a vacuum in the dining room. "And the flowers haven't arrived yet. We can't finish the tables without the flowers."

"I'll take care of it." Paula tried to sound soothing. "The cleaners will be finished momentarily, and I'll see to the flowers."

An answering glare from the cleaner suggested he wouldn't welcome any advice on finishing his job, and Janine didn't look as reassured as she hoped.

"We want everything to be perfect when we do a dinner," Janine said. "Everything."

"I'm sure it will be." Paula hoped she sounded calmer than she felt. "You can leave the dining room to me."

Looking only partially appeased, Janine disappeared into the kitchen.

Cleaners, florist, table settings. She shook her head, remembering the moment in which she'd assured herself that this would be easy. Give her thirty rambunctious five-year-olds, and she knew what to do. Making the arrangements for a formal dinner party was something else again.

Finally the cleaners were finished and out the door, taking their equipment with them. The florist had delivered the centerpiece, and delightful aromas had begun to float from the kitchen. Paula stood back, looking with admiration at the long table. Pristine white linen covered it, with not an errant crease in sight. Bone china reflected light back toward the chandelier, and cut-glass tumblers glistened.

Her gaze lingered on the massive chair at the head of the table. Alex would sit there, elegant and in control. Candlelight would flicker, while soft music played in the background. With a guilty start, she realized she was picturing herself seated at that table, too. Firmly putting that image from her mind, she began folding napkins.

Just as she finished, Alex came in. His swift gaze assessed the room.

"Is everything ready?" He frowned, looking at the table as if he expected a flaw.

"Everything is coming along fine," she said. "You don't need to worry." At least, she certainly hoped that was true. She ran her mind over her lists again, nervously checking to see that everything had been done.

"I don't see any place cards." Alex strode to the table, his frown deepening. "I told you we'd need place cards." His tone suggested that only the most inept of housekeepers would neglect something so important. And maybe that he hadn't expected any better from her.

Paula snatched up the calligraphy place cards she'd left on the window sill and handed them to him. "Place cards," she said.

He had the grace to look embarrassed. "I thought you'd forgotten them."

"You didn't tell me how you wanted the seating arranged, so I was waiting until you arrived to put them out."

She tried to feel resentment, because that was safer than looking at her true emotions. Unfortunately she knew what they were—longing, hurt, love.

Alex looked down at the place cards in his hand, because that way he didn't have to look at Paula's face. She'd hand-lettered each card in graceful script, and his guilt deepened. She'd done more than he'd asked, and all he'd done in return was bark at her.

"I'm sorry." *Sorry I snapped at you because I wanted to keep some space between us.* "Let's decide how best to arrange the table."

"Fine."

Her back was stiff as she walked to the long table, her tone making it clear that he wasn't forgiven yet.

"I assume you want Mr. Dieter on your right."

He nodded, handing her the card. He'd thought he knew what his attitude toward Paula had to be. But unfortunately, just seeing her had thrown his careful, well-ordered plans into disarray. He'd been so aghast at the surge of feelings she produced that he'd barked at her in self-defense.

Yesterday he'd let himself get too close, again. He'd almost let himself think a relationship between them might work. Then she'd brought up the crash and looked at him as if he were a hero. That attitude wasn't a recipe for happiness—it was a recipe for disaster.

"It's just not going to be perfect," Paula said. He gave her a startled look, then realized she was talking about the table.

"The arrangement?"

She shrugged. "Too many men and not enough women. Even I know the table should be balanced, but you just can't do it."

He didn't know what to say to the implicit self-criticism in her words. He hadn't intended to make her feel inadequate. She was doing a good job, and he hadn't realized before how difficult it was. Maida had always made things look easy.

"Do you think this will work?" She put the last card in place.

He saw the concern in her eyes, and it touched his heart. "It will be fine." He had a sudden picture of Paula in a soft evening dress instead of her usual jeans and T-shirt, sitting across from him at the table, the candlelight reflected in her deep green eyes. "If you—"

A commotion erupted in the hallway, composed of thudding feet and puppy yelps.

"Nugget, come back here!"

It sounded as if Jason had jumped down the last three or four steps, Alex thought. Jason had never come down the steps that way before Paula entered their lives. Why hadn't it ever occurred to him that a small boy wasn't supposed to be decorous?

Paula reached the hall a few steps before him and bent to corral the golden fur ball that was Nugget. She knelt, holding the puppy, until Jason reached her and grabbed Nugget's collar.

"Hey, Jason, I thought we decided Nugget would stay outside today." Her voice was soft, her face on a level with his son's.

Jason's lower lip came out in a pout. "Why can't he be in here? I want him to."

Paula stroked the puppy. "Well, mostly because there are a lot of strangers in and out today. That's upsetting for a puppy. And we put candy out in dishes for the guests. What if Nugget got some of it? Did you know it could make him sick?"

"I wouldn't do anything to let him get sick." Jason's pout disappeared. "Come on, Nugget. Let's go out back and play. I'll throw the ball for you."

Boy and dog pounded toward the door, not even noticing Alex, who tried to swallow the lump in his throat. Paula was so good with his son, so easy and unaffected. Jason responded to her better than he had to anyone in a long time.

"You must be a very good teacher," he said.

She looked up, as surprised as if she'd forgotten he was there, and got up quickly. "I am, as a matter of fact." She smiled, and the tension between them vanished. "But what brought that on?"

"You're good with Jason." He wanted to say more—to say she'd brought laughter back to his son—but he couldn't form the words.

Paula shrugged. "I like him. I think he likes me." Her gaze slid away from his, and he knew she was hiding something.

"And?" he prompted.

"I guess..." She hesitated. "I guess I feel I let him down, going away so suddenly the last time I was here. I'd like to make up for that, if I can."

Regret was a cold hand around his heart. He'd been the reason she'd left so abruptly then, he was sure of it. He didn't want to make the same mistake again. But he wanted to show her how much he appreciated her efforts for Jason. For him.

"About the dinner tonight—" He stopped. Was he doing the right thing? A wave of rebellion swept over him. This might not be the proper thing, but he felt quite sure it was right. "Will you do me the honor of joining the guests?"

Either she'd heard him wrong, or she'd misunderstood him. It almost sounded as if Alex were inviting her to be a guest at his dinner. "What did you say?"

"I want you to join us." Alex gestured toward the table. "You can easily fit another place setting there, since Dieter didn't bring as many people as I thought he might." He paused. "Can't you?"

"Well, yes." Pleasure swept through her. Alex wanted her to join in something that was important to him. *Don't read too much into this,* some part of her mind cautioned. "But why do you want me to attend?"

For a moment he looked disconcerted, as if he hadn't expected her to ask the question. "You said yourself the table was unbalanced. Not enough women."

"You could have asked another woman from the office."

"Yes, I could have, but I didn't." He gave her that rare smile. "I want you to come, Paula. Please."

A wave of warmth flooded her. "In that case, I'd like to." She turned back to the table, to hide any trace of embarrassment. "I can add another setting here."

She felt his gaze on her as she rearranged the place settings, and her hands became clumsy in response. What did he see when he looked at her?

"Paula, there's just one thing." He was frowning again, looking at her jeans. "You do have something else to wear, don't you?"

Well, that seemed to be the answer to how he saw her—as someone who didn't know how to dress. Before she could respond, someone did it for her.

"Alex, that's not a question to ask a woman." Anne Donovan came in through the kitchen door, amusement filling her deep blue eyes. She gestured toward the kitchen. "The caterers let me in. I hope you don't mind."

Alex smiled, kissing her cheek lightly. "You're always welcome. Is that for me?" He nodded toward the sheaf of papers in her hand.

"No, it's for Paula. A list with phone numbers of people who are going to bring food in or help out when Maida comes home. I thought she might be feeling overwhelmed at the moment." She shot a teasing glance at Alex. "And your insults don't help."

He raised his hands as if to shield himself from

attack. "I just thought Paula might not have come prepared for a dinner party."

Paula did a quick mental inventory of the clothes she'd brought with her. Was there anything suitable for dinner with Alex's business associates? Did she even *own* anything suitable?

"That's not a problem," Anne said. "If she doesn't have anything with her, we're about the same size. But Alex, if Paula is going to attend this business dinner, she has to have time to get ready. You can't expect her to make all the arrangements, take care of Jason, and then scramble into her clothes."

Paula tensed for one of Alex's polite putdowns, but it didn't come. Anne, like her husband, seemed to be one of the few people who could treat Alex like a human being. He shook his head, smiling.

"You're right as always. Paula, please take all the time you need. I'm sure the caterers know what they're doing, and I'll see to Jason."

"And the puppy," Anne prompted.

"And the puppy," Alex agreed. He shook his head. "I don't know how Mitch managed to survive before you came to town."

"Not as well as he does now," Anne said, her mouth softening at the mention of her husband. She linked her arm through Paula's. "Come on. Let's decide what you're wearing tonight."

Bemused at Anne's management, Paula let herself

be led through the kitchen and out onto the patio. There she stopped, common sense reasserting itself.

"Alex was right. I really don't have anything with me to wear." She looked down at her jeans. "And even if I did, it wouldn't be suitable for Alex's high-powered business types."

"Relax." Anne patted her arm. "We really are about the same size, and I have a closet full of clothes from when I used to work with some of those high-powered business types." She smiled. "Believe me, those clothes don't get much of an outing in Bedford Creek. I'll find an outfit for you to wear."

"But I couldn't. What if I spilled something on it?"

"Everything can be cleaned." Anne didn't seem concerned. "I'll run home and bring a couple of choices back. Meanwhile, you go run yourself a bubble bath." Her face lit with laughter. "We're going to knock Alex for a loop, believe me."

Paula still found the turn of events hard to believe two hours later, when she stood in front of the full-length mirror in Maida's cottage.

"That's it." Anne, sitting behind her on the twin bed, beamed with satisfaction. "That outfit was never quite right for me, but on you it's absolutely perfect."

Paula ran her hand down the length of shimmering aqua silk. "Are you sure you want to lend this? It's so lovely.'' It was the kind of dress she'd look at in the windows of the most exclusive shops—look at and walk on, knowing she couldn't afford it.

''I'm positive.'' Anne got up, a small box in her hand. ''I brought the jewelry I wore with it, since you probably don't have much with you for the summer.''

''What a tactful way of putting it.'' Paula smiled.

Anne held the dangling crystal drops at Paula's ears. ''What do you think? They're the perfect touch, aren't they?''

Paula looked again at the image in the mirror. If she blinked, that elegant stranger might disappear. She laughed suddenly. ''Aunt Maida would say, 'Fine feathers don't make fine birds.'''

''In this case, the fine feathers are just bringing out the beauty that's already there.'' Anne gave her a quick hug. ''You really will dazzle them.''

Paula glanced at the clock, and a wave of pure panic swept over her. ''It's almost time. What on earth am I going to say to those people? I don't know anything about business.''

''They're just people,'' Anne said. ''Encourage them to talk about themselves, and they'll be happy.'' She turned toward the door. ''You can't back out now. Alex is counting on you.''

''Right.'' Paula took a deep breath. She could do this. Anne was right—they were just people.

They walked back to the mansion together, but Anne stopped at the back door. "I'd better get home. Wish I could be a fly on the wall, though. I'd give anything to watch Alex's face when he sees you."

Hand on the door, Paula paused, thinking about Anne's words. That was why she stood here, half eager, half afraid. Because she wanted Alex to see her in a new way. Not as a housekeeper, not as a nanny, not as his assistant baseball coach. She wanted him to see her as a woman—a woman he could love.

Chapter Thirteen

Where was Paula? Alex wondered for perhaps the twentieth time, as he stood in the front hallway, greeting his guests. She'd done a wonderful job of organizing this affair. The old house shone with an unusually welcoming air. He tried to analyze the change. Perhaps it was the bowl of fresh-cut flowers on the hall table—from the garden, he realized, not the florist. Or maybe it was the way Janine circulated, at Paula's suggestion, offering shrimp and cheese puffs from a tray as guests arrived.

Paula had put her own stamp on this affair. The only thing missing was Paula herself.

He silently counted heads. Everyone else had arrived, including Christian Dieter and his staff. Dieter, a rotund elderly man whose cherubic expression was belied by a pair of shrewd ice-blue eyes, seemed genuinely pleased at being entertained in Alex's home.

Alex pressed down a wave of apprehension. No one must know from his demeanor how important this night was to him. He should be concentrating on Dieter, not worrying because Paula hadn't shown up yet.

Maybe she'd lost her nerve at the thought of participating. It hadn't occurred to him at the time that he might be putting additional pressure on her with his invitation. He'd just wanted to show her how much he appreciated her, not put her on the spot. She might have balked at the thought of coming to an elegant dinner party in a hand-me-down dress.

Just then, the door to the rear of the house swung open, and Paula walked into the hallway. She stopped directly under the crystal chandelier his great-grandfather had brought back from Germany.

The breath went out of him. She was beautiful. The blond curls that usually tumbled around her face had been swept back into a sophisticated style, and crystal drops dangled from her ears and around her neck, rivaling the chandelier for brilliance. The dress, an elegant length of aqua silk, molded her slender form, making her skin glow with a golden sheen, as if she'd brought the sunlight in with her.

He wasn't the only one she'd struck dumb, he realized. Dieter stood silent, interrupted in the midst of a story he'd been telling. With a brief nod, he dismissed the aide at his elbow and moved toward Paula.

It was high time Alex stopped staring, too. Anyone who'd been watching him would have known that Paula Hansen had just made him feel like an awkward kid instead of the company president.

He arrived at Paula's side in time to hear Dieter introducing himself.

"I am Christian Dieter." The man captured Paula's hand and held it in both of his. "I regret that I have not yet been introduced to you."

Paula's smile looked a bit strained. "I'm Paula Hansen, Mr. Dieter. It's a pleasure to meet you."

Dieter raised his eyebrows as he looked at Alex. "Where have you been hiding this lovely lady since our arrival?"

"I'm Alex's—"

"I'm afraid Paula has been very busy lately." Alex put his hand lightly on her waist, identifying his feeling with some surprise—possessiveness. He shouldn't feel that way about her, but he couldn't deny it. "Paula is a friend who's been helping me this summer."

"Lucky man," Dieter murmured, "to have such a lovely helper. And what do you do, Ms. Hansen, when you are not helping your friends?"

"I'm a teacher."

Paula drew slightly away from Alex, as if to put some space between them, but he increased the pressure of his hand, unwilling to let her go. He thought the faintest flush touched her cheeks.

"I teach kindergarten at a school in Baltimore."

"Inner Harbor," Dieter exclaimed, beaming. "I visited your city once on business. It's lovely."

Alex wondered, a little sourly, if there was anything Dieter didn't find lovely. Janine arrived at his elbow with a tray, distracting Dieter. As the man began asking Janine to identify the various tidbits, Alex drew Paula away from them a step or two.

She looked up at him, her eyebrows lifting. "A friend?" she asked softly.

He thought there was a slightly edgy undertone to her voice. "Aren't you a friend?" he countered, enjoying the way her green eyes sparkled.

Her chin tilted at a stubborn angle. "Maybe. But I'm also your housekeeper, remember? Are you embarrassed to tell Mr. Dieter that?"

She tried again to pull away from him, but he captured her hand. "Not at all. But tonight you're not my housekeeper. You're my guest."

Her hand twisted in his, and he tightened his fingers. They were engaged in a battle, locked in a private circle, just the two of them. The buzz of conversation in the hallway only served to isolate them together.

Paula looked up at him, emotions warring in her face. "I don't want people to get the wrong idea. They might think—"

She stopped, as if afraid to put it into words.

"They might think we're together," he finished for her. "Would that be so terrible?"

"I don't know." She met his gaze with a challenge in those clear green eyes. "Would it?"

Alarm bells seemed to be going off in his mind, and he ruthlessly suppressed them.

"Not at all," he said softly. He raised her hand, holding it in both of his. "Besides, if I don't lay claim to you, every man here will be trying to impress you. Then how will we get any work done at all?"

"That would be a problem." Her gaze never left his, and the things they weren't saying hovered in the air between them.

"We can't have that," he said. He brought her hand to his lips and kissed it, feeling her smooth skin warm to his touch. The others receded into the distance, as vague and insubstantial as flickering images on an old newsreel.

He heard her breath go out in a little sigh.

"No." She barely breathed the word. "I guess we can't."

Paula was adrift in an ocean in which only she and Alex were real. She knew the others were there, of course. She heard the murmur of polite conversation and the quiet background music she'd started. But all she really felt, all she really knew, was the touch of Alex's lips against her skin.

"Ms. Hansen." Janine's voice was low but insistent.

Paula forced her gaze away from Alex, made herself turn and smile. Janine, neat in a black skirt and white silk blouse, didn't look convinced. Her dark eyes held a certain speculative expression. Paula stiffened. What was the woman thinking?

For that matter, what was everyone else thinking? The whole room could have noticed the byplay between her and Alex. She took a cautious look around, but the others seemed engrossed in their own conversations.

"Dinner is ready to serve, Ms. Hansen."

Paula tried to look as if she received messages like that every day. She suspected Janine wasn't fooled.

"We'll be right in." She turned to Alex, trying to keep from blushing as her gaze met his. "Will you get people moving to the dining room?"

"I will." He touched her arm. "And you'll go in with me."

The wonder was that she actually arrived at the table without tripping over her heels. And she couldn't blame it on the fact that she'd been wearing sneakers all summer. Alex's grasp was sending messages tingling along her skin, distracting her so that the simplest action seemed difficult. Luckily she'd seated herself along the side of the long table, where she wouldn't have to meet his gaze throughout the meal.

But Alex led her to the chair opposite his, quietly indicating places to his guests as he did so. He pulled out the chair, and she shook her head.

"This isn't mine," she murmured.

He nodded to the place card. "It is now," he said.

He must have changed them around, and she could hardly try to rearrange the seating at this point. She slid into the seat he held out, very aware of his strong hands brushing her shoulders. He bent over as he seated her, his face so close to hers that she felt the warmth radiating from his skin.

"You're my hostess," he said softly, his breath caressing her cheek. "Naturally you'll sit opposite me." Then he straightened, and her skin felt cold where his breath had been.

She sat very straight as he went to the head of the table, trying not to watch him. How she was going to get through this evening without everyone there knowing she loved him, she couldn't imagine.

Love. The word echoed in her mind, shaking her. No, she couldn't let herself think things like that. Resolutely she turned to the man seated on her right.

Dieter's second-in-command looked far too young for his position, and much too stiff to carry on a conversation with her. After several futile attempts to find something they had in common, Paula remembered Anne's advice.

"Do you have a family back in Zurich?" she asked, not sure whether it was common for European men to wear wedding bands.

He beamed. "My wife and I have a baby daughter. She is just six months old."

It took very little prompting to get him going then. As he told her story after story designed to show that young Elissa was surely the brightest baby who'd ever been born, Paula decided that Anne had been right. He was really just a person.

He produced photos of a round-faced, solemn infant, and talked about how much he missed his family when he had to travel with Uncle Christian on business. She nodded, made encouraging noises and tried not to watch Alex.

But it was useless. She couldn't prevent her gaze from being drawn to him, any more than a compass could prevent its needle from pointing north.

She forced herself to look away, glancing around the table. Janine and her brother had outdone themselves, and the salmon *en croute* had been an inspired choice for the entrée. Dieter ate and gestured, his face growing more relaxed by the moment. He leaned to-

ward Alex, nodding, and she could tell by the smallest of things—the set of Alex's mouth, the movement
of his hand—that he was pleased.

Where had it come from, that unconscious ability
to read his mood? When had every line, every gesture, become familiar and dear to her?

Love, she thought again, and this time the word
didn't seem quite so frightening. Alex looked up just
then and caught her watching him. He gave her a
small, private smile.

Something strong and tangible seemed to run the
length of the table between them. The connection was
so palpable that she felt everyone at the table must
have been able to see it. It was so strong it gripped
her heart as if it would never let go.

"It has been a great pleasure. Thank you again."
Dieter beamed at Paula, clasping her hand, as he and
his entourage finally headed out the door.

She'd felt stiff, standing next to Alex in the gracious center hallway, telling his guests good-night as
if she and Alex were a couple. But Alex had made it
clear that was what he expected, and no one else
seemed surprised. Of course, Dieter and his people
didn't know what her true position was here, and
those who worked for Alex apparently accepted what
he did without question. It was his house, his company, his town.

When Alex finally closed the door, she should have felt relief, but she didn't. All she could think was that they were alone together, and there were too many conflicting feelings bouncing around inside her for comfort.

"I should check the kitchen," she began, but Alex caught her hand before she could move in that direction.

"Janine and her crew will leave everything spotless. They always do, and she wouldn't like the suggestion that you had to check on her."

"No, I didn't mean that." *I meant the excuse would get me out of your presence until I figure out what's happening between us.*

Alex loosened his tie. "It went well tonight. Thank you, Paula. For everything."

She nodded. Did "everything" include the way he'd teased her? The moment when he'd kissed her hand? Her skin tingled at the memory. Maybe she'd better find a safer topic of conversation.

"What about Dieter? I saw the two of you talking at dinner, and he looked receptive."

"Very receptive." His face relaxed in a smile. "I'm beginning to think we might pull this off. And if we do, I owe you thanks for that, too. I don't know how I'd have gotten through these past weeks if you hadn't been here."

"I was glad to fill in for Aunt Maida in any way

I could.'' That sounded hopelessly stilted, and it wasn't what she wanted to say at all. What she wanted to say was that she'd do anything for him. But how could she, when she didn't know how he felt?

She glanced at her watch. ''Well, maybe I'd better go.'' She gestured to the silk dress. ''I think it's time for Cinderella to turn back into a pumpkin.''

''That isn't how the story goes, is it?'' He still held her hand loosely, and she didn't want to pull away.

''Close enough,'' she said.

''I'll walk you out.''

His hand was warm against her waist as they pushed through the swinging door into the back of the house. From the kitchen came the clatter of pans and the sound of voices. Alex guided her out the back door to the patio.

The nearly full moon sent a silver path along the surface of the pool, and the stars clustered thickly, far brighter than they ever were when seen from the city. She walked beside Alex, hearing the faint unevenness in his steps that was the only hint of his leg injury.

They stopped at the end of the pool. The kitchen window cast a golden oblong onto the flagstones, but other than that everything was dark and quiet. The silver birch bent gracefully opposite them, its white bark sketching a ghostly figure against the gazebo.

"It's a beautiful night," she murmured. Maybe speech would interrupt the flood of feelings that surged through her. She shivered a little.

"You're cold," Alex said instantly. Before she could object, he'd shed his suit coat. "Put this on. Lovely as it is, I don't think that silk is going to keep you warm."

He draped the coat over her shoulders. It fell around her, still warm with the heat of his body. The fine wool carried a faint, musky scent that seemed to say his name.

She looked up. Alex was a dark silhouette against the darker night. She couldn't make out his expression, but whatever she imagined of his face took her breath away. She wanted to put her palms on his white shirt front, feel his heart beating....

"I should go in." Her voice sounded soft and uncertain, not at all like her.

"Maybe you should," he murmured, but his grip tightened on her hands.

"Jason will be up early. I really..." She lost whatever she'd been about to say when Alex drew her slowly against him.

His shirt was smooth against her hands, and through it she could feel the warmth of his body. For a heartbeat he just held her close. Then he stroked her face, his fingertips gentle against her skin, and emotion ricocheted through her. She cared so much for him. She'd tried to deny it, but it was no use.

He tipped her chin back, his touch insistent, and then his lips found hers. Gentle, so gentle. The kiss was tentative, questioning, as if he gave her every opportunity to draw away if that was what she wanted.

But she couldn't. Her arms slid around him almost without conscious volition, and every cell in her seemed to sing. She drew him closer. Paula's heart pounded, so full it seemed it could hold no more. She loved him, and she wanted to stay in his arms forever.

He pulled away, tearing his lips from hers. "No."

She could only stare at him, trying to read his expression through the gloom, trying to understand through the tumult in her heart. It was what had happened before. He'd kissed her in the moonlight, and then he had pulled away, apologized, tried to pretend it had never happened.

But he couldn't get away with denying it this time. Two years ago she'd let him, but not now. Not when she saw how he wanted to hold her. That gave her courage.

"Why?" She caught his arms when he would have pulled away, held him close. He couldn't break free without hurting her, and she knew he wouldn't do that. "Just tell me why. You can't say you don't want this, because I don't believe it."

His breath sounded ragged. "Maybe I do. But I'm not the hero you think I am, Paula. I'm not."

Her first impulse was to argue, to point out that he'd saved her life at the risk of his own. But some instinct told her that was the wrong thing to say. For whatever reason, he couldn't see himself in that light. And it was important to him. She could feel how important in the tension under her hands.

"That's good," she said quietly. "Because I don't want a hero. Just you, Alex. Just you."

Chapter Fourteen

Paula came awake slowly, trying without success to hold on to the fragments of a dream. She couldn't remember what the image had been, but she knew it was happy. She still felt warm and protected in its aftermath. Automatically she reached out for Nugget, but her hand didn't encounter a furry object in the puppy's usual sleeping spot.

She opened her eyes. Nugget wasn't there. Then she remembered. Alex had said the puppy could spend the night with Jason, so she could concentrate on the dinner party.

She sat up, memories flooding her—last night, the dinner, those moments on the patio when Alex had kissed her and she'd felt as if she'd come home.

Be careful, a faint, cautious voice urged in the back

of her mind. *Be careful with your heart. It's a long way from kisses in the moonlight to happily ever after.*

That was probably good advice. Unfortunately, she suspected it was far too late for her to heed it.

She glanced at the clock, then swung off the bed and reached for her clothes. She was late. Alex and Jason would be expecting their breakfast.

A few minutes later, she hurried into the kitchen, half expecting to find Alex already in search of his morning coffee. But the kitchen was spotless and empty. One of Maida's refrigerator magnets held a note in Alex's bold hand.

She snatched the paper, unable to prevent a silly little catch to her breath. But the brisk message, saying he'd had a meeting and had left early, didn't give any indication its writer had been thinking of late-night kisses.

Paula pressed down a surge of disappointment. She'd better get Jason up and have him take Nugget outside while she fixed his breakfast.

The front area of the mansion, back to its usual silence, seemed to reject the memory of yesterday's hustle and the evening's elegance. She went quickly up the stairs to Jason's room and called out his name, tapping as she opened the door.

But Jason wasn't there. And when she went to the

window that overlooked the pool and the back lawn, she still saw no sign of boy or dog.

Paula had just started down the stairs when she paused, listening. Something disturbed the stillness. Then she heard it—the smallest yelp, instantly shushed. The sound came from the circular staircase that led to the cupola on top of the house.

She went quickly to the steps and looked up, squinting against the sunshine pouring toward her through the windows of the octagonal cupola. "Jason?"

Nugget barked in answer. What was going on? Surely the puppy hadn't gone up there alone. She hurried up the steep, tight spiral.

She reached the top step and stood on the cupola floor, then instantly regretted it. The tall windows on every side of the octagonal chamber gave views of the town, the river far below, and the mountain ridges soaring above. Standing there was like flying above the valley.

Jason sat scrunched into a ball, his face turned away from her. She sat, scooting close enough to Jason to touch him.

Please, Father, please. Show me what this child needs from me.

"Hey." She touched his shoulder gently. "What's going on? You can tell me."

He moved slightly, then buried his face again, but not before she'd seen the tears in his eyes.

"Jason, what is it? Are you hurt?"

He shook his head, holding out against her for another moment. Then, quite suddenly, he looked up. "I saw you." He hurled the words at her accusingly.

"You saw me?" What on earth had him so upset?

"I saw you," he said again. "Last night. From my window. You were kissing my daddy."

Her heart turned over. Jason's bedroom windows overlooked the patio. He'd obviously been looking out. What he'd been doing up that late wasn't the point. He'd seen them, and he was upset.

She tried to respond calmly, not making too much of it. "Your dad walked out with me after the party. Yes, we did kiss. Grown-ups do that sometimes when they like each other. It doesn't mean…"

She couldn't make herself say that kissing Alex didn't mean anything, because that wouldn't be true. His kisses had meant a great deal to her. Whether they meant the same to Alex was still to be determined.

"It's just like before." Jason's face was blotchy with tears. "That's what you did before, and then you went away."

His words pierced her heart. Jason was right—although he couldn't possibly know or understand the reasons. She'd kissed Alex, and she'd left when he made it clear that kiss had been a mistake. What else could she have done? After all, she had a little pride—

She stopped, the word resonating to her very soul. *Pride*. Was that what it had been? Was that what had put her on that airplane, intending to scurry back to Baltimore? She didn't want to believe that about herself.

Jason's the important person now. Do your soul-searching later.

"Jason, I'm sorry I went away." She spoke slowly, choosing her words carefully. Each one should be as true as she could make it. "I made a mistake, and I let you down. I'm sorry."

He shook his head violently. "Everybody goes away. It's my fault."

She stared at him, appalled that this precious child could think it his fault people had let him down. *His mother. Then me. I let him learn to rely on me, and then I left. I ran away because I couldn't face the emotional pain of staying.*

"Jason, it's not your fault. Please, believe me. Talk to me about this." She tried to touch him again, but he shook off her hand and scrambled to his feet.

"I won't talk to you!" He shouted it, the hurt in his eyes turning suddenly to anger. "I won't! You'll just go away again!"

He turned and thundered down the steps.

She sat where she was, trying to grasp what was happening. Nugget stood at the top of the steps, whining, then came to her and nudged her hand. She gathered him into her arms, understanding why Jason had been up here hugging him. Comfort. The child had been looking for the comfort he wasn't getting from the adults in his life.

Is that what I've been doing, Lord? Asking the question was painful. *Have I been running away? Has my pride in being independent just been a cover for being afraid?*

She felt as if God had taken her heart, with all its pitiful little secrets, and held it up to His sunlight, pouring through the high windows. She wasn't very happy with what she saw.

She'd hurt Jason through her cowardice. She'd run away when she should have faced things. Faced Alex. If he hadn't cared for her then, if he didn't care for her now, she had to face it and go on. And right now Jason's needs had to come first.

Certainty pooled in her. She knew what God expected of her. The child was hurting, and he was trying to hide that pain, probably because he saw his father do the same thing.

It's my fault. Jason's words put a lump in her throat. He wouldn't tell her what he meant or why he believed that. His father was the only one who could possibly get to the bottom of this.

She had to make Alex see the truth about his son. Her heart seemed to cramp. It didn't take much imagination to know how Alex would react. Confronting him could put an end to any hope she might cherish that he returned her love.

She didn't have a choice. She had to do this, and soon, no matter what the cost.

Alex walked into the house, realizing he half expected to hear the noisy thud of Jason's feet on the oak stairwell or find Paula chasing an errant puppy across the Italian marble floor. But the Caine mansion preserved its silence, just as it had before Paula came back.

How had she managed to make such a difference in this place in a few short weeks? How had she managed to make such a difference in their lives? He'd told himself he no longer believed in happy endings. But Paula had begun to make a believer out of him.

If they shared many more moments like those out on the patio last night, he'd no longer have a choice about it. He'd tried, in the quiet hours of the night, to apply reason and logic to his reactions. But reason and logic didn't seem to fit the emotions Paula roused in him.

He carried his briefcase into the library, telling himself to concentrate on business. The meeting with

Dieter had gone better than he'd dared hope. The man's assistant had even dropped a hint that they'd enjoy an opportunity to become acquainted with a number of community leaders—perhaps an informal social event at the Caine mansion?

Alex had quickly agreed, making mental lists to line up the caterers and have his secretary send invitations. Town council members, business owners, police chief, doctor—he'd have to include them all. Dieter and his associates wouldn't suggest such an event, he felt sure, unless they were on the verge of signing the agreement.

He heard Paula's steps sounding in the hallway. A moment later she walked into the library, and he knew moonlight had had nothing to do with his feelings.

"Paula." He rounded the table, wanting to eliminate the distance between them. "I'm glad you're here."

She stopped in the middle of the oriental carpet, reminding him of the day she'd stood there telling him he had to let her stay. She looked just as determined now as she had then.

"I need to talk with you." She seemed guarded, folding her arms across the rainbow design on the front of her T-shirt.

"That's good, because I want to talk with you,

too.'' His news would wipe that concerned expression from her face. ''About last night.''

A warm flush brightened her peaches-and-cream skin, and he knew she was thinking of those moments on the patio. Suddenly he was there, holding her in his arms and wanting never to let her go.

''The dinner party,'' he added quickly. ''I wanted to thank you for everything you did to make it a success. Dieter was pleased.''

''That's nice.'' She shrugged her shoulders, as if to dismiss that as of no importance. ''But—''

''Nice? It's more than nice.'' He closed the gap between them with a quick stride. ''I've told you how important this deal is to the company's survival.'' He wanted to take her hands, but her body language set a barrier between them. ''I think they're almost ready to sign.''

The enthusiasm and encouragement he'd anticipated weren't there, and it annoyed him. Didn't she understand how important this was?

''They've asked for an opportunity to meet community leaders. That has to be a prelude to announcing a deal.'' Energy surged through him. He was going to pull this off. For an instant he imagined he'd look at the portrait of his father over the fireplace and read approval there. ''I want to hold a reception here next Saturday. My secretary will take care of the invitations and schedule the catering. You'll handle it the way you did the dinner party."

Again she responded with the briefest of shrugs, as if the most important deal of his life were a trifle. "Yes, good." Her mind was obviously elsewhere. "I'm glad it's working out, but I need to speak with you about something else."

Apparently he'd been wrong. He tried not to feel disappointment at her attitude. Paula didn't share his triumph. Apparently she didn't see this as anything more than just another job.

"What is it?" He took a step back, hearing his voice harden. "What's so important?"

"Jason." The muscles in her neck moved, as if she struggled to swallow. "I'm worried about Jason."

"Is he ill?" He glanced toward the hallway. "I assumed he was out when I didn't hear him."

"He is." She shook her head. "I mean, no, he's not ill. Rebecca picked him up to play with Kristie for the afternoon."

"Then what is it?"

"He's upset. I found him crying this morning." She hesitated, glancing away as if she didn't want to look at him. "He saw us last night. When we were on the patio. When we were kissing."

So that's what this was all about. "Paula, I'm sorry he was upset about it, but that's hardly surprising. I haven't…there hasn't been another woman in our lives since his mother left."

"It's not just that. I wish he hadn't seen us, but that's a minor part of the problem. He was genuinely upset, even angry." Color flamed in her cheeks. "He reminded me that we kissed the last time I was here. And then I went away."

Shame over Alex's behavior then reared its head, and he slammed it down. He couldn't let himself be sidetracked by past mistakes.

"Look, I know this is important, but I don't believe it's as serious as you're making out. I'll speak with Jason, explain it to him. He's a bright child, he'll understand."

Her soft mouth firmed in a stubborn line. "Alex, this is serious. You don't understand. Jason is troubled. He needs your time and attention right now."

Something in him tightened with annoyance. Paula was creating mountains out of molehills. Much as he appreciated her concern for Jason, she was letting herself get carried away. He tried reason.

"This summer hasn't been easy for Jason, I realize that. As soon as this business with Dieter is settled, I'll make more time for him. But this deal has to take priority. It will assure everyone's future, including Jason's."

She was shaking her head before he finished speaking. "Jason needs you now. He needs his father's attention."

His control slipped, and he felt himself reach for the protective barrier that was part of his Caine family tradition. "I'm doing what I have to for everyone, Paula, including Jason. I'm afraid you'll just have to accept the fact that I know best."

Alex's arrogant words were like a match set to the tinder of her emotions, Paula realized. He knew best, according to him. Whatever was happening, whatever she thought and felt, Alex believed, just as her father always did, that he knew what was right for everyone.

"No." The word came out with the force of an explosion.

Alex looked at her, eyebrows lifting, perhaps at her daring to question him. "What?"

"I said no." She took a breath, trying to hold on to whatever composure she had left. She had to make him understand. "I'm sorry, but in this situation you don't know best. Not if you think your business deal comes before your son."

He didn't move, but he withdrew. His frozen, superior expression told her she was losing him.

"My relationship with my son is not your concern."

"Yes, it is." She tried not to think about those moments in his arms, because if she did, she'd be lost. "I care about him." *And about you.* "I can't just stand back and ignore it when I see him hurting."

His dark eyes flickered, telling her that had touched him.

"I'm sorry." His voice softened. "Paula, I know you care about Jason. I shouldn't have said that. But you have to understand how important this is. The whole town will be affected by what I do in the next few days."

She knew he believed that. She could almost sense the heavy load of his responsibility for this town and its people. "Don't you see? The town needs you, yes. But not in the way your son does."

"Jason is just as affected as everyone else by the success or failure of this deal. It's his future I'm trying to assure."

He'd put up that shield that protected him from normal human emotions. She'd like to rattle him, but she knew that wasn't going to happen. Alex didn't get rattled. He'd just freeze her out, and she'd never be able to reach him.

"Is that what you think? That financial security is what Jason needs from you?"

He turned away, and despair gripped her. She looked from him to the portrait of his father, staring arrogantly out at the world as if he owned it.

"I suppose he'd approve of what you're doing?" She flung her hand out toward the painting.

Alex's jaw tightened until it looked made of marble. "My father's approval has nothing to do with this." The words were chipped from ice.

"Doesn't it?" She'd gone too far now. There was no going back. "Isn't that what this is all about, Alex? You're still trying to earn his approval, and you're doing it by repeating all of his mistakes. You're not thinking about Jason. You're thinking about the precious Caine family name!"

She stopped, suddenly breathless and exhausted. Alex stared at her as if from a very long distance. Then he walked to the library door and opened it.

It was over—that was all she could think. She walked out, passing him, trying to hold on to whatever composure she could. She'd tried to make him understand, tried to do what she thought God expected of her. And she'd failed. She wouldn't have another chance.

Chapter Fifteen

Paula's smile vanished as she closed the door of Aunt Maida's room in the rehab unit. She'd managed to maintain an air of normalcy during her visit, but she didn't think Aunt Maida had been fooled.

Leave it in God's hands, Aunt Maida had said as Paula was leaving. *Whatever the problem, leave it in God's hands.*

Unfortunately that seemed easier said than done. Paula stood for a moment, looking out at the courtyard of the rehabilitation unit, abloom with roses. She'd tried to turn her worries for Jason over to the Lord, just as she'd tried to relinquish her pain over the situation with Alex. But her rebellious spirit kept picking the burden up again. Surely there was something she could do—some way to make this right.

"Hi, Paula. How is she today?" Brett Elliot tucked a chart under his arm as he loped down the hall toward her. "Is she ready to get out of here and tackle the world?"

She had to smile, because that was an apt description of Aunt Maida's mood. "Just about. When do you think she'll be able to come home?"

"I'd like to hang on to her a few more days." He checked the chart. "Let's at least wait until after this reception Alex is planning. If we send her home before that, you'll have to tie her down to keep her from helping."

Even the most casual mention of Alex was enough to set the still-painful wound throbbing, but she managed to keep her smile on straight. "You know her too well."

"How is everything going with you?"

Brett's sympathetic tone was almost her undoing, and she struggled to suppress her worries. "I think the reception is under control." She deliberately kept the conversation superficial. He was Alex's friend, and she certainly couldn't discuss Alex with him, no matter how sympathetic he was.

"Alex tends to have a one-track mind about things like that," Brett said, his tone casual. "I've always thought he had way too much sense of responsibility. Of course, back in the old days, he said I had too little.'' He glanced over her shoulder. ''Speaking of Alex, here he is now.''

The warning gave her a moment to catch her breath and stiffen her spine before she turned.

''I didn't realize you were coming to see Maida this morning.'' *If I had, I wouldn't be here.*

Alex, dauntingly businesslike in a dark suit, came to a stop a few feet from them, as if he didn't want to get any closer to her than necessary.

''I had to come to town, anyway, to see an attorney about some business.''

''I see.'' At least Brett was there, so they weren't alone.

''I'd better be off. Duty calls.'' Brett was halfway down the hall before she could react. ''See you Saturday,'' he called over his shoulder, and left her alone with Alex.

Alex turned to her, and she tried to find some armor to protect her. There was something she had to say to him, if only she could get it out without betraying how she really felt.

''Brett says Aunt Maida can come home next week.'' She hoped that sounded as casual and cheerful as she wanted it to.

''Good. You can take off whatever time you need to get her settled.'' Alex glanced toward Maida's door, as if ready to move on at the earliest opportunity.

"I wondered…" She took a deep breath to still the quaking inside her. Was it better if his answer was yes or no? She really didn't know, so she'd better just get it out. "Once Maida is home, she might be able to supervise someone else doing the work. I'm sure we could work it out, if you'd prefer that I leave then."

He froze, but his well-bred mask didn't betray his opinion. "Is that what you want?"

Only the truth would do here, she knew. "No, it's not. If I leave now, I'll be doing the same thing I did the last time. That would just confirm Jason's fears, and I don't want to do that."

Do you? Talk to me about it, Alex. Please.

He gave a curt nod. "Fine. Stay until Maida is on her feet again." He turned toward the door. "I'll go in and see her now. Then I must get back to the plant."

It wasn't fine, but there also wasn't anything she could do about it. She'd stay until her aunt was well, and she'd try to ignore the pain that clutched her heart each time she saw Alex.

When Maida had recovered, when they'd had time to prepare Jason, she'd leave. And this time, when she left Bedford Creek, she wouldn't be coming back.

The reception spilled from the French doors as the crowd eddied through the downstairs of the mansion, out onto the sunlit lawn, across the patio. Alex made his way methodically from one group to another, encountering smiles and chatter. People seemed to be enjoying themselves, and that included the visitors from Dieter Industries.

A small group clustered around a table serving hot appetizers. He would have had the caterer set up a formal buffet in the dining room, but Paula had suggested a number of small serving stations, instead, scattered throughout the house and grounds. She'd been right. His guests mixed and re-formed again and again, and Dieter's people mixed with the rest.

He scanned the crowd—men in suits, women in colorful dresses that brightened in the sunshine like so many flowers. Where was Dieter? The man had proved remarkably evasive of late. Tension formed a knot in Alex's stomach, and he deposited the mushroom tart he'd been eating on the nearest tray. He'd expected, by this time, that Dieter would have—

"Dad?" Jason, wearing a dark suit and tie that replicated his father's attire, tugged on his sleeve and looked up at him questioningly. "Did you hear me?"

"Sorry, Jason." He tried to concentrate on his son, but his gaze kept straying to the surrounding crowd. Where was Dieter, anyway? "What did you say?"

"When is Maida going to come home?" Jason's small face tightened. "You said we'd talk about it, but we never did."

"Soon." Alex patted his shoulder. "The doctor says she can come home soon."

"But when?" Jason's voice took on a whining note. "When, Dad? I want to know now."

"Jason." He swallowed the tone of exasperation. "Look, son. I don't have an exact date, not yet. But she will be back. Just trust me on this, please."

"But what about Paula? Is she going to go away? I don't want her to." Jason's lower lip came out in a pout. "I want her to stay. Make her stay, Dad."

His tension went up a notch at the mention of Paula, until his very skin seemed to tingle with it. His hand tightened on the glass he held. Paula wouldn't stay long—he was sure of that. When they'd talked earlier, she'd made her feelings clear enough. She was staying because she felt Jason and Maida both needed her, not for any other reason.

"Da-ad!" Jason's whine was loud enough to attract attention.

He frowned down at his son. "Jason, this isn't the time or place to talk about this. We'll discuss it later. Everything's going to be all right, I promise."

For a moment Jason looked as if he'd flare up at him. Then he spun away and darted through the crowd.

Alex held out his hand, but it was too late to call Jason back.

Just as it was too late for a lot of other things.

He slammed the door on that morbid thought. He'd make this up to Jason. As soon as the deal was completed, he'd arrange a weekend trip for the two of them. He and Jason would find a way to talk the way they used to—the way he and his father never had.

Paula would see that everything he'd done was for the best. She'd see—

The crowd around him moved toward a server with a platter of chilled shrimp, the ruffle of movement creating an open path along the grass. Looking down it, he saw Paula.

His throat tightened. She looked like a daffodil in the yellow sundress she wore, and the sunlight gilded her warm skin with gold. She looked like everything he'd ever wanted in a woman—everything he wanted now and couldn't have.

The open space between them turned into a gap— a yawning chasm he didn't know how to cross. They were too far apart; they'd said too many bitter things to each other. There was no way back.

Paula stared at him what seemed a long moment. Then she turned away.

He'd wanted her to stop looking at him as if he were a hero, as if he were the prince in a fairy tale. Well, he didn't need to worry about that any longer. Now she looked at him as if he were the frog.

Paula's heart thumped painfully as she turned away from Alex. This was so difficult—so much harder than she'd dreamed it would be. Her remembered emotions for Alex had been sharp enough to hurt when she'd come back. Now the pain had intensified a hundred times.

She'd thought, or at least she'd hoped, that he'd be able to pull down the walls he held against the rest of the world. She'd imagined she could get close enough to make a difference in his life. That was clearly impossible. As far as she could tell, even Jason's mother hadn't been able to do that.

This wasn't just about what was best for Jason. If it had been that simple, there might have been a way through it. But she'd been fighting three generations' worth of Caine family tradition, and she'd lost.

It was ironic, in a way. She'd always thought her choices had been restricted by her family's working class background. Now she knew that Alex's life had been just as restricted by his family's wealth.

She made her way through the crowd, automatically checking the serving tables as she went. In one way or another, all of these people depended on Alex. That very fact set barriers between them and Alex, whether they realized it or not.

She'd reached the pool area when she realized the crowd was falling silent. Alex and Dieter, surrounded by Dieter's colleagues, stood near the gazebo, and Dieter clinked a spoon against a glass.

The businessman beamed as he held up his hands. "I wish to make a small announcement to my new friends here in Bedford Creek," he said. "I am pleased to tell you that we have come to an agreement joining Caine Industries with the Dieter Corporation in a venture we trust will bring increased prosperity to all of us."

So, Alex had done what he'd set out to do. Paula joined in the applause, trying to feel some genuine happiness for this result. Of course she was pleased. This meant a great deal to Alex personally, as well as to the town. But it was hard to join in the general celebrating when her heart hurt.

People started moving forward to offer their congratulations. Mitch and Anne got there first, closely followed by Brett with Rebecca. The sight of that close little group surrounding Alex just reminded her that she wasn't part of it. She slipped to the rear of the crowd, swallowing hard. She'd better try to get her emotions under control before she did anything else.

The housekeeper's cottage looked like a haven. She'd give a great deal to be able to go inside and close the door. But she couldn't forget she had a job to do. She had to—

She stopped, frowning. Some foreign odor mingled with the aroma of food and flowers—something vaguely unpleasant. Her stomach lurched. Smoke!

She smelled smoke, coming from the old gardener's cottage Alex used as a studio.

Quickly she hurried around the small building to the door, pulse hammering, trying to reassure herself. She must be mistaken. There wasn't anything in the studio that could be burning. And she certainly couldn't start a panic. She'd have to investigate.

She grasped the knob, relieved to find it cool to the touch. This was nothing—she was letting her imagination run away with her. Besides, the building was probably locked—

The knob turned under her hand. She yanked the door open.

Fire! Panic crashed over her, stealing her breath in an instant. Flames shot from the trash can, and the draft from the opening door sent gray smoke billowing toward her. She clenched the knob. A cry ripped from her throat in spite of her effort to keep it back.

Run, the voice screamed in her head. *Run, run!* Suddenly she was back in the plane, the flames sweeping toward her, the twisted belt trapping her in the seat. She'd never get out, she—

Then she saw something that cut through her nightmare like a knife. The half-finished carving of Jason, covered by its cloth, sat on the workbench. Next to it lay the design plans Alex had shown her. Almost against her will, her mind assessed the risk. They weren't in danger yet, but if the curtains caught, if she waited for help to arrive…

The fire extinguisher hung from a hook just inside the door. A prayer for help echoing in her heart, she grabbed the metal canister and advanced on the flames.

Please, God. Please. She wasn't trapped in the past any longer. A shudder ripped through her, but she shook it off. She wouldn't give in to the fear. With God's help, she never would again.

Chapter Sixteen

The moment Alex heard the cry, he knew it was Paula. Not stopping to wonder at the certainty that propelled him, he pushed his way through the crowd, ignoring their astonished stares. Paula was in trouble.

An acrid smell assaulted him as he rounded the pool. His stomach lurched. *Smoke!* He raced toward the studio, heart pounding, throat tight. Something was on fire, and Paula was there. She'd be terrified. He had to get to her.

The cottage door stood open. Gray smoke funneled out into the clean air. Behind him he could hear calls as others realized what was happening.

"Alex, wait!" It was Mitch's voice.

He couldn't wait. Paula was inside, maybe trapped, flames reaching toward her—past and present mixed in a dizzying, terrifying scenario.

He ran to the door, throwing his arm up to shield his face, and stumbled inside. ''Paula!''

She swung at the sound of his voice. Not trapped. Not terrified. Foam dripped from the extinguisher she held over the trash can. Even as he watched, the last wisps of smoke dissipated.

His mind seemed one huge prayer of thanks. She was all right. He went to her quickly, taking the metal canister from her hands.

''Are you hurt?'' He clasped her hands in his, wanting to pull her into his arms, but not quite daring.

Paula nodded, coughing a little. ''It's out. I put it out.'' Something like wonder filled her eyes as she looked at him. ''I put it out,'' she repeated.

''You certainly did.'' He felt a long shudder work through her, and his hands slipped to her arms. Again he wanted to pull her against him. But heavy footsteps pounded on the porch, and the small room suddenly filled with people.

''Paula, how do you feel? Any trouble breathing?'' Brett brushed past, elbowing him out of the way, intent on Paula. Mitch knelt by the soot-covered trash can. He picked it up gingerly and started toward the door.

Alex stepped back. His heartbeat should go back to normal now that the crisis was over, but that didn't seem to be happening. ''Why didn't you call me?'' He broke into Brett's series of questions. ''You should have gotten out of here. You should have let someone else handle it.''

Paula glanced toward the table, toward the carving of Jason. ''I couldn't wait. I couldn't risk losing that.'' She looked back at him, and it felt as if no one else was in the room.

''Paula...'' He let the sentence trail away. They were talking to each other without the need for words. They both knew what had just happened, whether anyone else did or not. Paula had faced the thing that terrified her most in this world, and she'd done it to save something important to him. His throat closed, and all he could do was look at her and think how dear she was to him.

''How did it start?'' Mitch frowned at the remnants in the can. ''I wouldn't think there'd be anything to spark a fire in here.''

Alex tried to pull his gaze away from Paula. ''It doesn't matter,'' he began, then became aware of a small figure in the doorway. *Jason.* His son shouldn't be exposed to this. It might frighten him. ''Jason—''

''It was me!'' Jason's face was white. ''It was my fault. All my fault!''

Alex didn't know which of them moved first. He and Paula got to Jason at the same time. ''No, Jason, no. It's not your fault, son. Don't think that.''

Jason jerked away from his hand. ''It is,'' he insisted almost angrily. ''I did it.''

Alex could only stare at the boy, totally at a loss.

"You were playing with matches." Paula said it softly, so softly probably no one else heard. "Is that what happened?"

A denial rose in Alex's throat, but before he could speak, Jason nodded. His small face crumpled.

"I'm sorry, Daddy. I didn't mean to. I'm sorry."

"Jason..." He stopped, reading the clear message in Paula's gaze. *Hold him.* She might as well have said it aloud. This wasn't the moment for analyzing or arguing. Alex knelt on the sooty floor. Feeling as if his heart might break, he drew his son into his arms.

For an instant Jason seemed to resist, then he flung his arms around Alex's neck, clinging as he hadn't in years. Sobs shook him.

"It's all right," Alex murmured, stroking his child's back. "It's all right, Jason."

His gaze met Paula's over Jason's head. The sheen of tears brightened her eyes.

"Is something wrong? What is happening?"

Dieter's voice had to be one of the most unwelcome things Alex had ever heard, when only moments before it had seemed so important. Aware of Paula watching him, he glanced up, not relaxing his grip on his son.

"Just a small accident," he said. His gaze caught

Mitch's. "Would you?" He jerked his head toward Dieter.

Mitch nodded, not needing any further explanation. "Everything's under control now, folks." He began ushering people toward the patio, his large frame protecting Jason from curious eyes. "Let's get back to the party."

A murmur of voices, the shuffle of feet, and they were gone. Beside him, he felt Paula move, too.

"I should go. "

He shook his head. "Stay. Please." He stroked Jason's hair, his hand unsteady. "We need you, Paula."

That was as true as anything he'd ever said. He needed her. He loved his son more than life itself, but he didn't know how to reach him. If he didn't do this right, he'd probably regret it the rest of his days.

Please, Lord. Please. The prayer was almost involuntary. How long had it been since he'd begged God on his knees? The thought startled him. He'd been raised to be self-reliant. Somehow that attitude had extended to his faith, almost without his realizing it.

Paula nodded, seeming to understand all the things Alex didn't say. She moved closer, touching Jason's shoulder.

"Jason, it's okay. I understand."

Jason burrowed against his father's neck, and his voice was muffled. "I promised you."

"You didn't mean to break your promise," she said.

Her voice stayed calm, and Alex could only guess at the effort it took. He wanted to demand answers, but this wasn't the time. He could only try to understand.

"Tell your daddy what happened," she said gently. "He won't be angry."

Jason shook his head.

"Come on," she coaxed. "Were you mad?"

Jason sniffled. "Everybody was busy with this dumb party." A sob interrupted his words. "I just wanted someone to pay attention to me."

Someone. The word rang in Alex's mind. He remembered that exchange with Jason, how he'd brushed off his son's worries in his own anxiety over the business deal.

"So you were playing with matches in here." Her gaze ordered Alex not to react.

He felt Jason's nod, and then finally Jason raised his head, his gaze searching Alex's face. "I'm sorry, Daddy. I didn't mean to start a fire. I guess one of the matches wasn't clear out when I threw it away. I didn't mean it."

Alex gently wiped away the tears on Jason's face. "Fires are pretty scary, aren't they."

Jason nodded again, and his lips trembled. "I'm sorry. I just needed to know. About Maida, and Paula, and everything."

"I know, son. I'm sorry, too. But..." He censored the automatic response that assured Jason not to worry. Obviously that did no good. Jason did worry, whether Alex wanted him to or not. "You know I love you, don't you?"

"Mommy loved me." The words burst out, as if Jason had been holding them in for a long time. "Mommy loved me, but she went away. It was my fault."

"Jason, no. Why would you think that?" Appalled, he could only stare at his son, feeling his heart shatter into pieces.

Jason hung his head, staring at the floor. He sniffled a little. "I wasn't good enough. That's why she went away."

How was he going to find the words? His son's pain wrapped around his heart, squeezing the life out of it.

Please, God. I've tried so hard to be the perfect heir my father wanted, but I've failed my own son. Please. Help me.

Paula watched the battle on Alex's face. His torment showed in his eyes so clearly. If he realized how much he was giving away, would he shut down again? Shut her out?

Alex stroked Jason's cheek. "Jason, that's not it at all. Of course your mommy loved you, more than anything. If she could have come back, I'm sure she would have. It wasn't your fault she went away. Mommy and I just couldn't seem to get along together. We made each other unhappy."

A strong fist seemed to grip her heart. Alex was opening up to his son. Maybe for the first time, he was being vulnerable to the boy.

Please, Father, don't let him pull back now. Help him to tear down the barriers between them.

Jason shook his head as if he couldn't let go of the responsibility. He and Alex were so alike in that quality, and Alex had never seen it.

"Yes," Alex insisted. "Don't you remember how she used to sing you to sleep at night?"

"She did?" That simple idea seemed to break through Jason's absorption.

"Sure she did—"

Alex glanced at Paula, as if looking for confirmation he was on the right track, and she nodded, smiling through the tears that insisted on falling.

"And she made you that little stuffed dog that's on your dresser."

Jason stared into his father's face. "But she went away."

"I know." She saw the muscles work in Alex's jaw. "I'm sorry I didn't talk to you about it more. I guess I thought you were too little to understand."

Jason straightened. "I'm big enough, Dad. I want to know what's going on."

"I see that now." Alex stood, holding out his hand to Jason. "Let's sit down and talk about it, okay?"

"Okay." Jason tucked his small hand into Alex's.

As father and son moved toward the bench against the wall, Paula slipped quietly out the door. Alex was doing it. He was taking down, stone by stone, the wall that separated him from his son. He could do that now without her.

She hesitated when she reached the patio. Snatches of conversation reached her ears, and the flurry of excitement was clearly over. Mitch stood on the pool deck, casually talking with someone, but his position was such that no one could go past him toward the studio. Brett had corralled several of Dieter's deputies near the gazebo, and Anne seemed to be keeping Dieter himself occupied.

She couldn't go back to the party, not until the last traces of tears were gone from her face. She moved softly across the grass and behind the shelter of the yew hedge.

The buzz of conversation turned into the merest background noise, quieter than the twittering of wrens in the hedge. Peace filled her.

Thank you, Lord. She glanced up, toward the mountain ridge cutting into the sky. *Thank you. I think I understand now.*

She and Alex were more alike than she'd thought. He'd been trying to prove he was the perfect Caine heir his father wanted. She'd thought she had to earn the approval her father had never given. The truth was that neither of them had to prove their value in God's sight. They were accepted, just the way they were.

She wiped away another tear. She wasn't the starstruck girl she'd been two years ago, who ran away from rejection and told herself she didn't need anyone. She'd like to believe that, if not for the loss of her memory, she'd have dealt with that failing long ago, but this was her chance. Perhaps this had been in Aunt Maida's mind all along, when she'd pushed Paula into the situation. This time she wouldn't run away, no matter how difficult the future might be.

She loved Alex. If he didn't care for her in the same way, if the differences between them were too great, she'd deal with that. But she wouldn't run away from it.

"Paula."

She turned at the sound of Alex's voice, her heart thudding. "Is Jason all right?"

He nodded. "He will be. Thanks to you."

"I didn't do anything." Her throat was tight with

longing. "You're the one he needed." *The one I need.*

Alex shook his head. "I'd never have known that without you. I'd have kept on trying to protect him, not realizing I was closing him out." He moved closer. "You understood me better than I understood myselt. If I succeed in being a better father, it will be because of you."

"I'm glad." She knew the love she felt for him was shining in her eyes, but she couldn't help it. There weren't any walls between them, at least not any of her making. Whether Alex could say the same, she didn't know.

His step closed the distance between them. He stood very close, not touching. "I don't think I'll ever be the perfect father I wanted to be."

"Jason doesn't need a perfect father. He needs you." It was much the same thing she'd said when he'd rejected the idea that he was a hero.

Perhaps he remembered that, because he smiled.

"Not a hero," he said quietly. "Not a perfect father. Are you willing to take a chance on someone as fallible as I am?"

Her heart seemed to stop beating for a moment as she looked up into his eyes. It took a moment to find the words. "I've always been ready to take a chance. And in case you haven't noticed, I'm not so perfect myself."

He drew her into his arms, and she was home. She rested her cheek against his chest and felt the steady beating of his heart.

"Will you marry me, Paula?" His breath stirred her hair. "Will you stay with us forever?"

She looked up at him, seeing the love so strong in his dark eyes that it took her breath away. Maybe they weren't perfect, but with God's help they could build a family that would last.

"I will."

He pressed his cheek against hers, and her heart overflowed. God had poured blessings on them, and all they'd had to do was open their hearts and hands. From now on the memories they made would be ones they could share, with God's grace.

*   *   *   *   *

Dear Reader,

I'm so glad you decided to pick up this book. The love story of small-town millionaire Alex Caine and his reluctant housekeeper, Paula Hansen, is one that has been teasing my imagination for a long time. I'm delighted to see it in print, and I hope you'll enjoy it.

Alex is the kind of person who thinks he has to be perfect for everyone, including God. It takes a near disaster to make him see the truth—that God's acceptance is already won for him. Once he understands that, he's finally ready for the happily-ever-after he always thought was an illusion. And he finds it in the surprise Cinderella who's right there in his own house.

Please let me know how you liked this story. You can reach me c/o Steeple Hill Books, 233 Broadway, Ste. 1001, New York, NY 10279.

Best wishes,

Marta Perry

A FATHER'S PLACE

Many waters cannot quench love;
rivers cannot wash it away.
                    —*Song of Songs* 8:7

This story is dedicated with love and gratitude
to my friends in Christ at First Church.
And, as always, to Brian.

Prologue

Prayers from Bedford Creek, Pennsylvania

Father, please remember my son, Quinn. He's so bitter now, and if only he'd come home, maybe I could help him....
Please, Lord, bless my brother, Quinn, and help him to see that he has to forgive....
And God bless my daddy, and bring him back home to stay. Please don't forget that I'd like a new mommy, and if it's okay with You, I think my Sunday school teacher, Ms. Ellie, would be just perfect....

Chapter One

He'd come home to the town where he no longer belonged, to break up his mother's romance. Put like that, Quinn Forrester decided it didn't sound like a creditable goal. It wouldn't impress the woman he was about to see, and he needed Ellie Wayne's cooperation. Either that, or he needed her surrender.

The tension that had driven him for days cranked up a notch. His natural instinct was to explode, demanding explanations, but that wouldn't work. He'd have to exercise diplomacy to get what he wanted from Ellie Wayne, and his talent for that had grown rusty over years of fighting nature's rampages in places considerably wilder than this one.

He glanced along the narrow street. Bedford Creek, Pennsylvania, spread up a narrow cleft in the mountains from the river. Its frame houses climbed the hillside in steps, as if they'd been planted there.

Ellie Wayne's craft shop was on the lowest street, along with the police station, a few other small shops and a scattering of houses. Opposite it, the park spread along the flood-prone land by the river. His practiced engineer's eye automatically noted the water level, higher now from the frequent rain than was usual for August.

The craft shop, the lower floor of a frame house, had been a newsstand when he was a boy, when Bedford Creek was a sleepy backwater where nothing ever happened. Then some energetic citizens had decided to capitalize on turn-of-the-century architecture and wooded mountain scenery.

Since then, like much of the town, the shop had been transformed into a quaint attraction for the tourists who deluged the village during the summer and fall. He stepped around a man with a camera, dodged two women laden with shopping bags and stopped.

Ellie Wayne had an eye for display—he'd give her that. An artfully draped quilt brightened the shop window, surrounded by handwoven baskets and dried-flower wreaths in colors that picked up the quilt's faded earth tones. A yellow stuffed cat snuggled into a needlework cushion.

He'd planned his visit for closing time on this busy summer Saturday, hoping to catch her alone after the last of the shoppers left. He didn't want any eaves-droppers on the conversation he was about to have.

He took a breath, tried to curb his impatience and reached for the door. A bell jangled, and the cool, dim interior invited him in. The woman behind the worn oak counter glanced up, her brown eyes registering his presence. But she wasn't alone yet. Two last-minute customers fingered a quilt that was spread across the counter, peppering her with questions.

He moved behind a display table heaped with woven tablecloths and inhaled the faint, spicy aroma of dried flowers. Every inch of the tiny shop displayed something—his first impression was clutter; his second, coziness.

He intercepted a questioning glance from Ellie Wayne and pretended interest in a stack of handmade baskets, tamping down his irritation.

"I'll be with you in just a moment." Her voice was as welcoming as the shop.

"No hurry." He forced cordiality into his tone. "I can wait." He could wait. When he talked to her, he wanted the woman's undivided attention.

Undivided attention—that was also what his mother and his six-year-old daughter wanted from him. They'd been reluctant to let him out of their sight since he arrived home yesterday, as if fearing he'd disappear back to the Corps of Engineers project that had occupied him for so long.

Too long, he realized now, far too long. It had been too tempting to bury himself in work after Julie's death, too easy to convince himself that Kristie was better off living with his mother in this comforting, safe place where nothing ever changed.

He gripped the oblong basket he'd picked up. Things had changed, and if he'd been a better father, a better son, he'd have realized that. Bedford Creek wasn't a safe little backwater any longer. The tourism boom had brought strangers to town—strangers like Ellie Wayne and her father.

He glanced toward the woman. Maybe it wasn't entirely fair to describe her as a stranger. She'd opened her shop four or five years ago, and he must have seen her playing the organ in church on his few visits home. But it was only in the last few months that Kristie had begun talking about Ms. Ellie so much, and even more recently that her innocent chatter had paired Grandma with Charles Wayne. And then his sister Rebecca had called, concerned about their mother's infatuation for a man she'd just met, and he'd known it was time to come home.

The customer produced a credit card. Apparently the transaction had been successful. Ellie smiled as she folded the quilt, her hands lingering as if she hated to part with it. A neat salesperson's gimmick, he decided. She probably hoped to sell them something else.

He assessed the woman, trying to look at her without preconceptions. Slim, tall, probably about thirty or so. A wealth of dark brown hair escaped from a woven headband to curl around her face. There was nothing conventional about Ellie's looks. Her face was too strong, her coloring too vivid, with those dark expressive eyes and the natural bloom in her cheeks.

Nothing conventional about her clothing choices, either. Today she wore a long skirt and an embroidered blouse that would look more at home in an artists' colony than in Bedford Creek. He shouldn't let that quick impression prejudice him against her, but he couldn't deny the feeling. She looked as if she didn't belong here.

The bell jangled as the customers went out, and he tensed. Ellie Wayne was an unknown quantity as far as he was concerned. He didn't want to do battle with her, but he would if he had to.

She came toward him with the quick, light step of a dancer. "I'm sorry I kept you waiting. May I help you with something? I have those with different colors of reed woven in."

He glanced down at the basket he'd nearly forgotten was in his hands. "I'm not shopping."

Her eyes widened as if he'd insulted her wares, and he reminded himself he'd intended to be diplomatic. "It's very nice," he added, putting it down.

Faint wariness showed in those expressive dark eyes. Maybe it was her eyes, maybe it was the ethnic flavor of her clothing, but a thread of song wound through his thoughts, its lyrics warm and yearning, something about a brown-eyed girl. He shoved the distraction away.

"Then what can I do for you?" she asked.

"I'm here about my mother." She still looked at him blankly, of course. She didn't know him from Adam. "I'm Quinn Forrester. Gwen's son."

"Quinn?" Her voice lilted with surprise. If he expected guilt, he didn't get it. "Gwen didn't tell me you were coming home."

It was almost as if she should have been informed, and irritation flickered through him. "Does she tell you everything?"

"I didn't mean that." Warm color rose in her cheeks. "I'm just surprised she didn't mention it."

"Especially since you see so much of each other." He didn't intend the words to sound accusing, but they did.

She stiffened, apparently sensing his attitude. "Your mother and I are cochairing a craft show next month for the church." She said it carefully, as if weighing each word. "So we have been seeing a lot of each other lately."

"It's a little more than that, isn't it?" He wasn't going to dance around the subject any longer. It was time the woman leveled with him. "The way I hear it, your father's the one who's spending a lot of time with her."

He couldn't be mistaken about her reaction to that—a flash of fear. She masked it, but not quickly enough.

Determination hardened inside Quinn. His father would have expected Quinn to protect his mother, not to bury himself in his own grief. But he hadn't, and now it looked as if Gwen Forrester, with her naive belief in people and her tempting little nest egg, was falling prey to a charming drifter who had no visible means of support and a murky background. Well, not if he could prevent it.

"I don't know what you mean." Her sudden pallor gave the lie to the words.

He shook his head. "I think you do. I want to know what's going on between my mother and your father."

The unexpected introduction of her father into the conversation sent Ellie's heart racing. What had Charles Wayne done now? Familiar panic flooded her. She'd known it spelled trouble when he showed up at her door after all these years. She should have told him to go away. She should have...

She took a grip on her frightened thoughts. This was ridiculous. She was overreacting. Something about Quinn Forrester's uncompromising expression had panicked her unnecessarily.

"I don't understand." She could only hope it came out calmly enough—that he hadn't seen that moment of fear.

Quinn leaned against the display table with what was probably meant to be a casual air. It didn't succeed. Nothing about his intensity was casual.

"It's not that difficult a question." He concentrated on her face as if he'd look right past her expression and into her mind. "What's going on between my mother and your father?"

"Going on?" She stared at him blankly. "Nothing. I mean, they hardly know each other. Why would you think something was going on?"

He moved toward her, bracing his hand against the worn wooden counter. He was too close, invading her space. She forced herself not to step back, knowing instinctively he'd interpret that as a sign of weakness.

"From what I've heard…" he began, when a yellow blur soared to the countertop next to him. Quinn snatched his hand back with a startled exclamation.

"Sorry." She took a steadying breath, trying to calm her stampeding pulse. "That's Hannibal. You're encroaching on his favorite place."

As this man was with her. This was her shop, she reminded herself. Her town, her place in the world. She belonged here now. She stroked the tomcat. Hannibal pushed his head firmly against her hand and then sat, folding front paws majestically under his white bib.

"I saw him in the window. I thought he was a stuffed toy." Quinn held out his hand. Hannibal sniffed cautiously, then deigned to let himself be scratched behind the ear.

She took another deep breath. *Calm down. Don't overreact.* Whatever Quinn wanted, it didn't necessarily have to be bad. She watched as he stroked the cat, giving it the same concentration he had her.

Quinn's daughter must have gotten her red hair and freckles from some other part of the family tree. His hair was a dark, rich shade of brown, the color of ripe chestnuts. Straight dark brows contrasted with surprisingly light eyes—not quite blue, closer to slate. His tanned skin and the feathering of sun lines around his eyes suggested years of outdoor work in a place far from this green Pennsylvania valley. He had a firm mouth and an even firmer chin that argued an uncompromising disposition.

He switched his gaze from the cat to her, and a little quiver of awareness touched her. That intent gaze was unnerving. It was much the same as the gaze with which Hannibal watched a bird before he pounced.

"As I was saying, about my mother and your father."

"Gwen is my friend." She hurried into speech, hoping to deflect whatever accusation was coming. "And my father is here for a visit. A brief visit," she added. "Naturally they've met each other."

"Because you and my mother are friends." His tone made it sound sinister.

She held her gaze steady with an effort. "Yes."

"It's a little more than that, I think." His concentration pinned her to the spot. "Each time I talk to Kristie on the phone, his name comes up. 'Charles and Grandma did this. Charles and Grandma did that.' He seems to have become almost part of the family in the last few weeks."

Her mind raced. When had all this been going on? She'd been busy, of course, but she should have known what her father was doing. Maybe she'd just felt relieved he'd found something to occupy himself in Bedford Creek. That way she didn't have to see him and constantly be reminded of the painful past.

"As I said, Gwen and I are working on the fund-raiser together." She hoped her smile looked more convincing than it felt. "My father has been helping out, so I suppose he and Gwen have spent some time together."

"Some time?"

His persistence sparked the anger that had been hidden beneath her fear. "This is beginning to sound like an inquisition."

He didn't bother to deny it. "I have a right to worry about my family's welfare."

Meaning he thought she and her father threatened it. She stiffened, meeting his eyes with as much defiance as she could muster. "Your family isn't in danger from us."

"When my sixty-five-year-old mother starts acting like a schoolgirl with a new boyfriend, I worry. Try hard. Maybe you'll understand."

The temper she'd fought to control escaped. "I can't imagine when you had the chance to observe your mother. You've hardly been back in Bedford Creek in the past few years."

His fists clenched, and she saw in an instant she'd gone too far. She knew about the death of his wife, of course. She'd barely become acquainted with Julie when the woman's death in a car accident had shocked the whole town. In the two years or so since, according to Gwen, Quinn had buried himself in his work, as if to find escape. Now she'd challenged that.

"I'm sorry," she said quickly, before the situation could deteriorate any further. "I didn't mean that. And I certainly didn't have the right to say it."

"My work has kept me away." He said it calmly enough, but a muscle quivered in his jaw with the effort. "That doesn't mean I don't care."

She seemed to be juggling dynamite. "I'm sure you do. But Gwen…" She hesitated on the verge of pointing out the obvious—that Gwen was a grown woman who could manage her own life.

His gaze hardened, and she suspected he knew what she'd been about to say. "My mother's led a sheltered life. My father always protected her from any unpleasantness."

A spasm of memory clutched her. She'd led a fairly sheltered life, too, once upon a time, until her father's betrayal had blown it into a million pieces. If Charles really was somehow involved with Gwen, it was probably the worst idea he'd had since that disaster.

She wouldn't believe it. Quinn was probably over-reacting, but she knew instinctively he'd be a bad enemy to make. She couldn't afford to antagonize him any more than she already had.

"My father is just here for a brief visit. He regards Gwen as nothing more than a casual acquaintance." She hoped.

His frown was uncompromising. "If there's anything more—"

The jingling of the bell cut off what sounded like a threat. Ellie turned toward the door, and her heart sank. Why on earth had her father chosen this particular moment to come into the shop?

She glanced cautiously back at Quinn, and tension zigzagged like lightning along her nerves. He looked like a predator about to strike.

* * *

Quinn looked from Ellie's suddenly guilty face to the man who'd just entered. So this was the father—it had to be. Why else would she look that way? He'd almost been swayed by her protestations, but now all his suspicions flooded back.

"Sorry, my dear. I didn't realize you were busy with a customer." Charles Wayne stood, hand on the doorknob, his expression mingling regret at interrupting with curiosity.

"I'm just closing," Ellie said. "Maybe you could set the table for supper."

She gestured toward the stairs at the rear of the shop, which must lead to the living quarters upstairs. Her desire to get her father out of his range was as clear as if she wore a sign announcing it.

He didn't intend to let that happen, not until he'd had a chance to see the man for himself. He took a step forward, holding out his hand. "You must be Ellie's father. I'm Quinn Forrester."

"Charles Wayne. What a pleasure to meet you. You're Gwen's son, of course. She talks about you all the time."

His smile was smoother than his daughter's, more practiced. He had to be in his sixties, but he had a quick, light step that made him look younger, as did the sparkle in his bright blue eyes.

"Gwen mentioned you were home when I ran into

her and little Kristie at the grocer's," he went on. "A delightful child, isn't she?"

It was the trick of either a good salesman or a confidence man—to ask a question that would bring an affirmative answer. "I think so, but then I'm prejudiced."

And prejudiced against the man in front of him, he realized. Maybe it was the ready smile, or the glib chatter, but Charles Wayne put his back up. He preferred the daughter's quick antagonism to the father's charm.

"Dad." Ellie nodded toward the stairs. "I have soup in the slow cooker for our supper."

"Then we can have it anytime," Wayne said, apparently oblivious to her desire to get rid of him. He smiled at Quinn. "I believe Gwen told me you're working out west someplace."

"Oregon. I'm with the Corps of Engineers." He'd like to tell the man his profession was none of his business, but that wasn't the way to find out about more about him. He'd already come within a hair of outright war with the daughter. Maybe it was time to take a step back. His mother wouldn't be inclined to listen to his concerns if he started by alienating her friends. "Are you familiar with the West Coast?"

"Been there, of course. Now, this little town where my daughter's settled is a far cry from our old stamping grounds."

The tension emanating from Ellie jerked upward, evidenced by the indrawn breath, the tightening of her hands. So, there was something about that mention of where they were from that bothered her.

"And where was that?" he asked. "I don't think I've heard much about Ellie's past."

"I don't find people all that interested in my history." Ellie's casual tone wasn't very convincing.

"Odd, isn't it? People's stories are endlessly fascinating to me," Charles said. "There was a man I met when I was working in San Francisco, or was it Santa Fe? Doesn't matter. In any event, this man had actually taken part in a Mount Everest climb. Think of that."

Quinn didn't intend to be distracted by mythical mountain climbers. "You were saying you'd lived where?"

Charles gave an airy wave. "All over the place. I'm afraid I'm the original tumbleweed. Just haven't been able to settle down in one place, unlike my daughter." He smiled fondly at Ellie, who looked strained. "Ellen has certainly put down roots here in Bedford Creek. Not that it isn't a charming place, but it's not the life I expected her to have."

"People have to make their own decisions about things like that." Ellie took his arm firmly and turned him toward the stairs. "I'll be up soon, Dad. How about checking the soup for me?"

"Of course, of course." Charles glanced over his shoulder at Quinn. "I'll look forward to seeing you again. We must talk longer the next time."

If Ellie ever wanted to embark on a life of crime, Quinn decided, she'd have to do something about that expressive face. It showed only too clearly her relief at having gotten rid of her gregarious father and her conviction that he and Quinn wouldn't be having any more little talks.

Ellie glanced pointedly toward the exit. "I should be closing now."

I'm not as easy to be rid of as all that, he assured her silently. "Your father's quite the charmer, isn't he? I can see how my mother might find him entertaining company."

He had a sudden longing for his own father's solid, quiet presence. No one would have used charming or entertaining to describe John Forrester, but he'd been a man of strength and integrity.

"My father's charming to everyone." She smiled tightly. "It's his way. I don't think you need to worry that Gwen is susceptible to it. She's got a level head on her shoulders."

"You think so? I love my mother dearly, but levelheaded is the last thing I'd say about her. My father was always the dependable one in the family."

She lifted her eyebrows, as if doubting his assessment. "And now Rebecca is, I suppose."

Guilt stabbed at him. Since his father's death Rebecca had taken on the duty that should have been his. Their other sister, Angela, had married, then gone off to Philadelphia when her husband's business sent him there. And Quinn had been so preoccupied with the twin burdens of his career and his grief that he'd let Rebecca handle everything.

Not anymore, he promised, not sure whether he was talking to himself or his father. It was time he took on the responsibilities he'd shelved for too long.

"Rebecca has enough to do with her husband, the clinic and a baby on the way. If my mother needs anything, I'll be the one to help her."

He wasn't sure whether anger or fear predominated in the look she gave him. "I'm sure she appreciates that," she said. "Now if you'll excuse me, I have a meal to get ready."

He clearly wasn't going to get anything more from Ellie at this point, so he let himself be ushered to the door. Her relief was almost palpable when he finally set foot outside.

He stopped, hand on the door to keep her from closing it. "Where was it your father said the two of you were from?"

"Ohio," she snapped, and closed the door so sharply he had to snatch his hand away.

Ellie wasn't the accomplished storyteller he suspected her father was. That had had the ring of truth about it.

He watched as she flipped the Closed sign into place. She went toward the stairs, so quickly she might almost have been running away. The yellow cat leaped into the window, stared unblinkingly at him for a long moment and then turned and followed his mistress.

If he'd gone to Ellie Wayne's shop seeking assurance that everything was all right, he'd come away knowing the opposite was true. And it wasn't his adverse reaction to Charles Wayne that had convinced him. He could chalk that up to personal taste.

No, he'd been convinced by Ellie's reactions. Ellie Wayne was afraid. Of him? Of something to do with her father? He wasn't sure, just as he wasn't sure of a lot of things about her.

She'd lived in Bedford Creek for close to five years. She'd become an accepted part of the town. But as far as he could tell, no one knew much about her life before she came here. And people knew even less about her father.

It was time that changed, and he intended to change it.

Chapter Two

"Ms. Ellie, do you really think God answers prayers?"

Ellie decided she'd never get used to small children's ways of asking the deepest spiritual questions. She sat down next to Quinn's little daughter the next morning. The rest of her Sunday school class had scampered out the door already, but Kristie had lingered, the question obviously on her mind.

"Yes, I think God does answer prayers." She brushed a coppery curl back from Kristie's cheek, sending up a silent plea for guidance. "But I think sometimes we don't understand God's answers."

Kristie frowned, putting both hands on the low wooden table. "I don't know what you mean."

"Why don't you tell me about your prayer," she suggested. "Maybe I can help you understand."

Kristie's rosebud mouth pursed in an unconscious imitation of her grandmother's considering look. "Well, see, I prayed just like you taught us. And I remembered to thank God and everything."

Their last few lessons had been on prayer. Kristie, at least, had been listening. "And what else?" she prompted gently.

"I asked God to make Daddy stay here for good." The words burst out. "And I thought it would work. But when I asked him, Daddy said he has to go out West again. And I don't want him to!"

Ellie drew the child close, heart hurting. Did Quinn realize how much his little girl missed him, even though a loving family surrounded her?

"Kristie, I know I said God answers our prayers, and I believe that." She spoke slowly. Caring for the spiritual well-being of the children in her class was one of the most important things she'd ever do, and she wanted to do it right.

"But God knows what's best for us. Sometimes the answer is yes, and sometimes it's no. And sometimes the answer is wait." She smiled into the little face turned up to hers so trustingly. "I think that's the hardest answer of all, because I hate to wait for things. But I remind myself that God loves me and wants what's best for me. Do you think you could remember that, too?"

"I guess so."

"I'm sure she will."

The unexpected masculine voice jolted her. Quinn stood in the doorway, and he'd obviously been listening for some time. Her cheeks flushed. Had he heard what Kristie's prayer was about? And was he angry that she presumed to give his daughter advice?

"Daddy!" Kristie raced across the room to throw her arms around his waist. "Are you going to church with me?"

"Sure thing, sweetheart." He gave her a quick hug, his face softening as he looked down at her.

Ellie's heart cramped. When he smiled at his daughter, the lines in Quinn's face disappeared. The marks of grief and bitterness were magically erased, and he looked again like the college graduate in the picture on Gwen's piano, smiling at the world as if he owned it.

"You run down to the parlor and catch up with Grandma, okay? I want to talk to your teacher for a minute."

Kristie nodded, the clouds gone from her face, and danced toward the door. "We'll wait for you," she said importantly. "Don't be late."

Yesterday it had been his mother; today it was his daughter. Quinn Forrester must feel she'd interfered with his family far too much.

Quickly, before he could launch an attack, Ellie shoved the Sunday school books onto the shelf. "I'm afraid I don't have time now." She started for the door. "I'm playing the organ for the service, and I have to get ready."

But if she thought she was going to get rid of him that easily, apparently she was mistaken. He fell into step beside her. A dark suit, pale blue shirt and striped tie had replaced yesterday's jeans, but he still looked like a man who belonged outdoors. And he moved as if the church hallway were a mountain trail.

"I'll walk with you, and we can talk on the way." He pushed open the double doors that led from the Sunday school wing to the church itself, his hand strong and tanned against the pale wood.

Maybe it was time to go on the offensive with him. "I suppose you think I shouldn't have spoken that way to your daughter." She certainly wouldn't apologize for doing what a church school teacher should.

Instead of counterattacking, Quinn tilted his head slightly as if considering. "No, I wouldn't say I think that. You're her Sunday school teacher. That's your job, answering the tough questions."

His unexpected agreement took the wind out of her sails, and she glanced up to meet his steady gaze. For now, at least, it wasn't accusing. "The questions are tough. Sometimes almost unanswerable."

"What do you do if you don't have an answer?" He really seemed curious.

She smiled. "Say so. Then I ask the pastor. That's his job, after all."

"I'm sure he appreciates that."

She'd never have thought, after yesterday, that she and Quinn would be smiling at each other in perfect harmony. The tension inside her eased. They'd gotten off to a difficult start, but perhaps they could begin again. She didn't want to be on uncomfortable terms with Gwen's son.

They reached the vestry before she could think of anything else to say. Was that all Quinn wanted to talk with her about?

She reached into the closet and took out the shoes she wore for playing the pipe organ. She held them for a moment, waiting for him to speak, wondering if she should say anything more about Kristie.

When the silence stretched out, she looked up at him. "I guess you overheard what Kristie's prayer was about."

He nodded, a muscle flickering near his mouth, but he didn't say anything.

She took a deep breath. This was definitely not her business, but she couldn't ignore Kristie's prayers. "I don't know much about your job, but I know she'd love it if you could work closer."

Quinn's expression closed to a stiff, impenetrable mask. "That's not possible. I go where the Corps of

Engineers sends me. Unlike your father, I'm not a gentleman of leisure.''

Her stomach clenched. There was the counterattack she'd expected. "My father is retired." She forced the words out through suddenly stiff lips.

Quinn leaned toward her, making her aware of how tiny the vestry was. He was much too close, and he took up all the available space. "What is he retired from?"

She turned away, slipping on her shoes, buying time. So the battle wasn't over between them. His brief friendliness had evaporated, and he wanted answers she had no intention of giving him.

A tremor of fear shivered through her. If anyone in Bedford Creek knew the truth about her father, everyone would know. And if they did, the love and acceptance she'd grown to count on would vanish in an instant. She'd be alone again.

She straightened slowly and looked at Quinn. If she were a better liar, she might be able to throw him off the track, but she suspected that was impossible. "Business," she said crisply.

She hurried through the door to the organ loft, knowing she was running away from him, knowing, too, that it was futile. Quinn Forrester wasn't the kind of man to give up easily. He wanted the truth, but if he got it, he could destroy her happiness.

*   *   *

Quinn stood frowning after her for a moment. He'd like to pursue her and drag some answers out of her, but he couldn't. The opening notes already echoed from Grace Church's elderly pipe organ. Where had Ellie trained? That was yet another thing he didn't know about her.

He walked back through the hallway to the parlor. It was surprising how little the people in Bedford Creek seemed to know about Ellie Wayne. Even his mother, who was usually a clearinghouse of local information, only seemed to know tidbits: that she'd worked in a craft shop in Philadelphia; that her mother died when she was young; that she was an only child. Hardly the kind of information Bedford Creek usually amassed about newcomers.

And as far as Charles Wayne was concerned, the slate was even blanker, if possible. That was what had upset his sister enough to make her call him. No one knew anything, according to Rebecca, except that he was Ellie's father. He'd never visited her before; no one had ever heard her speak of him; he'd arrived by bus and didn't seem to have a car. A man whose background was that vague must have something to hide.

Quinn entered the parlor, trying to push his concern to the back of his mind. At least Gwen would be safely separated from Charles Wayne for the next hour. After church, like it or not, he'd have the private talk with her that she'd managed to avoid for the last two days.

His mother and Kristie waited with Rebecca and her husband. He put his arm around Rebecca, kissing her cheek.

"How's my little sister?" He looked at her closely. "Kind of washed-out these days, aren't you?" He sent a mock glare in Brett's direction. "Have you been working her too hard at the clinic?" He knew Rebecca loved her work as a physician's assistant at the town clinic, especially since her husband was the doctor she assisted. Together they took care of the whole town.

Brett Elliot grinned, holding up both hands in surrender. "Not me, I promise. Blame your new little niece or nephew."

"Speaking of which…" Rebecca's face seemed tinged with green. She shook her head and rushed off in the direction of the rest room.

"What's wrong with Aunt Rebecca?" Kristie pulled at Brett's sleeve. "Is she sick?"

"Sometimes ladies have upset tummies when they're going to have a baby," Brett said easily while Quinn was still considering how to answer that question. Thank goodness for a doctor in the family. "I'll see if she feels like staying or wants to go home. Catch you later."

The choir passed them, heading into the choir loft,

and Kristie grabbed his hand. "Come on, Daddy. I want to get a story paper before they're all gone."

He let himself be drawn toward the sanctuary and followed his mother and daughter into the pew, automatically tensing. He glanced at his mother. Did she have the same thoughts he did each time he entered this space?

Kaleidoscopic images flowed into each other—standing at the communion table for his confirmation, holding Julie's hand while they said their vows, watching his sisters get married. Unfortunately the happy images were swamped by the sad ones of sitting in the front pew looking bleakly at his father's coffin and then, too soon, at Julie's. He swallowed hard, trying to get rid of the knot in his throat, and concentrated on the arrangements of roses on either side of the chancel.

A flutter of movement at the end of the pew distracted him, and he watched with disbelief as his mother half stood to wave to Charles Wayne. In another moment she'd beckoned the man to join them, and Wayne was sliding into the pew next to her as if it were the most natural thing in the world.

The organ sounded the notes of the opening hymn, and he stood, seething silently. So much for his assumptions about the way this morning would go. He sent his mother a look that he hoped conveyed his feelings, and she smiled back blandly, as if she enjoyed disconcerting him.

He tried to concentrate on the service, tried not to be distracted by Charles's presence in the family pew or by memories of the past. It wasn't easy.

Kristie pinched his arm, and he leaned over for her soft whisper. "Ms. Ellie plays pretty, doesn't she?"

He nodded. The organ was half-hidden by the pulpit, but he could see Ellie when she leaned forward. Her dark hair curled around her face as her hands moved to the organ stops. Her expression unexpectedly touched him. She was transported; that was all he could think.

His gaze lingered on the line of her cheek, the soft smile that curved her lips. If not for the problem posed by her father, he might be thinking how attractive she was. Not his type, but appealing, with her vivid coloring and quick grace.

In an instant he rejected the thought, appalled at himself. The pain of Julie's death at the hands of a drunk driver was with him every day, even after two years. On the job, preoccupied with work, he managed to hold it at bay.

But here in Bedford Creek, where they'd married, where she'd chosen to live when the corps sent him out West, it wasn't possible. Each time he came home he had to mount a guard against the sudden onslaught of memory, pain, anger.

He'd thought the anger would go away once the driver was in prison where he belonged, but that hadn't happened. Instead it had stayed, burning at the back of his mind, singeing his very soul.

He forced himself to pay attention to the message. *Just concentrate, and the service will soon be over.* He'd take his mother and daughter home, then sit his mother down for a serious talk about the danger to a well-off, naive widow posed by glib strangers.

The last Amen sounded, and he tried to hustle his little party toward the door. But at least half the congregation wanted to greet him, and he couldn't be rude, even though the sight of Charles lingering at his mother's side sent his blood pressure rising.

With a sense of relief he saw Ellie heading toward them, shedding her robe as she came. She'd probably detach her father.

"Ellie, dear, that was lovely." His mother hugged her, then turned to him. "Wasn't it lovely, Quinn?"

He felt about eight years old, being prompted by his mother to say the right thing. "Beautiful. You play very well. Where did you study?"

"Here and there." She caught her father's arm, tugging it a bit. "Come on, Dad, time to go home."

"But you're not going home," his mother exclaimed. "I've already talked to Charles, and it's all settled. You and your father are coming to Sunday dinner with us."

To do her justice, Ellie looked just about as appalled at that suggestion as he must. "That's very nice of you, Gwen, but I'm afraid we have to get home."

"Nonsense," his mother said briskly, linking her arm with Ellie's. "I know you haven't started dinner yet, and I have a pot roast cooking that's just about ready. We insist you come, don't we, Quinn?"

In other circumstances, this would be comic. Ellie clearly didn't want to come, any more than he wanted her to. Just as clearly, they were both stuck.

"Please join us," he said.

Ellie shot him one wary look, and then she nodded. Like it or not, the Forresters and the Waynes were having Sunday dinner together. Maybe this was his chance to get closer to her. He frowned. That should not be making him feel anticipation.

"Dad, please. Before we get there, you have to tell me about you and Gwen." Ellie turned onto the street where the Forresters lived, her stomach tightening. They'd be there in moments, and she still hadn't gotten a satisfactory answer from her father.

She felt him studying her face and kept her eyes on the road. "Princess, I..."

"Don't call me that!" The nickname took her relentlessly back to the past, to a time when she really had felt like a princess—pampered, sheltered, a popular figure in the social scene of their small Ohio city.

Foolish, she added. *Living in a dream world that was bound to crash.* It had crashed, all right, in a scandal that took away everything she knew.

She took a deep breath and managed to glance at him. He looked hurt.

"I know you weren't happy to see me here, Ellen. I know I let you down. But I'm a different person now."

"I hope so." She did hope it, with all her heart. Maybe that was why she hadn't been able to tell him to go away when he'd turned up after all these years, even though common sense said he'd only bring trouble.

"I've changed," he said, eagerness coloring his voice. "Believe me, prison changes a person."

"Don't." The word came out involuntarily. "Don't, Dad. I don't want to talk about it."

"But, Pr—Ellen, we have to."

"No, we don't." She pulled the car to the curb. "Just promise me you won't do anything to make Quinn Forrester suspicious of you. More suspicious than he already is."

"I told you, Gwen and I are just friends. I find her charming." He glanced into the rearview mirror, straightening the blue tie that matched his eyes.

Charming. Plenty of people had used that word

about Charles Wayne, including his daughter. Until the day he was arrested for embezzlement, leaving her bereft and alone, bankrupting herself in a futile attempt to pay off his debts.

There was no time to think about that now, not with Gwen already opening the front door of the rambling Victorian house. Her father took her arm as they got out of the car, and she felt a brief moment's pleasure in his courteous manners.

"I don't care who knows the truth, you know," he said quietly.

Panic shot through her. "Well, I do." She stopped on the walk, turning to face him, and spoke in a furious whisper. "I still feel the pain of what happened back in Winstead when people knew the truth. It took me a long time to find a place where I belong again, and I won't let you ruin it."

He nodded, and for an instant she almost imagined she saw the sheen of tears in his eyes. That was impossible. Charles Wayne took everything in life far too lightly to be brought to tears by her.

"I won't do anything to hurt you, Ellie. You can count on me."

She held back a despairing sigh. She'd counted on him before, and then found out he was living a lie.

"Come right in." Gwen waved them into the wide center hall of the gracious old house, and Kristie danced forward to hug Ellie. "Dinner will be ready in a few minutes."

"Let me help you, Gwen." She was uncomfortably aware of Quinn, standing silent behind his mother. He'd shed his jacket and tie and should have looked relaxed. Instead he looked unyielding. He was only too obviously not joining in the welcome.

"No, no, it's all under way. But I did want to show you those notes about the craft fair. Now where did I put them?" Gwen looked around, her soft rosy face puzzled, as if the papers should spring into her hand.

"You had them on the coffee table, I think," Quinn said. "Why don't you and Ellie take a look at them, and I'll see to things in the kitchen." His smile carried nothing of amusement in it. "Charles can help me."

Ellie had another moment of panic at the thought of her father alone with that formidable personality, but before she could say anything, Gwen swept Charles toward the kitchen, taking Kristie with them.

"You show Ellie where those notes are, dear. Charles and Kristie will help me."

The kitchen door swung shut, and Ellie thought she heard Quinn grind his teeth in exasperation. Then he gestured toward the living room.

"In here. I think that's where she left them."

She was uncomfortably aware of his tall figure looming over her as she glanced through the notes

Gwen had made about the craft fair arrangements. She didn't want to look up at him, but she couldn't seem to help herself. He was frowning, and his gray eyes had taken on the glint of steel. Her heart thumped, and she braced herself for another question about her father.

"It sounds as if you and my mother have taken on a big project."

For a moment she didn't know what he was talking about, and then she realized he meant the craft fair.

"We're cochairing it for the church fund-raising committee. The pipe organ desperately needs a complete overhaul, and we're trying to raise the money."

She'd much rather talk about the fund-raising project than her father, although maybe in the end it came back to the same thing. She'd conceived the idea of the craft show as a way of repaying her church family for their kindness and acceptance. And she wouldn't have been so desperately in need of that kindness if it hadn't been for her father. But Quinn couldn't know any of that.

She had a crazy desire to laugh at the situation. She was no more eager to see her father involved with Gwen than Quinn was, for several very good reasons. But she couldn't risk ever letting Quinn know why.

"I guess, as the organist, you have a vested interest in that."

She nodded. "It's a fine old instrument, but nothing more than basic maintenance has been done for years. I say a prayer each time I touch it that the mice haven't nibbled on anything crucial."

"You never did tell me where you studied." He slid the comment in casually, but his expression was watchful.

She suppressed a sigh. Quinn wasn't going to give up easily, that was clear, and he wouldn't be content with the carefully crafted version of her past she usually gave when pressed. Somehow she had to convince him that her father didn't represent a threat to his mother.

"Actually I started piano lessons when I was about Kristie's age. I didn't get interested in the organ until I belonged to a church in Philadelphia. The organist took me under his wing and taught me."

She sent up a brief, thankful prayer for the elderly man who'd shared more than his love of music. He'd shared his love of God, and his profound faith had brought her out of the spiritual low she'd been trapped in after her father's conviction.

"He meant a lot to you," Quinn said quietly.

"Yes, he did." She stopped on the verge of saying he'd given her back her faith. Quinn didn't merit that kind of confidence from her. She was giving too much away, and he was too observant.

She looked up at him, trying to find something

light to say, something that would take them away from dangerous personal ground. She realized in an instant she'd made a mistake. He stood very close to her, watching her intently. That single-minded focus of his was disconcerting. It robbed her of the ability to think.

Quinn frowned, his eyes darkening as their gazes held and they were silent too long. Awareness shimmered between them. Her breath caught. She shouldn't be feeling anything for Quinn. She couldn't. Of all the men in the world, he was the last one she should feel anything at all for.

Chapter Three

"Daddy, Grandma says dinner's ready." Kristie skipped to them and took Ellie's hand, breaking the spell that held them immobile. "She says I can sit next to you, Ms. Ellie. Okay?"

"That sounds great, Kristie." Feeling released, she turned away from Quinn.

She had to keep her mind on the problem, she lectured herself as Kristie led her across the hall to the dining room.

"Right here," Kristie said, pulling out a chair at the side of the oval mahogany table.

Ellie nodded, slipping into the seat, and then she realized Kristie wasn't the one pushing it in for her. Quinn's hand brushed her shoulder lightly as he settled the chair, and his touch both startled and warmed her. Then he rounded the table to his own seat. Directly opposite her, she saw with a sinking heart.

He sat down, unfolded his napkin, and his gaze met hers over the bowl of zinnias in the middle of the table. How on earth could she concentrate on anything else with him staring at her?

"The roast smells wonderful," she said, wondering how she'd manage to taste it.

"My daddy's favorite," Kristie announced. "We always have his favorite when he comes." Using two hands, she carefully passed the bowl of mashed potatoes to Ellie. "Do you like roast and mashed potatoes, Ms. Ellie?" She looked unaccountably anxious.

"Of course." She took a spoonful, feeling her stomach tighten. This couldn't possibly be a peaceful meal, not with her father beaming at Gwen and Quinn looking like a dam about to burst.

The conversation, accompanied by the clinking of silverware on china, didn't reassure her. Quinn probed into her father's past. Charles parried the questions with his customary skill, but her tension rose with every question, every comment.

How long would it be before her father said too much? She knew how he loved to talk. If he got started on any of his familiar stories, he'd give something away to a listener as acute as Quinn.

"You're going to be here for the craft fair, aren't

you, Quinn?'' Gwen must have decided that a change of subject was in order. ''I'm counting on you to help us out with it.''

''I guess so.'' His gaze turned inward, as if he consulted a mental calendar. ''I'm on leave from the project for a month.''

Gwen pouted prettily. ''You and that project. There's always a new one. This is the first decent vacation you've taken in two years. I'm sure there are plenty of jobs for engineers here in Pennsylvania.''

''I have to go where the corps sends me. The work we're doing is important.'' Quinn sent his mother a quelling look.

''Why don't you work here, Daddy?'' Kristie took up the offensive. ''Then you could come home every night. You could coach my soccer team, and we could go fishing and you could help with Bible school.''

Quinn looked a bit harassed, and Ellie had to smile. Maybe coping with his daughter's wishes would distract him from her father.

''Honey, I can't do that. Not right now. Let's just enjoy my leave, okay? Hey, we haven't talked about your birthday yet, and it'll be here before you know it. Have you decided what you want?''

He wasn't quite as skilled as her father in changing the subject when it got uncomfortable, but he'd probably improve with practice. She found herself wanting to tell him to answer his daughter's question, and reminded herself it was none of her business.

Kristie tipped her head to one side, considering the question. "I want a chocolate cake," she said firmly. "With white icing and lots of sprinkles."

"We can probably manage that," Quinn said.

"And a party with Ms. Ellie and her daddy." She tilted her head toward Ellie. "You'll come, won't you? Please?"

Ellie tried not to look at Quinn, knowing what she'd see in his eyes. "If we get an invitation." He undoubtedly wanted her to make an excuse, but she wouldn't lie to the child.

"What about your present?" Quinn's voice was even, but she could detect tension underneath. "A little bird told me you were thinking about a two-wheeler."

Kristie giggled. "That wasn't a little bird, Daddy. That was me!"

"Oh, yes, that's where I heard it. So, what do you think? Is it going to be a bicycle?"

She shook her head decisively. "I decided there's something I want even more."

Quinn looked surprised, and Ellie wondered if he'd already picked out a bicycle. A six-year-old's wants tended to change from moment to moment, but Kristie would probably be delighted with whatever her father gave her.

"Well, what is it?"

"I don't know if I should tell." Kristie wrinkled her nose. "Do you think it's sort of like wishing on your candles? I mean, if you want something really, really bad, maybe you'll get it if you don't tell."

"If you don't tell," Ellie pointed out, "Daddy won't know where to buy it."

"He doesn't have to buy it!" For some reason, Kristie thought that was hilarious.

A spasm of apprehension crossed Quinn's face. "Even so, sweetheart, I think you'd better tell me."

Kristie considered a moment, then nodded. "Well, see, it's something I was praying about. Ms. Ellie taught us about praying in Sunday school. And she said that God always answers, but sometimes He has to say no." She turned to Ellie. "Isn't that what you said?"

Now she was the one who was apprehensive, Ellie thought as she nodded. What on earth had she said that played into Kristie's birthday wish?

"So I decided I'd ask for it for my birthday," Kristie said confidently. "I always get what I want for my birthday, and if I do that and pray, too, I'm sure to get it."

"I don't think…" Ellie began, then fell silent when Quinn frowned at her.

"So what is it you want?" Quinn looked afraid to find out.

Kristie smiled confidently. "I want you to get married so I can have a mommy. Then you'll come home to stay."

"So, do you think you understand now?" Quinn concentrated on his daughter, seated between him and Ellie on the back porch swing. He tried to ignore the way Ellie's arm curved around Kristie, the way her hand brushed his as she patted the child.

Think about your daughter, he lectured himself. *Not about Ellie Wayne, no matter how attractive she is.*

Now where had that come from? He was *not* attracted to Ellie. Her hair tickled his shoulder, escaping as usual from its band, and the faint scent of roses teased his senses, mingling with the spicy aroma of his mother's marigolds. It looked as if he'd have to keep reminding himself he wasn't.

They'd just tried to explain to Kristie the difference between prayer and birthday wishes, and he still wasn't sure they'd succeeded. Maybe he'd have been better off doing this without Ellie, but he felt she carried some of the responsibility.

"I guess so." Kristie looked up at him with trust shining in her eyes. "But that's still what I want for my birthday, okay?"

He tried to suppress a sigh of exasperation. "Kristie..." he began, but she slid off the swing and patted his knee like a little mother.

"It's okay, Daddy. You think about it. I'll go help Grandma with dessert while you decide."

She danced across the porch, her white sundress flitting around her. The screen door slammed behind her.

He looked at Ellie. Her expressive face was perfectly grave, but he thought a trace of amusement lurked in her dark eyes.

"I suppose you think this is funny."

Her dimple showed. "Maybe just a bit. She is one very determined little girl. I wonder from whom she inherited that quality?"

She had a point there, though he hated to admit it. Certainly Julie had never been that way. Julie had been sweet, dependent, passive. But never determined.

"Do your spiritual lessons with six-year-olds always end up like this?" He firmly lobbed the ball back into Ellie's court.

Her expression clouded. "I hope not. I take it very seriously, and I try to put things in terms children can understand. But you just never know how they're going to interpret what you say."

"To an engineer, precision is crucial."

"Even when you're dealing with a six-year-old?"

"Especially when you're dealing with a six-year-old like mine." He frowned. Did he really have a clue what Kristie needed anymore? "I already ordered the bicycle. It's hidden over at Brett and Rebecca's house. Bright blue, with streamers on the handlebars."

"She'll love it. Really." She reached toward him, almost as if she wanted to comfort him. Then, just as quickly, she drew her hand back, apparently thinking the better of it. "I'm sure she knows you want what's best for her."

"I hope so." He looked at her, weighing the caring that shone in those bright eyes. He'd like to believe that was genuine. Unfortunately he couldn't ignore the instinct that told him she was hiding something. "I want what's best for my mother, too."

She knew immediately what he was talking about. He could see that in her sudden wariness. Her expression clouded, and she looked down at her hands, clasped in her lap. "Your mother seems to be perfectly happy with her life."

"You look at her as a friend," he said, trying to ignore the way her dark hair curled against the sunshine yellow of her dress. "At least I hope so. I look at her as the mother who's always been protected."

She bit her lower lip for an instant, then seemed to come to a decision. Her gaze met his with a certain amount of defiance. ''I've already told you that she and my father are just friends.''

''Are they?'' After his mother's performance this morning at church, he couldn't believe that.

''Yes.'' She said it so firmly that he thought she was trying to convince herself. ''And if it's any satisfaction to you, I don't want to see anything else between them, any more than you do.''

''Why?'' He shot the word at her.

For an instant she looked disconcerted. ''Because...because my father will be leaving soon.'' He sensed she edited her words carefully, and wondered what she'd say if she really spoke her mind. ''I just don't think it would work out.''

''That's good, because I intend to make sure nothing happens between them.'' He leaned closer, hearing the sudden catch of her breath at his nearness. They were so close he could see the fine vein tracing her temple, the curve of each dark lash. ''And since you agree that a relationship between them is a bad idea, you can help me.''

''I don't—I don't think that's necessary.'' She drew back, setting the swing vibrating with her tension.

''I do.''

She started to rise, as if to escape him. He caught her hand, holding her still for an instant. He felt her skin grow warm against his palm.

"And I think you do, too," he said.

"I don't know what you mean."

It wasn't the first time she'd said that to him. But this time they both knew it wasn't true. They seemed to be communicating through their linked hands. He felt the determination on his side and just as clearly felt the doubt and fear on hers.

Ellie's eyes widened, telling him the same instinctive knowledge flooded her. The moment stretched, weighted and silent.

She twisted away from him in a sudden movement and hurried into the house, the screen door slamming behind her.

Quinn took a deep breath, looking down at his hand as if it belonged to someone else. He wasn't sure what had just happened here. Maybe Ellie didn't know, either.

But one thing was very clear. He had to detach his mother from Ellie's father, and he had to guard his own emotions while he did so. Because Ellie Wayne had just roused feelings in him he'd never thought to have for any woman again.

Everything was going to be all right. Ellie had told herself that a dozen times by the next morning, and she still wasn't convinced. Her reaction to Quinn rattled her—she couldn't deny that. She just hoped she hadn't let him see how much.

She glanced around the Sunday school room, trying to focus on it instead of the shop. Her part-time help, young Janey Dean, would do fine without her for the mornings this week while she concentrated on vacation Bible school.

She'd pushed the tables to the side so she could set up a pretend camping area in the center for vacation Bible school. The kids would like that. Unfortunately thinking of the children made her think of Kristie, which led her thoughts right back to Kristie's father.

She had to stop this. There was a simple solution to the problem presented by Quinn Forrester. She'd avoid him, and she'd make sure her father did the same.

She knew Quinn's type, only too well. He might stay in Bedford Creek for a time, feeling guilty about his little girl. But then the need to achieve at his job would kick in, and before he even recognized what had happened, he'd be on his way back to the West Coast.

She bit her lip, thinking of Kristie. *Lord, I'm sorry. I'm being selfish. I shouldn't be hoping he goes away soon, not when his daughter wants so much for him to stay. But what can I do?*

There didn't seem to be any good answer to that question, and she suspected her prayers on the subject of Quinn had been a little self-serving.

She just had to stay away from him, she reminded herself firmly. Surely Bedford Creek was big enough to allow that. She'd stay away from him, and everything would work out fine.

The thunder of running feet announced the first arrivals for Bible school, and she turned her mind firmly toward her plans for the day.

Kristie bounced through the doorway with the earliest group, her small face beaming with pleasure. "We're here!" she shouted.

We? Ellie's heart thudded to her toes as Quinn appeared behind his daughter. He paused for a moment, his tall figure framed in the doorway. His faded jeans and white knit shirt were considerably less formal than the suit, dress shirt and tie he'd worn for church. Less formal, she found herself thinking, but not less attractive.

She forced a smile. "Good morning." She turned to the children. "Wow, you're here early. How would you like to help make a mural of Abraham's sheep?"

Luckily everyone would. She got them started with markers on the newsprint background she'd already prepared and steadfastly refused to look at the doorway. He'd go away.

Several sheep later she glanced up, and her stomach clenched. Despite her hopes, Quinn was still there.

Leaving the young artists to their work, she approached him cautiously, realizing she was being ridiculous. He wasn't going to start discussing their parents in the middle of Bible school.

"Kristie's fine," she said quietly.

"I can see that." He didn't move.

What was wrong with him? Didn't he realize parents were supposed to drop the children off and go? "You can come back for her at noon."

He arched his dark brows, as if in surprise. "Come back? I don't need to come back. I'm staying."

"Staying?" She couldn't help the way her voice rose, and she made an effort to control it. She couldn't let the children see what an undesirable effect Kristie's father had on her. "Why? If you're worried about Kristie adjusting to Bible school, you can see she's fine."

"No, of course I'm not worried about her. I know she loves coming here." Quinn's smile seemed tinged with a touch of malice. "In fact, she loves it so much she insisted I come along. She's talked me into helping with Bible school, so we can be together all the time. I'm your new assistant."

Chapter Four

For just an instant Ellie was speechless, and then anger took over. "Don't I have anything to say about who helps with my class?"

"Don't you want me?" Quinn gave her an innocent look that was belied by the satisfaction in his tone. "I thought vacation Bible school always needed extra help. I talked to the pastor about it, and he thought this was a wonderful idea."

Quinn obviously felt he'd covered all the bases, and her temper rose. "Fine." She clipped the word. "Since you want to help, suppose you supervise the class for a few minutes. I think I'd better talk with Pastor Richie myself."

She assumed he'd balk at being left alone with the children, but he just smiled. "Fine." He strolled toward the mural. "Take as long as you want."

Fuming, Ellie hurried down the hallway, passing classrooms whose teachers didn't have to worry about anything more than the lesson. *Or making visitors feel welcome.*

Her fists clenched. They always urged the children to bring a friend to Bible school. How could she turn Quinn away? But how could she possibly work with him?

She caught up with the pastor in the kitchen, where he was arranging trays of cookies and fruit for the children's snack.

"Don't we have a volunteer to do that?" she asked, diverted from her mission at the sight of Pastor Richie in an apron.

The minister's round, cherubic face creased in a smile. "Rebecca volunteered to set up refreshments before she went to the clinic, but she's feeling sick, I'm afraid. I told her we didn't require expectant mothers to help, at least not first thing in the morning." He popped a broken piece of gingerbread in his mouth. "Besides, I'm an expert on cookies."

"Speaking of help…"

He beamed. "Your new assistant, of course! Isn't it wonderful? I could hardly believe it when Quinn said he wanted to work with your class."

"Yes, well, you see…" In the face of the pastor's pleasure, it was amazingly difficult to say she didn't want him. "I'm not sure this will work out. Maybe he'd do better with a different class."

Pastor Richie wiped his hands on his apron, his gaze assessing her. He always seemed able to look right into people's minds, but never seemed surprised at what he found there.

No, not into hers. He'd never guessed the secret she hid, even from him, and for an instant she felt ashamed.

"I'm afraid a different class wouldn't work," he said slowly. "Quinn told me Kristie was counting on his presence. Poor child, she sees little enough of her father."

His words were arrows, hitting her heart. She tried to put up a shield against them. "But surely he'd feel more comfortable working with older children. Or he could help with the games."

Pastor Richie was already shaking his head. "Ellie, please. I realize it may be a little uncomfortable, having the father of one of your students there, but this is a special case. So many of us have been praying for Quinn."

"I know." How could she not? Gwen constantly asked for prayers for Quinn from her prayer partners.

Sympathetic pain flickered in Pastor Richie's eyes. "He's had a difficult time of it since his wife's death, and he hasn't let us minister to him the way we should. Don't you think God expects us to grasp this opportunity to help him if we can?''

He seemed to be putting a charge on her. Much as she'd like to avoid it, she couldn't. She tried to manage a smile. "Yes, of course, Pastor. You're right."

He squeezed her hand. "I knew you'd understand, Ellie. Perhaps God has guided Quinn to a point where he can be helped."

"I don't know that I'm the best person to help him." If the pastor knew why Quinn was here, he'd realize how true that was.

"Nonsense." He squeezed her fingers again. "Your warm heart will tell you what to do and say, my dear. Just follow it, all right?"

This situation had spun entirely out of her control, and she seemed to be out of choices. She tried to smile. "All right. I'll try."

"I don't think that's a good idea." Quinn caught the hand of the little boy who'd apparently decided he could extend the mural onto the wall. "Let's keep the markers on the paper."

The kid stuck his lower lip out. "Don't want to. You can't make me."

Okay, this was the first challenge to his authority as a teacher. Quinn suppressed a ripple of panic at the way all those little faces turned toward him. What had he gotten himself into?

''Then I guess you're finished,'' he said calmly, and took the marker away.

The boy flung himself into a chair, arms crossed over his chest, scowling fiercely. Quinn looked up to see Ellie in the doorway.

Trying to look as if he knew what he was doing, he strolled toward her.

''Trouble?'' she asked in an undertone.

''Just a little marker on the wall.'' The kid was still glaring at him. ''I hope I didn't create more trouble. He doesn't look too happy.''

''He'll get over it. A tantrum usually happens at least once a day with Robbie, no matter what we do.'' She smiled, so apparently Pastor Richie had smoothed things over for him. ''We're lucky he doesn't bite anymore.''

''Bite? Kristie didn't tell me I should come armed with a muzzle.'' He discovered he wanted to see her smile more often. It brought out a dimple at the upper corner of her mouth.

''You can always back out if it's too much for you.'' Her direct gaze challenged him.

That was exactly what he'd been thinking a few moments before, but her words made him perversely determined to stick with it, no matter what. ''Not at all. I think it'll be fun.''

Was that a shadow of disappointment in her face? If so, she masked it quickly.

''In that case, we'd better wind this down and get on to our story time.''

He watched as she gave the children a few minutes to finish what they were doing, then quietly guided them to put materials away. Kristie was among the first to stow her markers in the box, and then she danced over to him and flung her arms around him.

''I'm so glad you're here, Daddy. Are you glad you're here?''

His heart clenched as he returned her hug. ''You bet, sweetheart.''

No, he wouldn't back out on this. He watched her run back to the group, plopping down on the rug next to Ellie. His helping out this week meant too much to Kristie.

He settled on the floor at the back of the group. Besides, this was a golden opportunity to find out about Ellie Wayne and, by extension, about her father. He watched her draw the children closer to her as she opened the Bible and tried to ignore her soft smile and the way her loving glance touched each little face.

He hardened his heart. He would look at Ellie as if she were a technical problem to be solved, nothing more. By the end of the day, he should know everything he needed to.

The story was God's call to Abraham to set out for a new land. Ellie had a gift for communicating with the children, he had to admit. Her face grew even more animated, her voice changed to depict each character.

The children leaned forward, as intent as if they were watching the latest cartoon or playing a video game. Maybe they were drawn by the power of the story, or maybe by the warmth Ellie projected. Whatever it was, she had them hooked.

As the morning wore on, he found himself wondering how much she needed his help. His mother had assured him that an extra pair of hands was always welcome at Bible school, but Ellie seemed to have everything under control. She moved the class easily from one activity to the next. The most useful thing he'd found to do was to pass out crayons.

Then Robbie planted himself in front of Quinn. The scowl was gone, but the kid's look challenged him. What now? He felt a stir of unease.

"You're Kristie's daddy," Robbie announced.

"That's right."

"Why don't you have red hair like hers?"

This didn't seem the place for a lecture on genetics. "Kristie has red hair like her aunt. I have dark hair like my dad did."

"I don't like red hair."

From the corner of his eye he caught a flash of hurt on his daughter's face. His heart clenched involuntarily, and the depth of his anger astonished him.

Before he could say anything, Ellie steered Robbie back to the table. "God made all of us different," she said calmly. "It would be a pretty boring world if we looked the same. I happen to think Kristie's hair is a beautiful color." She touched her own dark brown curls. "Much more interesting than my plain old brown."

She'd handled it far better than he would have, he realized, and he wasn't sure how he felt about that. If he could, he'd protect his daughter from every bump in the road. Something winced painfully inside him. He'd already learned the hard way how impossible it was to protect the people he loved.

Ten minutes later Robbie was back, and he tensed. But this time the boy didn't look quite as belligerent. "Ms. Ellie says Abraham did what God wanted him to."

"Right." What was driving this kid?

"What I want to know is, how did he know what God wanted? She says God spoke to him, but I never heard God say anything."

He longed to look at Ellie for guidance. Or even to have her come to the rescue. But he wouldn't be much of a helper if he couldn't answer a simple question.

"Maybe not with your ears," he said, remembering a long-ago Sunday school class and his own questions. "But what about with your heart?" He touched the child's striped shirt. "Didn't you ever have a feeling right in here that there was something you should do? Or maybe something you shouldn't do?"

Robbie's face clouded. "I guess so. Sometimes."

"We have to learn to listen with our hearts," Ellie said, and he realized she'd caught their exchange, realized, too, that the rest of the class was listening. "That takes practice, but the more you try, the better you'll get." Her gaze met his, and she smiled approvingly.

He began to regret his quick words the day before about teaching spiritual lessons to kids. Maybe he understood her attitude a little better now than he had then. And maybe he'd bitten off more than he should, given his own distance from God in the last two years.

It wasn't until they'd taken the class outside for games that he finally had a chance to talk to Ellie without an audience. Several high school kids had been recruited as game leaders, giving the teachers time to catch their breath.

Ellie sat on the grass under one of the birch trees, her full denim skirt spread around her. He sat down next to her and leaned back on his elbows, surprisingly tired by the morning spent with the kids. And Ellie.

He glanced toward her to find her giving him a measuring look. "How are you holding up? Was it what you expected?" Her earlier anger seemed to be gone entirely.

"Well, it's not quite as tough as building a dam," he admitted. "But almost."

"I'm surprised you were able to take this much time off from your work." She plucked a few strands of long grass, plaiting them without looking, as if her fingers were on automatic pilot.

"I was due some leave." His thoughts flickered to the flood-control project, nearly finished now.

"You don't look as if it was that simple to get away." Ellie plaited a red clover flower into the braid.

"It's never simple." He inhaled the fresh scent of newly cut grass and found himself relaxing. "There's never a good time to get away from a project. That's part of the job."

"I suppose things were easier to handle when Kristie's mother was alive."

For an instant he wanted to flare out at her, to say it wasn't any of her business. But then something— maybe the warmth in her eyes, maybe the cheerful cries of the children playing in the distance and the soft hum of a bee buzzing in the clover—stilled his quick response.

"Not necessarily easier. Julie tried to support my

career, but she never wanted to go where the corps sent me.''

"That's why she and Kristie came here?''

"She didn't want to go out West.'' He tried not to sound resentful. "She thought they were better off here, where my family could support her.''

He clamped his mouth shut, pressing his hands flat into the warm grass. She probably knew the rest of the story. Julie, driving back from a shopping trip on a rainy night, the drunk driver who'd wiped her out with a careless swerve. Everyone in Bedford Creek knew that.

"I'm sorry,'' she said, her voice soft. Her hand brushed his with a butterfly touch. "I didn't know her very well, I'm afraid. And I can't say I understand, because I've never lost anyone like that.''

He nodded, not looking at her, but somehow soothed. Most people either avoided the subject entirely, as if embarrassed, or claimed they understood. Either response was hurtful, but generally he preferred avoidance. He could manage not to think about Julie when people who didn't know about it surrounded him.

He'd set out this morning to find out more about Ellie. As the children rushed toward them, their playtime over, he realized that he'd just revealed more than he had learned. He wasn't quite sure how that had happened.

* * *

"Dad, I'm just too busy to talk now." Ellie hoped she didn't sound as edgy as she felt. She glanced across the counter of the shop at her father late that afternoon. "I know you're trying to help, but I need to balance these books myself."

Her father looked wounded, as if she thought he couldn't be trusted with the shop's accounts. Maybe that was true, but she didn't want to hurt his feelings.

"There must be something I can do to help you. Any errands that have to be run?" Charles brightened a little at the thought. He really seemed to enjoy being out and about in Bedford Creek, accomplishing some small chore. Maybe it reminded him of the days when he'd been known and respected in another place.

Her gaze landed on the poster order for the crafts fair, ready to go to the printer. She'd intended to take it herself, but she'd been busy with Bible school. "Would you like to take this up to the printer's? I've already talked with them about it."

He seized the sheaf of papers. "Of course, Princess. I'll take care of that immediately. You don't need to worry about a thing."

Of course she'd worry, how could she help it? But she managed a smile. "Thanks. That's a big help."

It was much the same thing she'd say to a child who'd offered to erase the board, but her father beamed as if she'd given him a present. Somehow that happiness touched a long-forgotten chord in her heart, echoing with memories of the pride and love she once felt for him.

"Daddy..." The word came out without volition. She slid from her stool and took a quick step toward him, kissing his cheek lightly. "Thanks."

He blinked, then nodded and started out the door, clutching the papers carefully. He paused to hold it for the person who was coming in. Quinn.

Her nerves jangled in tune with the bell over the door. Why was he here? And how much of her confused feelings for her father had been written on her face when he walked in?

"Quinn. I didn't expect to see you again today." That probably sounded unwelcoming.

He'd been watching her father walk jauntily up the street, but he turned at her words and surveyed her. She resisted the urge to be sure her hair was tidy. It never was, and today wouldn't be any different. Anyway, she didn't care what Quinn thought of her looks.

"Your father helping out with the shop?" He sauntered over to the counter, and she retreated behind it.

"No." She resisted the urge to tell him it was none of his business. That would just make him more interested, if that were possible. "He's taking the craft show posters to the printer for me."

"Must be nice having him around. I understand

you hadn't seen each other for a long time." His words were casual, but his gray eyes were alert.

Hannibal, perhaps recognizing Quinn's voice, jumped lightly from the show window to the floor and rubbed against his legs. Quinn bent to scratch behind the cat's ears, giving Ellie a moment to regroup and decide how to respond to his unspoken question.

"My father had been working in another state for several years before he retired," she said neutrally. "Is there something I can do for you?"

He straightened. "I'm here to do the planning for tomorrow."

"Tomorrow?" She looked at him blankly.

"Bible school," he said. "Remember? I know I wasn't much help today, but I really can do more than just pass out crayons. I thought we could plan the lesson together."

That was the last thing she'd expected. She'd assumed he wanted nothing more than to be at Bible school with his daughter. That was certainly enough participation to satisfy Kristie.

"That's not necessary." She realized that sounded as if she thought he couldn't do it, and embarrassment flooded her. First her father, now Quinn. She seemed to be making a habit of clumsy words. "I mean, you don't have to do any of the actual teaching."

He raised an eyebrow, amusement showing in his face. "Does that mean you think I can't?"

"No, of course not." She was going from bad to worse. "I'm sure you can, but since your aim is to spend time with your daughter, you don't need to well, do anything more than be an aide."

"That is what I had in mind originally." He leaned against the counter, the movement bringing him closer to her. His long fingers brushed the basket of sachet that sat there, releasing the scent of last summer's roses.

"Well, then…"

"But I've changed my mind."

She wanted to tell him to change it back, but she could hardly do that. "Why?"

"Remember Robbie?" He smiled suddenly, his whole face lightening, and her pulse accelerated.

"I couldn't forget him. If anything, I'd think Robbie would make you want to run in the other direction. He usually has that effect on people."

"Tempting," he admitted. "But just for a minute there today I felt as if I reached him. That's a feeling I hadn't had for a while." His mouth quirked a bit, as if he mocked himself. "I think I'd like to feel that way again."

Something squeezed her heart, and she remembered Pastor Richie's words. She'd wanted to reject them at the time, but maybe he'd been right.

Unlikely as it seemed, perhaps God was giving her a chance to minister to Quinn Forrester. Little though she might like it, no matter how dangerous to her secret it might be, she couldn't turn away.

Chapter Five

Quinn waited, watching the thoughts chasing across Ellie's mobile, expressive face. This clearly wasn't how she'd expected things to go, and he suspected she didn't know what to make of it.

Fair enough. That's how he felt about the morning at Bible school. Something about Ellie, maybe the warmth and sympathy she exuded, had changed things between them.

If that warmth and sympathy were real, those qualities should work to his advantage now. She'd have to say yes. He waited, leaning against the counter as if he had all the time in the world.

Finally Ellie nodded, a reluctant smile tugging at her lips. "Okay. If that's really what you want. Believe me, it's harder than it looks. And I can get a bit possessive about those kids. Their spiritual well-being is important to me.''

''You think I'm not up to the challenge?'' He raised his eyebrows. ''Think I can't handle it?''

''I think you might be surprised at the questions they ask.''

''You're forgetting, I have personal experience of that with Kristie.''

Not enough, not lately, a little voice whispered in his mind. He thought again of Kristie's birthday wish, and guilt stabbed him. But he couldn't marry someone just to provide Kristie with a mother.

Ellie kindly didn't point out that he hadn't been around to answer many questions recently. ''Do you want to work on the lesson now?''

The cat leaped to the counter, and he stroked the animal, wondering if Ellie would try to put him off. ''I can come back later, if that's better. I know how hard it must be, juggling the shop and your volunteer work during tourist season.''

Later. He could practically see her mind working behind those dark-lashed eyes. *When her father would be here.*

''No, that's all right. We can do it now. Monday's not a busy day in the shop, and I have a good part-time helper when I need her. Have a seat.'' She gestured toward the round oak table in the corner of the shop. ''I'll get my book.'' She spun and disappeared quickly up the staircase, her heels clicking on the bare wooden treads.

One hurdle over, he thought, strolling to the table. He scanned the area behind the counter. Nothing there but business-related things, probably, and he wasn't about to start rifling through her books, even if he thought it would give him answers. Although if he continued to come up blank on the elusive Mr. Wayne, he might be tempted.

The oak table, its surface scarred by years of use, held a scattering of craft supplies. Ellie must have been using the breaks in her day to work on some of the things she sold in her shop. He brushed a skein of yarn from the spot in front of the chair. He hadn't been idle today, either, but she'd probably been more productive than he had.

He'd been trying to find out something—any-thing—about Charles Wayne. He'd been remarkably unsuccessful. The man seemed to have no history. So he was here, looking for answers.

What he'd told Ellie was true, as far as it went. He did find the kids intriguing. He did want to do some-thing more useful than pass out crayons.

But he had an aim that wasn't quite so altruistic. He intended, one way or another, to find out some concrete fact about the Wayne family. Something, one little bit of information, that would unravel their past and lead him to the truth.

He angled his chair a little closer to the one Ellie had obviously been using. Hannibal twined around his legs, then leaped lightly to the table and nosed inquiringly at a pile of corn husks.

"I don't think she wants you to get into those." Quinn lifted him away and sat down. He thought the cat would escape, but instead it settled on his lap, kneaded his jeans a time or two and purred.

"You're right about that." Ellie crossed to the table, her step light. "I don't know what the attraction is, but every time I work with corn husks, Hannibal tries to appropriate them." She tickled the cat's ears. "They're not on his diet, believe me."

"What on earth can you do with a corn husk?" He watched as she put the book down in front of him, moved her chair an inch farther from him and sat down with a rustle of denim.

Nervous—yes, Ellie was definitely nervous. Her color, always vivid, was a touch brighter, her movements a little quicker. Even her cloud of dark hair seemed to spark with nervous energy, as if it would shock him if he touched it. He suppressed the desire to find out.

"Corn husks? Lots of things." She seemed relieved to talk about a neutral subject.

He was happy to let her. Let her relax, feel at ease with him. Then she might relax her guard enough to say something useful.

"Lots of things like what?" He wasn't really interested in crafts, but it would keep her talking.

"Corn husk wreaths, corn husk flowers, corn husk dolls." She picked up something that had been partially hidden beneath the pile of loose husks. "Like this one."

He took it from her, turning it in his hands. "It's an angel." The tiny halo was braided from corn silk, and the wings cut from a single husk.

"People will start buying now for Christmas." She picked up another one, half-made. "I like to think of my angels on so many different Christmas trees, in so many homes."

He thought again of the way that her hands had caressed the handmade quilt the first time he'd seen her. That hadn't been a salesperson's ploy. She was doing the same thing now, with the half-finished doll.

"You make something out of nothing." He felt a little envious. His job was controlling things, not creating.

She shook her head, smiling a little. "Only God does that. I make something out of things other people would throw away."

"Why?" He wanted, suddenly, to know more than facts about her background. He wanted to know who Ellie Wayne was inside.

"Why?" She looked startled, as if she hadn't considered the question. "I don't know. I guess because it's satisfying. To take an object someone might consider useless and create a thing of beauty from it might not be great art, but it's creative. It makes me happy.''

For a moment they were still, her words hanging in the air between them in the cozy shop. The grandfather clock against the wall ticked, and the cat purred on his lap. *It made her happy.* He'd wanted to know what she was like, and she'd shown him a piece of herself.

Her gaze slid away from his, long dark lashes shielding her eyes. She dropped the doll and picked up the Bible school book. "We'd better get to work."

Before you give anything else away? Is that what you're thinking, Ellie?

She leafed through the book to the lesson for the next day, and he hitched his chair closer to hers. She glanced up, wary again, and he smiled.

"Can't see the book from over there."

"It—it's too bad we didn't order two teacher books for the class. But I didn't expect to have a helper." She spread the book flat and slid it toward him. "Here we are. Tomorrow's lesson is a tough one to teach children. They'll love the story of Isaac's birth, but the sacrifice is hard to deal with."

"Especially at this age." His mind flew, inevitably, to Kristie. "How do you handle it?" He lifted an eyebrow. "You did notice I said 'you.' I'm not going to touch that one."

Her generous mouth relaxed in a smile. "See? I told you it was tougher than it looked."

"Touché." He lifted his hands in a gesture of surrender. "You're the authority. I'm the rank amateur. Give me something I can't mess up."

She nodded, the smile lingering on her lips, and turned to the book.

They worked their way through the lesson, discussing each part, dividing up the responsibilities. With her attention on teaching, Ellie seemed to forget her wariness where he was concerned. She gestured, excited about a concept, laughing over something a child had said about a Bible story.

He liked it, he realized. He liked the way her face lit up, liked the caring that shone in her eyes. That couldn't possibly be faked.

And he liked more than that. That bountiful hair of hers, escaping as always from the tie that was supposed to hold it back, brushed his shoulder. It tickled his cheek when she leaned close to point out the memory verse for the day. Her scent teased him to identify it, something as fresh and natural as she was herself.

She glanced up from the book suddenly, her gaze tangling with his. Her eyes widened as if she'd just read his thoughts, and her hand clenched on the page.

"That's about it," she said quickly. "I can get the activity sheets ready. You don't need to help with that. I'm sure you want to get home."

"Not at all." He smiled blandly. "My mother took Kristie to play with a friend, so I'm on my own until supper. I'll help."

Her hand went down flat on a stack of construction paper. "You don't have to."

"If I can build a dam, I can certainly cut out a camel." He held out his hand for the scissors. "Give me a break, Ellie."

That was just what she didn't want to do—he could sense it. Her mouth tightened a little, but she handed over the scissors without another protest.

"So that is what you do?" She picked up a sheet of construction paper and snipped busily, not looking up at him again. A lock of dark hair fell dangerously close to the scissors blades, and she shook it back. "Build dams?"

"Mostly." He cut carefully around a camel's tail, feeling as if his hands were too big for the scissors. "I do flood-control projects. We're finishing up a big one out West."

"You like it out there." It was a statement, not a question.

He considered. "Like it? I hadn't thought of it that way. I like the work I'm doing. It's important." *And it keeps me too busy and too tired to feel.*

"I guess it must be quite a change from Bedford Creek."

She was leading him to talk about himself to keep the focus off herself, he realized. But there was more than one way to get where he wanted.

"Every place is a change after growing up in Bedford Creek," he said easily. "I didn't realize until I was grown what an idyllic childhood we had here. Safe streets, everyone knew us, we could go anywhere in town and have people around who cared for us."

"That must have been nice." Something wistful touched her voice.

He grinned. "I'd have to say we didn't always appreciate it, not when we were doing something we didn't want to get back to our parents."

"We?" She took her attention off cutting long enough to shoot him a sideways glance.

"My sisters first, then Brett and I after he moved in next door. We were in and out of each other's houses like we lived there."

Her mouth curved in a reminiscent smile. "My friend Libby and I were like that. All those endless pajama parties."

"Guys don't have pajama parties. Not macho enough. We camped out in the backyard. You still in touch with her?"

"Libby? No." There was a pointed finality in the word, along with regret.

"Too bad." He kept his tone casual. "Why not?"

"I—we moved away."

All his senses went on alert. Her tension was palpable. Something about that move was important.

"Too bad. It's tough to move away from your friends. How old were you?"

She shrugged with a pretense of unconcern that didn't work. "Not so young. And not so far away. I was eighteen."

"That's when you went to Philadelphia?"

"Not right away. I worked in Columbus for a while."

So, perhaps, that hometown Charles had mentioned was somewhere near Columbus. And she'd left there after something traumatic happened when she was eighteen. Could he risk another question without sending all her barriers up?

"Did your father go to Columbus with you?"

The shutters slammed down on her expression, closing him out. "No." She swept a hand across the table, gathering together the animals she'd been cutting out. "I think I'll finish this evening. There's some shop work I really need to get done now." She stood, and it was a clear invitation to him to leave.

He got up slowly. So he'd been getting too close, and she didn't intend to let him stick around. His gaze traced the taut line of her neck, the tension that clouded those bright eyes.

"Okay, Ellie. I'll be on my way, then. I'll see you in the morning."

"Fine." She didn't look as if the thought gave her much pleasure.

Actually, what he was thinking wasn't giving him much pleasure, either. The idea that had been floating around in the back of his mind settled into a reluctant certainty.

Ellie was hiding something about herself and her father. She wouldn't tell him what that something was, not of her own volition. So he'd have to do it another way. He'd hire a private investigator to trace Charles Wayne's past.

It was the logical thing to do, he assured himself as Ellie showed him to the door. He had to protect his mother. If the investigation didn't show anything harmful, Ellie need never know about it.

So why did the whole idea make him feel as if he was betraying her?

Ellie pulled the shop van carefully into Gwen's driveway the next afternoon. She'd rather be almost anywhere else than here, where she might run into Quinn yet again. But she and Gwen had arranged to drive to Henderson this afternoon to pick up the display panels for the craft show, and that needed to be done today.

Besides, Quinn probably wasn't here anyway. She'd pick up Gwen and be on her way, with no further chances for him to pick her brains or probe her past or upset her senses with his sheer masculine presence.

Now where had that come from? She wasn't upset by him, not in that way. She couldn't be. She wasn't attracted, didn't find her pulse accelerating when he smiled, didn't feel a flood of warmth when his hand brushed hers.

Yeah, right, a sarcastic little voice in her brain commented.

She turned off the ignition, wishing she could just honk the horn for Gwen. But that would be rude, especially since Quinn was right there in front of her, pulling a weed from the flower bed that overflowed with cosmos, phlox and marigolds.

As she slid from the van he straightened in a swift, smooth movement and stood looking at her. Her heart gave an odd little flutter, and she told it sternly to behave.

After all, they'd spent the morning together at Bible school, and she'd managed to keep working with him strictly businesslike. She wasn't going to let her guard down now.

"Hi. Is Gwen ready?"

He raised an eyebrow, causing another rebellious little flutter. "Ready?"

"We have an appointment to go to Henderson to pick up some things for the craft show." She glanced at her watch. "I'm a few minutes late, I'm afraid."

"She's not here."

She stared at him blankly. "Not here? But we made arrangements ages ago to go to Henderson today."

"She took Kristie shopping." He took a step toward her, and sunlight slanting between the big trees touched his face with gold. "They were going all the way to the mall in Cedarton, so I don't expect them back for hours."

"But…" She forced herself to concentrate on the problem, not Quinn. What was Gwen thinking of?

"Are you sure your plans were for today?"

"Of course I'm sure. We knew it would take two of us to manage the display panels, and this was the only afternoon that suited both of us."

"She'll be upset that she forgot." He frowned, as if it was up to him to solve the problem. "Any chance you can do it tomorrow?"

Frustrated, she shook her head. "We're borrowing them from a gallery there, and it's closed on Wednesdays." She'd have to go alone, that was all.

Quinn brushed off the knees of his jeans and turned

toward the porch. "Just wait while I leave a note for my mother."

She blinked. "What do you mean?"

"Isn't it obvious?" He lifted his straight brows. "I'll go with you."

"No—I mean, that's not necessary," she said quickly. She'd manage the job herself, somehow. Anything was better than going with Quinn.

"Don't be silly." Quinn's smile bore a hint of challenge. "You'll just have to make do with a different Forrester, that's all."

"You don't need to do that." The thought of driving all the way to Henderson and back alone with him in the van put a note of panic in her voice.

He ignored her protest. "I'll just be a minute." He took the porch steps two at a time. "Then we can get on the road."

She took a deep breath, suppressing the urge to leap in the van and drive away. Doing that would only make Quinn more suspicious than he already was.

She didn't want to spend the afternoon with him. She was afraid to. But before she could come up with an alternative, he was back.

"Ready?" He looked at her inquiringly.

She swallowed hard, then nodded and climbed back into the driver's seat. Quinn settled next to her, buckling his seat belt, and she started the van.

She backed out of the driveway cautiously, wishing for something that would dissipate her awareness of his solid form, just inches away. Something that would erase the warmth she felt when he glanced across at her. And the flutter of her pulse when he leaned close to switch on the radio, and the spicy scent of his aftershave as it touched her senses.

This had to stop. But she didn't know any way to make that happen. Like it or not, and she told herself fiercely that she didn't, Quinn seemed able to reach past the barriers she'd built around herself. He aroused feelings she'd thought were safely buried. And she didn't know what to do about it.

Chapter Six

"Are you hungry enough to share an extralarge?" Quinn glanced at Ellie across the red-and-white-checked tablecloth. The mingled aromas of tomato sauce and cheese filled the air of the small restaurant in Henderson.

Ellie shrugged, as if unwilling to commit herself. "We didn't need to stop for supper." She'd been saying that for the last fifteen minutes, and he'd been ignoring it just as long.

They'd finished the errands Ellie had to do that afternoon for the craft show. Then he'd spotted the pizza parlor, and he'd realized how long it had been since lunch. He'd overridden Ellie's objections, and here they were.

Apparently giving up the argument, Ellie accepted

a menu and flipped it open. She held it between them like a barricade.

"So what's it going to be? Pepperoni or mushrooms? Or are you a nontraditionalist when it comes to pizza? I see they have pineapple."

"Whatever you like." She closed the menu again. "I don't care." It was as if she feared sharing anything personal with him, even her taste in pizza.

"You must care. Everyone has an opinion on pizza." He kept his voice light.

She shrugged. "Okay, mushrooms." She said it as if determined to humor him.

"That wasn't so hard, was it?"

She met his gaze, startled, and he smiled. "It's okay to say what'll make you happy, Ellie."

"I'm already happy," she said quickly. "The panels are just what I hoped. They'll be perfect for the show. I really appreciate your help." Her gaze slid away from his, as if she remembered how reluctant she'd been to let him come.

"Glad to help." That wasn't quite true. To be exact, he'd been glad of an opportunity to be in her company. He'd figured they couldn't possibly do a forty-mile drive together without his learning something useful.

But so far it wasn't working out that way. Instead of probing, he'd found himself relaxing and enjoying the trip. Enjoying her company, without worrying about what he was finding out. When he'd seen the Italian restaurant, it had been too tempting to prolong the enjoyment.

He gave their order to the waitress, trying to shelve any other thought. When the woman moved away, he glanced across at Ellie again. She was busily folding one of the red-and-white napkins.

"What's the matter? Aren't you satisfied with the way they fold those?"

She stared at it, as if she hadn't realized what her fingers were doing. "Sorry." She set the napkin on the table, and he saw that it had been folded into the shape of a rabbit. "I guess I do that automatically."

"Very neat." He tweaked the bunny's floppy ears. "Is there anything you can't make?"

She tilted her head, considering. "Plenty of things, I'm afraid. I can't build a dam, believe it or not."

"But you can turn napkins into rabbits. Where did you learn how to do that? Don't tell me they have napkin-folding classes in school."

She shrugged, a touch of sadness in her eyes. "My mother taught me. She loved doing things like that."

"I thought it was always just you and your father." He thought of Kristie, also motherless, and his heart cramped. Still, she'd found substitutes for Julie in his mother and sisters, hadn't she?

"My mother died when I was eight." Ellie looked almost surprised that she was confiding in him.

"Just a little older than Kristie. Maybe that's why she's grown so fond of you. She recognizes the bond." They had a bond forged of shared experiences and similar pain. "No aunts and uncles and grandparents?"

"Just my father." Her mouth tightened on the words, as if she didn't intend to let anything else out.

"That must have made the two of you very close," he said quietly. For the first time, he wasn't mentioning her father in order to pry. He just wanted—he tried to analyze his motives. The truth was, he didn't know what he wanted. To understand her, maybe.

She seemed to weigh his words for a moment, then nodded. "Yes, we were close. He was everything to me."

Something pained and private showed briefly. He fought against the urge to touch her cheek, to caress that secret grief away.

Instead he wrapped his hand around his glass. That was probably safer. "I guess that's not what my daughter would say about me." Still, it was better, wasn't it, that she didn't have to depend only on him?

"Kristie's luckier than I was." Ellie seemed to hear the concern he didn't want to voice. "She has a loving family to count on, as well as her father. And she knows you love her."

"Does she?" He didn't intend to let his worries about Kristie out, but he couldn't help it.

"Of course she does." She reached across the table, impulsively gripping his hand. Their palms linked, fingers intertwined.

For a moment they looked at each other without barriers, as if they'd known each other a long time and were about to know each other even better. It might have been a moment full of promise, the kind of moment when a man and a woman realize that something good could happen between them.

But it couldn't. He had to remember that. Because just a few short hours ago, he'd hired a firm of private investigators to look into her father's past.

If—when—Ellie found that out, she wouldn't be able to forgive him. And he suddenly realized that mattered far more than it should.

"Do you know you're the most stubborn woman in the world?"

Ellie glanced quickly at Quinn, but amusement showed in his eyes, not irritation. She relaxed, balancing the awkward panel they were trying to put into the storage closet at the church. Being alone here with Quinn ought to make her wary, but instead it felt as if they'd been working together for years.

"I don't know what's being so stubborn about putting these away. I was sure we'd be able to store the panels here until after Bible school. Maybe it'll go in if we turn it sideways."

Quinn's gaze seemed to measure the panel, then the doorway, and he shook his head. "We can stand it on its head, if you want, but it's not going to fit. You can't put a six-foot panel in a five-foot opening."

"Is that the engineer speaking?"

His sudden smile made her heart contract. "Trust me. I'll get out my slide rule, if you like."

"Not necessary." She gave the awkward-size panel another frustrated push. It bounced harmlessly against the doorframe.

"Stubborn," he murmured again.

"We have to store them somewhere out of the way." She wiped her damp forehead. The August heat had built up in the church since the morning.

He sighed with elaborate patience. "Not even an engineer can fit a six-foot panel—"

"—into a five-foot opening. I know. I got that part." She liked feeling this relaxed around Quinn, liked the way the afternoon had gone. All her fears about this time together had been groundless.

Quinn glanced around the large room. "Why don't we just prop them against the wall? They won't take up much space."

"We have Bible school opening exercises in this room, remember? Do you really want them out where the children might knock them down?"

"We could put a Don't Touch sign on them."

She smiled. "Would that stop Kristie?"

His baritone chuckle seemed to vibrate in the air between them, almost as if it touched her. "No, I guess not. Okay, the engineer knows they won't fit in the closet, but the teacher knows they can't be left out. What do we do?"

Again she felt as if they'd been working together comfortably for years. "Well…" She glanced around the room, much as he'd done a moment earlier.

The cement block walls didn't offer any answer. But along the far side, a series of coat racks had been installed in wooden frames, forming a wide, high shelf on top. "What about up there?"

Quinn sized up the shelf, then lifted the panel. "Looks like it might work. We'll give it a try."

"Let me help carry that." She reached for the end of the awkward panel, but he hefted it easily.

"I've got it. You can bring a chair for me to stand on."

For a moment she stayed where she was, watching the ripple of muscles as he carried the panel across the room. His broad shoulders and lithe movements suggested that he'd managed far heavier burdens.

He put the load down, then looked at her with raised brows. "A chair?"

Sure her cheeks were red, she hurried to drag a metal folding chair across to him. What was wrong with her? She couldn't stand around watching him as if she were a love-struck teenager. All right, he was an attractive man. She'd been around plenty of attractive men without letting it throw her off balance.

Quickly, before he could take it from her, she climbed onto the chair. "You hand them to me, and I'll slide them up."

He frowned. "Maybe I should do that. It's not easy to lift something above your head."

"I'm perfectly capable of doing it. After all, if Gwen were with me, I'd be doing the lifting." She smiled. "Although she'd probably give me an argument."

"She probably would." His frown deepened, but he held the panel up to her. "I don't remember her being quite so assertive in the past."

Perhaps he was beginning to realize that Gwen wasn't the passive, protected mother he remembered. If so, that would be good for all of them.

"Maybe she's grown more independent since your father's death. She's probably had to take care of things she'd never done before."

He paused as he lifted the next panel. "You think that's a good thing?"

Whatever she said, it had to be tactful, bearing in mind his own grief. She breathed a silent prayer for guidance.

"I suppose," she said carefully, "that it can be an example of God bringing good out of something tragic. Your mother didn't need to fend for herself before. But now she's discovered some strength she didn't know she had.''

''Maybe,'' he said, but he didn't sound convinced.

She hesitated, wondering if she should say anything more—that she'd worked with Gwen on committees, that she'd seen her gaining confidence and trying things she hadn't attempted in the past.

But would anything she said end up sounding self-serving? She certainly didn't want to destroy the harmony between them by reminding him of his concerns about her father.

''Will this one fit?'' He lifted the last of the panels, and the opportunity slipped away before she could decide.

''I think so.'' She eased it onto the stack, shoving it as far back as possible so there'd be no danger of them sliding to the floor. ''There, that's done it.''

''A job well-done.'' He smiled up at her, the tension around his eyes relaxing. ''Congratulations.'' Before she could climb down, he grasped her waist and lifted her to the floor.

Her breath caught. His strong hands held her securely, and she automatically clasped his upper arms for balance. His muscles felt smooth and strong under the fabric of his denim shirt.

Don't look up. Don't meet his eyes.

But that caution seemed beyond her control. She

glanced up, to find his face very close to hers. His eyes darkened. The muscles under her hands tightened, as if he would pull her against him.

Then he snatched his hands away as if he'd touched something hot. Ellie took a quick step back from Quinn. Was she crazy? How had she let this happen?

"Maybe it's time we called it a day," Quinn said.

"I'll get my keys."

For an instant he looked disconcerted, as if he'd forgotten he couldn't just walk away from her. "I'd say I'll walk, but it's getting late."

"Of course I'll drive you." She grabbed her bag and fumbled for her church keys.

Quinn stood waiting while she found them, waited again while she shut off the lights and locked the outside door. They walked across the gravel lot to the van, their steps matching almost as if they belonged together.

No, they didn't belong together. They couldn't, no matter how appealing it might sound.

She stole a quick glance at Quinn's face. She'd been wrong when she told herself there wasn't any tension between them—very wrong. Tension sizzled in the very air when she looked at him.

It had to stop. It had to stop now. She couldn't let herself feel attracted to Quinn—she certainly couldn't let herself get involved with him.

She couldn't be honest with him. And she knew him well enough already to know that was the one thing he'd never forgive.

Ellie pulled into the driveway, coming to a stop near the side door that led into Gwen's kitchen. Thank him, let him out, and then she could go home and give herself a stern talking-to.

"Thanks again for helping me. I really appreciate it."

"It was a pleasure."

Even though she knew it was unwise, she couldn't keep herself from looking at him. That really was pleasure in his eyes, and it set her pulse fluttering all over again.

She glanced away again, before the moment could become too personal. "It looks as if your mother's home now." Yellow light spilled from the kitchen window in the gathering dusk.

"So it does." He reached across to close his hand over hers on the ignition key. "You may as well come in. She'll want to apologize and explain and hear all about it anyway."

What she ought to do was run the other direction. Instead she found herself switching off the motor, sliding out of the van.

"Just for a moment," she said, falling into step

with Quinn again. She wasn't sure whether she was telling him or herself.

He smiled, then touched her waist lightly as if to shepherd her inside when he opened the door.

They took two steps into the kitchen. Ellie felt Quinn freeze behind her.

Gwen sat at the kitchen table, the remains of a meal in front of her. But she wasn't alone. Ellie's father sat next to her, and they looked up with identically guilty expressions.

Her heart thudded to the soles of her feet. Oh, no. Why now? Why, when she and Quinn had grown so comfortable together, did this have to happen? He would think...

Ellie looked at Quinn. If Gwen's expression had been easy to read, Quinn's was even easier. Anger and accusation battled for supremacy. He obviously thought he'd been manipulated, and he'd just as clearly concluded that she'd been in on it.

The accusing look in Quinn's eyes cut Ellie to the heart. For a moment all she could feel was a sense of loss. The rapport that had begun between them had vanished as if it had never been.

Gwen's kitchen should have been a cozy place, with its old-fashioned glass-front cabinets and ivy in brass pots spilling over the shelves on either side of the sink. But the coziest setting couldn't dissipate the tension that crackled from Quinn, and Gwen's guilty expression didn't make things any better.

"What's going on here?" Ice coated Quinn's words.

"Going on?" Gwen's voice rose along with her eyebrows. "Nothing is 'going on.' We're having dessert and coffee."

The mingled aromas of coffee and cherry pie were normally appealing, but they'd lost their charm for Ellie. Her father had let her down once again. She'd asked him not to annoy Quinn further by pursuing his friendship with Gwen. He'd promised to be tactful. And now he'd gone behind her back and done something that made matters worse.

She took a breath, trying to still the tension that crackled along her nerves. Smooth the situation over; get her father out of there. That was the only thing she could do.

Please, Daddy, don't say anything that will rile Quinn even more.

Apparently her father didn't hear her silent plea. He gave Quinn his charming smile and rose, gesturing to a chair. "Won't you join us? I'm sure there's more coffee, and Gwen's pie is wonderful."

Ellie could almost feel Quinn's temper rising at her father's calm assumption of the role of host in his house, and for a second she wondered how she'd become so attuned to him. But this was no time to speculate.

"We'd better get home, Dad. I'll drive you." She didn't want to know what he was doing here, didn't want to know where he and Gwen had been that afternoon. She just wanted to be out of there before Quinn blew up.

"But Ellie, I'm not finished. You can't ask me to leave the best pie I've ever—"

Quinn cut across his praise for Gwen's pie. "Did you forget you were supposed to go with Ellie to Henderson, Mom?" His glare at Charles made it clear whom he blamed for her forgetfulness.

"Oh, my goodness!" Gwen's astonishment would be comical in any other situation. "Oh, Ellie, dear, I'm so sorry. I'm afraid it went completely out of my mind." She got up, fluttering around the table to hug Ellie. "Did you go and get those panels all by yourself? My dear, you shouldn't have."

"No, she didn't." Quinn's exasperation seemed to mount. "She was counting on you, and you weren't here. So I went with her."

"You did?" Gwen's round face creased in a smile, and she reached up to pat his cheek. "That was so sweet of you, dear. Well, it's all taken care of, then, and no harm's been done."

She turned away, seeming to consider the matter ended. For an instant, Ellie glimpsed a self-satisfied expression on her face, as if things had worked out just as Gwen intended, and a little jolt of tension pricked her. What was Gwen up to?

"Mom, that's not the point. You were supposed to help Ellie."

Gwen raised her eyebrows in surprise. "But Quinn, didn't you enjoy going with her?"

Ellie could only be glad the question hadn't been directed at her. She couldn't admit how much she'd enjoyed the afternoon in Quinn's company. The memory of those moments in Fellowship Hall flooded through her.

"Dad, I think we should leave now." She nudged her father, but he was doing a fine job of remaining oblivious to her hints.

Quinn's brows lowered as he glared at Charles, who got up from his chair. "Perhaps that would be a good idea. My mother and I need to talk."

That seemed to dent Charles's armor. His smile faltered, and he took a step.

"Quinn!" Gwen put a protective hand on Charles's shoulder. "That's no way for you to talk to a guest in my house. I'm ashamed of you." She looked like a pretty ruffled hen, shaking her finger at Quinn as she must have done when he was ten.

"Really, Gwen, we have to leave." Ellie tugged on her father's arm, trying to suppress a totally inappropriate desire to laugh at the ridiculous situation.

She and Quinn were united in one thing—they both wanted her father out of Gwen's kitchen immediately.

"Mother, I'm only trying to do what's best." Quinn sounded as if he'd gone too far and knew it.

"I'm perfectly capable of deciding what's best for myself, and so is Charles." Gwen's rare temper had been thoroughly roused. "You children have no business interfering."

Ellie's gaze met Quinn's. For a fraction of a second they shared a blend of exasperation and amusement, as if they were partners, colleagues. Friends. Then Quinn's eyes turned frosty as he seemed to remember that she was the cause of his predicament.

Charles finally moved, and she hustled him toward the door. "We really must be going." She glanced at Quinn, wanting to say... But what could she say? Nothing that would change his mind about her father, probably. "Thank you for helping me today."

Her father was finally out of the kitchen, but before she could follow him, Quinn's hand closed around her wrist. His fingers were warm and strong.

"We need to talk about this." His low voice made the words for her alone.

She tried to pin a smile to her face. "I'll see you tomorrow. At Bible school."

He nodded curtly, then turned toward his mother. Ellie escaped into the evening air.

There wasn't going to be anything pleasant about that conversation tomorrow, she could be sure. All the progress they'd made that afternoon had disappeared. She and Quinn were on opposite sides of a yawning chasm, and nothing was ever likely to bridge it.

Chapter Seven

Quinn leaned against the birch tree in the church-yard the next day, watching as Ellie put a platter of peanut butter and jelly sandwiches on the picnic table. The Bible school children were staying for a picnic lunch, further delaying any opportunity to catch Ellie alone.

He moved restlessly, feeling the rough bark through the fabric of his shirt. He'd thought it would be easy to have a private conversation with Ellie. He'd also thought it would be easy to give his mother advice. It seemed all his assumptions were wrong.

Across the table from Ellie, his mother poured lemonade into paper cups for the children. Her round face wore its familiar serenity. Everything about her was the same as it had been for years, and yet something vital had changed. She seemed to have developed a different personality since his father's death.

Ellie's words about Gwen discovering her own strength filtered into his mind, and he frowned. He didn't want to take advice about his mother from Ellie, of all people. Not even if he thought she had a point.

He'd tried to talk to his mother after Ellie and Charles had left the night before, but it had been useless. First she ignored his concerns, angry at what she called his interference. Then, when her anger cooled as quickly as the coffee on the table, she tried to talk about adjusting to the death of a spouse—her own, and his.

He pressed so hard against the tree trunk that it was probably leaving ridges in his skin. He couldn't do that. After all this time, he still didn't want to talk about Julie's death. Maybe some people coped with tragedy by discussing it, but he wasn't one of them. His mother, of all people, ought to know that about him.

It was easier to concentrate on his worries about Gwen, and certainly easier to blame Ellie and Charles. Fair or not, that was how he felt.

He watched Ellie again, as he'd been doing all morning. She bent over the table to cut a sandwich, and that untamed hair of hers swung in front of her face like a veil. She turned toward Kristie, laughing at something his daughter said, and his heart clenched at the sight of Kristie laughing back at her.

Ellie had a smile and a quick word for everyone at Bible school, it seemed. Everyone but him, that is. Oh, she'd been perfectly polite all morning. She'd also avoided any opportunity to share a word with him. She'd effectively frozen him out, looking through him as if he weren't even there.

Ellie picked up the empty lemonade pitcher and turned, making some comment to his mother. She walked quickly toward the building. Quinn pushed away from the tree. Like it or not, she had to talk to him. He was through being ignored by Ms. Ellie. He crossed the lawn and went after her.

The church basement was dim and cool after the bright summer sunlight. He stood for a moment, letting his eyes adjust, and then saw the door to the kitchen whisper shut. Ellie had obviously gone for more lemonade. The church kitchen would be a private setting for the conversation he intended to have with her.

She was turning away from the refrigerator with a full pitcher in each hand when she saw him. Her expressive face tightened, and for just an instant he wanted her to look at him the way she did everyone else—with caring and laughter lighting those dark eyes.

He dismissed the thought. No, that wasn't what he wanted from Ellie. He wanted answers.

She put the pitchers down, and they clanked on the long metal table. She stared at him defiantly. "Well, go ahead. Get on with it."

"With what?" He moved closer, watching her hands clench into fists at his approach. "Do you really dislike me that much?"

She looked at him blankly, and he touched her closed fingers.

"You look ready for a fistfight."

"I don't fight." She took a deep breath, opening her hands and lifting them, palms up. They were long-fingered, strong hands—a craftswoman's hands. "I suppose you want to talk about our parents again."

"No." His quick, negative answer obviously surprised her. It surprised him even more. What was he saying? That was why he'd come after her, wasn't it? "Not right now," he added.

She eyed him warily. "You had a reason for following me in here, I suppose."

"I want to know what happened to our working together."

"I don't know what you mean." She turned away, tracing a bead of moisture as it traveled down the outside of the pitcher.

"You know exactly what I mean." He leaned his

hip against the metal table, close enough to touch her if he moved his hand even slightly. "We're supposed to be working together on Bible school."

"Aren't we?" She still didn't look at him.

"Come on, Ellie. You kept me so far from the action today I might as well have been in Siberia."

The small dimple at the corner of her mouth made an appearance. "It wasn't that bad."

"It was worse." He gave a mock shiver. "I'm still cold."

She did look at him then, the smile taking over her face. "I guess I could have involved you more."

"We're supposed to be partners, remember? Helping each other."

Her smile stilled, and she gave him a frank look. "Are you talking about Bible school? Or about our parents?"

It was no good. He couldn't treat her as a friend, not when he was paying a private detective to investigate her and her father. For a moment he considered telling her that, telling her that if she had something to hide she might as well level with him.

He couldn't. His mother's happiness came first; it had to. He couldn't risk jeopardizing that on someone he didn't even know.

"Maybe both," he said lightly, wondering how she'd react.

She looked up at him with a flash of anger. "I'm

sorry if I didn't let you participate this morning. I'll do better tomorrow.''

''And the other?''

She stiffened, and he felt the barriers she put up against him. ''I told you before I don't want to see a relationship between my father and Gwen. But I can't keep him on a leash.''

That was just about what he wanted her to promise him. The realization made him angry, whether at himself or her he wasn't sure.

''I want your promise there won't be a repeat of yesterday,'' he said shortly. ''No more little excursions with my mother.''

She lifted her chin. ''There won't be if I can prevent it. I'm afraid you'll have to be content with that.'' She picked up the pitchers and brushed past him, the kitchen door swinging in her wake.

He looked after her. Content? That wasn't a state he'd enjoyed much lately, especially where Ellie Wayne was concerned. But at least he'd gotten her reluctant promise to cooperate.

That was what he wanted. So why didn't it make him any happier?

What had she expected? Ellie tried to control her hurt and anger as she carried the lemonade out to the picnic table. That one pleasant afternoon together would make Quinn's suspicions vanish? It was absurd. And yet that seemed to be exactly what she'd expected. Or maybe what she wanted.

She pushed that thought away firmly. There was no possible point in thinking she and Quinn could be friends, let alone anything more. She remembered, only too well, what happened to her last relationship when the man she'd thought herself in love with had found out her father was a criminal. He hadn't been able to get away from her fast enough. She didn't intend to repeat that experience.

And with Quinn—for a moment she looked at herself clearly, and was horrified at her own weakness where that man was concerned. Quinn was the last person in the world she could care about. With that iron determination of his to protect his mother, he wouldn't hesitate to make the Wayne family scandal public.

She knew only too well what would happen next. She'd already been through it. The people she thought were her friends, people she loved like family, would look at her as if she were a leper.

A shiver ran along her skin in spite of the summer warmth. She couldn't go through that again. Somehow she had to deflect Quinn's interest in her father.

Her gaze rested on Gwen, who was clearing the table as the children ran off for games. If she could show Gwen how uncomfortable the situation made her, maybe she'd help. All Gwen had to do was convince Quinn she wasn't falling for Charles Wayne, and the entire problem would disappear.

With a fresh surge of determination, Ellie started toward Gwen. Almost as if she wanted to elude her, Gwen scurried around the far end of the table.

"Gwen."

Gwen stopped, reluctantly it seemed, at the sound of her name. "What is it, Ellie? I want to take these plates to the kitchen."

"That can wait a minute, can't it? I need to talk with you."

Gwen shrugged, her round blue eyes looking everywhere but at Ellie. "I think we really should get the cleaning up done."

Ellie took the plates firmly from her hands and set them on the table. "Gwen, we need to talk."

That was what Quinn kept saying to her, and she wasn't any happier to hear the words than Gwen seemed to be. But she had to push on.

"I'm sorry Dad caused a disagreement between you and Quinn last night. That shouldn't have happened."

Gwen's rosebud mouth tightened. "It wasn't your father's fault, so don't blame him. I invited him to go shopping with us."

That was what her father had said, and she felt guilty for having doubted him. "You know, my father never stays long in one place. I imagine he'll be leaving Bedford Creek quite soon.''

''All the more reason to make his visit a happy one.'' Gwen's tone was righteous.

''Well, of course. But your son won't be here for an extended time, either. You should be spending your time with him.''

Gwen's frown disappeared. ''Now, Ellie, I just know Quinn enjoyed the day with you far more than he'd have liked shopping with me. And didn't you have a good time with him?''

''It was very nice.'' She said it with as little enthusiasm as she could manage. Gwen didn't need to know just how nice it had been. ''The point is that Quinn really doesn't like your relationship with my father. You don't want to upset him, do you?''

Gwen waved that off. ''Quinn can stand to be upset. He takes too much for granted. Besides, it will do him good to be worried about something that will keep him in Bedford Creek.'' She scooped the dishes from the picnic table and darted off before Ellie could say another word.

Maybe she wouldn't have had a response if Gwen had given her more time. What on earth did Gwen mean by that? Was she deliberately using the situation with Charles to keep her son in town?

No, that was ridiculous. Gwen wouldn't do that. But their conversation that night at dinner flitted through her mind. Gwen clearly thought it was time Quinn came back to Bedford Creek to stay. What might she do to accomplish that aim?

Ellie worried at it as she finished clearing the table, stuffing the used paper plates and cups into the trash can. Maybe she should ask Gwen point-blank if that was what she had in mind.

She'd almost screwed up her nerve to do that when Gwen came back from the kitchen, but before she could get the words out, Kristie came skipping to her grandmother.

"Grammy, guess what?"

"What, sweetheart?" Gwen put her arms around the child.

"Ms. Ellie told us a neat story this morning. It was all about how God picked out a wife for Isaac. He sent this servant, see, and when the man saw Rebecca, he knew she was the one God wanted."

It was nice to know someone had been listening to the story. She'd been so aware of Quinn's unblinking stare while she was telling it that it was a wonder she hadn't married Rebecca off to the servant.

"So I was thinking about when I prayed for God to give me a new mommy." Kristie wiggled her way free of her grandmother's arms. "I think God picked out a wife for Daddy, just like he did for Isaac. And I think the one he picked out is Ms. Ellie." Kristie beamed in satisfaction. "Don't you think so?"

The paper plates and cups Ellie was holding dropped from suddenly nerveless fingers. *Oh, no.* This couldn't be happening. Kristie couldn't possibly have come up with a conclusion like that.

But she had. And what was worse, Gwen smiled at her as if she agreed.

Lord, what am I going to do now? The only worse thing would be if Quinn had heard that.

She turned, hoping to escape before Kristie realized she was there. And found Quinn standing right behind her.

Ellie felt as if someone had dropped her into a vat of boiling water. Her cheeks burned, and all she wanted to do was run and hide.

She couldn't. She was an adult, and adults didn't do things like that. She had to pin a smile on her face and figure out how to deal with this, no matter how embarrassing it was.

If Quinn had heard... Well, if he'd heard, surely he'd understand. Kristie's longing to have a mother wasn't a secret.

"Ellie, is something wrong?" Quinn's straight dark brows drew into a frown.

"Wrong?" she echoed. Was it possible he hadn't caught his daughter's little bombshell?

"You look as if—" He stopped, shrugged. "I thought you looked upset about something."

He must not have heard. He wouldn't be able to

hide his reaction to that. She managed to breathe again.

"You mean about something else besides your obsession with keeping our parents apart?" She might as well go on the offensive. Trying to avoid the subject hadn't done her any good.

For an instant she thought he'd flare out at her, but then his mouth tightened, and he nodded. "Yes. Besides that."

Your daughter thinks God picked me out to be your wife. Well, no, she didn't want to say that.

"No, I'm fine." She sent a cautious glance over her shoulder. Gwen was still talking with her granddaughter, but at any moment she might look their way. Ellie could imagine her calling out.

Oh, Quinn, Kristie just said the cutest thing.

Could this situation get any worse? She walked away from the picnic area, forcing Quinn to move with her if he wanted to continue the conversation. They stepped from shade into sunlight, and she blinked, her eyes dazzled. Quinn seemed to loom like a dark shadow between her and the sun.

"Was there something else you wanted?" Her mouth went dry. She'd gotten him out of range of his mother at the cost of being alone with him herself.

He shook his head. "Guess tomorrow at Bible school we can decide what time I'm picking you up."

"Picking me up?" She had the sense that she'd

walked onstage in a play and didn't know her lines. "Why would you be picking me up?"

Now it was Quinn's turn to look confused. "Aren't we going up to White's Woods to gather something or other you and Mom need for the craft show?"

"What makes you say that?" This conversation went in more circles than a top. "Yes, Gwen and I intended to gather some wildflowers and cones, but I had no idea you planned to go." That sounded very unwelcoming, but she couldn't help it.

"Kristie said we're all going."

"When did Kristie tell you that?" She had a sinking feeling she knew the answer before he spoke.

He shrugged. "Just after story time this morning. What difference does it make? At least it'll give my mother something else to think about…"

He let that trail off, but she knew how that sentence would end. Besides her father. That was what he wanted to say.

She was a little more concerned with what Kristie was thinking right now. Kristie had probably decided this expedition was a perfect chance to help God along with what she'd decided was His plan.

"I'm not sure that's a good idea."

"Why not?" That stubborn jaw hardened. "I think right now it's a very good idea for me to stick close to my mother."

Why not, indeed. If she told him what Kristie had

said—no, she couldn't do that. It would be far better to discourage Kristie gently in private rather than to make a big deal out of an innocent childhood wish. But if she didn't tell Quinn, she had no good reason for avoiding the expedition together.

It looked as if she'd have to give up on this one. "I have to spend some time in the shop or my helper will feel overwhelmed. Let's make it around four, all right?"

Quinn nodded, then started back toward the church. She watched his tall figure until it disappeared into the building.

Another afternoon spent in Quinn's company, another time of keeping up her guard, trying not to let him see into her secret life. This was a bad idea.

So why did she have to try so hard to squash the soft voice inside her that insisted spending time with Quinn was exactly what she wanted, no matter how unwise?

Chapter Eight

"I'm glad we're going with Ms. Ellie, Daddy." Kristie wiggled in her seat belt, peering out the window as they approached Ellie's shop the next afternoon. "Aren't you glad?"

"I guess so." That didn't sound very gracious. "Sure," he added, and pulled to the curb.

Ellie came out so quickly, she must have been watching for them. She slid into the back seat before he could get out to open the door for her, plopping a large basket on the floor. Then she obviously registered the fact that someone was missing.

"Hi." She glanced from him to Kristie. "Where's Gwen? I thought she was coming."

"So did I." He suspected his exasperation showed in his voice. His mother and daughter had gotten him into this little adventure, and then his mother had backed out. Still, she'd had a good reason.

"Rebecca was feeling pretty rocky today, and the receptionist at the clinic didn't show up. Mom went to help out."

"I see."

Her candid gaze told him she wondered why he'd come in that case, but he didn't have a good answer. "Mom said you needed to do this, and Kristie was looking forward to it." He'd just given her two reasons instead of one—always a bad sign.

He didn't have to explain himself to Ellie. He made a careful U-turn in front of the police station, then started up the steep street that headed toward the mountain ridge. He didn't have to explain himself to anyone. His mother was safely involved at the clinic with Rebecca. There was no reason not to be here with Ellie.

No reason to be with her, either, a skeptical little voice in his mind pointed out. He'd heard a brief preliminary report from the private investigator that morning. When he'd mentioned trying to find out more himself, the man had politely told him to leave it to the professionals. They'd come up with any answers that existed.

He glanced into the rearview mirror. Ellie leaned forward, talking to Kristie about the Bible school program set for the next day. Her hair, escaping from its band as usual, twined on his shoulder and feathered against his neck.

So far, their investigation had focused on Ellie's history, since he'd had little to provide them about her father. He'd known she'd worked in a craft shop in Philadelphia for four years before coming to Bedford Creek to open her own shop, apparently drawn by less expensive property here.

The man had commented that she'd appeared to arrive in Philly from Ohio with nothing—no belongings, no furniture and very little money. She'd lived in a cheap, dreary, furnished room for over a year before she'd apparently made enough to get something better.

It only raised more questions. Ellie was obviously well educated. Anyone talking with her for more than a few minutes would, in spite of her propensity for casual, sometimes offbeat clothing, place her as upper middle class. So why had she been practically destitute?

"Turn right just ahead." Ellie touched his shoulder, pointing to the dirt lane half-hidden by a tangle of rhododendron bushes.

"I remember." He slowed, taking the turn onto the rutted lane slowly. He remembered. White's Woods was a local landmark—several acres of meadows, woods, a quarry—that had been a popular spot for hiking and picnics for a couple of generations. "My mother says my father proposed to her up here."

"Really? That's so sweet." They jolted over a pothole, and Ellie grasped his shoulder in an automatic reflex. She snatched her hand away immediately, but the imprint of it seemed to linger. "It's nice—" She stopped, as if she'd been about to say something unwise.

"What's nice?" He negotiated the curve into the meadow and parked by the rough-hewn picnic table that had been there as long as he could remember.

"That sort of tradition, I guess." For an instant Ellie's gaze seemed to turn inward. "Having a place that hasn't changed in so many years."

Isn't there a place like that in your life, Ellie? Before he could ask the question, Kristie opened her door and slid out.

"Hold it," he ordered, grabbing the bag his mother had provided. "You need bug repellent on first, before you go anywhere."

Kristie pouted. "I don't want to. It smells bad." She wiggled. "Don't want to wear this shirt, either. I'll be hot." She plucked at the long-sleeved shirt he'd insisted she put on.

"You'd feel even worse if you got stung by a bee." He tried to say the words lightly, but the memory of Kristie's terrible allergic reaction to a bee sting months ago haunted him.

"I'm wearing long sleeves, too, Kristie," Ellie said, getting out of the car. "I'd never go out in the woods without them." She wore jeans, hiking boots and a long-sleeved checked shirt that looked like a man's, except that there was nothing masculine about the way it looked on her.

Ellie smoothed some repellent on herself, then rubbed the rest of it on Kristie's neck. She glanced up at him. "I have an Epi-Pen in my basket," she said softly.

He had one, too, of course, but he was unaccountably touched that she was so prepared. "Guess we're ready, then. What's first?"

"I want to see the quarry." Kristie grabbed his hand. "Please, Daddy. Grammy wouldn't take me the last time we came. She said she didn't like it. But I want to see it. Please, can I?"

He tried to ignore the tension that knotted his nerves at the thought of the abandoned quarry. No sense infecting Kristie with his own feelings.

"Just a quick look. Then we have to get to work. This trip is business, remember?"

She nodded, red curls bobbing. "Okay."

They cut across a corner of the meadow, passing a stream bordered by river birch and weeping willows, and followed the path through the stand of hemlocks. Ellie walked ahead of him. She'd taken

Kristie's hand, and maybe that was just as well. He'd probably hold on to her too tightly.

The path ended abruptly, and Ellie stopped. The quarry yawned ahead of them, a vast gash in the peaceful landscape. Ellie drew his daughter close to her. He came to stand next to them and couldn't help grasping Kristie's shoulder. She was several feet from the edge, but it still set his nerves vibrating.

"It's deep." Kristie leaned forward against their restraining hands. "Is there water at the bottom?"

His gaze traced the rock wall down to its base. The water was so clear it seemed he could count every pebble on the bottom. "Some. Not much now, but if there's a lot of rain, it fills up fast."

Kristie glanced up at him. "Could you go swimming there?" She'd just learned to swim, and she tended to ask that question about every body of water she saw.

"No." It came out too sharply, but he couldn't help that. "It's a dangerous place, honey. Lots of rocks and holes. Nobody should ever swim there."

Or climb there, or do anything else there. He'd nearly lost three friends in that quarry, and that wasn't something a person forgot easily. A few scraggly trees clung to the lip of the cliff, and he could almost picture Brett, half-drowned and exhausted, hauling himself over the edge by grabbing one.

"Come on." He took Kristie's hand, reassured by

the way it curled trustingly around his. "We have a job to do. Let's get to work."

He'd meant that lightly, but he soon discovered that it really was work. Ellie had a very specific agenda, and she'd come as prepared to find what she needed as if she were shopping in the supermarket. Not just any flowering plant, or leaf or fern would do.

"Now look at this one." She spread a maple leaf out on her palm, smoothing the edges. "See, it's perfect. We'll use these for the leaf prints we're making with the kids tomorrow. Believe me, if they can argue about who has the best leaf, they will."

He thought of some of the disputes he'd refereed during Bible school and nodded. "Guess you're right. Okay, perfect leaves, coming up."

"Grammy says she wants flowers to dry," Kristie said. "Can I pick some?"

"We'll get those in the meadow," Ellie said. "They don't grow here where it's shady. Why don't you look for cones? You should find some under the trees along the path."

"Okay." Clutching her own small basket, Kristie darted toward the thick growth of hemlocks that overhung the path.

"I'm ashamed to admit I don't know, but why is my mother drying flowers?" Maybe the truth was that he didn't know a lot about what his mother was doing these days. "Don't teenage girls do that? I remember when every volume of the encyclopedia held a rose Angela or Rebecca was pressing. Made it tough to look anything up."

Ellie put a fern frond into the basket. "Your mom and I do a lot of crafts together, once tourist season is over and I'm not so busy. This fall we plan to make dried-flower pictures." She smiled. "You can probably expect to get one for Christmas, if hers turn out the way she wants."

"That should fit very nicely into the décor of the mobile home where I live out on the Oregon woods. It's kind of spartan rustic."

"You expect to be back there at Christmastime, then."

"Did I detect a note of criticism in that comment?"

She shrugged, not looking at him. "It's not my place to criticize."

Before he could agree with her, Kristie ran back to them. "We're almost at the meadow, Daddy. Now can I pick some flowers?"

He suppressed the urge to keep her by his side. He hadn't been brought up that way, and it wasn't fair to overprotect Kristie, either.

"Okay. But stay where I can see you. And don't go near the stream."

Her nose wrinkled. "But Daddy, how do I know you can see me?"

"If you can see us, then we can see you." Laughter threaded Ellie's voice. "Okay?"

"Okay." Kristie darted off, basket swinging so vigorously that several leaves dropped out.

He shook his head, smiling reluctantly. "She makes me laugh about every minute and a half, even when I'm worrying about her."

"Kristie's one of a kind. I guess all the children are, but I have to confess, she has a special place in my heart."

Ellie meant that, he realized. She cherished each one of the kids who came under her care. He'd seen that every day at Bible school, but the depth of her caring still surprised him. That warm heart of hers seemed to embrace everyone in town.

"I'm glad." He stopped, looking down at her. "Glad that Kristie has you."

For an instant there was something questioning in her dark eyes, but then she nodded. "And I'm glad to have her in my life."

She stood looking up at him. A shaft of sunlight wavered through the moving branches overhead. It touched her cheek, illuminating the warm color that flooded her skin, the sweep of thick dark lashes, the pulse that throbbed at the delicate curve of her temple.

Her skin couldn't possibly be as soft as it looked, could it? As if moving of its own volition, his hand lifted. He stroked the line of her cheek, feeling the smooth warmth like silk beneath his hand. Her eyes darkened, and her lips parted. He wanted—

"Daddy!" Kristie's shout was followed by a shriek, then a splash.

Shock flooded Ellie—shock and fear. Quinn snapped away from her as if he'd been shot, and in an instant they were both running toward the stream. *Please, God, please, God.* An incoherent prayer thudded in time with her racing steps over the rough ground. She stumbled once, and Quinn surged ahead of her. By the time she recovered her balance and hurried down the bank to the stream he was already ankle-deep in the shallow water.

Kristie, wailing, was on her hands and knees, her face muddy. He scooped her into his arms and carried her to the bank.

"Kristie, are you all right? Are you hurt?" His face was blanched with naked fear.

Ellie reached them and knelt beside the weeping child. "Kristie, honey, stop crying." It took an effort to keep her voice calm. "We need you to be a big girl and tell us if you're hurt." She wiped the mixture of tears and mud from Kristie's cheek with her hand. "Come on, now."

Kristie gulped and swallowed a sob. "I—I'm wet!"

Some of Ellie's fear subsided. "We know you're wet, honey. But are you hurt?"

Kristie looked down at herself. "My new jeans are all muddy," she said in a tone of outrage.

"The jeans will wash." Quinn sat down abruptly, as if his legs wouldn't hold him up any longer, and pulled his daughter into his lap. "Now, listen to me, Kristie. Does anything hurt?"

Kristie's lower lip came out in a pout. "No. But my new jeans are muddy."

Quinn's gaze met hers over his daughter's head, and his lips twitched. "That seems to be a recurring refrain."

Ellie smiled, relief sweeping through her. "I think that's a good sign."

"It doesn't explain what Kristie was doing in the creek." He held his daughter back so that he was looking in her face. "Kristie? Didn't I tell you not to go near the creek? Or out of sight?"

She sniffled. "I know. But Daddy—"

"Don't 'but Daddy' me. I want to know why you disobeyed."

"But I was just trying to help." Her voice quivered.

"Help who?" Quinn looked around, as if looking for someone in need.

"Help you and Ms. Ellie."

"I don't understand."

Quinn might not understand, but Ellie began to fear she did. If Kristie meant what she thought she meant, this was going to be uncomfortable.

"Remember the Bible story yesterday? About how God picked out Rebecca for Isaac to be his wife?"

Quinn nodded, still obviously puzzled.

"Well, you need a new wife, and I decided maybe God picked out Ms. Ellie to be her." Kristie clasped her hands together. "I was helping by letting you be together without me. So maybe you'd kiss Ms. Ellie."

She couldn't possibly look at Quinn. Maybe she'd never be able to look at him again—or at least not until the memory faded of that moment when they were standing in the meadow, and she'd thought that kissing her was exactly what he planned to do.

She heard Quinn give an exasperated sigh. "Kristie, what am I going to do with you? I told you. I'm not looking for a new wife."

"But if God picked her out for you—"

"Kristie, you don't know what God intends." Ellie breathed a quick prayer for the right words. "None of us does. Just because you want a new mommy, you can't decide that's what God has in mind for you."

Kristie grabbed her hand in a wet, muddy grip. "But don't you like my daddy, Ms. Ellie?"

She kept her gaze fixed on the child's face and willed her voice to be steady. "Of course I do. But that doesn't mean I'd be the right wife for him. That's something you have to let your daddy decide."

Quinn stood up, carrying Kristie with him. "We'll talk about this some more later, okay? Right now we need to get you home and into some dry clothes."

"But I don't want to go home!" That brought a fresh spate of tears.

Ellie patted her. "We can come again another day. The flowers will still be here."

"Promise?"

"I promise." But she wasn't sure the next outing would include Quinn.

Kristie wiggled. "I can walk, Daddy. Let me down so I can walk."

He put her down. She took a couple of steps, then stopped and giggled. "My shoes squish. Look, Ms. Ellie, my shoes squish." She danced ahead of them.

"I think she's recovered," Ellie said.

"I haven't." Quinn drove his hand through his hair. "She's going to turn me gray."

"I'm sorry I didn't tell you." The words came out impulsively, and then she stopped.

"Tell me? How could you tell me?" He looked

down at her, and his expression slowly turned cold. "You knew what she was thinking."

"I'm sorry." She could feel herself flush. "I heard her tell your mother yesterday at Bible school. I thought it would be better—"

"You thought?" He didn't raise his voice, but it was cold enough to send a chill down her spine. "Seems to me you didn't think. Kristie is my daughter. Anything having to do with her is my concern, not yours. It would be best if you remembered that."

He strode off after Kristie, his long, angry strides quickly catching up with her. Ellie stood where she was, abruptly conscious of her wet sneakers and muddy hands. She must look as forlorn as she felt.

Forlorn was definitely the right word. Because as she watched Quinn stalk toward the car without a backward glance, she recognized only too well what was happening to her.

She'd begun to fall for him. Unlikely as it seemed, she'd begun to fall in love with Quinn. And there wasn't the slightest chance in the world that he'd ever feel the same.

Chapter Nine

Ellie took another stitch and then let the doll she was working on drop into her lap. She should be enjoying these quiet moments at the end of the day. Usually she loved snuggling into the rocking chair in her cozy apartment above the shop, rain pattering against the windows, her favorite dulcimer music playing softly in the background. Usually. Not tonight.

How could she relax when her mind kept replaying, over and over again, those moments with Quinn in the meadow? Her every sense had been heightened, and it seemed she still felt it.

She stroked the soft print fabric she'd chosen for the doll's dress, loving the feel of it under her fingers. The trouble with handwork was that it didn't engage

her mind, or at least, not enough. Her restless imagination continued to work. It persisted in presenting
images of Quinn: of laughing with him, of talking
with him, of joining in his family parties and dinners
as if she really belonged.

You don't, she lectured herself firmly. *You don't
even belong in Bedford Creek. Not really. Not yet.
And if anyone finds out about the past...*

That didn't bear thinking about, and she'd worked
herself back to the hard lesson she'd learned when a
whole town had turned against her. She couldn't risk
letting people know the truth. She couldn't face the
rejection again. And that meant she couldn't possibly
let herself feel anything for Quinn, even if every
other obstacle between them disappeared like mist
rising from the river on a sunny day.

She'd just reached that dreary conclusion when the
back doorbell rang. Hannibal raised his head from the
couch, glared at her as if she were to blame for the
intrusion on his nap and closed his eyes again.

Putting the handiwork on the arm of her chair, she
glanced at the clock. Had her father forgotten his
key? No, the movie he'd gone to couldn't possibly
be out yet. She shoved her bare feet into moccasins
and went quickly down the back stairs.

Two steps from the bottom she could see through
the small glass pane in the door, and her heart gave
a little jump. Quinn.

He stood on the other side of her door, rain glistening on the windbreaker that covered his broad shoulders. The porch light touched damp dark hair and shadowed his face.

She opened the door with trepidation, extinguishing an involuntary flicker of pleasure at the sight of him. Had he come to lecture her even further about her relationship with his child?

"Quinn." That didn't sound very welcoming. "What can I do for you?"

"You can let me in." He brushed droplets of water from his hair. "It's wet out here."

She stepped back, making room for him in the miniscule landing at the bottom of the stairs. He stepped inside, bringing the scent of summer rain with him. She moved onto the steps to put a few more inches between them. He always seemed to invade her space, as if he had to take control of every environment.

"Is something wrong?" Her mind flew to Kristie's misadventure.

He shook his head, and a fine spray of rain touched her face. "No, nothing's wrong. I just want to talk with you." He glanced up toward the living quarters. "May I come in? Or if your father's here, we could go somewhere else for coffee."

He didn't sound antagonistic, but she wasn't taking any chances. "If this is about this afternoon, I don't know what else I can say. I'm sorry if you feel I took too much upon myself where Kristie's concerned.''

He lifted an eyebrow, his gaze intent on her face. ''Are you that reluctant to let me into your home?''

She could hardly tell him to go away, and at some level she didn't want to. ''No, of course not.'' She gestured to the stairs. ''Please, come in.''

She hurried up, very conscious of his firm footsteps behind her. Her mind raced ahead, doing a quick inventory of how her tiny living room looked. She hadn't expected to have company tonight, and clutter seemed to take it over at every opportunity, no matter how she tried.

''Your father?'' he said again, his voice carefully neutral.

''Dad is out. He went to a movie. I was just doing some sewing.''

The top of the stairs emerged directly into the living room. She gestured him to a seat, trying to decide how the room looked through his eyes.

Did he appreciate the fine handiwork on the double-wedding ring quilt she'd hung to disguise the stain in the wallpaper over the couch? Would he recognize the effort that had gone into the patchwork cushions, appreciate the deep pink of the cosmos filling the milk glass pitcher? Or would he think it all looked shabby and homemade?

Quinn glanced around, his only reaction a smile at

the sight of the sleeping cat. Then his gaze seemed to land on the doll she'd been making. Flustered, she reached for it, intending to stuff it into the workbag that sat next to her chair. But he got to it first.

His hands dwarfed the stuffed doll as he touched the curls made of vermillion embroidery silk. "Is this what I think it is?"

"I'm making it for Kristie's birthday."

He held it for a long moment, stroking the hair, his face unreadable. Then he put it into her outstretched hand.

She took the doll, slipping it carefully into the bag, and straightened again. She had no reason to feel embarrassed that he'd seen it, so why did she?

"She'll love it."

"I hope so. She told me once the only red-haired doll she had was Raggedy Ann, and she didn't know why there weren't any prettier red-haired dolls." She tried to say it lightly, but her throat tightened. It was so poignant.

"Thank you for thinking of it."

She nodded, trying not to imagine she heard caring in his voice. "You wanted to talk about something," she reminded him. She sat in the corner of the couch, leaving the rocker for him.

He turned the chair so that its curved arm touched the couch and sat, planting both feet on the worn carpet. He leaned toward her, face intent, and she braced herself for another lecture.

"I wanted to apologize for this afternoon. I shouldn't have been angry with you, and I didn't have any right to speak the way I did."

She'd been thinking that very thing, but once he said it she couldn't help protesting. "It was my fault. I should have told you."

"Maybe the truth was I was angry with myself." He smiled wryly. "I don't seem to be doing a very good job of meeting my daughter's needs."

His unexpected frankness startled her. "Please— it's all right. You don't have to apologize."

"Yes, I do. My mother told me to." His face relaxed a little, and the hand that had formed a fist on the arm of the chair relaxed, too.

"Seems to me you don't always do what your mother says." She could only be grateful the atmosphere had lightened between them.

"Maybe, but she had a point this time. She said I was overreacting. After all, she hadn't told me, either, and she was the one Kristie confided in."

Some of Ellie's tension seeped away. "I still think I should have told you. But it was just so awkward."

Awkward didn't begin to describe it. Her own feelings were all mixed up with Kristie's dreams of a mommy, and talking about this with Quinn wasn't safe. She might let her feelings show.

"Let's just forget the whole thing, all right? Kristie's falling in the creek had already upset us both. Especially when we'd just been looking at the quarry." She shivered. "I know it's beautiful, but it's also dangerous."

He nodded, mouth tightening again. "You do know about the accident there?" He made it a question, not a statement.

"Rebecca told me once about Brett and some friends nearly drowning in the quarry when they were in high school." She felt cold, suddenly, in spite of the warm summer night. "But I didn't think you were one of them, were you?"

"No." He clipped off the word. "That was Brett, Alex Caine and Mitch Donovan. I'm sure you know Alex and Mitch."

Everyone in town knew them. Alex was the richest man in town, owner of the factory that employed at least half of it, probably. And Mitch, the police chief...

She found she'd tensed, as she seemed to whenever she thought of Mitch. Mitch had never been anything but kind to her, but somehow just the sight of his uniform always reminded her of the secret she hid.

She glanced at Quinn, but his gaze seemed focused on the past. Judging by his expression, the memory wasn't a happy one.

"What happened?" she asked softly.

He shrugged. "They were on our class camping trip when a storm hit. It doesn't take much rain to flood the quarry, and they were trapped. It's a miracle they all got out alive."

Tension seemed to vibrate from him. Odd that it still bothered him after all this time.

"But they did get out." She tried to sound reassuring. "So it's all right."

He didn't seem to hear her. "I was supposed to be in their group that day. But I got out of it. I'd scheduled a college visit, so I left camp early that morning and missed going with them."

"You were lucky," she ventured, hoping she wasn't saying the wrong thing.

"Lucky? People said so at the time." His words were casual, but his hand tightened on the arm of the rocking chair until the knuckles were white. "But if I'd been there, maybe it wouldn't have happened."

"Why would you think that? If you'd been there, you might have been in danger, too."

"They were my friends. I should have been with them." His response was as swift as if it had happened yesterday.

Realization hit her with a certainty she couldn't question. Whether he knew it or not, Quinn might also be talking about his wife's encounter with a drunk driver on a rainy night. The patter of raindrops against the window no longer sounded soothing.

It was the sort of question that always haunted survivors: *Why wasn't I there, why didn't I do something.* How much more it must haunt someone like Quinn, who seemed to have such a need to control everything around him. That quality probably made him a good engineer, but it couldn't be easy to live with.

Her throat tightened until she couldn't speak. Pastor Richie had been wrong about her, she thought. She wasn't the right person to minister to Quinn's grief. She couldn't even get any words out.

"I'm sorry," she said finally. "I know. I guess we always want to be with people we care about when they're in trouble."

Quinn's face was bleak. "Then my record is perfect, isn't it? I've never been there."

The words were barely out of his mouth before Quinn realized what he'd said. He looked at himself, aghast. What was going on here? He'd never said anything like that to anyone, not even to himself. Why on earth had he said it to Ellie, of all people?

She was looking at him with a mixture of sympathy and distress in her dark eyes. She probably didn't know how to respond, for good reason.

"Sorry." That sounded curt, and he cleared his throat. "I didn't mean to get into that."

"Quinn, you shouldn't blame yourself. I'm sure your friends don't."

"Don't they?" He'd never been sure of that, and he'd never felt he could ask them.

"No," she said firmly. "And if you're thinking about Kristie... Well, she knows you love her."

Actually he hadn't been thinking about his daughter. He'd been thinking about Julie, dying on that wet road alone. About his father, battling cancer and not telling him, as if he shouldn't be bothered. He hadn't been there for either of them until it was too late. But he wasn't going to tell Ellie that.

"I know." He shook his head, trying to manage a smile. "You were right—I was upset about Kristie's falling today, especially after we'd just been looking down into that quarry."

"How is she?" She probably wanted to get the conversation back to a more normal level, and he couldn't blame her for that. "No ill effects, I hope."

"None the worse for her ducking." He tried to force a light note into his voice. "We had a talk about her interpretation of scripture. I hope she's beginning to understand she can't play matchmaker for me, but I wouldn't bet on it."

Her smile looked a little strained. That was hardly surprising. "I think I mentioned before how determined she is. We'll have to keep reinforcing the fact that we're just friends."

Friends, he thought. No, he wouldn't say they were friends. They'd started out as adversaries. Then, perhaps, they'd become reluctant allies. But that moment in the meadow—if Kristie hadn't yelled, he knew he'd have kissed her.

Would he? The thought startled him. He hadn't been consciously thinking of that when he came here tonight. But now that it was in his mind, he couldn't seem to think of anything else.

She'd stood there looking up at him with a question in her brown eyes, and the sunlight had kissed her skin and highlighted the rose in her cheeks. And he'd wanted to kiss her.

It had been a trick of the light, he told himself. The scent of wildflowers, the emotions stirred up by a familiar place. That was all. It could have been any other woman in that time and place, and he'd have responded in the same way. He was only human, after all.

Except that there was no sunlight here, only yellow lamplight and the sound of the cat purring. And he was feeling the same thing. He reached across the inches between them to clasp her wrist. Her pulse thundered against his hand. Her gaze met his, and he knew that she was remembering, too.

"This afternoon, if Kristie hadn't fallen just then…"

"Nothing," she said quickly, as if she could read

his thoughts. "If she hadn't, nothing would have happened." She seemed to be trying to convince herself.

"Wouldn't it?" He leaned closer. The rain tapped against the windows, and the plaintive sounds of a ballad came softly from the tape player. The yellow cat stretched on the couch and put one white paw over his eyes. He'd never been in a place that felt so much like home. "Seems to me something might have."

"It shouldn't."

He touched her hair, and the glossy strands wove around his fingers as if they were alive. He'd wanted to do that for days, he realized.

"It shouldn't," she said again, but her face tilted toward his.

"I think so," he murmured, and then his mouth found hers and stilled whatever protest she might make.

She was warm and sweet, and she smelled like the meadow had that afternoon. His palm cradled her soft cheek, and the blood pounded through his veins. He wanted to pull her closer. He wanted to go on kissing her for hours.

She drew back, her lips a whisper from his. "This isn't a good idea."

"Why not?" He felt as if he were continuing an argument he'd already started with himself. "We're both free."

She drew back another inch, and he was sure the movement was reluctant.

"Our parents," she reminded him. "Kristie. It wouldn't be fair to let her think her wish is coming true. Besides, you'll be leaving soon."

Leaving. Longing flickered through him, and he pushed it away. He would be leaving soon, and he didn't intend to walk away from problems when he did.

He stood quickly, before he could give in to the temptation to kiss her again. "You're right. I'll be leaving soon. And I guess that's what I'd better do right now. I'll see you in the morning."

He spun and thudded down the steps before he could give in to the longing to stay.

Quinn was escaping, Ellie thought as the outside door closed. He already regretted kissing her and just wanted to get away. Certainly she regretted that kiss.

His mouth had been warm and firm against hers. Feelings had tumbled through her, too quick to recognize. They'd swept away rational thought, until the only thing left in the world had been the touch of his lips.

She reached out a shaky hand to stroke the cat. "You should have stopped me, Hannibal. You should have stuck your claws in me before I got anywhere near him."

Hannibal yawned delicately, showing a pink tongue, as if to indicate he didn't believe a word of it. Then he closed his eyes again.

How had this happened? She glanced around the quiet room as if an answer had to be there someplace. She'd spent years being mindful of her secret past, holding it up as a shield against letting anyone get too close. She'd become an expert at rolling into a prickly ball when anyone attempted it.

Until Quinn. How had he gotten past her defenses? She looked back over the last week, but no answer appeared. She'd recognized Quinn for the threat he was, yet somehow he'd managed to touch her heart.

No, not her heart, she protested, panic-stricken. She might be attracted to him—any normal woman would be. But she couldn't let herself care for him.

She sat very straight, wrapping her arms around herself. That kiss had been a mistake. Quinn undoubtedly realized that just as well as she did. She regretted it, and she'd pretend it hadn't happened.

Liar, a soft voice spoke in her mind. *You don't regret it at all. And you won't forget it.*

Maybe she didn't regret it. Maybe she couldn't deny the feelings that stirred in her. But that didn't mean she had to act on them. Because if she did, the results could sweep away everything she cared about.

Chapter Ten

"It's time to sit down on the story rug now," Ellie announced the next morning. She could only hope she didn't sound as distracted as she felt. Overexcited children, the last day of VBS, the closing program for parents looming—those were all good reasons for her mood. Unfortunately none happened to be the cause.

She tried and failed to keep her gaze from straying to Quinn. He'd settled at the back of the braided rug as he usually did, preferring to let her tell the Bible story. He folded long legs in front of him and leaned back on his hands, strong face as impassive as if it had been carved from redwood.

The muscles in her neck tensed, and she cleared her throat softly. All right, she could get through this.

Maybe she did have feelings for Quinn. She'd simply accept that fact and move on. No more fairy-tale dreams for her. She wasn't the princess in the tower, and he wasn't going to ride up and rescue her.

She'd treat Quinn as impersonally as if he were a stranger. She'd be polite, friendly, and she certainly would not dwell on the shape of his mouth or the firm line of his jaw.

And she'd made a fortunate decision, since he apparently felt the same. All morning he'd watched her, but his impassive face hadn't given away a single glimmer of feeling.

So that was it. He'd obviously decided it was best to pretend last night hadn't happened. They were just two strangers forced into a temporary partnership that would soon end.

She opened her Bible, and a shaft of sunlight fell across the final VBS story—Jacob and Esau, and the reconciliation of the estranged brothers. *Forgiveness.* For a moment the words swam on the page.

She blinked the threat of tears away and began the story.

Half an hour later the children clustered at the door, ready to race into Fellowship Hall for their program rehearsal with Pastor Richie. If anyone could settle them down enough to remember their lines and their songs, he could.

"Hey!"

She turned at the sound of Robbie's peremptory challenge, but the boy had fixed his attention on Quinn. Well, good, let Quinn handle it. Maybe Robbie would jolt him out of his silent mode.

"Hey, what?" Quinn looked down at the boy.

"Ms. Ellie says that guy Esau forgave his brother for all those mean tricks."

Quinn nodded, not looking at her. "That's what Ms. Ellie said, so it must be true."

"Well, I wouldn't." Robbie planted his fists on his hips. "If I had a brother and he did that, I wouldn't forgive him, not ever. Would you?"

She waited for Quinn's calm answer, but it didn't come. He looked at the child for a moment, his face grim, then shook his head. "We don't have time to talk about it now. You can ask Ms. Ellie later."

The bell called the children to rehearsal, and they flooded down the hallway. Ellie stood where she was, looking at Quinn. The lines of his face seemed to deepen, as if he were worn down to the bone.

She remembered her intentions to keep things cool and impersonal between them, then pushed them away. She couldn't, not when he looked like that. "Quinn, what's wrong?"

Gray eyes, as hard and impervious as granite, met hers. "What could be wrong?" He grated the words, his tone denying their meaning.

She wanted to pretend she hadn't asked, pretend

she didn't care. *Impossible.* "I heard you with Robbie. You didn't answer his question."

If granite could harden, his expression did just that. "I didn't have time."

She longed to touch him comfortingly, as she would one of the children. Her imagination presented her with the warmth of his skin under her fingertips, and her hands tingled. She pressed her fists into the folds of her full skirt.

"We always have time to answer the children's questions. Why didn't you reassure Robbie about forgiveness?"

Anger flared dangerously in his eyes. "Don't lecture me, Ellie."

"I'm not." She had to steel herself not to take a step back from that bitterness. "I just want to know what's going on. We're teaching together, remember?"

"Not for much longer."

She nodded, conceding the truth. Not much longer. Something inside her wanted to weep at that. "That doesn't change the question, does it?"

His hand moved in a brief, dismissive chop. Then his mouth twisted a little. "Sorry if I didn't pull my weight as a teacher. Maybe you can talk to Robbie about it later. I'm not a good person to ask about forgiveness."

"But…" She reached toward him before she could tell herself it was unwise.

"Somebody killed my wife, remember?" He threw the words at her. "He got drunk. He got behind the wheel of a car and drove. He killed her. Do you expect me to forgive that?"

His pain seemed to grab her heart and wring it. "It doesn't matter what I expect." She struggled to keep her voice steady.

"You think God expects it, I suppose." His face twisted. "Well, if God thinks I'll forgive that, He's wrong."

He thrust her hand away with a quick, hard movement and charged out the door.

Pastor Richie had worried that Quinn hadn't opened up to anyone since his wife's death. He'd hoped she could minister to him. Ellie wrapped her arms around herself as if that would relieve the pain.

She hadn't ministered to him. The chance had flared up so suddenly she hadn't been prepared. She'd only made matters worse.

And if there had remained a tiny flame of hope in her heart about herself and Quinn, his words had extinguished it. Quinn didn't forgive. He didn't forgive the drunk driver, even though the man was in jail.

He wouldn't forgive her, if he ever learned the truth.

* * *

Anger drove Quinn halfway out of the building before he stopped, fists clenched, breathing as if he'd run a marathon. He hadn't let the anger out in a long time. He'd taken pride in controlling himself.

He took another breath. He certainly couldn't say he was under control now. He wanted to go outside, start running up the mountain and keep going until he'd tired out the anger that burned inside him.

He couldn't. Ellie could handle the children without him, but Kristie would be hurt if her daddy weren't there to watch her. He forced his fists to unclench. He'd slip into Fellowship Hall and find a spot at the back from where he could watch his daughter.

With a little luck, no one would bother him, and he wouldn't explode at anyone else the way he had with Ellie. He felt a twinge of regret. Even though she'd pushed him, she hadn't deserved to bear the brunt of his anger.

Parents, grandparents and friends already filled most of the metal folding chairs that had been set up for the program. Amazing, that this number of people could get away from their work at noon on a Friday to watch their children, or even someone else's children, sing a song or two and recite a Bible verse.

But that's how Bedford Creek was. That's how it had always been. If the children were doing something, the whole community turned out to support them, cameras in hand. The tourists would have to fend for themselves for the next hour.

Unfortunately, that same attitude prevented him from successfully disappearing into the woodwork. At least half a dozen people spotted him and stopped to chat—complaints about the wet summer weather, encouraging words about the tomato harvest, smiling approval at how the children had grown.

Had any of that changed in the last thirty years? The conversations sounded exactly the same, but people still felt compelled to make them. That was characteristic of a small town, and he told himself it was annoying. You could never be anonymous and alone. He propped his shoulders against the cement block wall and mutely ordered the program to start.

As if on cue the children filed to their seats. Kristie skipped to hers, her gaze scanning the audience. When she spotted him, her face lit with such pure pleasure that his heart cramped.

How many times had she looked out at an audience and found him missing? He kept telling himself that someday he'd make it up to her, but someday didn't come. How could he go away again? But how could he stay? Bedford Creek brought out the worst in him.

Pastor Richie bounded onto the small stage, consulted his notes, frowned and hurried back off again, to engage in a whispered conversation with several of the teachers. The children buzzed and stirred restlessly. If the pastor and teachers didn't get the program going soon, some of the smaller children would be wandering back to their parents.

"Looks like a glitch in the proceedings." Brett leaned against the wall next to him.

"Looks like," he agreed, wondering what Brett would say if he told him to buzz off. Probably just laugh. It took more than a minor insult to upset Brett. "What are you doing here, brother-in-law? Not enough patients at the clinic?"

Brett grinned. "I think they're all here at the moment. Besides, I had to come and watch my favorite niece, didn't I?"

"Looks as if you're not the only one. Half the town must be here."

Brett nodded toward the audience. "Look at Alex and Mitch down there, ready to beam at their offspring. Pretty soon it will be me. How did we all get old enough to be the grown-ups? I remember when we were the ones performing."

"You were always the one performing," Quinn corrected him. "The rest of us stood reluctantly in the back row of the chorus."

He discovered he was watching Ellie instead of the kids. From her place at the piano she smiled encouragingly at the children, then gave a hushing gesture. They settled back into their seats as if by magic. No matter how guarded Ellie might be with adults, the children walked right into her heart.

Whatever anger he'd been holding against her ebbed away. She hadn't been trying to pry—he knew that. She'd been trying to help. She just hadn't realized what a sore spot she'd touched.

Ellie got up from the piano, exchanged a few words with Pastor Richie and sat back down again. Apparently they were the right words, because the pastor's usual welcome speech got underway.

"Looks as if our Ellie got them straightened out," Brett said. He eyed Quinn speculatively. "She's a pretty woman. Seems like you've been spending a lot of time with her lately."

If that was a question, Quinn didn't intend to answer it. "Pretty, yes. But she's something of a mystery, isn't she? Nobody seems to know much about her past. And whenever anyone gets too close, she curls up into a prickly ball."

"Anyone?" Brett sounded amused. "Or you?"

"I'm trying to protect Mom, remember?" He shouldn't have to remind Brett of that. "Rebecca's the one who thought we had something to worry about."

"Much as I adore her, your sister worries too much." He punched Quinn lightly. "You do, too. Must be a family trait."

"I worry about keeping Charles Wayne away from my mother, if that's what you mean."

Brett shrugged. "He's something of an outsider, I have to give you that. But everyone likes Ellie. And if you're seeing a lot of her...well, why not?"

Rebecca waved, gesturing to an empty seat next to her, and Brett went to join her, leaving his question hanging in the air. *Why not?*

Ellie started down Main Street from the bakery, a still-warm loaf of seven-grain bread tucked into her already-full shopping bag. Bible school had ended successfully, and she actually had a small breather before she launched into final preparations for the craft show. She'd be feeling happy and relieved right now, if it weren't for one thing.

One person, a little voice corrected in her mind.

It was no use. She couldn't stop thinking about that exchange with Quinn in the Sunday school room. Each time she wasn't actively engaged in some other conversation, it started replaying in her head.

She shouldn't have said anything. If she'd just let it go...

But how could she? Pastor Richie was right—they had to try and minister to Quinn. But probably even the wise pastor didn't recognize the depth of Quinn's anger.

And his grief. She frowned, considering that. Of

course he must still be grieving, but that wasn't the overwhelming emotion that had rolled at her in waves when she pressed him. Instead she'd sensed anger, vengeance, maybe even guilt. And her questions certainly hadn't helped matters any.

Would she take it back, if she could? She'd had to say something, and possibly anything she'd said at that moment would have had a similar response. Whether Quinn realized it or not, the Bible story that morning had spoken to his soul.

Forgiveness. Thoughts of her father bumped uncomfortably in her mind. Maybe she had issues of forgiveness herself. She'd tried to forgive her father. She'd stood by him, visited him in prison and tried to repay his debts.

But when he'd been released, he'd promptly vanished. For five long years, she hadn't known where he was. She didn't understand it. Probably she never would.

"Ellie?"

She jumped, recognizing the hand on her shoulder even before she recognized the voice. "Quinn. What are you doing here?"

"Running some errands for my mother." He glanced at her packages, lifting an eyebrow. "Looks as if you have an armload. Can I take some of those for you?"

"You don't need to...." But he was already taking the shopping bag from her arm.

She took a breath, trying to still the jumble of feelings that invaded her at the sight of him. She hadn't expected to see him again so soon. But since she had, she owed him something.

"Quinn, I'm sorry for this morning." She rushed the words out, before she lost her nerve. "I shouldn't have said anything."

He shook his head decisively. "Forget it. I don't know why I was so edgy, but it wasn't your fault. Or Robbie's."

"I'm sure it rolled right off his back." She hadn't been able to forget so easily, but he didn't need to know that.

"Just like the directions you gave the kids about not rushing the refreshments line. He nearly knocked Mrs. Rolland off her feet, trying to get to the chocolate cake before anyone else."

"I noticed you intercepted him." By the time the program was over, Quinn had apparently shaken off his anger. He'd stayed for refreshments, talked to parents and generally behaved as if this week of Bible school had been the time of his life.

"I remember a thing or two about little boys and buffet tables." He gestured with the shopping bag. "Do you have other errands?"

He was behaving too nicely, too normally, and it

made her nervous. Whatever else you could say about their relationship, you wouldn't call it nice and normal.

She stopped in front of the print shop. "I have to pick up the posters for the craft show." She reached for her bag. "So if you have something else to do, I'll take that now."

"Not at all." He held the bag out of reach. "I'll help you carry them back to the shop. After all, that's partly my mother's responsibility, too, isn't it?"

"That's not necessary."

"Not necessary, but a pleasure." He held the print shop door for her.

Controlling, she thought, not for the first time. He just couldn't seem to help himself. *Determined.* A spurt of annoyance was quickly followed by a flicker of fear.

If he put that same persistence to work on her past, he'd find out the truth. And she already knew he wouldn't forgive.

Allen Kramer lounged behind the counter at Kramer's Print Shop. He didn't look up until Ellie stood directly in front of him. "Ellie. Is there something I can do for you?"

"I'd like to pick up my poster order."

Kramer's eyebrows rose. "Poster order? You don't have a poster order with us."

"Don't have... What are you talking about?" She

felt a wave of panic. "I talked to you ages ago about doing the posters for the craft fair. I sent my father up Monday with the design. They were supposed to be done today."

Kramer had started shaking his head at her first words, and he just went on shaking it. "Nope."

"What do you mean?" She herself felt like doing a little shaking of him. Kramer was always casual about deadlines, which probably came of being the only print shop in town. "I have to have those posters. The committee expects to put them up soon."

"Better talk to your father about that." Kramer drew himself up, clearly offended. "Came in here with that design and questioned my price. Said it was too high. So I said he could just take his business somewhere else, and off he went."

She couldn't let him see how disturbed she was. Even worse, she couldn't let Quinn see. She managed a smile.

"I guess we got our wires crossed, then." She probably should apologize, but the man was so smug she couldn't bring herself to do it. "I'll check with him about it."

Dad, what have you done now? I trusted you, I gave you the money.... Her heart twisted. Was that what this was about? The money?

She made it out of the shop, very conscious of Quinn on her heels. She turned to him, wanting nothing more than to be rid of him. She held out her hand for the bag. "It looks as if I don't have to pick those up after all. I'd better get back to the shop now."

The frown Quinn directed at her made it clear he wasn't going to accept her dismissal. "What's going on with the posters? Why didn't you know what your father did?"

She tried not to let her dismay show in her face. "I'm sure it's just a misunderstanding. I'll see Dad and straighten it out."

She grasped the shopping bag. He let her take it, then closed his hand over hers so that they stood locked. "Level with me, Ellie. I can see you're upset. Why?"

"If I'm upset, it's because you're making a mountain out of a molehill." She tugged at her hand. "People are watching us."

He glanced around, apparently realized that was true, and dropped her hand. "You looked like your worst nightmare had come true when Kramer told you what your father had done. If this affects the committee's work, my mother has a right to know."

"But you don't." She turned anger at her father into anger at him. "You're hoping this will make my father look bad, aren't you?"

His face hardened. "Sounds to me as if he's done that all by himself."

She wanted to argue, wanted to say he didn't know

her father, but she couldn't. Maybe she didn't know him all that well herself now.

But one thing she did know. She knew that the brief truce between her and Quinn had just been broken.

Chapter Eleven

Ellie shoved the shop door open so hard that the bell nearly jangled off its hook. She didn't know if she was angrier with Quinn or with her father. She just knew that it flared inside her like a physical pain. And beneath the anger was the thing she didn't want to recognize—fear.

"Ellie, what's wrong?" Her father stood behind the counter, looking as comfortable there as he once had in his corner office. "You look ready to bite someone." His smile held an edge of concern.

"I guess I am." Thank goodness the shop was empty of customers. "I just stopped at the print shop for my posters, but they weren't ready. Because you never gave them the order."

"Well, no." He flushed. "I was going to tell you about it."

"Dad, how could you? You know I need them to advertise the craft show! I'll never be able to get them in time now."

"Ellie, it's not what you think."

"Well, what is it, Dad?" She dropped her packages on the counter. "You tell me. This craft show is important. It's my way of repaying people here for their kindness. I trusted you to take care of ordering the posters, and you let me down."

She stopped abruptly, astonished that the words had actually come out of her mouth. *You let me down.*

It was what she'd always thought, always felt, and never said to him. She hadn't said it even in the worst of times, when the newspapers trumpeted his name and people avoided her on the street.

Her father, who never showed his age, suddenly looked very old. Shaking his head, he reached for something beneath the counter.

"I let you down once, Princess, in the worst way possible. I won't do that again." He lifted an unwieldy stack to the countertop. "Here they are."

Ellie took a step forward and pulled the brown paper covering aside. The craft fair posters stared up at her, their colors bright and appealing, looking even better than she'd expected.

"I don't understand." She touched them, as if to be sure they were real. "Where did these come from?

Kramer told me he didn't do them, and his is the only print shop in town.''

"I suppose that's why he thinks he can over-charge." Her father's voice regained a little brisk-ness. "I went to Henderson instead. Gwen lent me her car, They did them while I waited."

"You went all that way? Why didn't you tell me?"

"I wanted to surprise you." His smile was crooked. "I guess we were both surprised."

"Dad, I'm sorry." She didn't know what to say.

He shook his head and pulled a pale blue rectangle from his pocket. "Here's your check back. The post-ers are my gift to the craft fair."

She stared at it blankly. "You don't have to do that. I'm sorry."

"You thought I let you down." Tears glistened suddenly in his eyes. "It's all right, Ellie. I don't blame you. After all, that's what I did before. You have every right to be angry with me for that."

"It's not that. It's... You went away." The words burst out before she could stop them. "You got out of prison and just disappeared." She sounded like a lost child, crying for her parent. "How could you do that to me?"

"Oh, Ellie." He came around the counter to her. "I'm sorry. I was just so ashamed. You'd started a new life, and I didn't want to interfere with that. Be-sides, I had a debt to repay. I guess my pride got in the way. I didn't want to come back to you until I'd repaid every cent I'd taken—until I felt forgiven."

"You repaid…" She couldn't take it in. "All this time I thought…"

"You thought I didn't take responsibility for what I'd done." He took both her hands in his, and she felt him tremble. "Maybe I didn't for a long time. But God kept working on me, until He brought me to my knees. I believe He's forgiven me. Now I'm asking you. Please forgive me, Ellie."

Something seemed to break inside her, and her tears spilled over. She stepped forward into her father's arms.

"Please can't I have just one taste of icing? Please, please, please?"

Laughing, Quinn disentangled his daughter's arms from around his legs. "Don't you think your guests will notice if there's a great big Kristie fingerprint in the middle of the cake?"

She tipped her head, considering that, then spun around. "Maybe Grammy has some left in the icing bowl." She ran toward the kitchen.

He started to follow, but the doorbell rang. He glanced at his watch. Guests arriving already. Kristie's birthday party was getting underway, and she'd have the cake soon enough.

He swung the door open, and the welcoming smile

seemed to freeze on his face. Ellie and her father stood there, side by side, both holding packages. Given the way he and Ellie had parted the day before, he wouldn't have been surprised if she'd made an excuse not to come.

Her smile looked about as stiff as Quinn's, but Charles greeted him as if they were long-lost brothers. "Quinn, what a perfect evening for a birthday party. Where's the birthday girl?"

"In the kitchen, trying to con some extra icing out of her grandmother."

"No, now she's run outside to pick a few more mums for the table." His mother hurried in from the kitchen and enveloped Ellie in a hug. "She's so excited you'd think she'd never had a birthday before. I just hope she's not still thinking—"

"Of course not." He interrupted before his mother could blurt out anything potentially embarrassing. "We got that all settled." At least he hoped so.

"Perhaps you'd like to put our package with the other presents." Ellie handed him a box wrapped in pink, and his fingers brushed hers as he took it.

They both knew what was in the box. The memory of the night he'd seen the doll danced in his mind. Unfortunately it wasn't the thought of the doll that made his heart beat a little faster.

When Kristie had announced she'd wanted to invite Ellie and her father to her birthday party, his feelings had been mixed, to say the least. Maybe the truth was he'd like to have Ellie here, without Charles.

She snatched her hand away, the warm color in her cheeks deepening. Pointedly ignoring him, she turned to Gwen and held out the flat package her father had been holding.

"Here are the craft show posters you said you'd put around town. I've already taken them to the stores down at my end of River Street."

"Wonderful." His mother smiled. "I'll take them around on Monday, once this party is off my mind." She looked at Ellie's father. "Charles, would you like to help me bring out the plates?"

Charles shot a wary glance at Quinn, then followed her toward the kitchen.

Ellie made a move as if to go after them, but Quinn caught her hand. He wanted some answers before she disappeared. "I take it the poster snafu worked out all right?"

"It was a misunderstanding." She fired the words at him. "I told you that. My father got a better deal on the posters over in Henderson."

That couldn't be all of it, or she wouldn't have looked the way she had in the print shop. "He just forgot to tell you about it?" He lifted his eyebrows, knowing they were both thinking of those moments and her anger.

Her mouth firmed, as if denying him access to whatever it was she thought. "He wanted to surprise me. That's all. There weren't any problems."

"I'm glad."

"Are you?" It was a challenge.

"Yes." The truth of it astonished him. "I'm glad everything's okay."

They stood motionless for a moment, his hand clasped around hers. He had the sense of things unsaid passing between them—the sense that words trembled on her tongue, wanting to be said.

Then the doorbell rang again, and Kristie raced in to answer it. He let go of Ellie reluctantly and turned to greet the arriving guests, wondering what they might have said to each other, given the chance.

The party swirled around him for the next hour. Kristie had invited a mixture of family and friends that somewhat surprised him. Brett and Rebecca, of course, but also Alex, his fiancée, Paula, and his son, Jason. Maybe that was understandable, because Jason was only a year or so older than Kristie. Even Robbie was there.

But she'd also asked Mitch and Anne Donovan. Their foster son was a gangling adolescent, and little Emilie, the toddler, he'd think was too young to play with Kristie.

Family and friends, he thought again, watching Kristie find a balloon for Emilie. Kristie had created a party from the people who meant the most to her, including Ellie and Charles. How did they fit in?

Surprisingly well, he decided, watching them. No, he might as well admit the truth, if only to himself. Watching her. He couldn't stop watching her.

Something had changed between Ellie and her father, he could sense it. Some tension that had existed before was gone.

She glanced up, and her eyes met his as if she felt his speculation from across the room. Those dark, thick lashes swept down again, hiding her eyes, but she couldn't hide from him. They understood each other. He didn't know how or why, but they saw into each other without the need for words.

He turned away, confusion flooding through him. This couldn't be. What he was thinking was just plain crazy. He took a step or two and paused by the piano.

A photograph of his father sat on top of the piano, in the center, surrounded by pictures of him and his sisters at various stages of life. John Forrester looked out of the silver frame with the grave smile that had been so characteristic of him.

"I miss him, too." His mother's voice startled him. "Every day."

He put his arm around her soft shoulders. "I know. It doesn't seem fair that he can't be here to celebrate with us."

She patted his hand. "In a way, I think he is. I guess I need the comfort of feeling that."

He couldn't stop his gaze from straying toward Charles. She nodded, seeming to understand what he didn't say.

"I know. You don't like my seeing Charles. But it doesn't mean I'm forgetting your father. It just means that I need someone to share things with. Can't you understand that and be happy I've found someone?"

"I would be." He tried to believe that. "If I were sure you'd found the right someone."

"Isn't that my decision, dear?" Her voice was very gentle.

She turned and hurried off toward the kitchen before he could find an answer. Maybe he wouldn't have found one very quickly in any event.

He looked at Ellie again. She was organizing a game of Pin the Tail on the Donkey, laughing as she tied a blindfold on Brett. If he were able to let go of his suspicions of her father, if he could accept his mother's judgment and leave it at all, where did that leave him with Ellie?

"Goodbye, goodbye, goodbye!" Ellie watched as Kristie waved to her aunt and uncle, then spun and ran to the back porch. She crawled up onto the swing next to Ellie, hugging the new doll tightly.

"I just love her." She leaned against Ellie's arm. "Did I tell you that?"

She stroked the child's hair. "About a hundred times." She glanced at Quinn, who was tidying up the grill where he'd fixed hot dogs and burgers for supper. "You could probably tell your daddy again how much you love your new bike."

Quinn looked up, smiling, a lock of his usually neat dark hair falling onto his forehead. "I think she already did that."

Kristie had ridden the new bicycle up and down the driveway time after time, until she could do it with no help at all. The triumph on her face when she'd gone all the way on her own had been worth seeing. Quinn had to know how much she enjoyed her gift.

Did he also know how much Ellie had enjoyed the evening? The tension that usually disrupted the time she spent with Quinn had been absent, even when her father was near. It almost seemed that Quinn had accepted their part in his mother's life.

No, that was too much to hope for. Quinn had just been on his best behavior because all of his friends were at the party. And since everyone else had left, they should go, too.

"I think we'll say good-night now." She hugged Kristie. "I'm glad you like your doll."

"Amelia," Kristie corrected. "I'm going to call

her Amelia.'' Her face clouded. ''You can't go now.''

Quinn came onto the porch, wiping his hands on a towel. He tossed it over the railing. ''It's starting to get dark, honey. Time for you to get ready for bed.''

''No, no.'' Kristie shook her head firmly. ''Not yet. Charles promised to tell me a story about San Francisco.'' She slid off the swing. ''I'll go find him, okay? He can tell me the story, and then it will be bedtime.'' She scurried into the house, the doll tucked under her arm.

Ellie expected Quinn to intercede and waited for him to object. Instead he shrugged.

''Have you noticed how often she outmaneuvers me?''

''It had occurred to me.''

He sat down in the place Kristie had vacated on the swing, seeming in no hurry to put his daughter to bed. The wooden swing creaked under his weight, and he pushed gently with his foot. They swung back and forth, the creak a soft counterpoint to the crickets in the hedge. Fireflies began to rise from the grass, painting swirls of light against the deepening shadows.

Quinn's face was in profile to her, and she realized she was studying the crisp strong lines as if she needed to memorize them. Her nerves seemed to be standing at attention, as if every cell in her body was aware of him, sitting so close. She should leave, but she couldn't seem to make herself get up.

"You surprised me." She said the words without thinking.

He turned to her, raising straight, level brows. "How so?"

"Do you really want my father telling her stories? Isn't that a change?"

"I don't suppose a story or two will do any harm." The corners of his mouth quirked slightly. "Seems to me you're the one who's changed toward him."

She felt as if the porch floor had just tilted, leaving her stumbling for balance. "I don't know what you mean."

"Just what I said. Every time I've seen the two of you together, I've noticed a strain. Until tonight. Tonight, things are different."

"You're imagining it." Surely he couldn't see into her feelings that much. If he could, she was in more trouble than she'd thought.

"I don't think so. What's changed between you? Does it have something to do with the posters?"

She leaned back against the arm of the swing to give herself another inch or two between them. The wooden arm pressed, unyielding, into her back. "You like to ask questions so much maybe you should have been a lawyer instead of an engineer."

"Lawyers have to stay indoors too much. I couldn't handle that. I just like to know how things work. And people."

"You must have been the kind of child who's always taking things apart."

His slow smile made her heart turn over. "How else could I know what made them work?"

Keep it light, she ordered herself. *Don't let him see the effect he has on you.* "I'll bet your parents really enjoyed that."

"Mom got frustrated, I have to admit. Especially when I dismantled the toaster on the day she was having her church circle in for brunch." He shook his head, then casually stretched his arm along the back of the swing. It pressed against her shoulders. "I'll bet she's thankful every day that Kristie doesn't take after me in that respect."

"I suppose." She clasped her hands together in her lap, sure they were giving away the tension she felt at his nearness. "Kristie's like you in a lot of other ways, though. I'm sure your mother enjoys that."

"I hope so." He frowned. "I hope it's not getting to be too much for her."

She didn't know what to say to that. Gwen adored her granddaughter and loved having her here. But Gwen and Kristie both longed to have Quinn home for good.

He glanced at her, his eyes questioning. "No opinion on that?"

"My opinion doesn't matter," she said carefully. "It's how you and Gwen and Kristie feel about it that's important."

"Yes, I guess it is. And it was time I came home and figured that out." He turned his body to face her, and his hand curved over her shoulder. "You know, I seem to owe your father a vote of thanks."

"For what?" If she weren't so distracted by the strength of his arm and the warmth of his hand, she might be able to come up with an intelligent response.

"If I hadn't been worried about his relationship with my mother, I might not have come home when I did."

"You don't have to worry..." she began, but the words became trapped, then lost, when he touched her cheek. Her skin tingled under his fingers, and her breath caught.

"And if I hadn't come home when I did, I wouldn't have gotten to know you." His voice grew husky, and he leaned closer. "I wouldn't want to miss that."

She couldn't speak, couldn't think, couldn't even breathe. All she could do was lift her mouth to his.

His hand slid into her hair as his lips found hers, and his arm tightened around her, drawing her close against him. She couldn't have pulled away if she'd wanted to, and she didn't want to. Her arms went around him, touching the strong, flat muscles of his back.

She was where she wanted to be, and she never wanted this moment to end.

Chapter Twelve

Ellie found herself singing as she wiped down the counter in the shop on Monday morning. She tried telling herself she was singing praises because God had given this lovely day, but that was only part of the truth. The rest of the reason was both more complicated and more selfish—Quinn.

Silly, wasn't it? She looked out the window at what she could see of Bedford Creek. The maples in the park across the street waved in the light breeze, and sunlight glinted on the river. Beauty did surround her, but Quinn filled her mind.

He'd let down his guard with her. He'd kissed her. For a few minutes she'd felt closer to him than she'd ever felt to anyone in her life. Surely she wouldn't feel that way if something weren't meant to be between them.

But the barriers hadn't disappeared just because Quinn had kissed her. Even though she'd resolved the strain between herself and her father, that didn't change history, however much she might want it to.

Her father had embezzled, he'd been caught, he'd been sent to prison. Charles honestly believed that wouldn't make a difference in how Bedford Creek viewed her. He was wrong. She'd lived through that revelation before, and she knew.

Nothing had changed. She had absolutely no reason to be so happy. But she sang another chorus of "Bringing in the Sheaves" while she swept the wide wooden floorboards.

The bell above the shop door jingled. She stood, dustpan in her hand, and tried to control the joy that flooded her.

"Quinn, I didn't expect to see you this morning." But she'd hoped.

He stood motionless just inside the door, a silhouette with the light behind him. Then he moved, and she saw no answering smile. Without speaking, he flipped the sign to Closed and turned the lock.

Something chilled inside her. "What are you doing? Why…"

His grim expression dried up her words. He took a step toward her. "Why? Because I don't think either of us wants the conversation we're about to have interrupted."

Something was wrong, very wrong. She tried to swallow the apprehensive lump in her throat. "What is it? What's happened?"

He glanced toward the expanse of glass across the front of the shop. A pair of early tourists looked at the sign, then peered through the window. "Maybe we'd better go upstairs."

Mutely she nodded. She turned and forced herself to walk up the steps, feeling as if she were mounting a scaffold.

What was it? Her mind darted from one possibility to another. Something about Kristie, something about her father? Had Charles done something else to upset Quinn?

She emerged into the living room. The sunlight that had brought joy moments before now only seemed to make the room look shabby. She turned to face him.

"What's happened?"

The lines in his face deepened, and his granite stare turned implacable. "You lied to me." He threw the words at her like four separate stones.

"I don't know what you're talking about." She tried to keep her voice calm while her mind twisted and turned. "When did I lie to you?"

His right hand made a short, chopping motion. "Don't play games with me, Ellie. I know the truth.

The private investigator I hired found out everything there is to know about you and your father.''

"Private investigator?'' For an instant sheer anger swamped every other emotion. ''You hired someone to investigate me? How could you?''

His mouth twisted in what might have been a smile, except that it held nothing but mockery. ''Funny, that's the question I started asking myself last night. How could I investigate Ellie, the person everyone loves? How could I be so suspicious? So I phoned the firm this morning, intending to call them off. But they already had a report for me. Shall I tell you what it said?''

Something inside her seemed to shrivel up and die. She didn't need to worry any longer about telling him the truth, did she?

''I suppose it said that my father had a prison record.'' It took all her strength to keep standing upright, looking at him.

''You suppose right.'' His body was stiff with anger. ''A prison record for embezzlement—for stealing from his employer. And you brought him to Bedford Creek, introduced him to people who had befriended you and never said a word of warning.''

She took a breath, trying to suppress the tears that threatened to clog her voice. Be angry. It was much better to be angry with him. That way she could hold the pain at bay for another moment or two.

"My father's past is no one's business. Should I have taken out an ad in the paper, announcing his failures? Or maybe you think he should wear a sign."

"Failures?" His eyes flashed. "Crime, Ellie. Call it what it is. Embezzlement is a crime."

"Yes, it's a crime." She threw the word back at him. "I'm sure your private investigator filled you in on all the details. But did he tell you my father spent the last five years working to repay every single cent? My father has changed, whether you believe it or not."

If that mattered to him, it didn't show. "What I believe isn't important, but the truth is. My mother is supposed to be your friend, yet you let her become involved with him and didn't tell her. What kind of a friend hides a secret like that?"

"I care about Gwen." She turned away from him, suddenly too exhausted to keep on fighting. "But I couldn't tell her. I couldn't tell anyone."

"So you lied."

Her fury came raging back at his contemptuous tone. She swung on him. "Lied? I tried very hard never to lie to anyone, but I certainly didn't volunteer anything. I knew what would happen when people found out. I've been there before—believe me, I know."

"What are you—"

"You don't know." She swept on, carried on a

wave of pain. "You don't know because you've always belonged. You can't begin to imagine what it's like when everyone you care about turns against you. And now it's going to happen all over again."

She turned away, fighting back tears. He had to get out of there, now, before she broke down completely in front of him.

"Ellie…"

"Please, just go away." Her voice broke on the final word, and she took a shaky breath that ended in a sob. "It's over."

Her pain reached out and wrapped itself around Quinn's heart. He didn't want it to cut through his anger and touch him. He didn't want to, but he couldn't help it.

"Ellie…" He said her name again, his voice tight. Before he could think about it, he grasped her shoulders and felt the anguish that wracked her. He turned her toward him and pulled her into his arms.

"Don't, Ellie." He murmured her name into her hair. "Don't hurt so much."

He wasn't sure she heard him. Sobs shook her, and he felt hot, wet tears against his shirt. He didn't know whether to blame her father or blame himself. All he seemed able to do was hold her.

"Shh." He stroked her back as he would Kristie's. "It's going to be all right." He murmured soothing words, not sure she was hearing him, not sure he even meant them. This wasn't going to be all right. How could it be? But he couldn't stand the pain she was in.

Finally the sobs lessened. She took a long, shuddering breath and pushed away from him.

He let her go reluctantly. But she clearly wouldn't want him to comfort her, not if she could help it. She wiped her eyes with the back of her hands, as a child would.

"I'm sorry."

"Don't be." He had to find a way to deal with this. He took her arm, leading her to the couch, and sat down next to her. "I was angry. I came here intending to hurt you." He looked at that truth bleakly. "I just didn't realize how much you were already hurting."

She took a breath, interrupted by a small sob. "Everything you said was true."

"Yes." Everything he'd said had been true, but he'd had a choice about what he did with it. He'd used it to strike out at her, and that didn't exactly make him proud of himself. "Tell me, Ellie. Tell me what happened."

She shrugged, then wrapped her arms around herself as if cold. "You already know, don't you?"

"Facts, that's all. I don't know how it hit you."

He took her hand. It felt like ice. "You couldn't have been very old when he was arrested."

For a moment he thought she wouldn't respond, but then she seemed to force out a word. "Eighteen."

He swallowed. When he was eighteen, he'd felt as if he had the world at his feet. "How did you find out?"

"We were at a dinner at the country club, with all our friends, my father's business associates." Her hands twisted convulsively in his. "I didn't have any idea that anything was wrong, until the police came in and arrested him."

She stopped, as if that was the end of the story. His imagination presented him with the picture, unrolling in front of him as if he'd been there. A younger Ellie, vulnerable and innocent, lost when the father she loved turned out to be a criminal.

"You must have had someone to help you—family, friends."

She shook her head, pulling her hand away from his. "No one. We didn't have any other family. And when it came out, the people I'd thought were our friends acted as if he'd cheated them personally." Her mouth firmed. "That wasn't surprising, I guess. His employer owned the mill that supported the whole town. He was like a little king. No one would go against him to support an embezzler."

"You didn't do it. They couldn't blame you." He

wanted her to say it wasn't so. To say she'd had friends, people to support her. He didn't know why it was important, but it was.

She started to shake her head and just went on shaking it. "I was tarred with the same brush as my father. That's how it was. That's how it will be again, when people here know." Her face grew bleak. "I'll have to leave."

An hour ago, he'd have welcomed those words. But then he'd been blind with anger. He'd told himself that anger was for his mother's sake, but it wasn't. Truth was, he'd been furious because he felt betrayed.

He'd begun to care for Ellie. He'd never intended to. He didn't know how it had happened. But he had, and the knowledge that she'd deceived him cut through his pride to his heart.

"People here aren't like that." He'd like to believe that. "No one will turn against you because of what your father did."

She looked at him as if they came from different planets. "Why not? You did."

He wanted to deny it, but there was too much truth in what she said. He'd been suspicious of Charles from the beginning, and that had inevitably colored everything he said and did.

"All right, maybe you have a point. Maybe, if people knew you hadn't been honest with them about your father, it would change how they look at you. But they're not going to know about it from me."

Her startled gaze flew to his face. "Not?"

"What did you think, that I'd start a whispering campaign about you? Of course I'm not going to blab it around town."

Something that might have been hope began to dawn in her eyes. Quickly, before she could say anything, he went on.

"But there's one person who has to be told. My mother."

"You haven't told her?"

"It should come from you." *You're her friend.* But he wasn't going to beat her with that anymore. She'd taken enough from the father who'd betrayed her and the so-called friends who'd let her face it alone. Anger seared along his nerves.

She took a breath, seeming to call on some reserves of strength deep inside. "All right. When?"

He stood. "Now."

Not sure her legs would support her, Ellie forced herself to her feet. She made herself take a breath, then another. How could she possibly keep going when it hurt so much? She pressed her fist against her diaphragm, trying to control the pain, and started down the stairs. Quinn's footsteps thumped out a dirge behind her.

She'd lost. She'd lost the battle to keep her secret, and she'd lost him.

The thought drove the pain deeper. *No.* She couldn't lose something she'd never had, and she'd never really had Quinn's love. Maybe, if things had been different for both of them, it might have been possible. But it wasn't.

Quinn held his car door for her, and she got in. She tried to put a glass barrier between them as he drove. If she could just keep her heart walled off from him, maybe she could get through the ordeal of telling Gwen.

A fresh wave of pain assaulted her. Gwen's face, angry as Quinn's had been, formed in her mind. She'd deceived Gwen. How could she possibly forgive that? And once Gwen knew the truth, how long would it be before everyone in town knew?

Panic fluttered at the thought of what would follow. She couldn't—she couldn't go through that again.

Maybe Gwen wouldn't tell. The thought formed in her mind, and she clung to it. Maybe, if she understood why Ellie had kept her secret, Gwen wouldn't tell. That might be the only hope she could salvage from this disaster.

By the time they reached the house, that faint hope was all that kept her going. Then Quinn opened the side door and stepped into the kitchen, and they relived the past all over again. Gwen and her father sat at the kitchen table together.

Quinn's fists clenched, and anger rolled off him in waves. "What are you doing here?"

"Quinn!" Gwen's feathers ruffled. "I won't have you talk to my friend that way."

"Gwen, please." Ellie forced the words out past the lump in her throat that threatened to choke her. "Dad, I think you'd better leave."

In an instant he'd reached her side. He put his arm around her, drawing her away from Quinn. "Princess, what is it? What's wrong?"

"Dad, just go home." She tried to detach herself. "It's better."

"Maybe he should stay." Quinn grated the words, all the anger back in his voice. "This is about him. Go ahead, Ellie. Say it."

She leaned against her father's arm for a moment. "I'm sorry, Dad." She looked at Gwen. "There's something I have to tell you about myself. About my father."

"Ellie, honey…" Her father hugged her. "You don't need to."

"Yes, I do." Didn't he understand that it was over? Couldn't he see that Quinn knew? "I have to."

"No, you don't." Gwen's voice took command. "You don't have to tell me, because I already know.

I know all about Charles's conviction and his prison term. I've known for days.''

Ellie could only stare. Gwen's soft, round face hadn't changed. Her hands still fluttered. But determination shone in her eyes. "You know? How do you know?"

Gwen looked at Charles, and her expression softened. "Charles told me himself."

Her father stroked her hair. "Honey, I know you didn't want me to tell anyone here about the past. But when Gwen and I became friends, I couldn't keep it from her. That wouldn't have been fair."

Fair. She was the one who hadn't been fair, either to Gwen or her father. He'd had the courage she didn't.

Lord, how am I going to get through this? What can I possibly say?

"Ellie, it's all right." Gwen patted her hand. "I haven't told anyone, and I won't." She looked at Quinn. "And neither will Quinn."

Quinn looked as if he'd been hit with a brick. "He told you?" He focused on his mother. "Mom, I appreciate the fact that he leveled with you, but that doesn't change anything. He still committed a crime."

"And he paid for that. He went to prison, and when he got out, he worked until he'd repaid every single cent." Her gaze softened as she looked at her son. "You have to let me make my own decisions, Quinn. I'm not a child, and I don't need to be protected."

"Dad..." Pain crossed Quinn's face as he said the word.

"I know." Gwen reached for his hands. "It was always so important to him to take care of me. So I let him." She focused on him, face intent. "But I don't need you to step into his shoes. I can take care of myself. Can't you let me do that?"

Ellie could see the struggle in him so clearly, even though none of it showed in his face. How had that happened? Her heart hurt even more. How had she become so close to him that she could see into his heart?

Finally he nodded. "All right, Mom. If that's what you want, I won't stand in your way."

"And you won't tell anyone, will you?" She clutched his hands for emphasis. "That's what Ellie wants, and we have to respect that."

His face tightened as he looked at her. "I've already told Ellie that."

"Thank you." Her lips were almost too stiff to form the words. "Dad, I think we'd better go."

He didn't argue. His arm around her, he piloted her to the door. He didn't speak until they were safely outside. "Princess, I'm sorry." Tears filled his voice. "I've hurt you again. I'm sorry."

She leaned against him. "It's all right. You did the right thing, telling Gwen."

"She won't say anything." She felt the hesitation in him, as if he weighed saying something more. "But Ellie, don't you think you should?"

"I can't." Surely he realized that. "I don't want to lose people I care about." *Anyone else I care about.*

"Honey, I know. Don't you think I've been there?"

What was he saying? "I don't understand what you mean."

He held her close. "Princess, I got into trouble because I tried to live a lie to impress people, and the only way to maintain that lie was to take money that didn't belong to me. I just don't want you to make the same mistake I did."

"It's not the same."

"In a way, it is," he insisted. "If you love these people, you have to stop living a lie. Don't you think their love is strong enough that you can trust them with the truth?"

His words hit uncomfortably close. She'd like to believe him. But she'd seen how Quinn reacted, and she couldn't.

If Quinn couldn't hear the truth and still care for her, no one else would. And Quinn, despite his sympathy for her pain, had made it perfectly clear that any feelings he'd had for her had vanished.

Chapter Thirteen

Two days. It had been two days since the truth had come out, and she hadn't seen Quinn in all that time.

Just the thought of him was enough to send her heart into spasms of pain. Surely it wasn't possible for a heart to hurt this much and keep on beating, but it did.

She sought for something good to cling to—her renewed relationship with her father, the strength of her faith. Those would carry her through.

At least Quinn had apparently kept his word. He hadn't told her secret.

Ellie ducked under the portico sheltering the church door and folded her umbrella, shaking it. The rain had been relentless all day. She could only hope enough of her volunteers had braved the weather to

452   *A Father's Place*

work on the booths for the craft fair. And if she could concentrate on that, maybe she could stop thinking about Quinn.

She hurried inside to find Fellowship Hall abuzz with activity. People scurried back and forth, carrying boxes of craft items, arguing over jobs, hammering together the wooden booths they'd hoped to set up on the church lawn. Then all of the action seemed to freeze, and she saw only one person.

Quinn stood, a hammer in his hand, in the shell of a booth. Mitch held out a board to him. Quinn didn't take it. He didn't move. His gaze fixed on her, his expression unreadable. Then the moment broke. He turned away, taking the board, making some comment to Mitch, and everything flowed on.

She pressed her hand against her rib cage, feeling as if he'd hit her. But what else could she expect? She'd deceived him. To his way of thinking, she'd betrayed him. Maybe he'd felt reluctant sympathy when he'd seen the depth of her pain, but that was all.

"Ms. Ellie, Ms. Ellie!" Kristie skipped over, her red hair as wiry in the damp weather as if it was spiked with electricity. "I'm helping with the craft show. Grammy said I could."

"That's wonderful, Kristie."

The child's voice had drawn other people's attention to her, and she was immediately besieged with questions about the fair. Pastor Richie hurried over, waving them off.

"All right, all right, we'll make a decision. Just give us a moment." He smiled at Ellie and shook his head. "Everyone has an opinion, of course. What do you think? You're the committee chair. Can we have the fair outside, the way we planned?"

"Ask me an easy question." She grimaced. "The weather forecast says the storm is going to move off the coast by tonight, but do we want to count on that? Gwen, what do you think?"

Gwen handed the sign she was making to Charles. "I'm just not sure. What if the forecast is wrong? Then what?"

What if Quinn saw his mother and her father together? She reminded herself she didn't have to worry about that any longer. The truth was out between them now. In a way, it made things so much easier.

For a brief moment the thought of letting the whole town know about her father's history flickered through her mind. Her father would be all right with that. Even Gwen would.

She was the only one not brave enough to risk it. She hadn't even been brave enough to pray for guidance, afraid of what that guidance might be.

She forced herself to concentrate on the discussion. "The problem is, if we wait, we might not have time to finish all of the booths.'' Pastor Richie frowned. "But if we finish them in here, we won't be able to get them through the doors to take them outside.'' He shook his head. "There's no good answer.''

They were all looking to her for a solution. She took a breath. *Think about the job at hand. Don't think about Quinn. Don't wonder if he's listening or what he's thinking.*

"I say we'd better commit to having the fair in Fellowship Hall. I know it's not what we planned, but I don't want to take the chance of ruining it entirely. Okay?''

Pastor Richie nodded. "That's what I like. Someone who's not afraid to make a decision. Okay, everyone, let's get this done. We're going with inside.''

Not afraid to make a decision? She wanted to laugh. If he only knew the truth.

For some reason the story she'd told the children about Abraham popped into her mind. She heard again Kristie's question. *But wasn't Abraham scared to go off on a long journey just because God told him to?*

She'd told the children Abraham trusted God enough to do what God wanted. That had been easy to say, but it wasn't so easy to do. Here she stood, afraid even to take her problem to God—afraid to hear His answer, let alone trust it.

Pastor Richie nipped his thumb with a hammer. "Ouch." His eyes twinkled. "I'm not sure carpentry is my strong suit."

She took the hammer from him. "We could probably find you something safer to do."

He shook his head. "I want to help." He glanced toward Gwen and Charles. "Your father seems very handy with tools. Was that what he did before he retired?"

The innocent question hung in the air. Ellie tried to breathe—tried not to let the thought into her mind. But it came anyway.

She could evade the question. Or she could let the truth come out. She could, like Abraham, trust the Lord.

The words pressed on her lips as if they wanted to be said. She took a breath, reaching out in prayer.

I'm stepping into deep water here, Lord. Please don't let me drown.

She opened her mouth, not sure what was going to come out. "My father was assigned to the carpentry shop for several years while he was in prison for embezzlement. He says it was the only positive thing about the experience."

The words came as easily as if she'd been talking about the rain. No one would guess the leap of faith they represented.

She heard a startled gasp somewhere behind her and knew what it meant. Her long-held secret would be all over the room in minutes. She forced herself to meet Pastor Richie's eyes.

She discovered nothing but sympathy there. "I didn't know."

"I've hidden it for a long time." She felt an odd sense of release at admitting it.

He patted her shoulder. "Secrets can be heavy burdens. You have to use up a lot of energy keeping them from escaping. Maybe it's better this way."

Some of the tension she'd been carrying for days slid away. Maybe it *was* better, although she couldn't expect other people to take her revelation as calmly as Pastor Richie did. He took everything calmly, as if he'd seen it all. Still, for better or worse, it was out.

Thank you, Lord. Now please, help me deal with the fallout.

She straightened, looking around the room, feeling the murmurs spread from person to person. Her gaze tangled with Quinn's. Her heart gave a momentary leap of totally irrational hope, and then she quashed it.

Quinn stared back at her, totally expressionless. He wouldn't care that she'd finally exposed her past. It was too late now.

For a moment Quinn didn't believe his ears. He blinked. Just like that, after all the secrets and lies, Ellie had told.

"Whew." Mitch spoke softly. "That's quite a little bombshell from our Ellie."

"Isn't it, though?" He tried to sound noncommittal.

But Mitch had known him too long. His dark eyes surveyed him, and Quinn realized that his friend the cop was somewhat like Pastor Richie. He saw things other people didn't.

"You already knew," Mitch said.

Quinn shrugged, pounding a two-by-four into place. "I did some investigating into Charles Wayne's past. After all, Charles has become quite a friend of my mother."

"I see." Mitch glanced across the room. "Looks like your mother isn't bothered by his record."

"No." He clipped the word and slammed the hammer with unnecessary force. It didn't help.

"Guess this explains something that always puzzled me about Ellie." Mitch grinned. "She's never really warmed up to me. Not that I'm the most lovable guy in the world, but still…"

"Yeah, right." Quinn found himself smiling back, feeling again like the kid he'd once been, kidding around with his friend. "That's why you ended up married to the smartest, most beautiful lawyer Bedford Creek has ever seen."

"That was luck," Mitch said. He glanced at Ellie and sobered. "Ellie will need a little luck, I'd say. Some people won't take this as well as Pastor Richie."

"I guess not." The words pricked him like a nettle. That wasn't his problem, Quinn told himself. Ellie had brought this trouble on herself.

It took a lot of courage to come out with it, a small voice remarked in his mind. *She's already suffered enough for something that wasn't her fault.*

Ellie wasn't his problem. But he couldn't keep from watching her, even as he turned back to his work. He couldn't help wondering what she was feeling. What had made her blurt it out, after all this time? Did she already regret it?

His mother moved to Ellie's side, murmured something in her ear, then gave her a quick hug, exuding strength and compassion.

Had his mother really changed? Or had that strength been there all along, and he'd just never seen it? Maybe he'd been guilty of looking at her simply as his mother, instead of as a person with a mind of her own and the will to use it.

His mother had moved off, and another woman paused by Ellie. Next to him, Mitch straightened.

"Uh-oh," he said.

"What?"

Mitch raised his eyebrows. "Don't you recognize Enid Lawrence? You've been away too long, buddy, if you were able to forget her. That woman has the bitterest verbal attack in three states. I should know. She's turned it on me often enough."

"I'd forgotten. My dad used to say she'd curdle milk just by looking at it."

He couldn't hear what Enid said to Ellie. But he could guess at the content. Ellie's expressive face went white, and then as scarlet as if she'd been struck.

He was still telling himself it wasn't his concern when he was halfway across the room. By the time he got there, Enid had said a word or two to Charles and gone on her poisonous way.

Quinn stopped in front of Ellie, searching for words. He didn't know what to say, and he hadn't realized Mitch was behind him until his friend spoke.

"Let me give you a hand with that, Charles." Mitch lifted the end of the board Charles held. "I'll help you get it up."

Charles shot him a thankful look, nodding. Something, maybe a sense of relief, ran through the room. Quinn could almost feel what people were thinking.

If the police chief accepted the man, he couldn't be too bad.

Ellie's dark eyes filled with gratitude, and Quinn had to suppress a spurt of jealousy. He could hardly expect her to look at him that way.

"Are you all right?" he said in an undertone, not especially wanting to advertise his concern to the whole town.

Her expression turned wary. "I'm fine."

He reached for the stack of boxes she held. "Let me help you with those."

She pivoted, setting them down, her back stiff. "I don't need any help."

A spurt of anger—or was it hurt?—flared at her quick dismissal. He didn't want to look too closely. "So you're grateful to someone who helps your father, but you reject anyone who tries to help you."

Her cool stare seemed to put him at a distance, as if she was looking at him through a telescope. "I don't need your pity, Quinn."

"I'm not…" What could he say? That he didn't feel sorry for her? She'd know it wasn't true, and she'd reject that, too.

She was still looking at him as if he were the guilty party. His jaw clenched. The truth was, he couldn't tell her what he felt because he just plain didn't know. And that was a pitiful admission to make.

* * *

A few drops of water, left from the all-day rain, pattered from the trees in the park onto Ellie's hair as she walked that evening. She tilted her face back, enjoying their cooling.

This had been one of the longest days of her life. She had desperately needed a few minutes alone, and the rain and the drawing in of evening had emptied the park.

She paused under the lifted branches of a river birch and glanced back at Bedford Creek. *Her town,* she thought as she had so often over the last few years.

Was it? She loved it here, but was it really her place now that the truth was out? She still wasn't sure.

As for Quinn... She turned and walked swiftly toward the river, as if she could outrun her thoughts. She didn't want to think about Quinn, because that hurt too much.

The split-rail fence that guarded the riverbank felt wet and smooth under her hands. She leaned against it, trying to concentrate on the gray water, trying not to think it was the same color as Quinn's eyes.

That was a useless exercise. She couldn't stop thinking of him, and it was foolish even to try. Maybe, after he'd gone away again, the pain would lessen. At least then she wouldn't have to be constantly keyed-up, expecting to see him around every corner.

"A little wet out for a walk, isn't it?"

She hadn't heard Quinn's approach across the wet grass, and she spun around to face him, heart pounding. He wore the shuttered expression that told her nothing of what he thought or felt.

"What are you doing here?" She hugged herself, suddenly chilled through the light windbreaker she wore.

He stopped next to her, leaning his side against the fence as he looked down at her. "I came to see you. Your father told me where you were."

She turned toward the river again, planting her hands on the wet rail. It was much easier to look at the high water than to look at him and wonder what he was thinking. "I'm surprised you're speaking to my father."

She felt, rather than saw, his shrug. "Charles isn't a person to hold a grudge, is he? He greeted me like a long-lost friend." Quinn turned, putting his elbows on the fence next to her, looking out at the river as she did. "He's worried about you."

His arm brushed hers, and she had to stifle the impulse to spring back as if she'd received a shock. *Be careful*, she warned her fragile heart. *Don't start imagining he cares about you. He feels sorry for you, that's all.*

"No one needs to worry about me." She tried to sound as if she believed that. "I'm fine."

"Are you? This can't have been an easy day."

That sounded like genuine concern in his low voice, and she tried to hold up a barrier against it. If she let his concern in, believing it was real, she might crumble. She'd done that once with Quinn, humiliating herself by crying her heart out. She wouldn't do it again.

"I didn't expect this to be easy." No, not easy. *But the worst part is you, Quinn. Don't you know that?*

"How did people behave the rest of the day?"

Her cheeks went hot at the memory of Enid's barbed comments. "Luckily everyone isn't as bitter as Enid." She shrugged. "Some people were all right, others hostile. Some were just cool, as if they reserved judgment."

"I'm sorry."

"Don't be." To her surprise, she meant it. She wouldn't blame him for this. "Actually, it wasn't as bad as I expected. As I remembered. Maybe because it's old news, or maybe because I'm a little more mature now than I was at eighteen."

"Maybe you're stronger than you know." His arm pressed against hers, sending a thousand messages along her nerves that she tried not to heed.

"Pastor Richie said a secret is a heavy burden. It

feels good not to be carrying it any longer, no matter what happens.'' She forced herself to look up at him. ''So I guess I have to thank you.''

He lifted his dark brows, and his eyes gleamed with what might have been humor. ''Is that comment sarcastic, by any chance?''

''No.'' Some of the tension she carried slipped away. ''I mean it. If you hadn't forced the issue, I might not have found the courage to let it out.''

His hand closed warmly over hers. ''I'm still sorry for the way I went about it.''

''But not for doing it.'' She shook her head quickly, before he could speak. ''That wasn't a criticism, really. You wanted to protect your mother. I understand that.''

''You wanted to protect your father.''

''And myself,'' she admitted.

His fingers tightened around hers, and she felt their warmth all the way up her arm. ''There's nothing wrong with that,'' he said softly.

She tried to think through the jumble of feelings roused by his nearness. Was he saying he was able to forgive? Had she actually made a dent in that implacable nature of his?

''I don't...'' She lost whatever she was about to say in his intent gaze. He was so close that her emotions welled up, catching her by surprise. She wanted... She wasn't sure what she wanted.

Liar, her heart retorted sternly. *You want to be in his arms.*

His eyes darkened suddenly, like a storm moving up the river. "Ellie." His voice roughened on her name.

She shook her head, not sure what she tried to convey. Her lips parted, but no words came out.

He released her hand, and for an instant she felt cold and lost. Then he touched her face, hands slipping under her hair, thumbs brushing her cheeks. Emotion filled her—need, longing, tenderness.

He was so close, so close. Then his mouth claimed hers, and the world spun off in a dizzying spiral. She heard the rush of water from the river, and it seemed to be sweeping her away to a world where only she and Quinn existed.

He drew away for an instant, brushing kisses against her cheek, the corner of her mouth. "Ellie." He murmured her name against her lips.

Be careful, she tried to tell herself, but it was no use. She couldn't possibly be careful where Quinn was concerned. She couldn't guard her heart. She could only hold him close and know she loved him.

Chapter Fourteen

"Where does this go, Ellie?"

Ellie decided she must have answered that question fourteen times in the last hour, but the craft fair was finally shaping up. She glanced around the church hall the next morning with a sense of satisfaction.

Fewer volunteers had shown up this morning than the day before, but she wouldn't let herself speculate on whether that was due to yesterday's revelations or today's even wetter weather. Only one absence really bothered her—Quinn hadn't come yet.

Just the thought of his name brought a warm glow to the heart she'd assumed was broken for good. When they'd stood locked in each other's arms by the river, she'd felt more cherished than she ever had in her life. Maybe she even felt loved.

The feeling went to her head, banishing the sober cautions she probably should heed. She didn't care about that. She didn't want to be cautious, or careful, or have to guard her heart from pain. She wanted to shout her love aloud for everyone to hear.

Instead she went sedately across the room to where Gwen was arranging a display of crocheted pot holders in one of the craft stands. Kristie had been helping her grandmother a moment ago, but now she chased Jason Caine around and around the funnel cake stand.

She could ask Gwen where Quinn was, couldn't she? There was nothing wrong with that.

"That looks nice." She admired the rainbow array of pot holders Gwen had hooked onto a sheet of Peg-Board. "Are all of those from Isabel Strong?"

Gwen nodded, smiling. "She can't see too well now, poor old dear, but she says her fingers still know how to make pot holders, since they've been doing it for nearly ninety years."

"At that price, everyone who comes through the door should buy at least one." She touched a pink knit baby bonnet lightly, hoping her voice wouldn't change. "By the way, I noticed Quinn isn't here. Do you know if he's coming?"

"Oh, I'm sure he is, dear." Gwen's eyes twinkled. "He wouldn't miss helping, I know. But he had a phone call just as we were leaving. It must have been business of some sort.''

Business? He surely wasn't going to cut his leave short, was he? Her heart sank. ''What made you think it was business?''

''He just looked so serious, I thought it must be.'' Gwen squeezed her hand. ''I'm sure Quinn will be here any minute now. He knows we're expecting his help today. Don't you worry.''

She considered protesting that she wasn't worried, but decided it would just draw more attention to her feelings for Quinn. *Her love for Quinn,* she corrected. She might at least be honest in her thoughts.

Was it possible Quinn had said something to Gwen the night before about his feelings? No, Gwen's knowing look probably had nothing to do with that.

''I'll catch up with him later,'' she said, and went quickly off to check on the soft drink machine.

She'd just convinced the soft drink vendor to cut his prices in view of the charitable nature of the fair when she heard the creak of the door opening. She glanced up to see Quinn's tall figure framed in the opening.

While she was still considering the advisability of going to him, his gaze swept the room and settled on her. He indicated the outside with a jerk of his head and held the door invitingly.

Trying not to hurry, she crossed to him. Quinn caught her arm in a firm grip and hustled her outside.

"It's a little wet out here, isn't it?" She repeated his remark from the night before, but he didn't smile in response. The gray rain streaked down relentlessly. They stood in the shelter of the portico, close against the church building. "Looks as if the weatherman was wrong again."

He didn't answer, and his grim expression sent a chill down her spine. "What is it?" She caught his hands in hers. "Quinn, what's wrong?"

"I had a call this morning."

"You don't have to go back to Oregon to the project, do you?" She probably sounded as plaintive as Kristie would. How could he go away again when they'd just begun?

"The project?" He looked startled for a moment, as if he'd forgotten about that. "No, it's not that." His mouth tightened, lines bracketing it.

No, not the project. This was obviously something much worse. Tension jerked up a notch inside her. "What is it, then?"

"The call was from the prosecutor's office." At her blank look, a muscle jumped in the hard line of his jaw. "The ones who prosecuted the driver who killed Julie."

"Why were they calling you now?" She'd assumed that was over and done with long ago.

"They wanted me to know the driver is up for parole. It looks as if he may be released early."

She wasn't sure how to respond to that. Quinn had obviously been glad the man was in jail, but she hadn't thought beyond that.

He didn't seem to expect a response. He gripped her hands until they hurt. "I can't let that happen."

"Quinn…"

"I can't," he snapped. "He killed Julie."

Her heart cramped. He'd loved Julie that much— so much, the thought of the driver's release tied him in knots. Maybe he still loved her, loved her too much to give himself to someone else.

She tried to put her own pain aside long enough to deal with his. "What can you do? It's not up to you."

Quinn, can't you let it go? Can't you forgive? But she already knew the answer to that one. He couldn't.

"That's where you're wrong." He wore his need for vengeance like a mask. "Family members can testify at the parole hearing. I'm going. By the time I get done with him, he'll be lucky to get out in twenty years."

She stroked his hand the way she'd comfort a

child. "Quinn, I know how much you must miss Julie, how wonderful your marriage must have been."

She had to force the words around the lump in her throat. She couldn't expect he'd ever feel that way about her.

"Wonderful?" For the first time he seemed to look past his anger and focus on her as if he really saw her. His mouth twisted. "I don't suppose Julie thought it was too wonderful. If she had, maybe she and Kristie would have come with me on the job. But she didn't want to change her life, didn't want to move to a new place or have new experiences. The lure of being with me wasn't enough to change that."

She tried to adjust her image of their marriage. Apparently it hadn't been the perfection she'd imagined. "I'm sorry. But you...you can't change the past by seeking revenge."

Did he even want revenge, in his innermost heart? Or was he trying to assuage the guilt he felt for what his marriage hadn't been?

"Justice," he snapped, pulling away from her. "Not revenge, justice. Look, I have to leave. I'm sorry I won't be here to help with the fair. Tell my mother for me, will you? And Kristie."

The wind whipped a spray of water across her face like tears. He was going. "Aren't you going to say goodbye to them?"

"I have to leave now," he repeated. "If I tell her, Mom will try to talk me out of going, and I'll be lucky to make it in time for the hearing as it is. I just wanted you to know."

"Why?" She caught his hand as he turned away, preparing to run back out into the steady rain. "Why me, Quinn?" She had to know that, at least.

She read the struggle for an answer on his face. "Because I want to know you'll be waiting for me when I come back." He blurted the words out as if almost afraid to say them. "Look, I don't know where this is going between us." He gripped her forearms. "I don't know. But I want... I guess I want to know you're with me."

Her heart gave a leap of hope, and then turned to lead. What he was really saying was that he expected her to approve of what he was doing. And she couldn't—she couldn't. If he wasn't able to forgive and put the past behind him, he could never be whole again.

The temptation to say nothing sang sweetly in her ear. *Just let him go,* it whispered. *You're not his conscience. Let him believe you approve, and save what you have with him.*

No. If she'd learned anything from the situation with her father, it was that only honesty would do between people who loved each other. But if she were honest with Quinn now, she'd lose him.

You'll lose him anyway, her heart responded. *He can't love you when he's caught up in the need for revenge. Either way, you lose.*

Quinn shifted impatiently, waiting for her answer, not sure why it was so important to him. He had to get on the road, but somehow he hadn't been able to go without seeing Ellie. The pressure to leave was a physical drive inside him, surging along his nerves.

"Quinn, can't you let it go?" Ellie's dark eyes were huge and troubled. "This isn't going to do any good for anyone."

"I have a responsibility. Don't you see that?" Why couldn't she understand?

"Your responsibility is to your mother and your child now, not to Julie. I can't believe she would have wanted you to seek revenge for her death." She clutched his hands, her eyes pleading with him.

He pushed her hands away, rejecting the words, anger riding him. "You barely knew Julie. You don't know what she would want. Besides, I owe it to her."

"Why?"

She wouldn't leave it alone. He couldn't think why he'd believed she would understand.

Because I let Julie down. Because whatever it was she wanted, I couldn't provide it.

She'd been so sweet, so young, when they'd met, with a touching willingness to rely on his every word, unlike Ellie, with her determined questions. It was only after they were married that he realized Julie wasn't going to grow any stronger.

"Why, Quinn?" Ellie repeated.

"I just do, that's all. I thought I could count on your support."

Her mouth trembled for an instant, then firmed. "I can't tell you to do something I think is wrong."

He struck out with the only weapon at hand. "You weren't all that righteous when you lied to everyone about your father."

Pain flickered across her face, shaming him. He wanted to take it back, wanted to make things right with her, but he couldn't. The anger he'd been carrying around for nearly two years burned along his veins.

She lifted her chin, looking at him steadily. "All I can say is that I've learned from that. You have to forgive before you can accept forgiveness. Living your life in search of revenge isn't right, any more than living a lie is. You're only going to hurt yourself and the people who love you."

She didn't understand. He'd been a fool to think she would.

"Then I guess I'll have to learn to live with that." He turned and ran through the rain to his car.

Pain was a huge, angry knot inside her chest, so big it threatened to suffocate her. Ellie watched Quinn's car turn, then spin out of the parking lot, spraying gravel. He turned up the mountain road and vanished into the gray mist.

She tried to swallow, but her throat was choked with tears that echoed the pelting rain. Tears she couldn't let fall. Whatever might have been between them, it was gone now. She'd had a chance at his love, and she'd turned it away. She wouldn't have a chance again.

She pressed her hand against her mouth, willing back the tears. She didn't have time to grieve now. People depended upon her, and she had a job to do.

Father, are You going to make something good come of this? I confess I can't see how, but I'll try to trust anyway.

She took a steadying breath, then another. When she thought she'd conquered the tears, she pushed the door open and went inside.

"Ellie?" Gwen came hurrying to her. "I thought I saw Quinn with you. Where is he?"

"He left." She pressed the pain down again. Obviously she'd have to keep doing that. "He asked me to tell you he had to go."

"Go? Where?" Gwen's voice rose. "I don't understand."

Ellie glanced around to be sure no one was within earshot. "He found out that the driver who was in the accident with Julie is up for an early release. He's going to the hearing to try and prevent that."

Quick tears filled Gwen's eyes. "Oh, dear. Why did this have to happen now, of all times?"

She blinked back her own tears. "I don't know."

"He seemed to be doing so well. I really thought he was letting go of his bitterness, especially since..." She stopped.

"Since what?"

"Well, since you, dear." Gwen patted her hand. "I thought you were good for him."

"I wish that were true." Oh, how she wished it. "I tried to convince him not to go, but I'm afraid I just made things worse."

Gwen blotted the tears that escaped onto her cheeks. "It's not your fault, Ellie. I've prayed and prayed Quinn would come home so we could help him get rid of his bitterness. When I finally got him to come, I thought everything would work out all right."

"You got him to come," Ellie echoed, wondering. "Gwen, did you use your relationship with my father to goad Quinn into coming home?"

"Of course not!" Gwen's cheeks went pink with indignation. "Well, only a little bit. I mean, when I saw that it upset Quinn, I decided that was a good thing It did bring him home, didn't it?"

She wouldn't have thought Gwen could be so devious. "Wasn't that a little unfair to my father?"

Gwen flushed a bit deeper. "Oh, Ellie, I do care for Charles on his own account, you know."

"I know." She squeezed her friend's hand. "He's a lucky man to have you care about him."

Gwen sighed. "I confess, I thought Kristie's prayers were finally going to be answered. I thought she was right—that you were the one God picked out for Quinn."

She felt as if she were bleeding inside. "I guess God must have something else in mind."

She tried to say it lightly, but Gwen must have heard the pain underneath, because she wrapped her arms around her. Ellie leaned her head on Gwen's shoulder, trying to hold back the tears that wanted to overflow.

The door swished open behind her, and she swung around. Quinn... Hope blossomed in her heart, to be quickly trampled. It wasn't Quinn, it was Mitch.

Bulky in his police slicker, Mitch glanced around the room as if he couldn't believe his eyes. "What are all of you doing still here?"

"What do you mean?" Ellie asked. The room slowly became quiet.

"You haven't heard the radio?"

She shook her head, feeling bad news coming.

Mitch's face was grim. "This storm's not going anywhere. It's stuck right over us, and they're saying now we'll get a good ten inches of rain before it's done. The weather service has issued a warning— river's going to crest well above twenty feet. We're in for a flood, folks."

For a moment silence greeted his words. Then a clamor of questions and exclamations burst out. Ellie's mind raced. Twenty feet—she'd lived through a couple of minor floods since she'd come to Bedford Creek, but nothing anywhere near that. The shop...

"Ellie, I expect you want to get down to the shop and start taking stuff to the second floor." Mitch was briskly efficient. "Maybe Gwen can keep a crew here to be sure everything's up on tables."

Ellie nodded, her mind starting to function again. The church was high enough to be safe from the river, but even here, ground water could cover the floor.

Mitch raised his voice above the babble. "Anybody who's able to had better report to sandbagging detail. We'll meet down by the bridge. We've got to get organized quickly. Looks like the flood is going to be a bad one.''

Heart pounding, Ellie grabbed her jacket and hurried out into the rain. It slanted into her face as she ran to the car.

Flood, she thought again, the word echoing in her mind. They were going to have a flood, and Quinn was out somewhere on the road on his mission of revenge.

Lord, protect him, please. Bring him back to us. She stood for an instant, staring at the road he'd taken. *Please, Quinn, come back. Please.*

Chapter Fifteen

Rain pounded against the windshield so fiercely that the wipers couldn't keep up with it. Quinn leaned forward, peering through the murky grayness that was barely pierced by his headlights, trying to make out the lines on the two-lane back road that led to the interstate. Anyone would think it was midnight instead of early afternoon.

He glanced at the clock on the dash. Time was running out. If he didn't arrive at the courthouse by four, his chance to speak at the hearing would disappear. Anger burned along his veins.

Did the prosecutor even care if that happened? Why hadn't they let him know sooner about the parole hearing? When he'd fired that question at the person who'd called, the answer had been evasive.

She'd claimed some sort of bureaucratic mix-up, but he didn't quite buy it.

Maybe the truth was that no one cared—no one but him. Julie hadn't had anyone else to care. The man who'd taken her life with his carelessness had served less than two years, and people had already forgotten. The prosecutor's office had moved on to other cases. Friends and family told him to forgive and forget. *Ellie* told him to forgive and forget.

No, that wasn't fair. He saw again the caring and pain in her face as she talked. Ellie hadn't looked for an easy answer. She wanted what was best for him. They'd just never agree on what that was.

He tried to find some feeling inside, but there was only numbness when he thought of her. Maybe that was best. He didn't seem to have anything to offer that she wanted.

A truck roared past him, going the other way too fast on the narrow mountain road, and sent a torrent of muddy water sluicing across his windshield. The car swerved, and he struggled with the wheel to right it, heart suddenly pounding.

Ridiculous. He'd driven in much worse than this. Why was he letting it affect him?

Then he knew why. Julie had been out on a road like this, on a night like this—wind whipping the rain, branches slashing, the pavement glittering like black ice. She must have seen the headlights coming toward her on the wrong side of the road. She wouldn't have known what to do. She'd have panicked.

Stop it, he ordered. *Thinking like that does no good at all.*

Ellie wanted him to forgive. He saw her face again, dark eyes pleading with him, the mellow stone of the church behind her. He'd wanted to pull her into his arms and bury his face in her hair. He'd wanted to hold her forever.

But she didn't understand. How could she expect him to forgive?

She forgave, a voice whispered in his mind. *Her father destroyed her whole life, and she forgave.*

He grappled unwillingly with the thought. He wanted to believe Ellie didn't know how he felt, but he couldn't. She'd been where he was, and she'd forgiven. She looked into the darkness in his heart, and she still loved him.

Love? He looked at the word cautiously. It hadn't been said between them. How could he believe that was what she felt?

Red taillights ahead of him signaled a warning. He pumped the brakes, sliding a little, and came to a stop behind a lineup of cars on the narrow road. A figure in a black slicker battled through the rain toward him, and he rolled down his window.

"What's happening?"

"Mudslide on the road ahead." The state trooper wiped his wet face with a wetter hand. "They're trying to clear it now. Shouldn't be too long."

The need to move surged through him. Time was ticking away, and any delay could mean he wouldn't get there in time. "Any other way I can get onto the interstate headed east?"

The trooper looked at him as if he'd lost his mind. "East? Haven't you been listening to the radio? The interstate's closed going east. The governor's declared a state of emergency for ten counties. We're dealing with a major flood."

The man turned to wave down a car behind Quinn's, and Quinn snapped the button on the radio, apprehension clutching his throat. He listened to the news, and a slow, sick feeling spread through him. Creeks and rivers were rising at an alarming rate. Flooding was inevitable, maybe as bad locally as the Agnes flood of '72. Bedford Creek sat right in the path of it.

Kristie, his mother…Ellie. *They* were right in the path of it.

"We're right in the path of it." Mitch Donovan stood just inside the shop door, shaking water from his slicker. "The good news is that the rain's slacking off a little upstream. It looks as if the river will crest some time overnight."

"And the bad news?" She feared she knew what it was.

"Bad news is, the crest is going to be well above flood stage."

A low murmur greeted his words, but no one stopped working. They weren't surprised. Ellie had turned the radio on as soon as she reached the shop, so they'd listened as they worked. Local stations had stopped playing music to air a steady stream of flood-related news.

Mitch looked around the shop, seeming to weigh what remained to be done. "Do you have enough help? I'm afraid I can't spare anyone else right now."

"We're fine," she assured him.

She gestured toward the people packing wreaths and candles into boxes and carrying them upstairs. Some had come with her from the church. Others had simply appeared and started working, not waiting for directions.

"We'll have it all on the second floor within the hour." She managed a smile. "I don't even know all these people, but they're helping."

"Nothing like an emergency to bring out the best in people." Mitch glanced at Enid Lawrence, who was folding quilts and putting them in plastic bags. She was also complaining in a querulous voice about the ineptitude of emergency management and flood control, but she worked while she complained. "Even some surprising people."

Ellie nodded. She'd stopped being surprised an hour ago. Now she was just thankful. She wouldn't let herself think beyond that.

"As soon as we're done here, I'll be out to join the sandbagging."

"Good." Mitch shoved the door open and flashed her a smile. "We'll get through this, never fear. We've been through worse."

Her father slid his arm around her waist. "Are you all right, Princess?"

She glanced around at the denuded shelves, wondering if she'd ever see the shop that she loved back to normal again. She shook off the fear and gave him a quick hug. "I'm fine, Daddy. I'm glad you're here."

He blinked rapidly, as if to hold back tears. Then he straightened his shoulders. "Well, now, let's get the rest of these things moved. By the time the water comes, we won't leave anything here for it to ruin."

She had her father back. No matter what else happened, she had him back. *Thank you, Lord.* She tried not to think about the person she didn't have back, but it was useless. *Why couldn't I help Quinn, Lord? Even if a relationship between us wasn't meant to be, even if he could never love me, why couldn't I help him?*

The question echoed in her mind while she cleared the store, sandbagged the doors, thanked the friends and strangers who helped. It continued to reverberate in the back of her mind an hour later, when she joined the sandbagging crew by the bridge.

She surveyed the line of sandbags marking off the lowest, most vulnerable sections of the bank. They looked small and helpless. And the river—

Her breath caught. She'd been so busy, she hadn't had time to look. Now she did, and she couldn't look away.

The clear water had turned a muddy brown. Swollen, sullen, it rolled relentlessly, carrying branches, crates and fragments of what had probably been someone's shed. A picnic table floated past, to shatter into matchsticks against the bridge pilings.

Could they possibly stop something that powerful? She seemed to hear the prayer Pastor Richie had said earlier. The Israelites must have thought it was equally hopeless when they'd faced the sea with an army at their back. Encouraged, she went to the pile of sandbags to start carrying.

She soon found herself working in tandem with the pastor, carrying bags as quickly as they could be filled.

"Do you think this is going to work?" She lugged a sandbag into place, starting the second layer.

Pastor Richie straightened, hand on his back.

"Maybe. I hope so." He shook his head, and water streamed from his hat. "All we can do is our best, Ellie. Beyond that, we have to leave it in God's hands. Do you remember the lines from the Song of Songs? 'Many waters cannot quench love; rivers cannot wash it away.' I find that a comforting thought right now."

Many waters cannot quench love. Her heart contracted.

Quinn, where are you? Are you safe? Why aren't you here with the people who love you?

Quinn pounded the steering wheel in frustration, staring blindly out at the row of stationary cars washed by the rain. Where were the people he loved? Were they all right? Were they taking precautions?

His mind presented him with a terrifying image— a wall of water sweeping down the valley, carrying everything in front of it. He'd seen that once, in a canyon in Colorado. He knew the implacable nature of a flood confined in a narrow valley. He knew the devastation it could bring.

He forced his engineer's mind to zero in on flood-control measures upriver from Bedford Creek, trying to assess how well they'd work. Piecemeal. They were always piecemeal. No matter how the professionals tried to stress the importance of the whole area cooperating, it didn't happen. No one knew what effect the floodwall at Barclay would have on the towns downriver—towns like Bedford Creek.

If the rain kept falling, if the wall held in Barclay, forcing the river into a narrower channel—if, if, if. This could be worse than the flood in '72, when the whole lower end of town had water up to the second floor. Ellie's shop, across from the park, had no protection.

She'd have moved things to the second floor by this time, wouldn't she? He imagined her struggling to save her shop, putting herself in danger, and pain wrapped itself around his heart. He should be there. Instead he was stuck here while people he loved faced danger without him.

Like always, the soft voice of his conscience commented. *That's what you did before, isn't it? You let the people you loved face danger without you.*

His friends, facing death in the flooded quarry; his wife, facing death on a rain-swept road—he hadn't been there.

God, what have I done? For the first time in too long he cried out to God. *I thought I'd find peace by punishing the person who drove the car that killed Julie. But I'm the guilty one. I'm the one who wasn't there. I'm the one who needs forgiveness.*

His hands clenched the wheel so tightly, its ridges seemed to burn into his palms. Ellie had known. She'd seen it, when she'd told him he was hurting himself by not forgiving. He couldn't have God's forgiveness for himself if he didn't forgive others.

Hot tears stung his eyes. He'd been clutching his need for revenge too long. It had become a part of him, and it was hard to let go. But he had to, or he'd never be whole again.

Help me, Father. Forgive me, and help me forgive.

Someone tapped on the window. He took a breath, searching for calm, and opened the window.

The state trooper stood there. "They've got the road clear now, sir. You can get through, if that's what you want."

"No." Peace filled him as he said the word. "I don't need to go forward. I just have to go back. I have to go back home."

Chapter Sixteen

How much longer could they keep going?

As long as they had to. Ellie tried to steel herself. They didn't have a choice. Maybe a cup of coffee would help, she thought as she dragged herself toward the makeshift food stand that had been set up in front of the police station.

At least the rain had slacked off to a thin drizzle. That had to be good news, didn't it?

Then she looked back at the river and knew it might be too late to make a difference. Sullen and heavy, it rolled inexorably over the park. The pavilion roofs poked above mud-colored water like tiny green islands.

Despair washed over her. Half an hour ago the water had not yet reached the top of the support poles. Now it was well over. The river was still going up. The worst wasn't over.

"Ellie, dear, you need something hot to drink." Gwen, behind the folding table that had been set up under a tarp, forced a plastic cup of coffee into her hand.

"Have you heard anything from..."

Gwen bit her lip, her blue eyes filling with anxiety. "Quinn hasn't called, not yet. But I'm sure he's trying to get back."

"I'm sure he is." Ellie's throat tightened at the thought. Quinn, trying to get back, probably blaming himself again for not being with the people he loved in a crisis. Did he even begin to realize how much his anger was driven by his own sense of guilt? Could he ever let that go?

"Have a piece of apple cake." Gwen forced the paper plate on her, obviously driven by her need to feed people when trouble loomed. "This was baked for the craft fair, but I didn't think you'd mind if I used it."

"Of course not." Her notion of repaying people for their kindness by putting on the fair paled into insignificance when they were all fighting for survival. "The fair isn't important now."

Gwen nodded. "Funny how your priorities change, isn't it? If only I knew Quinn was safe, I wouldn't ask for anything more."

A cold hand clutched her heart, but she managed to smile reassuringly at Gwen. "I'm sure he's fine. He's probably just stuck somewhere. So many of the bridges washed out on the back roads, it'll be hard to get home. But he'll be here—you'll see."

Gwen brightened, as if Ellie's words had helped, and she turned to urge coffee on another weary worker. Now if Ellie could just believe them herself—

Of course I believe. Lord, please keep him safe. Bring him back to us.

She downed the rest of the coffee and headed back to the sandbags.

An hour later it was nearly full dark. Circles of light from rigged-up spotlights played across the scene, turning it into something from an old movie. *A horror movie,* Ellie thought numbly, trying to lug a sandbag that had become inexplicably heavy. Was this never going to end? No matter how many bags they piled up, the water kept rising.

A trickle of muddy water snaked across the road like an advance warning. If the river got much higher, the makeshift floodwall couldn't possibly hold. The water would pour across the road, smash into the buildings—

She stumbled, and a strong hand grabbed her arm. "What are you doing?" Quinn's voice was rough with emotion. "You're exhausted. Let me have that."

"I'm fine." She snatched at the sandbag, then realized how ridiculous she must sound, fighting over a sandbag. "You're back."

She looked up at him, feeling as if she'd never get enough of looking. He was back, safe and sound. Shadows darkened his eyes, and worry had etched lines in his face. But he was back.

"Took me too long. I should have been here hours ago." He looked around at the nightmare scene. "My mother? Kristie?"

"They're fine," she said quickly. "Gwen's helping with the canteen over by the police station, and Kristie is with your sister up at the clinic. She's taking care of Hannibal for me, so that's keeping her occupied. Brett's running the first-aid station here."

"Good. I got trapped behind a mudslide and never even made it to the interstate."

So he hadn't made it to the hearing. He'd come back because he had to. Nothing had changed, except that this time he wouldn't have to blame himself for not being here.

"Look, Ellie, I have to talk to you, but I've got to go and help Mitch. Go find something safer to do, will you please? If the water breaks through, I don't want you here."

Before she could argue, he kissed her quickly, his

lips warm against her cold ones. Then he was gone, running after Mitch, and she was left standing with her fingers pressed against the place where his lips had been, trying to believe she could hope.

Quinn hurried after Mitch, holding a picture of Ellie in his mind—wet and bedraggled, wearing rubber boots and a too-big poncho, dark hair plastered to her face, a streak of mud on her cheek. She was beautiful. His heart cramped. Beautiful.

But this situation wasn't beautiful. He joined Mitch and a handful of others behind the fragile barrier of sandbags.

''...afraid the bridge might go if the pressure is too great,'' Mitch was saying.

Quinn frowned at the old iron bridge that should have been replaced long ago. ''I think we've got a more immediate problem.'' He pointed. ''Look at the debris stuck against the center piling. If that mess doesn't break free, it could turn the bridge into a dam, sending all that water surging right for us.''

Mitch caught on quickly. ''If it does, we'll be lucky to have anything on River Street left standing.''

Quinn nodded, fear clutching his heart. Had Ellie done what he told her and moved to safer ground? Probably not. She wasn't a person who'd seek safety when she thought she was needed here.

''Let's take a closer look.'' He grabbed a metal

pole from the debris washed to the bank and jogged toward the bridge, hearing Mitch's footsteps splash along behind him.

The iron bridge trembled under their feet, shaking in the onslaught of water. The roar of the river was so loud, Mitch had to shout to be heard. "What do you think?"

"I think the state should have replaced this relic years ago." Quinn reached the center and leaned over the railing, scanning the expanse of brown water roiling below. The root system of a massive spruce had caught on the middle piling, with smaller debris stacking up behind it with terrifying speed.

"We've only got another foot or so between the water and the deck. It's not going to take much to turn the whole bridge into a dam." Quinn reached for the pole, and Mitch put it in his hand.

He leaned over, the metal railing hard against his stomach, poking at the mass. "No good." He straightened, shoving the hood of his poncho back. "I can't get a good enough angle. I'll have to get outside the railing to do it."

"No, you don't." Mitch grabbed his arm before he could move. "I'm the police chief, remember? They pay me to do the dirty jobs."

"Wait. Maybe we should get more help." Quinn glanced toward the shore.

Mitch slung his leg over the metal rail. "No time

for that.'' He flashed a grin. ''Just hold on, buddy, unless you want to chase me all the way to the Chesapeake Bay. I'm counting on you.''

Mitch knelt on the narrow ledge outside the railing, taking the pole in both hands. Quinn grabbed his belt and braced both feet against the metal post. No time to look toward the bank, no time to wonder if Ellie and his mother were watching. Only time enough to breathe a wordless prayer.

Then Mitch was leaning perilously over the river, poking at the mass of debris with both hands, the only thing between him and disaster the grip of Quinn's hands.

''Almost got it.'' Mitch grunted, shoving harder, his weight putting an almost unbearable pressure on Quinn's arms. Pain burned along the muscles, and he gritted his teeth.

I won't let him down, Lord. I've got another chance here, and I won't let him down.

A final shove, a final scream of exhaustion from his aching muscles. Then a creak, a crash and the debris washed free.

Mitch lurched, dangling over the edge for an instant. Quinn hauled him back, both of them stumbling as he came over the railing. Quinn found his balance and clutched Mitch's arm. ''You okay?''

''Thanks to you.'' Mitch pounded his shoulder. ''Let's get out of here.''

They stumbled back off the bridge, to be met by a rush of people. Quinn could hear Mitch giving orders to post watchers on the bridge to prevent any further pileups, but he didn't pay attention.

There was only one voice he wanted to hear. He pushed through the crowd, scanning faces. Only one face he wanted to see.

Ellie splashed through the muddy water toward him and ran straight into his arms.

Dawn streaked the sky with pink and gold. Ellie sat on a pile of sandbags and leaned back wearily against the side of the police car. She glanced around. Everyone else seemed to be doing the same thing— too tired to move, probably. Not that there was much more they could do, except wait for the river to crest.

She looked at the man who sat next to her. Quinn stretched and rubbed reddened eyes, then passed his hand over a stubble of beard, leaving a streak of mud in its wake.

"You should go up to the house," he said again, as he'd said several times during the night. "Mom has a room ready for you."

"I need to be here until we know it's over." *With you.* But she couldn't quite say that, not yet. Quinn had held her in his arms, he'd kissed her with a kind of hungry gratitude when he'd come off the bridge after risking his life for all of them.

But she still didn't know what his return meant for her. And she couldn't ask. It was for him to say.

Quinn wrapped his hand around hers. "At least it hasn't gone up any more in the last two hours. If there's not a problem upriver, maybe we're going to get through this one."

Maybe. She glanced toward the shop, standing inches from disaster. "And the next one? How often can we go through this?"

"Not again." His grip tightened. "Not if I can help it."

Hope began to stir, a faint flutter in her heart. "What do you mean?"

He managed a smile. "Like my mother said, there's plenty of work for an engineer in Pennsylvania. I'm going to ask for a transfer to the local corps district. It's time I came home."

"Your mother and Kristie will be so happy." A sobering thought struck her. "Of course, then you'll be close if they reschedule the parole hearing, too."

His mouth tightened as he stared out at the brown water, and then he faced her. "No. I won't be going to any parole hearings."

Her gaze clung to his. "Are you sure?" She could barely breathe for hoping.

He nodded. "I had time to think about it, sitting out on that back road while everyone I cared about was in trouble. God had a hard lesson for me to learn about forgiveness. But I think He finally got it through my thick head.'' Warmth lightened his gray eyes. ''Thanks to you.''

Tears trembled on the edge of spilling over, and she blinked them back. ''I'm glad.''

''Ellie, I—''

The siren blared on the police car, making both of them jump. Quinn got up, pulling Ellie to her feet. Her heart thumped uncomfortably. Bad news?

Mitch stood on the seat of the police car, hanging on to the roof, as people turned toward him, faces apprehensive.

''News from upriver,'' he shouted. ''They just checked the gauges again. The crest has passed—the water's going down. We've done it!''

The crowd erupted, hugging each other, shouting and cheering and crying. Ellie choked back a sob as she turned to Quinn. ''We're safe. We came through it.''

He held both her hands in his. ''What is it Pastor Richie always says at baptism? Through the water, into new life.''

He glanced at the people surrounding them, then drew her behind the police car, hidden from the crowd.

''New life,'' he said again. ''That's what I want, Ellie. A new life, with you.'' He touched her face gently. ''My wise little daughter always knew you were the wife God picked out for me. It just took a little longer for me to get the message. I love you, Ellie. Will you marry me?''

She looked up at him, heart full, and saw that all the bitterness had disappeared from his face. The steady light of love glowed in his eyes, so intense it took her breath away. She could only nod and lift her face for his kiss.

Epilogue

An autumn leaf drifted into Quinn's lap as he sat on a folding chair in the park two months later. They had been months filled with changes, months of hard work. The park was just beginning to look normal again, with the fences replaced, the pavilions repaired and new grass sprouting up through the layer of mud left by the flood. Funds from the belated craft fair had paid for that. And now the community had gathered to thank God that they'd come through the water, to new life.

A lump formed in his throat as he reached to his right to take Ellie's hand. Her fingers closed around his, and her engagement ring pushed into his skin, reminding him again just how fortunate he was. She smiled at him, and her face held such happiness and contentment that it seemed to shout.

Kristie leaned forward from her seat on the other side of Ellie. His daughter had been taking a proprietary air toward their engagement, apparently convinced that only her prayers had brought it about. Well, maybe she had a point there.

"Isn't it going to start soon, Daddy?" she asked in a stage whisper.

"Soon, sweetheart," he murmured, smiling at her. "Be patient."

As if he'd heard, Pastor Richie stepped to the makeshift platform. The sun slanted on the peaceful river behind him, turning its rippling surface to gold. He raised his hands.

"Let us give thanks to the Lord, for He is good. His steadfast love endures forever." A smile lit his face. "My dear friends, God truly is good, and His love does endure. In all the hours we fought the flood, one verse kept coming back to me. 'Many waters cannot quench love; rivers cannot wash it away.' We are the living proof of that."

Quinn clasped Ellie's hand tighter as he looked at the faces surrounding him. His mother, serene as she locked hands with Charles, and beyond them Brett and Rebecca. His sister's hand was curved across the maternity blouse that announced new life. Mitch and Anne Donovan were together, with their children close at hand. Alex Caine and his new bride, Paula, had their son between them. The rest of Bedford

Creek filled the chairs and stood around the edges of the seats. Even young Robbie, fidgeting on his seat, turned around to smile at him.

Many waters cannot quench love; rivers cannot wash it away.

Quinn's heart seemed to overflow with gratitude for the love surrounding him. He'd spent too long running away from this place. He squeezed Ellie's hand again. He'd come home at last, to the place where he belonged, and he'd found the love that waited here for him.

*   *   *   *   *

Dear Reader,

I'm so glad you decided to pick up this book. The love story of Ellie and Quinn lets me, like Quinn, return to Bedford Creek and find out what's been happening there. I'm delighted to revisit old friends, and I hope you will be, too.

I felt the HOMETOWN HEROES miniseries wouldn't be complete unless the town faced a flood, since the flood in the past ran through all the stories. Writing about it made me relive our own experiences in the Agnes flood of 1972. Those of us who were there will not forget!

But I suppose all of us face flood times in our lives. My hope for you is that, like the characters of my story, you'll come through the water to new life.

Please let me know how you liked this story. You can reach me c/o Steeple Hill Books, 233 Broadway, Ste. 1001, New York, NY 10279.

Best wishes,

Marta Perry

2 Love Inspired novels and a mystery gift... Absolutely FREE!

Visit

www.LoveInspiredBooks.com

for your two FREE books, sent directly to you!

BONUS: Choose between regular print or our NEW larger print format!

There's no catch! You're under no obligation to buy anything. We charge nothing—ZERO—for your first shipment. And you don't have to make any minimum number of purchases.

You'll like the convenience of home delivery at our special discount prices, and you'll love your free subscription to Steeple Hill News, our members-only newsletter.

We hope that after receiving your free books, you'll want to remain a subscriber. But the choice is yours—to continue or cancel, anytime at all! So why not take us up on our invitation, with no risk of any kind!

LIGEN05

Love Inspired

THE HAMILTON HEIR

BY

VALERIE HANSEN

Heads turned when Hamilton media heir Tim Hamilton was seen squiring his assistant Dawn Leroux around town. Since he'd accidentally wrecked her car, Tim had offered to help with her meal-delivery route, and he saw a new side of Dawn—a very appealing one.

Davis Landing

NOTHING IS STRONGER THAN A FAMILY'S LOVE.

Available October 2006 wherever you buy books.

Steeple Hill®

Love Inspired®

TIDINGS OF JOY

BY

MARGARET DALEY

The Ladies of Sweetwater Lake: Like a wedding ring, this circle of friends is never ending.

He came to Sweetwater to repay a debt, but Chance Taylor never expected to have feelings for his new landlady, Tanya Bolton. They had a chance for a fresh start together, but Chance's secret obligation could put an end to their new beginning.

Available October 2006 wherever you buy books.

Steeple Hill®

Love Inspired.
CLASSICS

TITLES AVAILABLE NEXT MONTH

Don't miss these stories in October

UPON A MIDNIGHT CLEAR
AND
SECRETS OF THE HEART
by Gail Gaymer Martin

Enjoy a little Christmas cheer with two timeless
stories of love, faith and redemption.

A GROOM OF HER OWN
AND
THE WAY HOME
by Irene Hannon

Two very special couples say their vows in
these stories of unexpected love from
RITA® Award winner Irene Hannon.

LICLASSCNM0906